EAGER SEDUCTION

"You were worth waiting for," he murmured as he bent his head, put his other arm around her, and kissed her.

Sassy gasped at the hot domination of his mouth on hers. She stiffened just a moment and he whispered, "Don't fight me, Sassy. You're mine now. Relax and let it happen. Relax . . ."

For this he had gotten her tipsy, she thought in a daze. She could give herself to him as wantonly as she pleased and he'd think it was the wine. His mouth went to the pulse point at her throat and she gasped for air. It unnerved her to think he could take control of her emotions like this.

Then she couldn't reason anymore, only feel . . .

FEEL THE FIRE IN CAROL FINCH'S ROMANCES!

BELOVED BETRAYAL (2346, $3.95)
Sabrina Spencer donned a gray wig and veiled hat before blackmailing rugged Ridge Tanner into guiding her to Fort Canby. But the costume soon became her prison—the beauty had fallen head over heels in love!

LOVE'S HIDDEN TREASURE (2980, $4.50)
Shandra d'Evereux felt her heart throb beneath the stolen map she'd hidden in her bodice when Nolan Elliot swept her out onto the veranda. It was hard to concentrate on her mission with that wily rogue around!

MONTANA MOONFIRE (3263, $4.95)
Just as debutante Victoria Flemming-Cassidy was about to marry an oh-so-suitable mate, the towering preacher, Dru Sullivan flung her over his shoulder and headed West! Suddenly, Tori realized she had been given the best present for a bride: a night of passion with a real man!

THUNDER'S TENDER TOUCH (2809, $4.50)
Refined Piper Malone needed bounty-hunter, Vince Logan to recover her swindled inheritance. She thought she could coolly dismiss him after he did the job, but she never counted on the hot flood of desire she felt whenever he was near!

GEORGINA GENTRY
HALF-BREED'S BRIDE

ZEBRA BOOKS
KENSINGTON PUBLISHING CORP.

ZEBRA BOOKS

are published by

Kensington Publishing Corp.
475 Park Avenue South
New York, NY 10016

First Printing: May, 1993

Printed in the United States of America

DEDICATION

*Secrets. Everybody has one; some big, some small. Have you ever lain awake at night, worrying about what **might** happen if your secret should be discovered, especially by the one you love? If so, dear reader, I wrote this story just for you. . . .*

Prologue

A ship-load of mail-order brides. It is one of the strangest true stories to come out of the old West.

Washington Territory immediately after the Civil War was a raw but booming frontier. All it needed to further its development, some thought, were respectable white women to become wives for the rough pioneers.

What type of man would send for a mail-order bride? What kind of girl would leave back-East civilization to move forever to a primitive wilderness to marry a man she had never met? Sometimes both were driven by necessity and sheer desperation.

James Hunter was such a man: a wealthy, darkly handsome rogue hiding more than one secret. His requirements for a bride were strict: she must come from a blue-blooded, aristocratic family and have a spotless personal reputation. He saw it strictly as a business deal. He offered marriage, wealth, and power. She would preside over his empire and provide sons to carry on his dynasty. He didn't even care if she were pretty as long as her reputation was spotless. The cold, moody half-breed sneered at love and romance. After all, the girls at

Lulu's Lovelies, the local bordello, could provide for a man's physical needs. A meek, mild-mannered maiden was what James Hunter expected—no, demanded—a prim, pedigreed virgin. Above all, she must be a *lady*.

That's what he expects. What he's about to get is a fiery little Irish whore on the run in fear for her life. Hunter will never be the same once he's clashed with Sassy Malone . . .

Chapter One

March, 1865
Seattle, Washington Territory

"Hell, I'm not sure if I even want a mail order bride!" Hunter confessed, looking from the letter in his hand to the half-dressed whores sitting around Lulu's office.

The fat madam leaned her elbows on her desk and waited. "If you're havin' second thoughts, handsome, any one of my girls would be happy to marry—"

"No thanks," Hunter snapped. "The type of wife I had in mind—"

"We know; we know." Lulu drawled as she pulled her purple satin wrapper around her huge bulk. "You're picky."

Hunter looked at the letter again, misgivings in his soul. What the hell was he letting himself in for? He leaned to hand the paper to the plump madam of Lulu's Lovelies. "Here, girls, I called you all in to get your opinion. Lulu, read it aloud and see what they think."

Lulu took it, rolling her eyes. "I'll swan! Honestly, Hunter, if you weren't one of my establishment's best customers . . ." Her voice trailed off and she cleared her throat. " 'To Whom It May Concern:' "

Blanche fiddled with the soiled lace on her corset cover. "That ain't too romantic, is it?"

The girls all tittered. Hunter paused in lighting a thin cheroot and frowned at her. "This is not about romance, Blanche; it's a business deal." He shook the match out, broke it in half. A man who spent as much time as he did around timber always thought about fires.

Lulu's double chin quivered as she began again in her thick southern accent. " 'To Whom It May Concern: The bearer of this letter has been authorized to present it to a prospective bride whom he has deemed suitable.' "

The whores all giggled and Lulu rolled her eyes, the lamplight reflecting off the rings on her fat fingers. She reached for the pen on her desk. "Maybe I could make some changes. I told you before it won't attract—"

"It may attract the kind of wife I'm looking for." He crossed his long legs and shrugged his wide shoulders. "Hell! I want her to know up front what she's getting into."

Lulu sighed as if she knew it was useless to argue with such a stubborn man and turned her attention again to the letter. " 'By suitable, I am in need of a wife of sturdy stock, good family, spotless personal reputation, and capable of bearing children.' "

Blanche giggled again. "Hunter, Lamby Pie, why don't you just ask her to bring her pedigree with her, the way you'd do if you was buyin' a mare?"

"In effect, that's just what I'm doing, buying breeding stock." He didn't laugh. Hunter seldom laughed. Life

10

had been a serious, uphill fight to success and power. Now he had both. "If this mail-order bride is to be my wife and the mother of my sons, she has to have a spotless reputation. I won't be snickered at or have other men laughing behind my back."

Like they did my father, Hunter thought bitterly and absently ran his hand through his black, curly hair. Some things money couldn't buy. "Finish reading, Lulu, I haven't got all night. I've got to get this letter to Mercer before he sails."

"What about love?" Claire demanded.

"What about it? Overrated, if you ask me," Hunter scoffed, blowing smoke toward the ceiling. "That's what you girls sell here. I'm not into silly mooning and sappy poetry. This marriage is going to be a solid business deal, just as the letter states. For my part, I get a back-East blue blood to preside over my empire and produce sons for me. She gets money, security, and—"

"Does that mean you won't be comin' here no more?" Claire stuck out her lower lip.

"I told you this marriage is a business deal, plain and simple." He shrugged. "I don't suppose a prim lady wants a man botherin' her any more than necessary to produce children; at least, that's what I've heard. Finish reading, Lulu; it's getting late."

Lulu read, describing Hunter's house with a real piano and how he would be waiting on the dock when the ship arrived, and ended with a description of him: " 'I am tall, dark, and not bad looking. I will be dressed in black with a black western hat. Expecting a mutually rewarding life together. Sincerely, James Hunter.' "

Blanche studied her long nails. "If a guy sent me a letter like that, I'd throw it away."

11

"No, you wouldn't," Claire challenged. "Not if it were Hunter, no matter what it said."

The whores all laughed and even Lulu smiled.

Hunter frowned, reached to take the letter from her fat fingers. "I should have known I couldn't count on you girls to be serious." Life was totally serious to Hunter. He stood up. "Lulu, what do I owe—"

"Never mind, never mind." She waved his thanks away and leaned back in her chair. It creaked under her weight. "A little out of my line, but I was happy to help. God knows you and all that crew of yours do enough business in my establishment." The girls giggled again.

Hunter, looking at Lulu with her heavy layer of white face-powder and scarlet rouge, wondered if she had ever been pretty in her younger days.

"I'll swan! I just have to warn you, Hunter, I can't imagine what kind of girl would consider such a cold marriage proposal as that," Lulu drawled.

"The kind of no-nonsense, mature woman I'm looking for—prim, highly respectable—who'll appreciate my honesty as I'll appreciate hers." He took a final puff of his cigar, tossed it into the spittoon, then tucked the letter in the pocket of his fine, black broadcloth coat.

"But, Hunter," Lulu reminded him as she reached for a cookie from the plate on her desk, "you didn't really tell her much about yourself—"

"I told her all that's important," he snapped. "A marriage is a business contract and should be handled as such. I don't want some silly female with dreamy ideas about romance. Much obliged, Lulu. Good night, girls."

"Aw," Blanche pouted, "don't go. I thought maybe after a little rest, you'd—"

"Sorry, girls, I've got to get this letter to Mercer; his

12

ship leaves at dawn." Turning, he took his black Western hat off the rack and went out into the rainy, cool night.

Lulu stared after the darkly handsome man whose eyes were the bright color of an azure sky. He was a strange one, all right, dressed in fine clothes cut to hang well on his big frame. He hadn't told the prospective bride about his background and Lulu had not dared suggest it. In fact, he might be furious if he knew how much she knew about him. Hunter was a very private, lonely man who kept everyone at arm's length. Such a contrast to his suave brother, Lulu thought. Not many people except Swede even knew he had a brother, and Hunter didn't know she knew.

Lulu pulled her purple satin robe around her bulk. "It's gettin' late, girls. Get yourselves fixed up. Customers will be comin' in soon."

"It ain't as if we have any competition," Blanche complained. "Except for a few squaws over at the *Illahee* and a few respectable wives from that last little bunch of mail-order brides, there ain't any women in Seattle."

Lulu began to clear off her desk. She put away the pen, paper, and ink and shook her head, thinking. Stubborn son-of-a-bitch. Ask for help with a letter, then won't take it. Independent as some damned Yankee. Aloud, she said, "We're about to get some competition if Asa Mercer succeeds in bringin' in that whole shipload of brides; and he may, what with the war almost over and his friendship with President Lincoln."

Blanche pouted and pulled up her stockings. "What kind of girl do you think will accept that letter?"

"Maybe no one," Claire yawned and pushed back a dark curl as she paused in the doorway leading to the hall, "but he ain't gonna marry you, Blanche, or none of us. Hunter wants a lady."

"No lady can give him the fun we do." Blanche grinned and winked. "He'll be back; you wait and see. The lady might get the ring and that big house, but as long as he keeps comin' in here a couple of times a week and slippin' big money in my stocking top—"

"I'd like him to slip a big something in more than my stocking," Sal said wistfully. "He never chooses me."

"Ya'll give him time." Lulu made a soothing gesture. "After all, we ain't been open but a few months. I reckon that big stud'll get around to all of you." Lulu knew why the lumber king craved respectability. Lulu knew more about Hunter than he would want anyone to know. When she'd met his older brother in New Orleans, he'd snickered about Hunter.

Lulu looked in the mirror on her office wall. Another gray hair among her blond locks and, despite the thick powder and rouge, her wrinkles showed. Once she had been young, thin, and pretty, but that was a long time and a lot of men ago. "At least the girl who comes to marry Hunter won't expect romance, just marriage."

Blanche giggled again as they left the office to greet the first customers of the evening. "Maybe he'll change his mind and pick one of us."

Lulu smiled wryly. "Don't ya'll hold your breath 'til that happens. Hunter's pride would never let him marry a slut." Knowing what she did, Lulu was sure of it.

Outside on the muddy street, Hunter turned his coat collar up against the damp wind and pulled his hat down over his blue eyes. He could feel the marks of

14

Blanche's nails on his broad back and still taste Claire's hot kisses. Lulu's Lovelies had seen a lot of him and the other loggers in the few months the place had been open.

Hunter felt for the letter in his pocket. Just what the hell was he getting himself into? It isn't too late to throw it away and forget it, he reminded himself with a frown.

Slowly he lit a cigar and blew out the match, broke it in half, and tossed it. Hunter, you damned fool. He stared at the glowing tip of his smoke. What kind of man would propose marriage to a stranger? Well, weren't these mail-order brides going to be carefully screened? With so many men dead in the Civil War, word was that a lot of respectable women had been left widowed or orphaned and were desperate enough to go thousands of miles to marry men they'd never met.

Hunter wasn't getting any younger; he had passed twenty-five. What good was being one of the richest men in the Territory if he had no children to inherit it? He thought about his father and shivered, wondering if that terrible thing ran in the blood, could be inherited? He'd never discussed that with anyone; Hunter wasn't sure he wanted to know. Maybe he shouldn't want children, but he did. For that reason alone, he could stand to bed some cold little aristocrat once a year. No doubt she'd be relieved if he took his virile appetites down to Lulu's, because ladies weren't supposed to like making love.

Was that what had driven his father into the arms of a beautiful Indian whore?

Hell. He didn't want to think about that because it reminded him of his nightmares. No one knew about the nightmares; he'd never discussed them even with Swede.

15

If he married, what would his wife think when he woke up shaking, drenched in sweat? He took one last drag on his cheroot and stared at the glowing tip as he tossed it in a puddle. Then he started briskly for Asa Mercer's place before he changed his mind and listened to his own misgivings.

Asa Mercer was the president of the new university, which had no students. Hunter allowed himself a rare smile. In lieu of teaching, Mercer was taking donations to bring back a ship-load of brides from back East. Hunter decided that he would double the three hundred dollars the others were giving Mercer so he would get the choicest lady on board. In a few months, Mercer would return with a hand-picked bride for Hunter, and maybe the lady need never know his own shadowy secrets. All Hunter had to do until then was build his wealth, pick out a name for his son, and wait for the future mother to be delivered.

Boston, Massachusetts
January, 1866

Sassy Malone hugged her burly father once more and looked into the five little, freckled faces so much like her own. "Aye, don't be so sad. We'll meet again someday." In her heart, she wasn't sure it was true; and, judging from her brothers' and sisters' expressions, none of them thought so either.

"Aye," Mike agreed in his thick Irish accent, "sure we will. Now you children don't be makin' Sassy feel bad. 'Tis hard enough for her to go."

A big lump came up in her throat that she thought would choke her, but she tried to keep tears from over-

16

flowing her brown eyes. "By the saints, 'tis a grand adventure I'll be having accompanying Miss Merriweather; and I'll keep sending money, just like always." Sassy prayed her father would never learn how she had been earning her money before she found a respectable position as a lady's personal maid a few months ago. She had only done what she had to do, yet Mike Malone was a proud, old-fashioned man. The family had been desperate, but Papa would have starved before he'd have taken money earned that way.

Papa's weather-beaten face reddened as he looked at his scarred arm. "I'm only glad your mother didn't live to see what a pretty pass I've brought to her children. It is a shameful thing indeed that the whole family becomes the responsibility of a mere slip of a girl."

"Now, Papa, I'm almost nineteen and didn't mind helping out after you were hurt on that construction site. Now that you're well, there must be someone who'll hire the Irish."

"Nobody's hiring the Irish," little Megan piped up. "They chase us home when we leave the neighborhood, calling us 'shanty Micks.' "

"We're as good as anybody, we Malones. All you children remember that," Sassy snapped, stroking Megan's dark red hair.

"Aye," Mike agreed, "your mother was a lady; a real highborn lady." His rough face saddened. "She gave up a lot to run away to America with me." He slipped Maureen's ring from his little finger, his own from his left hand. "Sassy, here's the Claddagh rings we gave each other the night we wed. I want you to have them."

"But, Papa, the rings mean so much to you—"

"She'd want you to have them, me darlin' girl." His

17

callused hand pressed the two gold rings into her palm, closed her fingers over them. She felt his hand tremble as if he couldn't bear to think of his dear, dead Maureen. He cleared his throat. "Remember the saying that goes with a Claddagh ring: 'Let love and friendship reign.' May they bring you love and luck."

She leaned to kiss his weathered face one more time. "If they bring me a man like you, Papa, I'll be more than blessed."

He made an awkward, dismissing gesture. "Get along with you now before you miss your train back to New York. Maybe you and your Miss Merriweather will both meet very eligible gentlemen."

Little Ian said proudly, "There's no one good enough for our Sassy!"

The others set up a chorus of agreement, and Sassy had to fight to hold tears back as she kissed them all, thinking she might never see them again. "I—I'll write and I'll send money when I can." Sassy put the rings on a small chain around her neck, then reached to rumple the reddish hair of Paddy, the youngest brother, named for Papa's brother, Patrick. Patrick's family was supposed to have immigrated just before the war started, but they'd lost track of him and his family's whereabouts. One more tragedy for Mike.

"Oh, daughter," Mike's face furrowed, "are you sure now you know what you're about? The papers have been full of talk about this Asa Mercer. Some say Washington is a wild place full of savages and trees as big around as a house. Some say the girls will be used for . . ." He glanced at the big-eyed children, then his honest face reddened and he didn't finish.

Sassy closed her eyes momentarily. If Mike had

18

known how she had disgraced the Malone na—
wouldn't have touched the money she had sent home
this past year. Only a short time ago, she had fled both
New York and Brett James and found honest work in
Philadelphia as a lady's personal maid. "Papa, I told you
Miss Merriweather has exhausted her money and is determined to go. If I don't go with her, I won't have a
job. You know how hard work is to come by with the
war ended and things slowing down, especially for the
Irish."

He nodded and sighed. "Aye, I know, but me heart
won't accept it."

Besides, Brett James was looking for her, Sassy
thought. And when he found her, no doubt he'd kill her.

Little Megan said, "Maybe we can come to Washington, too, someday."

"We'll all ask Our Lady to intercede for us," Sassy
said a little too brightly, touching the rings. Her gaze
caught Mike's, and his sad expression told her he was
thinking the same thing she was: passage for a big family
would be expensive. The Malones would never be able
to raise that much money.

Mike patted the child on the head. "Maybe someday."

Sassy looked around the cramped tenement. The
dirty streets of a teeming Boston slum were no place for
children to grow up. The best she could do was hope
that she would be able to send them a little money, although Miss Merriweather was as tight as a cork in a
bottle. "I must hurry. My employer is short-tempered
and doesn't like to be kept waiting." She hugged and
kissed each one again.

Sassy managed to hold back her tears until she descended the dingy stairs and walked into the cold afternoon, then they made warm trickles down her freckled cheeks. She had probably seen her family for the very last time, yet she had promised her mother on her deathbed that she would look out for them. Big Mike Malone had seemed to disintegrate like a frightened child with his beloved Maureen gone. Sassy reached to touch the gold rings with the small heart motif. Even Queen Victoria wore a Claddagh ring. *Love and friendship.* Sassy never expected to find that kind of marriage—especially not if the man found out about her unforgivable past. Maybe not even God could forgive it. She hurried down the street, shivering in the cold. At least now Sassy had an honest job. If she hadn't been so naive and innocent, she would never have gotten mixed up with Brett James. Sassy pulled her worn coat collar up around her dark red hair. She wasn't innocent anymore. The handsome, dapper saloon-owner had seen to that.

By lifting her skirts and running, Sassy climbed aboard the train just as it was ready to pull out. Miss Sophia Merriweather scowled as Sassy rushed down the aisle breathlessly.

"Well, Shawnna, it took you long enough!" the thin-faced aristocrat snapped. "I've been waiting for you to get me a cup of tea. I'm not feeling well."

Sassy had to force herself to hold her temper, reminding herself that she needed this job; Holy Mother, how she needed this job! It wasn't for nothing her family had nicknamed her 'Sassy.' She sat down. "If you please, ma'am, I was only gone two hours. Little enough time to say goodbye to my family—probably forever."

A scowl crossed the elegant lady's plain face. "You Irish! So sloppily sentimental."

"Aye, we are that." She tried to feel sympathy for Miss Merriweather. After all, what could the sour spinster know about families? She had been reared in a boarding school called Miss Priddy's Academy after her parents died. During the war, the executor of her father's estate had made some unwise investments, impoverishing his ward. Miss Merriweather was fast running out of money and hoped to find a rich husband in Washington Territory, where women were scarce and beauty not so important. Otherwise, there was no way that very civilized lady would have considered becoming one of Mercer's mail-order brides. Desperate circumstances called for desperate decisions, Sassy thought. "I'll get you some tea, ma'am," she said docilely and stood up; but just then the train puffed and lurched as it began to move, sending her falling back into her seat.

Miss Merriweather's thin lips set in a grim line. "See? Now it's too late. I won't get any tea until the next station."

Sassy bit her lip to keep from pointing out that Sophia Merriweather could certainly have gotten herself a cup of tea in the station during these two hours while she waited for her maid to return. Miss Merriweather had the disposition of a wounded lioness and might fire Sassy on the spot. "I—I'll do better."

"I should take it out of your pay."

"You owe me three months back wages now," Sassy muttered.

"What did you say?"

Remember how much you need this job, Sassy reminded herself. *And how hard it is for an Irish girl to get a position at all. Sooner or later, she'll pay you, and at least you've been getting board and room.* "I said I'm deeply sorry for my shortcomings." She settled back in her seat and looked around at the people traveling in the coach.

Miss Merriweather's gaze followed hers. "My father would roll over in his grave if he knew his only child was now forced to ride with all these poor, ragged immigrants." She sniffed in disdain and then put a dainty handkerchief to her nose to keep from smelling the odors around her. "In the old days, I had *real* servants. Dear Daddy would be so upset if he knew I was almost penniless, having to make do with one Irish girl. Daddy would never hire the Irish; he thought we should send them all back where they belonged."

Sassy forced herself not to reply. She must change the subject. "Are you looking forward to Washington Territory? I hear it's beautiful."

Her choice of subjects was poor. She realized it immediately as Miss Merriweather frowned again. "If I weren't down to my last few dollars because of the idiot who invested my money in that Huntington Uniform Factory, I wouldn't have lost everything." The spinster touched her chest. "It just gives me pains to think about it."

Huntington, Sassy thought. Could that be Albert Huntington, the man Brett James killed? No, couldn't be; too coincidental. "Perhaps you'll meet a rich husband—"

"Imagine someone of my family background having to marry some uncouth frontiersman!" Miss Merriweather put her handkerchief to her mouth, annoyed.

"Well, now, you could get a job like I did," Sassy blurted without thinking.

Sophia Merriweather scowled and her thin lips curled into a sneer. "That's all right, I suppose, for a common Mick, but a *lady* doesn't go to work. How dare you even use that nasty, unthinkable word to me!"

Sassy touched the rings hanging under her dress collar, thinking Maureen had been twice the lady Miss Merriweather could ever be and when construction jobs were hard to come by for Papa, Maureen sometimes had done housework at the fine Van Schuyler estate in Boston. However, Sassy held back her fiery retort and reminded herself that Washington Territory might be a fresh start for her, too. She certainly couldn't afford to go except with her employer buying the passage. Sassy apologized again.

Miss Merriweather coughed as she looked out the coach window at the snowy landscape whizzing by. "I'm not feeling at all well, but then *real* ladies have such delicate constitutions."

Sassy decided to ignore the jab, leaned back in her seat, and closed her eyes, pretending to be asleep. No matter what she did or how hard she worked, she couldn't seem to make Sophia Merriweather like her. She had heard another lady's maid say it was because Sassy was pretty and Miss Merriweather was not. Sassy's beauty was what had taken Brett's eye and gotten her into that nightmare existence she was now trying to escape.

They reached New York City and checked into a modest, but respectable hotel on a cold January night. The ship was due to sail tomorrow. Sassy dealt with all the luggage and arrangements while Miss Merriweather

23

sat and complained; but then, Miss Merriweather always complained. No wonder she couldn't get a husband, Sassy thought with exasperation. Only in some area where there was a shortage of women would mail-order brides like her be sought after.

Miss Merriweather ordered dinner sent up to their room. It was a skimpy meal, but then, Sassy knew the money was getting low. Sassy didn't get quite enough to eat, but she didn't reach for seconds. The prim spinster took the extra for herself and then complained all evening that she felt bloated and had heartburn.

Sassy prayed for patience and decided not to point out that the lady probably didn't feel well because she had eaten so much. "Ma'am, should I call a doctor?" Sassy asked politely.

"No, you idiot! I don't want to spend the money. I'm sure I'll feel better tomorrow."

Sassy nodded, helped her into her nightgown, and then packed their things. The ship was leaving tomorrow. Sassy wouldn't feel safe until she was on it and it sailed out of New York harbor. There was always just the slightest chance one of Brett's henchmen might have seen Sassy coming from the train station or would spot her as the pair went to catch their ship. Sassy wasn't even sure whether Brett's Black Garter was closed permanently. She did know he and Marylou would still be looking for Sassy since her testimony could put nooses around their necks.

She went to bed and lay there in the dark, unable to sleep even if her employer hadn't been snoring in a most unladylike way. Some lady. Maureen Malone had taught her own daughter about proper manners and Sassy had been struggling to do away with her Irish accent because it annoyed the sour spinster so. Why, if she ever got the chance, she could certainly be more of a lady than Sophia, for all her blue blood.

At least her employer had said she had bought the tickets in advance, so they had their ship passage already paid for. She wondered why Miss Merriweather was even bothering to take an Irish maid whom she didn't like all the way to Washington Territory? Knowing how prejudiced the prim lady was, she probably didn't want to put up with an Indian servant and, besides, she'd have to train a new girl. At least she needed Sassy to fetch and carry for her until they got on the ship; ladies didn't make tea and pack their own luggage.

It was a long time before she dropped off to sleep with Miss Merriweather snoring away.

Sassy awoke with a start. It was still dark and the hotel room felt cool. What time was it? She'd have to get up early to fix Miss Merriweather some tea. At least Miss Merriweather had finally stopped snoring.

Sassy sighed and sat up slowly. It must not be long 'til dawn. She wished she could lie in the warm bed a few more minutes; but she had always worked hard, even when she was a small girl, because the Malones were so poor. Mama had once had a fine house, too, and had given it all up for Papa when her father had said she couldn't marry Mike. Sassy had seen her mother die because there was no money for medicine, seen her little brothers and sisters hungry and ragged after Papa had his accident. Desperation had driven her out to find work and she had walked innocently into a nightmare.

Thinking about the danger Brett James posed to her,

25

she decided the sooner she got on that ship, the safer she would be. She got up and dressed in a plain, frumpy dress—one of Miss Merriweather's discards—and tried to be grateful that they were both almost the same size so she could wear the lady's hand-me-downs. She checked to make sure everything was packed up, then made a pot of tea on the little oil burner and sipped a cup. It was warm and bracing in the cool room. She wished she had thick cream for her tea and a warm sugar-bun covered with melted butter and homemade jam. Ah, well, maybe someday. . . . Sassy finished her tea.

Now all she had to do was wake Miss Merriweather and get her ready. She'd just as soon wake a sleeping bear, but it was part of her job. She tiptoed over to the bed. "Miss Merriweather? Time to get up."

The grumpy spinster gave no sign she was even considering answering, much less complying.

"Ma'am, remember? We've a ship to catch."

The woman lay with her back to Sassy. She didn't move.

Sassy reached out, touched her shoulder. "Miss Merriweather, we'll have to get ready to . . ." Sassy's voice trailed off as she shook the lady.

"Miss Merriweather?" With growing horror and disbelief, Sassy reached to touch the lady's hand then recoiled at the feel of icy flesh.

"Holy Mother of God!" Sassy gasped and crossed herself. Miss Merriweather would never shout or curse at Sassy again.

The prim lady was dead.

Chapter Two

Horrified, Sassy crossed herself again and backed away from the bed. Holy Mother of God, what should she do? A doctor. She should get a doctor. Whirling, she ran for the door. Halfway there, she stopped and looked back at the body. No, a doctor wouldn't do any good. The coldness of Miss Merriweather's skin told her the lady had been dead for hours. Oh, why hadn't she called a doctor last night? Miss Merriweather complained so constantly, Sassy hadn't taken her seriously.

The police. Of course she must notify the authorities. Heart pounding hard, she paused with her hand on the knob. Dear God, suppose they accused her of killing her employer?

What to do? Sassy leaned against the door and trembled. Outside, a raw north wind whipped around the building, wailing like a banshee.

If she went for the police, at the very least there would be an investigation and Sassy might get her name in the paper. Suppose Brett James saw it and came looking for her? As a witness to the murder he had committed, she represented a threat to him. A poor Irish girl

27

could disappear in this big city without a trace. She had no doubt Brett would have no qualms about silencing her any way he could.

Sassy went to the window and looked out. Few people were on the streets in the cold January dawn. The leaden sky was spitting snow. She could just run away and. . . . She shook back her reddish hair. No, that wouldn't work, either. In only a couple of hours, a cleaning woman would come to the room, find the body, and raise the alarm. The desk clerk might remember Sassy. She could be arrested for murder.

Poor Sophia Merriweather. Now that Sassy's initial panic had passed, she could pity the arrogant, mean woman. Her mother had always said try to find the good in everyone and understand them. Sassy had tried to do that for her employer, although, praise the saints, it strained the temper. The aristocrat had so looked forward to starting a new life in Washington Territory. So had Sassy—a fresh start on life with a clean slate where no one knew her secret past; maybe even a sweet, kind husband for herself.

What to do? She forced herself to remain calm as the seconds ticked away. Miss Merriweather hadn't paid Sassy any wages in weeks, claiming she was almost penniless and Sassy had been powerless to do anything about it. Now she had no money, was on the run from Brett, and had to decide what to do about a body.

If nothing else, Sassy had nerve and was as scrappy as an alley cat. Her mother had taught her a few of the fine points of being a lady, but coming up in the worst section of Boston had made her a scrapper. Most ladies at this point would get a case of the 'vapors' and faint, but Sassy decided that wouldn't help. Instead of collapsing and wailing, Sassy was going to have to act. Where to begin?

She should notify some relative or friend of Miss Merriweather's to make funeral arrangements. Sassy pursed her lips and shook her head. No, the lady didn't have any family left and she was too sour to have any friends. That left Sassy to deal with the funeral. She had no money and no idea what such things cost. A priest. A priest would know and certainly Sassy could use the lady's own money, no matter how small an amount was in the lady's reticule.

Hastily, Sassy found her employer's purse and, with some hesitancy, opened it. Holy Mary, there was a nice sum of money inside. Could Miss Merriweather have lied about not being able to pay Sassy her back wages? It wasn't her place to judge the dead woman. Maybe she hadn't yet paid for the pair of ship passages. Aye, that had to be it. Strange, she would have sworn Miss Merriweather had said she had taken care of all that. Maybe there'd be enough to pay for the funeral. Sassy took the purse and as she did, her gaze fell on the lady's monogrammed carpet bag. *S.M. Sophia Merriweather. S.M. Sassy Malone.* A thought crossed Sassy's mind, a daring idea born of sheer fear and desperation. Could a leprechaun or her own personal guardian angel have put the answer in her mind?

Sassy took Miss Merriweather's coat, luggage, and purse, taking care to leave her own few clothes behind. She looked one more time toward the bed and said a small prayer for the soul of the departed. Then she slipped out the door and closed it softly behind her.

Out on the street, the wind whipped through her clothes and snow flurries blew along the sidewalk. Sassy

29

asked several people and found her way to a Catholic church, not quite sure what to do next. If she tried to pay for a funeral for an aristocratic lady, there would be questions. However, if a lady took care of funeral arrangements for a poor Irish serving girl, who would bother to investigate?

Could she possibly pass herself off as a fine lady? She tried to remember everything her mother had taught her; all the niceties she had learned from Sophia Merriweather these past few weeks. If she were careful about her accent and her grammar, remembered all she knew about proper behavior, she just might pull it off. What she would do once she made funeral arrangements for Miss Merriweather, Sassy had no idea. She only wanted to escape her desperate troubles.

A chill ran down her back as she recalled arriving in New York last night. She had seen a stout woman entering a carriage who bore some resemblance to Marylou Evans, the hostess at Brett's Black Garter. 'Hostess' was a polite term, Sassy thought with a shudder. Marylou was the madam for the more profitable upstairs business. If that woman had been Marylou, had she seen Sassy? If so, Brett might be searching the city even now. The thought of what he would do if and when he caught up with her made her tremble. Marylou Evans had been an accomplice in that murder and risked jail or a hangman's noose, too, if Sassy testified. Hadn't the authorities hanged a woman last summer, that one who was part of the Lincoln assassination plot?

Keeping her face shadowed and hiding her dark red hair beneath the hood of her cloak, Sassy awakened a sleepy priest at the church. In her most lady-like masquerade, she explained she was leaving town and that

30

her Irish maid, Sassy Malone, had died during the night. Since the girl was an immigrant with no relatives in New York, could the priest possibly see to the arrangements so Miss Merriweather wouldn't be inconvenienced in her travels?

Sassy gave him most of the money from the purse and the hotel's address. Ignoring his disapproving gaze and questions, she gathered up her things and hurried from the church.

'Tis now I need luck more than love and friendship. She reached for the comforting feel of the twin rings on the thin gold chain around her neck. If she weren't careful, she'd burst into tears and break down. No, she didn't have time for hysteria; that was for fools or elegant ladies. Sassy was shaking as she walked away into the cold dawn. She had done all she could do for the dead woman. But what should she do now?

Sassy paused, the cold, raw wind whipping her fiery hair around her freckled face. If she could get a refund on the ship passages, it would surely cover the back wages she was owed. She had given her last small sum to her father. Sassy hurried to the port.

The *Continental* was loading in preparation for its trip down around the tip of South America and on to Seattle. Wistfully, Sassy thought of her big plans for going to Washington Territory, landing a rich and loving husband, making a fresh start and bringing her family out of the dirty slums of Boston. La, she could forget about that dream now, couldn't she?

Asking about the tickets, she was directed to a Mr. Asa Mercer, the balding, bearded young man who had thought up this Washington trip. "I—I'm Miss Merriweather," she said regally, "I believe you are holding

31

passage for me and my personal servant? The girl has decided not to—"

"Servant?" He scratched his beard, looked from Sassy to the list in his hand. "No, Miss Merriweather, your passage is paid, but don't you remember your note?"

"Note?" Sassy blinked.

He flipped through all the papers in the stack. "Ah, yes, here it is." He handed it to her. Sassy recognized the handwriting. Aye, it was Miss Merriweather's, all right. It stated that there was money enclosed for one passage, that she intended to fire her personal maid on the morning of the ship's departure. After all, why go to the expense of taking a maid along since surely an Indian girl could be hired and trained in Washington Territory much cheaper?

Sassy had to stifle a gasp. So Miss Merriweather had intended to leave Sassy behind, probably without giving her the back wages she owed her.

"Of course," she fumbled for words, "I—I had forgotten I hadn't paid for her ticket, but of course I fired her which is the reason she isn't with me."

Mr. Mercer shrugged. "Miss, I'll have someone show you to your quarters. We hope to be under way before three this afternoon."

"Wonderful!" She heaved a sigh of relief. "Did you really end up with a ship-load of brides?"

He laughed and looked a little embarrassed. "To tell the truth, no. Everything was going well with the early plans since my friend, President Lincoln, promised his help."

"And he was killed," Sassy thought aloud, remembering.

"Yes, just a few weeks before I arrived." Asa Mercer

sighed. "Next the army decided they couldn't legally help me with a ship; and finally Ben Holladay, the stagecoach king, got involved, bought the ship, and offered passage."

It occurred to her he hadn't answered her initial question. In fact, Sassy had a distinct feeling he was avoiding it. "Mr. Mercer," she looked him in the eye, "just how many ladies are on this journey?"

He combed his beard with his fingers, avoided her direct gaze. "We had such bad newspaper publicity, bunch of scoffers. The President's assassination delayed us."

"I heard about it," Sassy nodded.

"Well, the papers have not been kind," he admitted. "Some of them have been printing wild tales of how the ladies who embark on this daring adventure are really taking their reputations lightly and are slated to end up in . . ." He paused, stammered, and his face turned red.

"I'm not foolish enough to believe that!" Sassy said with spirit. The man looked too naive to know such things. "Sir, you still have not answered my question."

"I haven't?" He turned away as if he had just thought of important matters that needed his immediate attention.

"You'll find I'm quite stubborn." She caught his sleeve. "Now answer my question. Hundreds of prospective brides are supposed to be on this trip, a whole shipful. Just how many did you end up with?"

"I managed to get a number of families who hope to relocate to Washington," he said and took out a handkerchief to mop his brow even though the morning air was cold.

"How many girls?" Sassy insisted. Papa had always

33

said she could hang onto a subject like a terrier to a bone.

"Indeed, you are a very stubborn, spirited young lady!"

"Mr. Mercer, how many?"

"Uh, about fifty or so; more or less."

"Fifty? Did you say only fifty?" The undertaking suddenly seemed much more perilous as Sassy realized hundreds of women had had second thoughts about the whole project and backed out. Perhaps she should do the same.

"Not a lot, Miss Merriweather," he stammered, "but I'm sure those will have their choice of husbands, since there are several hundred eager men."

She hesitated, looked out toward shore. Somewhere in that very city, a murderer might now be searching for Sassy. Then, too, the priest might have somehow discovered that the dead woman was an aristocrat and the authorities might be looking for her maid. Sassy wondered again if she were making a mistake? What would her mother have done? She reached to touch the rings under the neck of her coat. It was too late to turn back now. For good or bad, Sassy was for all intents and purposes Sophia Merriweather, highly respectable lady from back East. Sassy Malone was being buried along with her past in a churchyard in New York City.

"All right, sir, I'm both brave and stubborn; I'll take a chance on this new frontier of yours."

She saw admiration in his eyes; and he studied her a long moment, then finally nodded. "Yes, I think you'll do, although you're prettier than he's expecting to get." He reached in his coat and handed her a letter.

"I beg your pardon?" She took it and looked at the envelope, wondering what he was blathering about.

"Just read it," Mercer said. "I assure you the prospective bridegroom is everything he says he is, although . . ." He paused as if there were things not in the letter that he hesitated to bring up.

A little bewildered, Sassy opened it and stood there in the cold wind reading it. "Sounds as if he's buying a horse or closing a business deal."

"Ah, he is a bit blunt and perhaps not as romantic as some ladies would prefer," Mercer conceded, red-faced, "but he's wealthy and some would call him handsome."

"I must give it some thought," Sassy stammered. "I—I'll be in my cabin," she turned and strode briskly across the deck.

Once below decks, she said prayers for cold-hearted Miss Merriweather, who had plotted to leave Sassy behind with no money and no references. Then she threw herself across her bed and wept from sheer terror and relief that she was finally safe. At last, exhausted, Sassy dropped off to sleep, still clutching the crumpled letter.

The throb of the engines awakened her. On a cold January afternoon, 1866, the *Continental* steamed out of New York Harbor. Sassy went to the porthole and stared out at the receding skyline. Relief mixed with sadness and brought tears to her brown eyes. Aye, she was safe now, but she would probably never see her papa and her five little brothers and sisters again.

She looked at the letter in her hand, reread it. This James Hunter was rich and powerful. Sassy's struggling family needed financial help badly; enough so that Sassy was willing to make any sacrifice—even if it meant marrying some backwoodsman who was no doubt uncouth, elderly, and ugly. If James Hunter were rich enough to help her family and wanted to buy himself a bride as coldly as if he were buying a mare for breeding stock, maybe she should do it. At least the old codger might not know anything about aristocracy, so he wouldn't know Sassy was no lady. It was thousands of miles and several months before they would reach Washington Territory, which gave her plenty of time to polish her grammar and manners. Besides, she didn't have to make a decision yet; she'd think on it.

After what she'd been through at the Black Garter, she really never wanted another man to touch her. The thought of marriage, submitting her body for some man's use, made her shudder. Naive and young, she had thought she was in love with Brett. He had plied her with drink and seduced her only weeks after she had answered his advertisement for a waitress. And he had repaid her love by forcing her to work upstairs in his brothel.

As the days passed on the ship, she had a chance to meet and mingle with the other passengers. What really unnerved her was discovering there was a young reporter from the *New York Times*, Roger Conant, on board, coming along to cover the story of the brides' trip. Suppose he found out who she really was?

Then the weather turned bad, the seas got rough, and many people became seasick. At that point, Sassy didn't care if anyone found out her secrets; she just wanted to die and get it over with. However, there were others more ill than she and when she realized that, she pulled herself to her feet and went to help them. The prospective brides ranged from very young to rather old; some widowed, some with children. They told sad tales of fathers or husbands killed in the Civil War and spoke of a shortage of prospective husbands because of all the deaths. The women had joined this daring adventure out of desperation since there were few available jobs for them back East. She found herself watching the ladies, wondering idly if any of them were hiding secrets, too, trying to close the door on their pasts, hoping to make fresh starts as Sassy was doing?

The trip settled into a routine. Some days it was exciting, others dull with little to break the tedium. Sassy had intended to keep to herself, but she was too friendly and fun-loving to sit in her cabin while the other women were up on deck. Sassy found herself sharing recipes and talk with the women and playing with fretful babies. Sassy loved children and had always hoped someday she would have a houseful of her own.

Everyone seemed to accept her at face value when she passed herself off as Sophia (everyone calls me 'Sassy') Merriweather—even that reporter, who flirted with all the girls, but most assuredly with Sassy.

At times she ached to tell everyone the truth. Would she have to be Sophia Merriweather forever? Basically an honest person, Sassy's conscience pained her, but her very life might be at stake should her whereabouts ever get back to Brett James.

Brett James. There was one more thing left to do to close the door forever on her past. The first time the ship stopped at a port down the coast, she sent Brett a letter telling him Sassy Malone was dead and buried in

New York. As her employer, Miss Merriweather was responding to Sassy's request to notify him if anything happened to her. Brett wouldn't recognize her handwriting and maybe he would believe the letter and stop looking for her.

Rough weather and boredom made everyone gloomy. Sassy took it upon herself to cheer everyone up with games and music. She could play the piano, but not very well, and she played all the popular songs of the day. Asa Mercer himself took a shine to one of the prospective brides, Annie. As the weeks passed, some of the girls looked with more than a little interest at the ship's crew. Sassy could tell by Mercer's worried expression when the ship put in at San Francisco and a bunch of the passengers got off and refused to go any farther that he was concerned that he might end up with no brides to deliver to Seattle at all.

He approached Sassy hesitantly. "You are going on with us, aren't you, Miss Merriweather? I've accepted a lot of money from possible bridegrooms in Washington and they are going to be angry if none of the ladies arrive."

"Of course I will." She didn't tell him that, to her, San Francisco posed a possible danger: Brett James had said he had lived there once. She was afraid he might return someday. She couldn't risk running into him on the street in that bay city.

He wiped his sweating face although it was a pleasant spring day. "Holladay's ship won't take us any farther without more money, so I wired Governor Pickering."

"Oh? He's sending money for us to continue?"

Mercer shook his head, looking a bit embarrassed.

"All he sent was a collect message wishing me luck and telling me I was on my own."

"Perhaps some of these lumber vessels I see might be willing to take us for little or nothing."

His bearded face lit up. "What a good idea! I'll look into it right away." He started to turn away, stopped. "Oh, Miss Merriweather, what have you decided about the letter?"

Sassy hadn't made a decision. She wrinkled her freckled nose. "I keep wondering: Why me?"

He hesitated, stroking his beard. "You strike me as a little fiestier than most of these ladies, someone who isn't afraid of the devil himself."

Sassy felt an uneasiness sweep over her. "That's not too reassuring, sir. Somehow I feel you are warning me."

"Oh, no," he answered hastily, "nothing like that." His averted gaze made a liar of him. "Mr. Hunter is quite rich and very choosey. Mind you, you're under no obligation if you decide he isn't for you."

She was intrigued that Asa Mercer was evidently a bit frightened of the man. "What is it you aren't telling me?"

He hesitated again, rubbed his hands together. "Remember James Hunter is quite wealthy and powerful."

Once more he had deliberately avoided her question. She thought again how much wealth would mean to her ragged family in Boston. "Jim," she mused aloud, "I like the name."

"No one calls him that," Mercer said with a shake of his balding head. "Hunter. Just Hunter."

Hunter. That name sounded menacing. She stared at him. Merciful saints, what was she getting into? On the

39

other hand, if this mysterious Mr. Hunter were indeed rich and powerful, she would have the protection of his name and position and everything that went with it. She would be safe at last. "I—I'll think on it."

Mercer gave a sigh of relief, turned, and fled across the deck. She stared after him a long moment, then went below to study the letter again.

She was more than troubled; his tone made her outraged and angry. Just who did this James Hunter think he was? Aye, she had half a mind to rip the letter to shreds and throw it overboard. Except that money and power made him a man to be reckoned with. Sassy paced her cabin. Perhaps she had misunderstood his tone.

She stared at the words. At least he had nice handwriting for a man. Maybe he was more sensitive than he seemed. Somehow Sassy doubted that. She reread the letter, trying to imagine what kind of a man would write it. He sounded cold, opinionated, and pig-headed—just the kind of man that she would clash with. This wasn't what she had in mind for a husband at all. She imagined what James Hunter would expect in bed and grimaced. No doubt he was just like the upstairs customers at Brett's Black Garter.

Sassy decided she would look him over for a day or two without letting him know she had the letter. After all, she didn't have to make any commitment or decision yet. However, from his tone, she was certain he wasn't a man she would want to marry, money and power be damned!

Finally, Mercer talked a lumber boat into hauling the ladies up the coast for nothing. Several of the belles decided to stay in San Francisco despite Mercer's pleas, although Roger Conant, the reporter, stayed aboard to see the outcome of the long trip for his newspaper.

Sassy would have been tempted to stay in San Francisco herself, but suppose Brett returned here? Could marriage to James Hunter possibly be so bad, especially when her family needed financial help? She read the letter again, decided it could. When she tried to question Asa Mercer further, he was evasive and quickly changed the subject. That made Sassy even more uneasy. She had a distinct feeling there was a lot about the mysterious suitor that Mercer wasn't telling.

In spite of everything, Sassy watched the coastline with increasing excitement as the hours passed. The giant trees and the rocky coastline looked wild and beautiful to her after all the years she had spent in cramped city slums. She loved the salt spray blowing in her face. The farther up the coast they churned, the surer she was that she had made the right choice. Already the beauty of the country appealed to her. She was glad she had had the courage to continue on instead of staying in San Francisco.

The May weather was clear and beautiful, the sea spray blowing cold on her face as they entered Puget Sound and cut through the water along the coast. In the distance, a snowcapped mountain a crew member identified as Mount Rainier gleamed in the morning light. At last they neared the harbor and the passengers set up a cheer. "Seattle! Seattle!"

With mounting excitement, Sassy ran to the railing and took her first look at the village nestled among the towering trees. It didn't look like much, she thought, but maybe some hearty settlers could gradually create a

41

great city. A crowd of men had gathered on the dock, cheering and waving their hats. Sassy scanned the men's faces, wondering which was James Hunter?

Was she about to view her future husband? With heart beating hard and fingers trembling, she put her hand above her eyes to shield them from the sun while looking over the men on the dock. Which one was he?

A man on horseback rode out onto the dock just then—a very tall, dark man wearing a black coat and western hat. He would have stood out in any crowd even if he hadn't been riding the biggest horse Sassy had every seen, its silver-trimmed saddle and bridle reflecting the sunlight. A fine stallion, ebony, with a snowy white rump and black spots.

Sassy turned to the first mate as he hurried across the deck. "I've never seen a horse like that one before. What do you know of it?"

"Ah, 'tis one of those fancy ones the Indians raise. Appaloosas, I think they call them. Here, Miss, use my spyglass for a better look."

"Oh, thank you." Eagerly, Sassy took it from him, straining for a closer look at man and horse. It was a fine stallion, all right, its bridle and saddle decorated with heavy silver. She swept the glass over the man. Holy Mother of God, he was a big one! The waistcoat, expertly cut, suited his wide-shouldered form. The brim of his hat shadowed his face for a long moment, but then he looked up and seemed to be staring directly at her.

"An Indian savage!" she gasped and turned to confront Mercer. All the wild stories she had heard came back to her. "I knew the men out here would be frontiersmen, but I didn't expect to worry about my scalp!"

42

"Now, now," Mercer reassured her, "he's not quite half-Indian, his mother had white blood, too."

With trembling hands, Sassy trained the spy glass on the man again. He seemed older than she had hoped for, or maybe he had just lived hard. A lock of black, curly hair hung down on his swarthy forehead.

A handsome face, she thought, but a mouth that looked as if it didn't know how to smile. She took a closer look at the eyes, so moody yet blue as the Pacific. Dark and dangerous as the devil himself. At once she had an uneasy feeling and automatically crossed herself. "Mr. Mercer, by Our Lady, who is that richly dressed, scowling rogue?"

He hesitated before answering. "James Hunter."

Chapter Three

Taken aback and a little afraid, Sassy returned the spyglass to the first mate and took a deep breath for courage. Saints preserve her, maybe God was about to get even with her for all her past sins by handing her over to the devil himself!

Now wait a minute, Sassy, she reminded herself as the ship dropped anchor and people scurried about, getting ready to disembark, you don't have to marry this James Hunter if you don't want to. He's waiting for you to present yourself because he won't know which girl has his letter.

Quickly, Sassy looked around the deck. Maybe she should give the letter to another one of the prospective brides. No, she shook her head. Most of these women seemed like such meek and mild ladies. In their sheltered lives, probably they had never come across a man who looked so stormy and forbidding. They would all be terrified of him. Besides, she wasn't obligated just because she had his letter. She'd look over the other men and choose one more to her liking or find herself a job, if there were any available.

She pasted a prim smile on her face and joined the others moving down the gang plank. The men on shore cheered and threw their hats in the air. However, the big dark man did not move or even dismount. He leaned on his saddle horn and watched the women coming onto the dock with the detached air of one who was watching a herd of heifers unload. He did not look ill at ease or eager or even a trifle embarrassed as some of the others did.

Once they all stood on the dock, Asa Mercer gestured for silence and cleared his throat. "Fellow citizens of Seattle, this is indeed an auspicious occasion! More than a year ago, you sent me off on a noble mission. I am back today with that mission done. Right now, we are a mere village of a few hundred souls, but who can know the future?" He grasped his coat lapels. "Why, I predict that someday Seattle might even be as important to the commerce of the west coast as San Francisco with a population in the thousands!"

Again the rowdy men cheered and threw their hats in the air. Asa Mercer droned on and on, but Sassy suspected not many were listening. Already the men and the girls were glancing at one another, sizing up possible mates. Several men smiled shyly at her. When they caught her eye, they looked timidly away, not meeting her gaze. She sneaked a look at the dark man on the Appaloosa. His gaze moved across all the women, studying them as frankly as if choosing a filly at a livestock auction. Worse yet, his bold stare left no doubt that he was mentally undressing each one, judging her physical attributes.

Bless the saints, Sassy thought with annoyance, the

next thing he'll be doing is moving through the crowd, asking to see the women's teeth!

His cold expression annoyed her and she glared at his profile. He seemed to feel her indignation and turned his head in her direction, his ice-blue eyes burning into hers.

He would not stare a Malone down! Sassy glared back defiantly. He looked surprised, then annoyed.

It occurred to Sassy that while an Irish servant-girl might appraise a man so frankly, a prim lady from back East would not. She must remember to act like Miss Sophia Merriweather from Boston. Demurely, she forced herself to look away. Still she felt his cold stare sweeping over her from head to toe in a curious, impertinent manner. She couldn't stop herself from sneaking a glance at him. His gaze moved slowly over her generous swell of breasts almost as if his hands touched her there. She felt naked, although she wore a prissy blue dress of dainty flowered lawn with a high, lacy neck. In spite of herself, Sassy felt the blood rush to her face.

Now just the slightest hint of an amused smile tugged at his grim mouth. He knew he had unnerved her and caused her to retreat, she thought, unable to keep the flush from spreading down her neck. His look moved from her face, down her neck, and onto her breasts again. Damn him for a scoundrel! No doubt he was wondering if she could nurse the children he would put in her belly. Or maybe he was thinking . . .

She felt her face burn hotly again as she saw a sudden vision of herself naked and in bed with this lithe, virile man, his face dark against her snowy, full breasts, his mouth hot and demanding on her nipples. The image sent an unaccustomed warmth from her neck down to the vee of her thighs. Now she was really thrown for a loss. Sassy had been used as a plaything for lustful, wealthy men, but she had never felt anything but indifference and shame when they touched her. She didn't like the way James Hunter's look affected her emotions.

Furious both with him and with herself, she turned away and pretended to listen to Mercer's speech, but now she thought she felt his smoldering gaze burning into her back. It seemed to start at her waist and caress her hips as if his big dark hands were warm on her naked flesh.

She had never been so unnerved by or disliked a man on sight as much as she had this one. She prayed to the saints that he wasn't the punishment that had been arranged as a penitence for all her past sins. Stubbornly, Sassy decided she wouldn't even do him the favor of letting him know she had his letter. There were plenty of other men here to choose from: old, young, handsome, ugly, rich, and poor. She looked around. Some of the other ladies were looking the big man over rather coyly. There was something about his savage masculinity that drew females, Sassy thought, like moths to a flaming torch. Did the silly moths understand the danger but just couldn't resist the fire? Aye, here was one who did!

Mercer finished his speech to cheers and applause. A pair of big wagons creaked down to the dock to take the passengers to the hotel where they would be quartered while the men wooed the ladies or the ladies found jobs.

Hunter sighed as Mercer made his speech. He leaned on his saddle horn, coolly assessing the bevy of females on the dock. Now just which one had Mercer picked for

47

him? As much money as he had given Mercer, his mail-order bride had better be the cream of the crop. His gaze went to one and then another, sizing them up as he would a filly he was considering buying. A good investment would be one of top bloodlines and the right breeding age. There were several that looked like they might fit his requirements. What about that one? She was small and slight with hair as dark red as glowing coals. Of course she had a very unladylike smattering of freckles across her nose and looked a bit younger than he wanted. Then again, she certainly had the equipment to nurse a fine strong son. His curious gaze went from her small waist to her generous expanse of bosom.

She had caught him looking her over and those brown eyes flashed with fire. In fact, she looked quite annoyed. That meant she had a temper; most unladylike and, anyway, he didn't want a woman who was headstrong and would defy him instead of behaving like a proper wife. He wanted a mild, refined type to decorate his house—a female who would fit in with the carpet, his paintings, and the local gentry. On the other hand, if she were a bit spirited, could she pass that trait on to her sons? The idea intrigued him.

She was glaring at him now as if she were about to come over and give him a piece of her mind. The other women looked demurely away when his frank gaze swept over them. He looked the pert one over again. No, she wasn't the prettiest of the lot . . . or was she? And she was hardly more than a school girl. What Hunter had ordered was a demure virgin of about twenty-two or three who would obey his every demand. Wasn't that what a wife was supposed to do? He would be master in his own house and the sweet maiden would produce children and tend her wifely duties. Of course he expected to be bored, but weren't proper women always boring? He expected to take his pleasure down at Lulu's place. Everyone said respectable women were relieved if husbands discreetly took their animal appetites elsewhere.

He took one more long look at the small redhead and shook his head. No, he certainly didn't want that one. Not only did she look like she might have a mind of her own, she looked as if she could be as independent and stubborn as hell if she dug her heels in and decided not to budge.

She stuck her pert, freckled nose in the air and turned her back on him, pretending to listen to Mercer's dull speech. How dare she do that? Didn't she know who he was? He had wealth and power and even the men of Seattle feared and respected him. How dare this snip of a girl turn her nose up at him?

Hunter pushed his hat back and shifted his weight in the saddle. He looked over the crowd of women again and wondered which one was his? Thank God some other man would have to deal with the fiery little redhead. No doubt she would lead some man a merry chase before he tamed her . . . if he tamed her. Probably there wasn't a man in the crowd who was up to that challenge. He himself might be able to do it, but that wasn't his problem.

If he could ever get Mercer aside, he would ask which one had his letter. He had expected too much, maybe, in thinking the woman would come forward in a no-nonsense manner so he could claim her. Of course that was how females behaved, he supposed. It occurred to Hunter that he really didn't know very much about women at all. He thought about his mother and frowned. The only women he had ever known were whores of easy virtue like those at Lulu's Lovelies. Having been raised in the company of men, Hunter had never had much of a boyhood. He looked toward that area of town known as the Sawdust. Of course the whores wouldn't come down to see the respectable women arrive.

Mercer seemed to drone on and on. Hunter pulled out his pocket watch on its big gold chain and checked the hour. He didn't have much time allotted for this securing a wife. He had business back at the mill and out on the lumber leases. If Mercer would just shut up and point out the female, Hunter could be married in a couple of hours and mark that off his list of tasks to do. He could take her virginity and install her in his house tonight. Tomorrow he could be back running his empire and the new wife could be seeing to the running of his household.

That thought made him frown. Damn, he hadn't thought about a woman coming in and changing his life. She'd probably put lace on everything and hang her drawers across the kitchen stove. Old Cookie wouldn't like that a bit. Swede had tried to talk Hunter out of it and was no doubt sulking out at the timber camp or enjoying himself as he so often did at Lulu's. Swede said three men and an elderly tomcat had gotten along just fine for several years now with good whiskey and bad women and they didn't need no prissy gal coming in to change things, by jingo.

Hunter took out an expensive cheroot, lit it, inhaled the fragrant smoke while breaking the match in half, making sure it was out before he tossed it away. Any man in the timber industry learned early to be careful with fire.

As Mercer talked, Hunter looked over the women again. Which one? His eyes returned to the redhead in spite of himself. Idly, he wondered which man would get her. Thank God it wasn't going to be him! Mercer wouldn't have been stupid enough to give his letter to that sassy little piece. He breathed a sigh of relief at the thought. Still his gaze lingered on her small waist, trim enough for a man to put his hands around—if his hands were as big as Hunter's. Did that mean she couldn't produce children? His gaze went to her hips. Those looked capable of birthing a baby. He wondered suddenly if her naked body was as creamy pale as her face and whether there were freckles on those big breasts? He had a sudden vision of his dark face against their pale nakedness, her pink nipples offered up to his greedy mouth.

Hunter shifted his weight in the saddle, sudden desire making his manhood go taut against his pants. He ought to be ashamed of himself, thinking that way about a very proper virgin. Of course a respectable wife wouldn't even let her own husband paw and kiss her body. He had heard that respectable women only submitted, never gave way to lust, not like his own mother . . .

The memory of the ridicule he had endured as a child hurt so much that he forced it from his mind. A lady. Yes, that was what he wanted on his arm and in his parlor, a chaste matron to whom other men tipped their hats with respect when she passed by.

A round of applause and cheering brought Hunter out of his thoughts. Mercer had finished his speech and the women were ready to board the wagons. Men crowded close, eager for the excuse to touch the prim females as they helped them upon the wagons.

Hunter swung down from his saddle, the leather creaking under his big frame. This would give him a chance to look over the available females more closely. Hunter crushed out his smoke and then elbowed through the men. They made way for him; some out of respect, some from fear. Hunter had cracked more than a few of their heads on a rowdy Saturday night when he and his crew brought a load of logs down the Skid Road to Yesler's Mill at the bottom of the hill. He looked over the girls as he lifted one and then another up to the wagon bed. Each blushed and thanked him prettily. Hunter only nodded, not smiling as he assessed their possibilities.

The freckled-faced sassy one seemed to see him coming. Rather than wait for him to lift her as the others had done, she tried to scramble up on the wagon herself, almost as if she didn't want him to touch her. He hated the obstinate stubbornness of her expression. No, this one he definitely wouldn't consider. Marriage to her would be like battling a forest fire, exhilarating but tiring. What a man wanted in his home was peace and quiet.

He watched with amusement as she struggled to get up on the wagon, but she was too small. Hunter couldn't resist reaching out to grasp her waist to lift her.

Hell, she was lighter and smaller than he had first thought—and probably younger, too. She was only chest high on him and his big hands almost completely spanned her waist. For just an instant, he was keenly aware of the heat of her body through the thin fabric of her dainty flowered dress. In fact he could see the barest outline of her nipples through the cloth.

He took a deep breath and smelled a slight scent of demure cologne; the type a lady would wear. Hunter paused with her half off the ground. He had a sudden wild vision of lifting her slim body up so he could put his mouth on her breasts and then kiss those dewey-looking lips.

"Sir, do you mind?" Her cold, prim words cut into his consciousness and he realized suddenly that he held her in his two big hands with everyone watching.

"Excuse me, Miss." He put her on the wagon and touched the brim **of his** hat politely. "I don't believe I caught your name?"

Her glare was as cold as a winter's day, despite her big brown eyes. "I am Sophia Merriweather, lately of Boston."

Sophia Merriweather from Boston. He'd heard the bluest bloods came from there, in spite of the pert turn of her nose and that impertinent expression. Most certainly a proper lady. He glared back. No, this one he definitely didn't want. "You don't look like a 'Sophia,' " he blurted.

Was that uneasiness or annoyance on her face? She paused, looking up at him, her expression one of impatience with his rudeness. "My family calls me 'Sassy.' "

She watched his somber face. He didn't smile, only gave her a curt nod. "Sassy. Now that fits you!"

"You, sir," she said in her most scathing tone, "are no gentleman."

He winced as if she had hit a very sensitive spot. "I didn't claim to be," he admitted softly. "That's something no one ever accused Hunter of."

Hunter. So much for Irish luck! She had hoped against hope that Mercer might have been teasing her and this dark savage wasn't James Hunter. The way things had been going for her the past year-and-a-half, what could she expect? Sassy made a deliberate gesture of looking about at the other men and the landscape, anywhere but into his face. The wagon lurched forward and the driver clucked to the oxen. They headed for the main street of the town with the men trooping along behind. All except Hunter. He made an angry gesture of pulling his hat down squarely on his head, almost as if dismissing her, and returned to his big Appaloosa.

Praise the saints, how fortunate she hadn't identified herself as the holder of his letter. Now she could either give the letter to another girl or throw it away. No, she shook her head as she felt for the reassurance of the Claddagh rings around her neck, there wasn't a woman in the bunch she would wish him on. He was rude, abrupt, and even a little dangerous looking. What she required was a nice, dependable, even though perhaps a little dull, gentleman for a safe marriage. After all she'd been through, what she didn't want was some primitive, passionate savage.

Why, he had looked Sassy over in a way that brought heat to her face just as if he were some aroused stallion selecting a mare to be bred. Aye, even his nostrils appeared to flare when he picked her up off the ground. She took a deep breath, remembering now the strength and the heat of those large hands on her waist. As the wagon bounced along, Sassy had a sudden vision of him throwing her across a bed, ripping her dress down the front, and proceeding to mount her with all the tender ness of a range stallion siring a colt. By Hunter out of Sassy, the pedigree would read.

Mildred, the sour little milliner from Cincinnati, adjusted the big hat she wore all bedecked with flowers and fruit. "My stars, Sophia, what on earth did that handsome man say to you? Both of you looked furious!"

"I didn't think he was handsome at all. He has no manners," Sassy said crisply.

Gertrude, the widowed mill-girl from Vermont, pushed her little gold-rimmed spectacles up and smiled, hugging her little boy, Timmy, to her side. "But such great possibilities!" She glanced over at the plump, older widow from New Hampshire. "Ellie, don't you think he would be a good catch?"

The plain, black-clad woman hesitated. "If he were as fine a husband as my Henry."

"But of course no man is," Mildred said sarcastically. "My stars, Ellie, Henry's dead and you've got to find another man or starve!"

Sassy winced. "Mildred, go easy."

Gertrude brushed Timmy's hair out of his eyes. "I'm not looking for a love match." Her voice was very soft. "I had a wonderful man and he's buried at Bull Run. I'm looking for a man who wants a son."

"Aye." Sassy smiled with encouragement. "You'll find a man like that here; Timmy's a wonderful little boy. What about that big, dark fellow?"

"Too wild for me." Gertrude pushed her glasses up. "I think you could deal with him, Sassy. Imagine what a challenge it would be to tame that one and turn him into a civilized gentleman."

Sassy wrinkled her freckled nose. "It would be more than a challenge; it would be a miracle."

55

Mildred hung on to her hat so it wouldn't blow away. "My stars! It could be done. I'll bet he's rich! Did you see the cut of his clothes and that horse he rode?"

Sassy had a sudden impulse. "Here, you try it then." She opened her purse, took out the crumpled letter, and put it in the startled Mildred's hands. "Just tell the surly beast that you were given his letter."

Gertrude strained to read over Mildred's shoulder. "Sounds as if he's buying livestock."

"Ha!" Sassy snorted, "Having met Mr. Hunter, there's no doubt in my mind that's just what he feels he's doing."

Mildred tucked the letter away carefully. "I think he can be brought to heel by the right woman."

Her smugness annoyed Sassy. She didn't think silly little Mildred was up to the task of dealing with Hunter. He looked like the type of assertive male who'd cause most women to cower in their tracks. It would take a stubborn woman with as strong a personality as his own to deal with the big half-breed. Otherwise, the wife would soon be reduced to a sniveling, whining little wretch and Hunter would be so bored, he would leave. Besides, more than half his primitive appeal to a female must be his untamed maleness. However, that was no longer Sassy's problem.

She looked around at the men trooping along behind the wagons, trying to pick a likely one. Hunter didn't bother to follow them into town. He had remounted his stallion back on the dock, glaring after her. Perhaps he wasn't used to having anyone stand up to him. She felt a bit smug at having given him tit for tat. In spite of her boasting, sour Mildred probably didn't have that much nerve.

56

The two-story, white frame building had a sign across the porch denoting it as the Occidental Hotel. The wagons took their passengers there. Asa Mercer announced there would be a social that night in the hotel dining room for Seattle's men to make the acquaintance of the ladies. The men set up a rowdy cheer that unnerved some of the women.

The four women and the sleepy little boy followed the others up the stairs.

"Goodness!" Gertrude whispered, pushing up her glasses. "If they could see this back home, they would never believe it. They must not have seen a woman for years."

Mildred pulled the big hat pin out of her hat and took it off. "Oh, I'd imagine this town isn't so small it doesn't have one of those places."

The plump, older widow looked from one to the other innocently. "What places?"

Mildred shrugged, "You know, Ellie, where men can, well, you know, with girls for money."

"Goodness!" Gertrude's nearsighted eyes widened. "I'd die first. No woman needs money that bad!"

Sassy opened her mouth to say something, thought better of it. In Gertrude's more sheltered life, she no doubt had never been desperate to provide bread for a disabled father and five younger brothers and sisters. She nodded toward the little boy. "Remember little pitchers have big ears. Let's get our things unloaded. I'm really tired."

The ladies were shown to their rooms and Sassy lay down to rest awhile before the evening's social, but she couldn't sleep. As hard as she had tried to forget, the discussion about the local bordello brought back a nightmare of memories. Could she ever be a real wife to any man? She had been used as a plaything for wealthy men and had never felt anything but horror and disgust at what they expected her to do night after night. However, the innocent Irish girl had soon learned that if she feigned passion, her customers tipped well; and that money had gotten her family through the leanest of times. Papa had believed she had a good job clerking in a New York City ladies' dress shop.

A lady. Thank the saints her mother, who had been a *real* lady, hadn't lived to know how poverty had brought degrading fate to her oldest daughter. Now again Sassy was left with nothing more than her own wits and daring to survive. Oh, dear God, would there ever be an end to it? Would she ever feel secure and safe? She could almost envy poor Sophia Merriweather, who no longer had to worry. Then she quickly said some prayers for the dead woman's soul. Sassy wasn't the type to give up the fight to survive. Her family needed any help she could give them; and if that meant marrying some elderly, comfortable lumberman, so be it. Sassy would be an honest, faithful wife to him.

However, she wasn't looking forward to her wedding night and most nights thereafter. Deep in her heart was a fear she had been afraid to give much thought: would a man be able to tell she wasn't a virgin and what would happen if he did? Could a proud man ever love a woman enough not to care if he hadn't been her first? Worse yet, could even the most liberal of husbands overlook it if his wife had been a whore? No, that was expecting too much. Secrets; everybody has one. This secret was a heavy burden she would take to her grave.

She recalled the way that big man had looked at her

as if she were a slave on an auction block and he were trying to decide whether she was worth the price. However, he had made it clear what kind of wife he demanded. No doubt he would be delighted to find out Mildred had his letter of introduction.

Now which of all those other men would be a good catch? Sassy struggled to remember some of the others. Try as she might, except for James Hunter, they were all just a nameless blur in her memory. Tonight she would look over all the eligible bachelors. There were bound to be some lumber kings among this large group of men. A generous and wealthy man would not mind sending money regularly to his wife's family. She was determined that her sisters not end up as she had and that her brothers be educated and get out of the slums. The chance she might find a job and be her own woman was pretty slim.

She heard a stir from the other rooms as ladies began to dress for the social. What on earth was she going to wear that might attract a husband? She had water sent up for a bath, washed her hair and brushed it until it caught the light like burnished copper. Now what was she going to wear?

She went through the luggage. Everything Miss Merriweather had owned was of the finest fabric and well made, but as bland and without style as the spinster herself. Poor Miss Merriweather! Sassy could only pity her, but she couldn't have done anything else except see to the burial. She wondered if Brett James had received her letter and stopped searching for her? Even the thought of that dapper rake sent a shudder through her slight frame.

There was absolutely no dress here that would take

any man's eye. Then which had any possibilities? The pale green lawn with lace insets on the neck and throat. Quickly, Sassy grabbed a pair of scissors. She could cut away the high neck and leave her shoulders bare with the merest hint of the swell of her breasts showing.

After she improvised, she slipped the dress on over full hoop skirts and tied her hair with a green satin ribbon in a cascade of curls on top of her head. She inspected herself in a mirror critically. Yes, she looked like a lady, a desirable but innocent lady. Sassy put her mother's ring on her right hand, the small crown turned inward. She left her father's big Claddagh ring on its tiny gold chain around her neck and it rested against the swell of her breasts. A man would have a hard time keeping his eyes off it, dangling where it did.

Even after she was really ready to go down, Sassy hesitated, fooling with her hair, putting a dab of dainty perfume behind her ears and in the cleft between her breasts.

Out in the hall, she heard the rustle of skirts as women went downstairs.

A knock. "Sophia?" Mildred's voice. "Gertrude, Ellie, and I are ready to go; are you?"

"Go on, I—I'll be down in a moment," Sassy felt completely unnerved as if she were about to stand on an auction block, the winner getting her body for his exclusive use. Sassy said a prayer to her patron saint that after all she'd been through, things might finally work out for her family's sake.

The noise and conversation from downstairs increased to a mild buzz. Probably all the men in Seattle and the surrounding timber country were here. It certainly sounded like it, judging from the laughter and music. Sassy took a deep breath for courage and looked at herself in the mirror. She appeared to be a real lady. All she had to do was remember to act like one, a bit haughty and cool. She still felt uncertain and apprehensive as she walked slowly to the stairs. She paused halfway down and surveyed the milling crowd. A small band played slightly off-key from the bandstand. She felt many men turn and stare at her as she hesitated. She looked over the crowd, her mouth dry, her heart beating nervously.

Hunter stood talking to Mildred and several ladies at the refreshment table. It was impossible to miss him; his big frame towered head and shoulders above most of the others. He turned slowly and looked up at her. If she had felt self-conscious before, she felt doubly so now because he inspected her from head to toe as cooly as a master about to bid on a slave. The question was did he want her. And how high was he willing to go?

Chapter Four

As she watched, Sassy wondered what the dark man was thinking now. She had a distinct feeling he was imagining her naked. He didn't move, but his eyes swept over her and left her feeling as if his hand reached out and ripped her bodice away so he could appraise her breasts. Was he handsome? Some women might think so with that black curly hair and bright blue eyes contrasting so starkly with that dark skin. A bit too rugged, maybe. She thought of Brett with his dapper, sophisticated good looks, his penciled mustache. He had dark hair, too, but his eyes were brown. She realized that the half-breed stared at her. His arrogant expression infuriated her. How dare he look at her so! Sassy tossed her curls and finished descending the stairs.

Immediately she was surrounded by eager men of all ages, introducing themselves, asking her to dance, offering to bring her some refreshments. Sassy laughed, fluttered her eyelashes, and flirted outrageously. Even as she flirted, her mind was busy appraising them. A handsome, but gangling, young lumberjack who said his name was Will asked her to dance and she nodded. They waltzed past the refreshment table and she heard Mildred say, "My stars! Oh, Mr. Hunter, you are just so clever, a poor little ninny like me could never understand business!"

Sassy made a moue. Surely James Hunter wasn't stupid enough to fall for that kind of flattery. He had seemed smarter than that. Being too busy attempting to overhear that conversation, she misstepped and almost tripped her partner, who apologized gallantly. "It's my fault, Miss. I'm just so nervous about having a pretty girl in my arms."

"Sir, you are too kind." She glanced at Hunter. Had he seen what had happened? He looked back at her, slight amusement on his dark face while Mildred prattled on.

"Now, Will, tell me about the lumber industry and Seattle." She brought her attention back to the young lumberjack, angry with herself that her gaze kept straying to the tall, grim man in the smartly cut waistcoat.

"Oh, I wouldn't want to bore you with money talk," he said. "After all, women have no head for business."

Sassy managed to hold back a retort. Of course Hunter would treat her with the same biting condescending attitude. Or would he?

The dance ended and Sassy fanned herself with her lace kerchief. "I'd love a cup of punch."

"Yes, ma'am. Let me get it for you." Will headed toward the refreshment table, thinking Miss Merriweather was a beauty, but too fiery for his taste. Now, that quiet, shy friend of hers, the gentle one wearing glasses who had the cute little boy, she looked Will's type. Would any of these women marry him if they knew he'd been in prison for robbery? He'd been hungry and desperate or he never would have committed such a shameful crime. Now Will had paid back the money and come out here to make a fresh start and an honest living. He'd never be able to tell his secret—not unless he found a very special woman.

Sassy watched Will threading his way toward the refreshments. She was immediately surrounded by men. She smiled, flirted, and glanced at Hunter. He had smoothly handed his trio of ladies over to Will at the refreshment table and begun to work his way through the crowd toward her. Several girls cast admiring glances his way, but he didn't seem to notice them. Oh, saints preserve me, he was definitely headed over here!

What was she to do? Suppose he asked her to dance? The music started again and Sassy took a bearded, older gentleman's arm. "Why, I believe this is the dance I was saving for you, sir."

"My pleasure, Ma'am." He grinned and danced her out into the crowd.

Hunter paused and scowled. Sassy watched him out of the corner of her eye. He seemed to realize what she had done and was evidently annoyed. He stood near the open French doors that led out onto the veranda. Sassy threw her head back and laughed gaily as if her partner were too clever and amusing for words. As she danced past him, Hunter caught her arm. "I believe this was to be our dance, Miss Sassy."

About to protest the bearded man, looked Hunter over, shrugged in defeat, and melted away into the crowd.

She made an airy gesture of dismissal. "I don't remember promising you a dance. And anyway, I'm waiting for a gentleman who promised to bring me some punch."

Past his wide shoulder, she saw Will approaching with two dainty cups. Bless her luck, she was saved. However, when the lumberjack saw Hunter, he hesitated and stopped. Sassy fumed. Was everyone in Seattle intimidated by this big brute of a man? The music started again and Hunter took her hand. "I believe this is my dance."

His hand was large and callused, completely enveloping her small one. Sassy looked at the other men, but they dropped their gaze and backed away. Even Will stood there looking ill at ease with a cup in each hand, unsure what to do. She'd get no help from this bunch of puppies. There was no way out without creating a scene. "All right, you'll have your dance."

"I mean to." Even as he took her in his arms, he whirled her out the French doors and onto the veranda in the warm May night.

For only an instant she was in his embrace, feeling the heat of his hand on her waist, his chest brushing against her breasts. He smelled slightly of brandy and tobacco and soap. She looked up at him and for just a split-second, she thought he would kiss her and she wasn't sure what she would do to stop him—or even if she wanted to stop him. Time seemed to stand still, but dimly in the background, music played and people laughed. A night bird called in the distance and she smelled the scent of the sea, wild flowers, and pine trees carried on the warm breeze.

"Sir," she pulled away from him, unnerved by the feel of his virile body against hers. "This is highly irregular."

"Is it? I know nothing of how gentlemen should behave."

"That's obvious," Sassy said. "I agreed to a dance."

"I don't know how," he whispered.

"You don't know how to dance?" She didn't believe him. James Hunter looked like a man at ease in a ballroom.

He shrugged, "All I've done since I was a small boy

65

was labor from dawn 'til dusk. There's not much except lonely men, sweat, and hard work out in the woods."

She remembered then the calluses of his dark hands. "You certainly didn't bring me out here to give dance lessons." She turned toward the door, but he caught her arm.

"I don't usually tell anyone that," he blurted, "I wouldn't want to be thought a fool."

What a contrast, she thought. Such a hard man, yet so vulnerable, afraid of being laughed at. Why? She looked down at his hand on her arm. "Coming out here alone with you will cause gossip."

Even in the darkness, she could see his grim face. "I would kill the man who smears a lady's reputation."

"You'd do what?"

"You heard me." His tone left no doubt in her mind that he meant it. "There aren't many real ladies around; a frontiersman reveres them."

Sassy took a sharp breath. Oh, Holy Mary, forgive me my sins, she thought. If he only knew the truth . . .

"We need to talk," he said urgently.

She had to tip her head back to look up at him. "Sir, I know of nothing we need to discuss."

He didn't let go of her arm. "Asa Mercer tells me he gave you my letter, yet you chose to pass it on to another girl once you'd seen me. I don't meet a lady's standards?"

"No."

"Why not?"

A lady. He had hurt her with his words, now she wanted to wound him for his arrogance. "You—you are entirely too uncivilized and blunt. I dare say you have a habit of taking what you want; you're ruthless and primitive."

"It's what it took to claw my way to the top; whites taught me how." Something about his tone made her take a long look into his blue eyes. For a split second, she imagined she saw something soft and vulnerable there. She had a sudden vision of a lonely half-breed boy who didn't fit into civilization now determined to show his success.

Her heart softened, then she reminded herself that he wanted a lady, a *real* lady. Why it was so important to him, she could only wonder. How he would spurn her should he ever learn she was nothing more than Sassy Malone, an Irish whore on the run. The painful knowledge of what she was made her lash out at him. "Mr. Hunter, I find you presumptuous and annoying. Why, with all these women so evidently eager for your attention, do you insist on forcing yourself on me?"

Immediately he turned loose of her arm. "Forgive me," he said. "I suppose I was intrigued because you evidently find me unacceptable while all the other women are flirting outrageously because I'm a rich man."

"In polite society, people never discuss money."

"You see?" He shrugged. "That's because they always had plenty and don't have to worry about it. I'll bet a well-bred lady like you knows all about such things."

She didn't, but she knew enough to fool him, she thought. Inside at the social, there was some safe, nice man waiting for her to charm him. And here she was stuck out on the veranda with this unpredictable renegade. "What is the point of all this?"

"We have things to discuss. Why don't we go for a stroll and we'll talk."

"We will not talk. Just being out here with you alone is doubtlessly enough to start tongues wagging."

"I'm sure they all know you're too much of a lady to be attracted to a scoundrel like me."

She brushed back a loose tendril of hair. "Are you telling me you're bad?"

"Ruthless is perhaps a better description." He stepped closer, standing near enough to put his hands on her bare shoulders and, for a moment, she thought he would. Then he hesitated and his arms went to his sides. "When I see something I want, I usually get it, no matter what it costs."

Cost. Only last year he could have bought Sassy's charms by the hour or for the night. If he knew that, he would spit on her, call her names.

His hand came up, caught the ring she wore on its chain. "What's this?"

She was giddy with the warm touch of his fingers across the bare swell of her breasts. "A ring."

"Damn it! I can see that. It's a man's ring; whose?" His tone told her that if she said a sweetheart's, he might tear it from her neck.

His big hand continued to turn it over, his fingers touching her throat in a way that sent goosebumps all over her in an unaccustomed rush. She was hesitant to pull away, afraid of breaking the delicate gold chain. "It's a Claddagh ring. You see it matches the one on my hand."

"And?" His fingers brushed against her throat as he studied the ring.

"It's an old tradition from the town of Claddagh, Ireland, that goes back hundreds of years."

"I see hands clasped around a heart with a crown above. What does it mean?"

" 'Let love and friendship reign.' You can tell if a lady's taken by looking at the way she wears her ring. If the crown above the heart is turned toward her, she still hasn't made her choice."

Now his hand went to grasp hers, to study her ring. "You wear the man's ring around your neck, yet your heart is still your own?"

"My late mother gave it to my father when they wed."

"I'd not wear a ring like some bull with one through his nose," Hunter snapped.

"No one asked you to," Sassy reminded him, thinking only of how close he stood to her. "Some men love a woman enough to wear a wedding ring. My father did."

He looked sympathetic. "They're dead then?"

Sassy didn't want to reveal any more about herself. She made a noncommittal reply.

He nodded silently and his face softened as he let go of the ring. "So are mine. You're trembling. Are you cold?" His voice was so gentle it surprised her.

"No." Could anyone understand this mysterious man? Dark and dangerous; yet almost as gallant as a knight of old.

"Let me give you my coat."

"No." Putting on his coat, still warm from his virile body, would be almost like letting him pull her into his embrace and, abruptly, she feared that. Was it because she feared him . . . or her own response to him? Her mind and heart were in utter disarray. Never had she felt emotions like these before. A bit dazed, she stepped away from him.

"Turn completely around," he said.

"What? A lady does not take orders like some servant."

69

"Then consider it a request. Please, will the lady turn completely around?"

What would happen if she refused? Very slowly, Sassy made a circle.

He looked her over, gave a grunt of satisfaction. "How old are you?"

"N—Nineteen."

"I doubt that. I'd say seventeen or eighteen. What I had in mind was more mature."

She had to stifle an urge to slap him. "There are dozens of ladies inside who are older than I; several must be forty or fifty."

"Too old. Are you healthy and able to bear children?"

"Mr. Hunter!" Sassy felt her face flame.

"I'm sorry," he said. "I suppose a lady wouldn't think those were polite questions."

"Hardly!" Her voice dripped sarcasm. "Not that it matters, sir, because I wouldn't even consider you as a possible husband."

"I haven't asked you," he pointed out as he took out a slender cheroot. "Do you mind if I smoke?" When she shook her head, he struck a match, lit up, and broke the match before he tossed it away.

She was seething. "Is it your intention to bring every lady out in the moonlight, ask her intimate questions, and inquire into her pedigree?"

"I have been very choosey about picking a bride," Hunter said coldly and blew smoke. "I want to make sure I get a girl of the best breeding who will give me healthy children."

She couldn't believe this conversation. "And what do you intend to give her?"

70

"What every genuine lady wants, I suppose: wealth, position, security. As my wife, she will have respect and anything her heart desires."

"What about love?"

Hunter leaned against the shadowy wall behind her and smiled, the tip of his cigar glowing red as he smoked. "I'm a realist, Miss Sassy; I can buy love by the hour. Pardon me for being so indelicate, since I'm sure you haven't the slightest idea about women like that. An enduring marriage is like a successful business deal—comprised of logical choices, not willy-nilly emotions and romantic hogwash."

"Just the kind of words to cause a woman to swoon with delight," she snapped. "I'll bet Mildred can hardly wait for the preacher."

"I also didn't really want a redhead," he said as if he hadn't heard her caustic remark and frowning at Sassy's curls. "Temper is bad in a wife."

"Mildred is a brunette," Sassy reminded him.

"Mildred? She's a silly fool," Hunter said. "You don't seem to be."

"I also have all my own teeth," Sassy seethed. "I presume you'll want to inspect them as you would if you were buying a filly at auction."

"I'll take your word for it. Can you read poetry, do womanly things like needlework, and play the piano?"

"Mr. Hunter, your questions are demeaning! I will not be interviewed as if I were applying for a position as a housekeeper or governess." Whirling, she took half-a-dozen steps out into the street and paused uncertainly. He remained where he was, shadowed by the roof. Sassy had a distinct feeling that if she tried to get past Hunter to reenter the dance through the French doors,

71

he would stop her. Perhaps she could run around the hotel to the front entry and return that way.

As she paused, a man stumbled out of a door down the street and came toward them. She would ask that gentleman for assistance. Before Hunter could move, she ran over and caught the man's arm. "Please, Sir, would you—"

He was a big, rough-looking character, and quite drunk. She realized that instantly as he grinned down at her and she caught the strong scent of cheap whiskey. "Hello, Girlie."

A chill ran over her. How many brutes like this one had she been forced to submit to in that brothel? Too many. "I'm sorry, Sir. I mistook you for someone else."

She tried to pull away from him, but he caught her arm. "Hey, Girlie, don't leave. You and me'll have a little fun."

Sassy glanced over her shoulder toward the safety of the social. She didn't want to create an embarrassing scene. How many millions of women had been raped since civilization began because they hesitated to create a scene?

Hunter stepped out of the shadows, silent and deadly as an Indian warrior. He dropped his cigar in the dirt, ground it out carefully with his boot, and crossed the distance between them, his shadow looming large across the pair in the moonlight. When he spoke, his voice was almost a whisper but it had the threat of a rattlesnake's warning. "Get your hands off her. Don't you know a lady when you see one?"

"Lady? He swayed on his feet. "This can't be no lady. She's out soliciting like a common wh—"

In one quick move, Hunter set her to one side as he hit

the drunk, knocking him backward with such force that the man hit the ground hard and rolled before coming to a stop against a horse trough, half-conscious. Hunter flexed his hand. "Mister, you need to learn how to treat a lady." He turned now to her. "I apologize for the violence, Miss; hope it didn't upset you. Are you all right?"

"Y—yes . . . no. I—I don't know." The horrible memories of her past nights dealing with men like this drunk rushed back to her, and she wanted to faint, block it all out. Even as she swayed, Hunter scooped her up in his arms.

"I—I'm all right. Put me down," she ordered.

"Sure you are." He started walking back toward the veranda, obviously with no intentions of doing as ordered.

Damn him. He was maddening. She ought to slap him and insist, but she was helpless against his strength. She felt his fine broadcloth coat against her face, the warmth of him, the sound of his heart beating in her ear. She closed her eyes as he carried her to the veranda. When she opened them, he was looking into her face with an intensity that unnerved her. "If you weren't a lady," he whispered, "if you weren't a lady . . ."

The passion and desire etched on his dark face left no doubt what he was thinking, what it was he wanted from her. A need she had never felt before caused her to open her lips. She almost reached up her mouth to his, then remembered in time. A lady. That was her attraction for him. He thought she was a pure virgin that no man had ever touched.

How very, very funny! Then why were tears gathering in her eyes? Because if he only knew what she was, what she had been, he would spit on her and call her names. He might even carry her off into the shadows, rip her dainty dress away, and rape her with that savage passion she could see pent up behind his troubled eyes.

If only she could change her past. Oh, God, she would trade half her life to be able to erase it. Only once in a lifetime can a woman give her virginity, and Sassy had wasted hers on a scoundrel who didn't love her. What a naive little fool she had been!

No respectable man, certainly not this one, would want her for his wife. She would have to spend the rest of her life fearing her secret might leak out. The thought of that made her sad and then angry. "Mr. Hunter, please put me down before someone sees us and my reputation is ruined."

Slowly, almost reluctantly it seemed, he stood her on her feet. "I told you what I'd do to a man who smeared a lady's name." He still wasn't smiling.

"You belong on a white horse with a lance in your hand, Sir Galahad."

"Who?" He looked puzzled and she realized he'd never heard of the knights of the round table.

"Never mind. He put ladies on pedestals, too."

"You laugh at me." He sounded more than hurt; he was angry. "I can stand anything but looking like a fool."

She started to deny it, but already he had turned and strode away into the night. Hunter was a proud man—too proud, but vulnerable under that hard surface. Sassy had found his weakness. If he married a whore . . . as much as he worshiped ladies . . . if it ever came out. . . . She shuddered at the dire consequences for everyone concerned. Secrets like hers had a way of surfacing. It was just as well that this stormy relationship ended before it really began. No doubt one of the innocent little ninnies like Mildred would suit his needs for a wife.

Sassy was suddenly very tired and her head hurt. She slipped quietly through the French doors during a rousing square dance and no one except maybe Mildred saw her come in. Mildred's expression was set and angry, but Sassy pretended not to notice.

Ellie stood talking to another woman. Gertrude was dancing with Will; and as they passed, she heard him say, "I wouldn't mind at all raising another man's son. I'd like lots of kids."

Men surrounded Sassy again and she was at her best, charming them all, flirting a little with each one. She needed a husband, but it wasn't going to be that smoldering half-breed.

Hunter strode down the street to Lulu's place where the off-key piano banged away. He marched in and bellied up to the bar. "Gimme a bottle."

The elderly bartender complied while Lulu moved from her position near the noisy piano and the whores singing: "Buffalo gals, won't you come out tonight, come out tonight, buffalo gals, won't you come out tonight, and dance by the light of the moon."

"Hunter, what the hell you doin' in here?" the stout madam drawled. "Almost every man in town is over at the social."

Hunter gulped his drink. "Not me."

"I can see that, Handsome. What happened?"

He poured himself another, leaned against the bar, listening to the off-key piano and looking over the bored girls standing around with nothing to do. "Who needs a prissy lady anyhow? Not me!" He drained his glass, getting angrier by the second. All he could think of was the warmth of Sassy's skin as his fingers brushed her. It made him go hard just thinking about her. He had the strangest urge to both rape and protect her. "You got any redheads, Lulu?"

She twisted her rings. "You've had them all, Hunter. You know none of my girls are red-headed."

"Good!" he muttered and poured himself another drink. "They're stubborn and contrary. Give me a blond or a brunette any time."

He noticed several of the half-dressed girls eyeing him from across the parlor. Hunter had a hunger for a woman that sassy one had built in him. Damn her, she was haughty! He hadn't expected that but maybe he should have. Maybe high-toned ladies were like that. Worse yet, he hadn't expected some prim, mail-order bride to build a fire in him.

Hell, Blanche could put out any man's fire. He gestured to her, picked up his drink. "I'll start with her, then I'll take Claire and then Sal."

Lulu laughed and her double chins quivered. "I swan, Hunter, you're really on the prod. There doesn't seem to be much action tonight; all the men are either down at the *Illahee* with the Injun whores or drinking lemonade with those respectable ones."

"I tried 'respectable.' "

"And?"

"Never mind." He sipped his drink, unsure whether he was the most angry with the prim schoolgirl or himself for lusting after her.

"Is this the one who got your letter?"

He nodded. "Hell, I don't care. All a man needs, your girls got, Lulu." He gestured to Blanche and she

76

sauntered over. "Let's go to your room, Honey, then when I wear you out, I'll take on Claire."

Blanche rubbed up against him in her black-lace chemise. "Sugar, you got to wear me out first and I intend to make a night of it." She smiled as she took his arm and led him down the hall.

He was more than a little drunk, he knew that, but Blanche suddenly didn't seem as desirable as she used to. Maybe it was because he could smell the scent of other men on her. There was no telling how many had already lain between her thighs today. He thought about that as they went into her room. She closed the door and slipped her arms around his neck, rubbing her breasts against him. He let her kiss him, but his mind was on that fiesty virgin with the freckles on her nose. Her mouth had looked so innocent and soft.

Damn, here he was with a big-breasted, half-dressed whore in his arms, the kind of girl who always clawed his back and bucked under him like an unbroke filly, and he was thinking about one who would probably slap him if he kissed her hand. He must be crazy. The thought sent a chill of remembrance down his back. No, he wasn't crazy; just drunk.

Blanche whispered in his ear, telling him what she was going to do to please him once she got his clothes off, once she got out of that lace chemise. She was whispering dirty, intimate things to him, words an innocent like Sassy probably didn't even know. Tonight, he didn't want a dirty-mouthed whore; he wanted a lady; a woman who wouldn't let any man but him make love to her. Blanche was too much like his wild mother. He felt his manhood soften. The knowledge infuriated him and he kissed Blanche again, pulling her against him so he could feel her breasts against his chest. His traitor body wouldn't co-operate. It wanted that innocent red-haired schoolgirl.

He pulled away from Blanche, cursing softly.

"Hunter, Sugar, what's wrong?"

"Nothing. I—I just changed my mind; that's all."

"Changed your mind? I'm ready to give you the hottest night you've ever had, and you've changed your mind?"

"Forget it. I'm tired and I've had too much whiskey. I'll be back when I've slept it off." He staggered toward the door.

"Who is she?" Blanche asked with a sigh. "It can't be one of those prim ones from Mercer's belles that's got you roaring around like a wild stallion."

"Mind your own damn business, Blanche," Hunter snapped.

She stood with her hands on her hips. "No little lady type can give you what I can, Hunter. In a few days, you'll be back, pounding on my door, and I'll be waiting."

Hunter didn't bother to answer as he staggered out the door and down the hall, past the off-key piano banging away. Hell, he had a blasting headache and he was going home. His common sense told him Sassy could be stubborn and hot-tempered. She would spend her life leading some poor devil on a merry chase, and he would never know what she'd do next. Tomorrow, he promised himself as he staggered out to his big stallion, Poker Chips, and mounted up; tomorrow, he'd take a fresh and cool appraising look at all those other demure belles. One of them was bound to be just the proper wife for him.

Chapter Five

Sassy felt much better the next morning as all the ladies gathered in the hotel dining room for breakfast. She had a distinct feeling that several were sneaking curious looks at her.

Gertrude and little Timmy slid into the chairs next to her. She pushed her wire-rimmed spectacles up. "The ladies are all curious about that handsome, rugged gentleman."

Sassy shrugged and sipped her coffee. "He's a little rough-hewn, I'd say, to be thought handsome and he certainly doesn't know the first thing about being a gentleman."

Mildred plopped down at the table across from her. She wore a silly-looking hat with fruit on the brim. "I'd be willing to teach him," she said pettishly, "so if you're not interested, you ought to leave him for someone who is."

Holy Mother of God, she wished she would hear the end of this man. When she thought about him, that abrupt manner of his, she got angry all over again. "Look, Mildred, I want to make it very clear that I have absolutely no interest in the big, churlish beast. Absolutely none. I've also made that quite clear to him."

"My stars, then what were you doing out on the veranda so long?"

She should say he couldn't dance and asked her to teach him. Sassy paused. She was too kind-hearted to make anyone look like a fool, even an annoying character like Hunter. "You know how men are; he's in the timber business and wanted to talk about it." She shook her hair back. "I thought the lumber industry was fascinating compared to him. He isn't my type at all: too bossy and opinionated."

The fruit on the hat bobbled as Mildred nodded, then smiled slowly. "That's good to know because I'm interested."

Gertrude's big eyes widened behind her glasses. "I hear he's rich. Will says gossip among the men says Hunter's dad used his wife's family fortune to build an empire in timber and land then left it to be divided between his two sons."

"The money doesn't make him any less attractive." Mildred's eyes gleamed with greed.

So that was the main attraction. Sassy liked her less for that remark. "I hope his brother is more sensitive." Surely there couldn't be another one around like him; he was definitely one of a kind. "So are we going to meet the other Hunter?"

Gertrude shook her head. "He's back East somewhere, and he's only a half-brother."

"Too bad he's not here." Sassy grinned. "That would be one for each of you."

Gertrude leaned closer, a bit sheepish. "Oh, I've already met one who took my eye, that Will."

Sassy searched her memory. Oh, yes, the earnest young lumberjack. "I hope it works out for you," she said warmly.

"I—I hope it does, too." Gertrude put her arm around her little boy. "Will likes children and I think my husband would have liked Will."

Mildred adjusted her hat. "What about you, Sassy? What are you going to do?"

"I think I'll try to get a job."

"A job!" They both looked aghast. "Didn't any of the men take your eye? There's plenty to choose from."

Sassy gave an airy wave of her hand, dismissing them. "It'll give me more time to look the prospects over."

Ellie had just joined them. Sassy liked the plump, older widow who seemed so quiet except when she was talking about her wonderful husband who had been killed in the war. "Ellie, what about you? Did any man appeal to you?"

The woman smiled and Sassy realized she was almost pretty, even if she must be in her fifties. "Oh, I don't think any of them would be interested in me."

"By all the saints, that's not true." Sassy said and Gertrude backed her up with a nod. "Ellie, there's bound to be a man in Seattle who would appreciate your good points."

"I'm afraid they all want younger, prettier women," Ellie sighed, "not an old widow like me."

"You aren't old!" Sassy protested, "and there're lots of men who'd be interested. You just need a little self-confidence. After all, your Henry chose you."

Ellie brushed a wisp of graying hair back, started to say something, paused. "Well, keep an eye out. I'm a good housekeeper and I'm looking for a man I can feel

81

comfortable with, one who likes plump women. I wouldn't mind if he had children; and I'd like one who loves cats."

Mildred had taken no part in any of this, Sassy noticed. Mildred stared off in a dreamy fashion as if lost in thought. "Mrs. James Hunter," she sighed. "It has a nice ring to it."

Not to Sassy it didn't. The thought of him set her teeth on edge, the pig-headed, aggressive, stubborn—

"So, Sassy," Gertrude asked, "what kind of job are you looking for?"

"I—I don't know." Sassy held out her cup for the balding waiter to pour more coffee. Seattle didn't appear to need ladies' personal maids and there didn't seem to be enough children around for a governess. In this day and age, there were few options open to respectable women. "I play the piano, although I'm not an expert. Perhaps I could go to local homes, give lessons."

The balding waiter shook his head. "Afraid not, Miss. There's only three pianos that I know of in the whole area, and the two here in town are in the kind of establishment that real ladies like yourself would never enter."

At least, never again, Sassy promised herself.

Gertrude looked around at everyone. "Saloons?"

The waiter fumbled for words. "Well, I suppose they also sell whiskey there." He retreated in embarrassment.

Mildred giggled and leaned closer. "My stars, Gertrude, you simpleton, don't you know what kind of places he's talking about?"

"No." Gertrude leaned closer. "What kind?"

"Mildred," Ellie cautioned, nodding toward Timmy, "there's a child present. Right, Sassy?"

Sassy winced, remembering the Black Garter and the bordello upstairs. That was one thing she'd never do again if she starved first. She gave the little milliner a disapproving look. "That's right. Please, Mildred, there are some things we shouldn't discuss."

Gertrude's eyes widened in sudden comprehension. "Oh, my! What kind of girl would do that for a living?"

A desperate one, Sassy thought, one who isn't given a choice. But even though her heart screamed the words, she said nothing.

Mildred giggled. "I'll tell you what kind they aren't: they aren't ladies!"

Ladies. That word again. It made her think of Hunter and the pure virgin he was searching for. To change the subject, she signaled the waiter as he passed. "You said there were three pianos. Where's the other one?"

"In Hunter's home."

"That big, uncivilized brute plays the piano?" Bless the saints, maybe he was more gentle than she thought.

"Oh, no, Ma'am, I didn't say that!" He laughed and ran his hand over his bald head. "I've never been inside Hunter's house, but I did see the piano being unloaded from the ship some months ago."

Sassy couldn't contain her curiosity. "If he doesn't play, why would he buy a piano?"

The waiter lowered his voice to a whisper and leaned closer. "They say Hunter has fixed up his place all ready for a wife: piano, books of poetry, fancy Victorian furnishings, just like back East or San Francisco."

Mildred sighed and the fruit on her hat jiggled as she shook her head. "My stars, isn't that the sweetest thing!"

83

Gertrude's glasses slid down her nose. "He didn't look that sensitive."

"Sensitive!" Sassy snorted, "He'd probably feel more at home in a cave!"

"I'll bet he has the finest house on Puget Sound," Mildred mused. "Imagine being the lady in that home: nice things, expensive china and silver."

Probably the kind of home Sassy's mother, Maureen, had given up for Mike Malone, Sassy thought, as she put down her coffee cup. She tried to imagine James Hunter sitting at a white-linen-covered table balancing a dainty teacup in one of his big hands. The picture was amusing, but also a bit sad. Was there more to the half-breed than she realized?

Mildred smirked. "I don't play the piano and I don't want to learn, so he'll have bought it in vain."

"In that case," Sassy brightened, "maybe he'd sell it. With it, I could give piano lessons in my own little place and support myself. Sometime soon, Seattle is bound to become more civilized and there'll be other women and maybe children who'll want lessons."

Gertrude's nearsighted eyes grew wide as she took off her spectacles to clean them. "Great idea! Sassy, do you have the money to buy Hunter's piano?"

"You know I don't." Sassy shrugged. "Perhaps he would extend me credit."

"My stars!" Mildred giggled. "He looks like a sharp businessman to me, and you've no collateral for a loan."

Sassy wrinkled her freckled nose. "Good point. A true gentleman might go out of his way to aid an impoverished lady, but then we've already agreed that Hunter is no gentleman."

Mildred sighed. "That's what I like about him! I have

the feeling that if he were overcome with passion, he would sweep a girl up in his arms and kiss her in a way that made her forget everything else. They would ride a skyrocket to ecstasy together."

Gertrude paused in cleaning her spectacles. "What does that mean?"

Ellie colored and cleared her throat. "Remember little pitchers—"

"I'm not a pitcher," the chubby toddler piped up. "I'm a boy. Miss Sassy, what does it mean?"

Sassy winked at the towheaded child as she threw down her napkin and stood. "It means that Mildred has been reading too many novels. I suspect that James Hunter is not in the least bit romantic; forget the skyrockets." She tried not to remember that emotionally charged moment in his arms last night when it had almost seemed as if he would carry her off and overwhelm her with his need . . . and hers. No, not hers. The thought of a man making love to her brought back too many memories Sassy wanted to forget.

Asa Mercer came into the dining room just then and clapped his hands to get everyone's attention. "Attention, Ladies! We are having a little picnic up in the hills this afternoon so you can see our beautiful Territory. You are all invited and the wagons will be here at noon. Until then, you are on your own."

The ladies applauded daintily and began to disband.

Gertrude said, "I believe I'll wash some clothes and write a letter home telling my mother we made it all right."

"Good idea!" Mildred giggled. "I've got to pick out something very special to wear and get it pressed if I'm to catch Jim Hunter's eye at the picnic."

Ellie sighed. "Maybe I'll just stay in the hotel; I'm not sure I'll go to the picnic."

"Now, Ellie," Sassy said, "you can't meet a husband if you don't go where the men are."

"Suppose I go and no man pays any attention to me?" Ellie looked miserable.

"My stars," Mildred said as she got up from the table, "even if you are past your prime and overweight, there's bound to be some man—"

"Thanks, Mildred," Sassy snapped, "your kind words will work wonders for Ellie's self-esteem." She patted the older woman's arm. "You and I can eat together at the picnic, okay?"

"All right." The widow looked relieved.

Gertrude pushed her glasses up again and caught Timmy's chubby hand. "And you're certainly welcome to join Will and me. Sassy, what are you going to do with your morning?"

"I think I'll go find out what jobs are available," Sassy said. "Besides, I'd like to see Seattle and learn what kind of a town we've chosen to spend our lives in."

The group of ladies broke up and Sassy went to the front door and stepped out onto the sidewalk. Down the street, the big Appaloosa horse stood tied to the hitching block out in front of the general store. There couldn't be more than one horse like that one. Whatever Hunter was doing in town, Sassy decided she didn't want to run into him yet. First she would try to find a job. Giving piano lessons would be a last resort. She slipped back inside and watched from the window. The tall half-breed came out of the general store and strode toward the ladies' store across the street. She watched him pause in the street for a moment, tip his black western hat over

86

one eye. From his expression, she'd say he had a bad hangover; she'd certainly seen enough of them. Now why would he be going into a ladies' shop? Maybe he was opening an account for his future bride. After a few minutes, he came out, mounted up, and rode away. Even his back looked arrogant, she thought with annoyance.

At least he was gone, and she could look for a job without any danger of running into him. Sassy spent the next two hours inquiring about possible work around the small village. Each proprietor would visit with her politely and some even seemed interested in hiring her. However, when she would give her name, the owner would abruptly get very busy and tell her to come back another time or let her know he couldn't afford to hire anyone just yet.

Discouraged, Sassy tried every store and even the lumber mill. No one needed any help. Somehow, the way some of the men refused to look her in the eye while they talked to her made her wonder if they were lying? A chill went up her back. Were the refusals because someone had found out her secret and soon everyone in Washington Territory would know she was really only a little Irish whore?

No, she wasn't that and never would be ever again, Sassy thought with a stubborn shake of her head. She was going to forget her past and make a fresh start; everyone deserved a second chance. Would she ever feel safe with this secret that she must keep forever? She almost envied those other Mercer belles. They all seemed so respectable, so free from scandal. Was she the only one in the world, or at least in this wilderness, with a secret past?

87

By the end of two hours, Sassy had walked all the steep streets, exhausting all the possible businesses except the hotel, so she returned to the Occidental. There she offered to work as a cook or a cleaning girl. The owner, all smiles yesterday, was polite but a bit terse in his refusal. He didn't think those were proper jobs for a lady. What she should do, he suggested, was get married.

Sassy, tired from the steep hills of the town, felt too discouraged to even return a snappy retort. Maybe he was right. She trudged upstairs. She didn't really want to go to the picnic, but she had promised Ellie. What was she going to do if she couldn't find a job? She was almost out of money and doubted anyone would extend her credit. That left her few options.

Aye, she would go on the picnic; maybe she'd get a chance to look over the other bachelors or talk to Hunter about the piano—if he weren't too stubborn to consider her offer. Sassy wrinkled her freckled nose. That meant she'd have to be charming to the brute. Since he had such a no-nonsense approach to choosing a wife, by now his amorous attentions were certainly centered on another girl. Maybe the two of them could stop this clash of personalities and talk business like two reasonable people. She was the reasonable one, of course. Hunter was not; he was opinionated and hard-headed.

Sassy took a bath, put on a crisp green gingham dress and a big straw hat. Lord knew she had enough freckles without getting her face sunburned. She looked in the mirror at her reflection and touched the Claddagh ring hanging around her neck. "Oh, Mama, there just isn't a man for me in Seattle—or at least, there doesn't seem to be," she whispered. "Not the kind of man a woman could love enough to sacrifice everything for."

Love. She didn't really know what it was about. She knew what it wasn't; it wasn't submitting to some stranger's lust and being sick inside your very soul. No, love was two people who cared only for each other. Nothing—not pride, not money, not life itself—would be as important to her as that love and that man.

A knock at the door. "Sassy, Mildred and Ellie and I are ready. Are you coming?"

"Just a minute." Sassy took one more look at herself in the mirror and pinched her cheeks to make them rosy, dabbing on a light, floral cologne. Sassy could choose one from all the dozens of eager men who had flirted with her last night and marry him, and she'd be the best wife she could be. Maybe she could learn to love him. She tied the ribbons of her hat under her chin, squared her shoulders, and joined the other ladies going down to the waiting wagons.

Many of the men were outside already, slicked up and self-conscious, awkward in new clothes. A few were on horseback; others helped the ladies up into the wagons. She craned her neck, looked up and down the steep streets. She didn't know whether she felt relieved or a bit disappointed not to see that distinctive Appaloosa stallion with its snowy white hips and black spots. Maybe Hunter wasn't planning on coming to the picnic. She should have approached him about the piano this morning.

Mildred looked around at the crowd gathered near the wagons and said, "Have you seen James Hunter? I thought he'd be here."

Sassy shook her head.

However, Will had just joined them and answered, "Oh, he'll already be out there; after all, this picnic is on his timber lease."

"My stars!" Mildred's eyes gleamed. "Does he own everything around here?"

Will grinned and squeezed Gertrude's hand. She turned a pleased pink. He said, "A man can homestead 160 acres, 320 if he's married. Because the Indians only take orders from Hunter, he seems to control just about everything else. People, too."

Sassy couldn't stop herself from wrinkling her nose. "It's time someone bucked him a little."

Will laughed. "He's a fair employer and a soft touch when a man needs a job. Even those who are afraid of his power respect him."

Sassy didn't comment, remembering the way the big half-breed had dispatched the drunk the night before. Aye, he was formidable, all right.

Gertrude and Will looked into each other's eyes as if no one else in the world existed, and an older man had struck up a conversation with Mildred. Ellie, talking to little Timmy, seemed too shy to look at any of the men. Sassy turned her attention to flirting with some of the bachelors, just in case she had to choose one. Funny, none of them seemed interested in visiting with her. Oh, they were polite enough, but each only spoke a few words and then drifted away. Even the ones who had appeared so taken with her last night barely gave her a passing nod today. She began to feel as unwanted and unsure of herself as poor Ellie.

Especially right now. Sassy looked around for a gentleman to assist her up into the wagon, but no one rushed to help her as they had before. She didn't know what to think. Was she not as pretty and charming as these other women? Last night, many of these same men who were now ignoring her had been buzzing around her like bees around a flower blossom. She managed to climb up by herself as the others boarded. Even waspish Mildred in her silly hat had three eager men vying with each other to assist her.

The wagons creaked away up the steep hill, headed out of town. Everyone but Sassy and Ellie seemed to be having a wonderful time; the women talking and laughing, the men flirting. None of the men even seemed to notice Sassy. It dawned on her that many of them had seen her go out on the veranda last night with Hunter. Was being seen with him the ultimate in ruining a lady's reputation?

Maybe it was just her imagination; maybe they weren't ignoring her. She set her jaw with Malone stubbornness and decided that when they arrived at the picnic site, she would be twice as flirty as any of the girls and giggle if it choked her. Holy Saint Patrick, the way the men were treating her, she was beginning to think maybe she couldn't land a husband if she wanted one. Stop that kind of thinking, girl, she told herself with spirit. You're getting as bad as Ellie.

The wagons wound their way through scenic pine and fir trees. Washington Territory was wild and beautiful country, Sassy thought with awe. A breeze blew in from Puget Sound, mixing the scent of sea air with the scent of wild flowers and fresh-cut timber from the sawmill behind them. The sun felt warm as a lover's kiss on her skin and somewhere a bird called. She could really learn to love it here. They drove several miles through the wooded hills before they came to a pretty clearing where the wagons halted.

Sassy heard a gasp and turned to see what all the ladies were murmuring about. Hunter sat his stallion on a nearby rise overlooking the picnic site. He did not smile as he watched the scene and in his black hat and coat, mounted on the giant Appaloosa stallion, he looked as forbidding as Satan himself suddenly appearing out of the dark·woods. Hunter nudged his horse and came toward them slowly, the silver bridle and saddle gleaming against the ebony horse.

She heard Will say softly to Gertrude, "We're on Hunter's timber lease."

"Will he mind?"

The young lumberjack laughed nervously. "If he did, his men would have already run us off. Nobody messes with anything that belongs to Hunter."

Bless the saints, was every person in the whole Territory afraid of that man? The thought rankled Sassy and she glared at him as he rode into the clearing. Their gaze met and held a moment, and he almost smiled, but not quite.

"Welcome," Hunter said. "Enjoy yourselves, but be careful with fire; the woods are unusually dry this year."

Immediately everyone relaxed and the men began helping the ladies down from the wagons. Even Ellie had gained an admirer. Sassy waited expectantly, but the men acted as if she didn't exist, gathering up picnic baskets and blankets to sit on and trooping off toward the clearing. Baffled, Sassy stared after them. Had she suddenly become invisible?

Even the drivers had tied the teams and left. Was everyone really walking away as if she weren't there? She felt his eyes on her. Very slowly, she looked up. Hunter still sat his horse, leaning on his saddle horn, only a few feet away. He watched her, his expression arrogant. She had never felt such apprehension. Either her shameful secret was out or being on the veranda with him last night had created such talk that now no man thought her respectable enough to consider as a prospective bride. With as much dignity as she could muster, Sassy struggled with her full skirt, which was caught on the wagon bed.

"Wait, Miss Sassy. I'll help you." He swung down off the big horse.

"No, thank you, I can manage." Damned if she was going to let him put his hands on her! She hadn't forgotten how they had seemed to burn through the fabric of her gown and into her flesh last night. "No, thank you," she said again, yanking at the skirt. "I'm perfectly capable of getting myself down."

When she tried to move, she realized her dress was snagged on a splinter. Even as she pulled on the fabric, he reached up, put his hands on her waist.

"I said 'no thank you,'" she snapped, tearing the dress free of the wood.

He didn't answer, but he never took his gaze off hers as he slowly lifted her down. For a long moment, she hung in midair and again she marveled at the immense strength it must take for a man to hold a woman off the ground at arm's length the way Hunter was doing. Very slowly, he lowered her feet to the grass, but he didn't take his hands away. She was placed in the vulnerable position of looking up at him. Her hat slipped off the back of her head and hung by its ribbons. Why hadn't

93

she noticed before the sensual curve of his mouth? His hands tightened possessively.

She had a sudden feeling that he was going to pull her to him and kiss her. He stood so close she felt the heat radiating from his lithe frame, the steel of his grasp on her waist. The air seemed almost charged with electricity as she waited. What should she do if he tried? Object loudly? Pull away? Return the kiss? She didn't know the answer to that herself. Sassy felt she was about to faint from lack of oxygen, but if she took a deep breath, her breasts would surely brush against his chest. She mustered enough dignity to break the animal magnetism between them. "Please, let go of me."

Perhaps he would not oblige her request. His eyes burned with intense passion, and she had a flash of intuition that he might throw her across his shoulder, carry her into the woods, and make love to her in a shadowy glade.

Hunter took a deep, shudding breath, removing his hands with evident reluctance. "A lady should always wait for a man to help her."

"Thank you for your assistance, Sir," Sassy said dutifully and took a step backward. Her own heart pounded against her breast. Surely he could see it under the checked cotton. She felt vulnerable and foolish. "Let's join the others."

"Are you afraid being seen with me will damage your reputation and good name?" He didn't smile.

"Should I be?" She returned the volley, attempting to put her hat on as she met his gaze.

"Both are the most valuable possessions a lady has; you should remember that."

And the major difference between a lady and a

94

whore, Sassy thought, but she didn't say it. He was a strange man, almost daring her to be attracted to him. He offered her his arm and she hesitated, feeling to ignore it would be churlish. She took it and they walked leisurely toward the picnic site a few hundred yards away. Sassy reminded herself that she had to be at least cordial to him until she found out if he would even consider letting her have the piano. "I hear you have a lovely home."

"It's better than anything in the area," he said, "but a lady from back East might think it primitive by comparison. Someday I intend to build a fine mansion on that far hill." He nodded toward the distant peak.

She thought with a pang of her father. Mike Malone was a great construction man. There were so many opportunities if she could only bring her family out here. But to do so would expose the web of lies she had built to protect herself from Brett James. God did punish people after all, Sassy thought miserably. Her punishment might be having to live with fear of exposure the rest of her life and never seeing her family again. "People say your house is wonderful, full of fine furnishings and pretty things."

He shrugged. "They mean little to me. I accumulated them to give to my bride."

A shrine, Sassy thought. He's creating a shrine to hold some perfect pristine virgin. What was the motivation that drove this man? "I understand you even have a piano."

He glanced at her. "I was told most ladies like them."

"Do you play?"

He shook his head. "I don't even dance, remember?"

"What do you do for fun?"

"Fun?" He said the word as if he didn't know its meaning. "Fun is for rich white boys. If you mean 'how do I occupy my time?' I work and add to my empire. When I do go into town, there's gambling and . . . well, other things."

Whores. Of course there would be a bordello even in the smallest town. She felt her face burn, knowing Hunter would not mention such a place in front of a respectable woman. Sassy had a feeling that even as a small child he had worked while other boys played. She took a deep breath, decided to plunge in. "If I had a piano, I could give lessons and support myself."

He raised one eyebrow at her. "But you don't, and the only other two pianos are—well, not at places a lady would be familiar with."

"But that you know quite well!" she snapped, letting her temper overcome her judgment.

"That goes without saying." He smiled ever so slightly. "But I am, after all, a bachelor."

There was a slight warning in his tone and she felt her own hackles rising, too. What was there about this man that put them at each other's throat within minutes each time they met? Were they so very much alike then? Sassy pulled her arm from his and faced him. "Mr. Hunter, I'll be quite honest with you—"

"Will you, Missy?" His tone was almost cynical. "I suspect most women never are, although I keep looking. They all seem to be nothing more than bits of fluff and fans and flirting. I've never found one who's genuine, who could also be a friend to me."

Sassy looked away. If he only knew what a lie she was living, he would be even more cynical and mistrusting.

96

"Mr. Hunter," she said softly and gave him her most appealing, vulnerable look, "I want to buy your piano."

"It isn't for sale." Hunter dismissed her curtly.

"I don't have much cash, but if you'd extend me credit, I'd pay you with interest as soon as I could once I got started giving lessons."

He tipped he hat back, so arrogant, so in control, and began to laugh. "Missy, you have to be the brassiest little thing I ever met! You're demanding I sell you something on credit? That's not very good business. Besides, I doubt you'd have any more luck giving piano lessons than you've had getting a job or a husband. My piano is not for sale."

"And you, Sir, are the most obstinate and stubborn man I have ever met. Pity the girl who finally agrees to marry you!" She whirled and flounced toward the picnic, angry with him for any number of reasons, some of which she wasn't sure she could name. Damn him. He was as stubborn as any member of the Malone clan— maybe even more than she was herself. Of course in her case it was an admirable trait. She was resolute; he was pig-headed. Besides controlling everything in the area, he must also have spies throughout Seattle reporting to him. Otherwise, how would he have heard she wasn't having any luck landing either a job or a husband?

Sassy hurried to join the crowd, hoping to lose herself among the laughing couples. She glanced back over her shoulder. Hunter stood where she had left him, feet wide apart, his expression dark as a thunder cloud under the black western hat. One strand of curly hair had fallen on his dark forehead. His lips moved as if he were swearing, then he wheeled and strode toward his horse. The ramrod set of his back made it clear he was angry. In moments, she heard the echo of hooves as he galloped away.

She sighed. Well, she had tried. Now what should she do? She had neither the money to stay or leave Seattle and was too proud to tell the other ladies her problems, although they might be willing to try to help her. She was a Malone, she reminded herself. Having gotten herself into this mess, she had to get herself out. Sassy took a plate of food, then sat down dejectedly on the blanket next to Ellie and little Timmy. The plump widow paused with a fork halfway to her lips. "Where have you been? I was about to send Will back to look for you."

"Hunter escorted me through the woods." Sassy bit into a crusty slice of freshly buttered bread.

"If I'd known that, I would have really been concerned," Ellie said. "He's a strange one. I'd be terrified of him."

"Hunter? He's quite gallant. A lady is perfectly safe with him," Sassy said without thinking, then wondered why she felt an urge to protect him from detractors. He was like a lone lobo wolf that did not quite fit into the pack.

Gertrude nodded toward Mildred, who sat with two young men. "Even Mildred's decided he's untamable, which makes him fascinating but scary. She said she'd have to get to know him better before she would consider marrying him."

For some reason, it annoyed Sassy that Mildred thought she might have a chance with the half-breed. Sassy reached for a fresh strawberry, anticipating its sweet taste. "I doubt anyone will ever know the man very well."

No, that wasn't true, Sassy decided. A very special

woman might finally cause the big man to open up his heart to her. If that woman turned out to have feet of clay or betrayed him, it would destroy Hunter. Sassy looked at Mildred in her silly, ornate hat. How dare she be so snide and sure she could capture his heart?

They finished eating and the ladies cleaned up the picnic debris. Now there was time for socializing. With no other recourse open to her, Sassy assessed the available men, drifting from group to group. However, it almost seemed as if she had typhoid, the way the gentlemen reacted to her. Oh, they were polite enough, but constrained. Men who had rushed to flirt with her last night avoided her this afternoon. Sassy's face ached from keeping a smile on her lips. All the other women had at least one beau; some had more than one.

So what was wrong with Sassy that no man was now interested in her? Somehow it seemed to her the picnic would never end. Finally people began to gather up the food baskets and head for the wagons. Will helped her up into the wagon, but no other man paid her the slightest attention. The wagons pulled away with the picnickers singing: *"Oh, the camptown ladies sing dis song, doodah, doodah."*

Back at the hotel, the ladies rested, changed clothes, and visited.

Ellie Kravet went to her room, tidied things up, and washed out a few things. She sank down in a chair and stared at her wedding ring. Was she the only woman in the entire ship-load with a secret? She had felt so guilty

99

lying to Sassy and all those other sweet, innocent girls. Maybe God would forgive her for her sin. It would be so humiliating if anyone here knew the truth; divorce was so rare.

Ellie wasn't a widow; she was a divorced woman looking for a fresh start at the age of fifty-two. Her supposedly saintly husband, Henry, whom everyone thought had been killed in the war, had in reality left her for another woman. It was Ellie's only child, Henry, Junior, who had been killed at Gettysburg.

The tears came in spite of everything she could do and she put her face in her hands and shook a long moment. Coming here with the mail-order brides had been a big mistake, but she'd been desperate for a fresh start. Ellie had tried to work after the divorce, but all she knew how to do was clean and run a house and there weren't many housekeeping jobs available. Ellie wanted to marry; she was so very lonely. She wouldn't expect a man to be either rich or handsome. If she found someone, would she ever tell him her secret? Ellie thought about it. He'd have to be more than a husband; he'd have to be a friend that she felt comfortable and secure with. Secrets. Surely she was the only one of the belles who was hiding something. Tonight she was sitting with Timmy so Gertrude could court with Will. All those pretty young innocents like Sassy and Gertrude didn't know what real trouble was!

Sassy hardly tasted her food at supper. She noticed Ellie didn't eat much, either. Gertrude talked with excitement because Will was coming over later. As dusk came on, a number of the ladies had gentlemen callers.

Sassy couldn't bear to sit in her room on such a lovely evening, so she strolled down the street with Mildred. There was a scent of rain on the breeze and, in the distance, lightning crackled, bringing electricity to the air.

Sassy said, "It's getting dark; maybe we should return to the hotel."

"Besides," Mildred simpered, "I have a gentleman caller coming this evening."

Sassy wondered if she were the only one besides Ellie who didn't have a gentleman caller. She wouldn't have admitted it for the world.

They turned and started back up the steep street as dusk turned into darkness and thunder rolled ominously.

"My stars," Mildred said, "it's going to rain. We'd better hurry."

They quickened their steps, lifting their skirts to keep them from dragging in the mud. Within a few hundred feet of the hotel, a big shape loomed out of the darkness blocking their path; it was the Appaloosa stallion with Hunter astride. "Excuse me, Ladies." He touched the brim of his hat politely and they started around the horse. "No, not you, Missy," he said. "You aren't going anywhere."

Sassy stared up at him, then at Mildred. A chill went down her back. Mildred shrugged helplessly and, hanging onto her silly hat, scurried past Hunter like a frightened mouse, deserting Sassy to look out for herself.

In the moonlight, his dark shadow fell across her and she took a step backward. He weaved slightly in his saddle. He's been drinking, she realized uneasily. "That was quite rude; you scared Mildred."

"But not you?"

"Of course not," she lied. "I'm not afraid of you."

101

"Then why are you backing away? You have spirit," he said. "There's more to you than fluff and fans and flirting. I'll apologize later, I never intended to scare her."

"But you did," she challenged.

He didn't debate that point. "I've looked them all over, you know, both last night and at the picnic, trying to choose one."

He was drunk, she decided; she'd better humor him. "Good for you! I hope you and your bride will be very happy." Sassy started around the horse, but he nudged it and it took a step, blocking her path again.

She felt her uneasiness deepen. A man full of whiskey was unpredictable. "What is it you want?"

He leaned on his saddle horn, looking down at her. She had seen that look a hundred times on men's faces as they closed the bedroom door and unbuttoned her bodice. "Missy, you know what I want. Why do you bother to ask?"

Chapter Six

Hunter looked down at the girl who glared back at him like a defiant kitten with its back raised, waiting to take on a big, dangerous dog. It knew it couldn't win, but it would make a valiant effort anyway.

For a moment in his hazy mind, he realized he was scaring her and almost felt regret. At least he was arousing some emotion in her; and he was too drunk to be ashamed at the perverse pleasure it gave him to see emotion, any emotion, in her face.

"I know what you want," Sassy said and nodded toward the bawdy houses in the distance. The sound of music and laughter drifted faintly on the air. "Those women will sell you what you need."

"I've already been there," he blurted out, "but when I got inside . . ." His voice trailed off as he remembered last night's humiliation. "I—I couldn't," he admitted, thinking she was too innocent to even understand what he meant. "All I could think of was a fiesty lady with hair the color of a forest fire who won't have me. I'm not used to that."

She looked up at him, soft and rustling in her pink calico. The light from the occasional flash of lightning caught the color of her hair. "So you got drunk. Did it help?"

"Damn you, you know it didn't! Only one thing will put out this fire!" Before she could react, he leaned over and grabbed her, lifting her onto the saddle. He had forgotten how light and fragile the girl was. She trembled in his arms as she struggled against his strength. He was past shame, consumed by the hungers raging within him that the flame-haired girl had stoked and coyly ignored since the first moment he had seen her. Her nipples thrust against his chest through her thin dress. His hat fell off as he kissed her savagely. What he couldn't do to her with his maleness, he could do with his mouth.

Sassy struggled a moment, undone by the suddenly unleashed passion of the man. His mouth covered and dominated hers, forcing her lips slowly open as he held her so tightly she wasn't sure she could breathe. His other hand tangled in her cascading hair which had come loose from its pins. She pounded against his chest as his mouth forced hers open and his hot tongue plunged into its depths, caressing and claiming that velvet softness with a hard, rhythmic thrusting.

She was giddy with the taste and heat of the man. Sassy had never felt physical desire before, not even with Brett, whom she had thought she loved before he forced her into earning money with her ripe body.

His hands—what was he doing with his hands? Wave after wave of heat swept over her like a fever as his hands touched and stroked. She had to escape before these feelings overpowered her. Yet even as she pushed against his muscular chest, she realized that fighting his physical strength was useless. Now he sucked her tongue into his mouth and he tasted of brandy and tobacco. There was nothing she could do against his superior strength. Her body actually wanted him. The thought frightened her. She had never wanted a man before; not even Brett had aroused anything in her as she lay there, thighs apart, while he pleasured himself with her body.

Hunter's mouth pillaged hers freely now, asking— no, demanding. She threw back her head and let him taste deep, wanting him to caress even more with his tongue. In spite of herself, she found her body weak in his embrace, pressing against him while one of his hands tangled in her hair, the other at the small of her back molded her even more tightly against him.

His manhood felt hard and throbbed against her body, her breasts crushed against his muscular chest. In that long extended kiss, she felt her tender nipples swell at the friction and wondered if he could feel that, too, through the thin, delicate rose-colored fabric.

The thunder rolled again and the horse snorted and stamped uneasily. Sassy managed to pull away from Hunter, literally gasping for air. Lightning crackled across the sky, lighting up his dark, intense face.

"How dare you! Put me down!" She slapped him then, the sound as sharp as a clap of thunder in her ears. She wasn't sure whether she was furious at him or at herself for almost giving way to her own emotions.

He rubbed his cheek. "I deserved that. I'm sorry; I'll take you back to the hotel."

"Never mind. I'll walk!" In a sudden move, she pulled away from him, slid to the ground. She whirled and, with a flounce of petticoats, stalked toward the hotel.

Behind her, she heard the creak of the saddle as he

dismounted and picked up his hat. "Sassy, wait. I—I don't know what got into me to treat a lady like that."

She kept moving, back ramrod stiff, head in the air. She heard him stumbling behind her, struggling to overtake her although he was unsteady on his feet. He caught up with her, but she didn't look at him and kept walking. In truth, she was more than a little angry with herself. No man, not even Brett, had ever stirred her as Hunter had just done. It not only angered her, it frightened her that he could exert that much control over her emotions.

The thunder rolled again as she walked up the muddy street, Hunter and his horse at her heels. Just as she reached the hotel, he said, "Sassy, wait!"

"Is that an order, Sir?" She turned on him sarcastically. "Everyone else in Seattle may take orders from you, Mr. Hunter, but I don't have to."

"All right, *please* wait." He ducked his head, took off his hat, fumbled with it.

"I'm waiting," she said, wondering what held her here, why she didn't turn and run into the hotel. It would be raining soon.

"Damn it, Missy, what is it you want of me?"

"Nothing. Nothing at all. You're the one who's following me."

For a moment she sensed he was fighting a battle with himself, that he was trying to decide whether to mount up and ride out.

He swayed on his feet and she realized how very drunk he was. "I'm used to getting what I want; I buy, bargain, or just take it."

She winced at his words. If he knew her secret, he'd have her flat on her back out there in the shadows without a qualm. "That's not the way to treat a lady."

"You think I don't know that?" He played with his hat, one black lock hanging down on his forehead. "I—I was out of line, grabbing you like a common whore." He brushed his hair back out of his eyes. "I—I was like a kid seeing something sweet I wanted and couldn't have. The liquor got the best of me and clouded my judgment."

"Are you saying you're sorry?"

He slapped his hat against his leg. "You want me to crawl? All right, damn it! I'm sorry I treated you like a cheap whore," he admitted grudgingly, "but the taste and the scent and the feel of you. . . . Hell, you shouldn't be so desirable."

"That's not an apology." She whirled to go inside.

"What does it take?" he said behind her. "I've done everything I can think of with no results. Tell me in God's name what's it gonna take?"

She paused again. "I don't know what you're talking about."

"Yes, you do." He tied his horse to the hitching block. "I want you for my lady, Sassy, want you worse than anything I've ever wanted in my life. What will it take?"

"That's not a proper way for a gentleman to propose."

"I never said I was a gentleman, remember? I'm even more of an uncivilized savage than you realize. What do you want to share my bed?" He moved closer.

"I don't understand you," she shot back, trying not to remember the heat of his hands, the taste of his brandy-sweet mouth. "Most of these women would jump at the chance to marry you, but you show no interest in any of them."

He shook his head. "A man always wants what he can't have, what he has to fight for." Very slowly his hand reached out, played with the lace on her pink collar.

She didn't pull away, not wanting to tear the dress. "You're doomed to disappointment, Hunter. You're looking for a fairy-tale princess you can put on a pedestal so high she'll faint from lack of air and land in the mud at its base."

"I can't believe I'd ever be disappointed with you for my lady," he whispered, and his forefinger went under her chin to tilt her face up. "I want you Sassy, bad enough to do whatever it takes to get you."

She looked up at him, the sensual curve of his mouth, his dark, troubled face. "We're too much alike, Hunter, hot-headed, stubborn. It would be better for us both if I chose another husband."

His expression hardened. "I will take your virginity or no one will. You'll bear no man's sons but mine!"

She was taken aback and pulled away from his hand. "Is that a threat?"

"No, Missy, that's a promise." She didn't doubt his tone or his expression. "I'm a proud man, Sassy; do you expect me to beg for your favors? You've got me crawling on my belly now and that's not my way."

The thunder cracked loudly and the lightning cut a jagged slash through the distant sky, silhouetting his dark face.

"And what if I say 'no, never?' "

He put both hands on her shoulders. "If you weren't a lady, I'd be tempted to carry you off and hold you like a captive princess in my big home on Hunter's Hill."

The thought intrigued her. She had the prince with all his power and wealth asking for her hand. Why did she hesitate? Because he was stormy as a summer squall and she sensed his tortured soul held dark secrets of his own. Something more. When he finally discovered his princess belonged in the gutter, there was no telling how uncontrolled his wrath might be. "I—I'm thinking of getting a job," she said. "I don't want to rush into marriage—"

"You'll find no job. You've been turned down by every employer in the area, and no man has offered to marry you but me. Be my lady, Sassy Girl; make me respectable; give me sons. I can buy you anything you want; position and power and wealth are at your disposal."

Power, position, and wealth. She would be safe and secure as Mrs. James Hunter. And yet . . .

"It can't work," she murmured. "It just can't work. We're too much alike."

He shook his head. "In some ways, maybe; but in others, we're miles apart. You're a lady and I'm just . . ."

His voice trailed off and she waited, wondering what he had almost said. Such a strange, proud, and lonely man. Why did she hesitate? A voice deep inside reminded her that the first time he took her, he would know he had bought used goods. It was a long way from that pedestal on Hunter's Hill down to the mud of the streets where a whore belonged.

Regrets. Oh, such bitter regrets. Try as she might, Sassy couldn't stop the tears from pooling in her brown eyes. When she tried to blink them away, they made hot, crooked trails down her cheeks.

"What is it, Missy?" He was drunk and fumbling as he wiped the tears from her eyes with a gentle finger. "You're trembling. Have I said something—?"

"No." She shook her head and swallowed the lump that threatened to rise in her throat and choke her. For a long moment, she wanted to blurt out the heavy burden of her secrets, hear him say that it didn't matter, that he wanted her anyway. She couldn't expect that from such a proud man; he wanted her because he thought he would be the first. Maybe she could fool him. She was desperate enough to try. "All right, as you've pointed out, I don't seem to have many alternatives."

"No, you don't." He took her in his arms, brushed a wisp of hair away from her forehead. "I'll see to it that you'll never regret it."

She regretted it already, knowing what an eternal burden her secret would be. How many, many women went through life like that? It was a form of personal hell. She said a silent prayer that she was doing the right thing. "We can make plans for next Saturday night—"

"No, Sassy, tonight." His voice brooked no argument. He pulled her against his chest, his muscular arms like a barricade around her. "Judge Stone will still be up."

She leaned against him, caught between feeling imprisoned and protected by his strength. "Tonight? We can't get married tonight!"

"We can and will."

"But it's impossible tonight," she protested. "All the ladies will want to attend the ceremony, and there's food for the guests, and I'll have to get something to wear, and—"

"Tonight," he said firmly. "I want you tonight."

She looked up, startled by his frankness and the urgency of his tone.

"That wasn't a gentlemanly thing to say, was it, Sassy Girl? You'll have to teach me some manners. I haven't had the raisin' that you've had. I'm blunt, aggressive as a bull on the prod, and plain-spoken."

Aye, and drunk as an Irish lord, she thought with a sigh. This wasn't the wedding she had always dreamed

110

of. But at least he had offered marriage, even Brett hadn't offered that.

"Men hate all that pomp and ceremony with the ladies running about pouring punch and throwing flowers." He untied his horse and Sassy took his arm. They walked down the street with an occasional raindrop falling on her face.

Was he afraid that if she thought it over, she might change her mind?

She almost turned and ran when they stopped at the small, plain house down the street. Hunter tied up his horse and rapped sharply on the door. It was answered by an old man with a shaggy white mustache. He took the pipe out of his mouth. "Why, Hunter, come in. So here's the bride and a pretty one, too! I thought you'd be here last night."

The half-breed looked over at Sassy, smiled wryly. "The lady didn't want to get married yesterday. She needed some convincing."

The judge laughed and motioned with his pipe. "I'll bet Hunter can be very convincing, young lady. Come on in."

So Hunter had made his plans without any thought that she might say no, even tonight. What a pig-headed . . . They followed the old man into a small living room lit by an oil lamp. A plump grandmotherly woman jumped up from her chair, laid her knitting aside. "Lands sake, are you two the first of all those marriages we're going to see from Mercer's brides?"

Sassy could only nod dumbly through the introductions. She felt she was being rushed into this before she had time to think it over. Hunter had decided he wanted a bride; she fit the bill, and he intended to bring

111

this matter to a quick close. She looked from the elderly couple to Hunter, still drunk as an Irish wake. She almost gave in to the urge to turn and run out into the rainy night. This marriage wouldn't be blessed by a priest and she couldn't use her real name. Would marrying under another woman's name mean this marriage wasn't even legal?

Judge Stone cleared his throat. "Hazel, Dear, wake Grandpa up. We'll need him as a second witness."

"It's a shame to wake him," Sassy interjected. "Perhaps we could come back tomorrow."

Hunter smiled at the old couple. "Bridal jitters."

Hazel Stone nodded, a twinkle in her eye. "Bless your heart! Grandpa won't mind." She left the room.

The judge knocked the ashes from his pipe out against the hearth. "They call you Sassy instead of Sophia?"

She nodded, remembering the real Sophia. Was this God's way of punishing her for not reporting Sophia's death?

The judge reached for his Bible, winked. "That ought to be a warning to you, Hunter. With that red hair, I'll bet she's more than a match for you."

"I'm counting on it. I ordered a fiesty lady with a little fire to her."

Mrs. Stone bustled out of the other room leading a bent, yawning old man in a faded bathrobe. "Here, Grandpa, you stand right here." To Sassy, she said, "I'm sorry, my dear, we won't have any music; we should have had the wedding at Hunter's house. He has a piano, you know."

Grandpa cackled, showing toothless gums. "There's

112

pianos down on the skid road and, as well as those girls know Hunter, I'm sure they would be glad to—"

"Grandpa, please!" Judge Stone glared at the old man. "Miss Merriweather is a lady; I'm sure she isn't interested in past history."

Sassy glanced around in big-eyed innocence as if she hadn't the slightest idea what was being discussed. Hunter looked uneasy, embarrassed, and drunk.

"Hazel," the judge said, "can't we do a bit more for Miss Sassy? Flowers or something?"

"Of course. Lands sake, how absentminded of me. There may be a few blooms in the window box." She hurried outside, returned in a moment clutching a handful of wild flowers. "It's gonna storm later on, I think."

Sassy took the flowers. She had dreamed of white roses in her wedding bouquet, but these straggly little blooms would have to do.

The plump lady surveyed her a moment. "At the very least, you need a veil."

Before Sassy could protest, Hazel Stone jerked an old lace tablecloth off the table and draped it over Sassy's head. "Hunter, what do you think?"

He turned and looked down at Sassy. "The most beautiful bride in all of Washington Territory," he whispered, and Sassy had a sudden feeling he had forgotten anyone else was even in the room. His expression was so tender, so gentle, that she almost couldn't believe this was the same stormy man who had frightened her only moments before.

Judge Stone cleared his throat. "Everyone take their places, please. Is there a ring?"

Hunter looked askance. "I didn't think about it."

Sassy looked down at the ring on its chain, the one on her finger. "Aye, double rings; my parents'."

"How sweet," Mrs. Stone cooed as Sassy took the worn little gold ring off her finger and handed it to Hunter.

Sassy didn't think it was sweet at all. It seemed sacreligious to use her mother's wedding ring in a marriage that was only a sham and was bound to be a disaster: No priest, marrying under a dead woman's name, a handful of wild flowers, and a faded lace tablecloth for a veil.

She unhooked the chain around her neck, but Hunter shook his head. "No. Hell, no. I'm not gonna wear a ring like some bull with one through its nose."

The judge said, "I think a double-ring ceremony is the coming thing, Hunter."

"I won't wear it," he said again, then noticed Sassy's disappointed face. "Well, maybe on my watchchain."

Let love and friendship reign, Sassy thought with a sigh. He wanted her body, but he wasn't willing to make a total commitment. Well, what had she expected from any man?

The judge pulled at his mustache and cleared his throat again. "All right, let's get on with it; Grandpa's dozing off standing there."

Mrs. Stone nudged the old man. "Just one minute, Grandpa, and you can go back to bed."

With Grandpa grumbling, the judge began: "Dearly Beloved, we are gathered here tonight before God and these witnesses to unite James Hunter and Sassy Merriweather in Holy Matrimony."

The thunder rumbled outside as if God and the saints were protesting this sham of a wedding. Hunter took her

114

arm, sensing that she was ready to turn and run out into the night. The judge's words were a blur to her. What a mistake she was making!

"Do you, Sassy, take Hunter as your lawfully wedded husband, to have and to hold, in sickness and in health, forsaking all others, till death do you part?"

She nodded. If she opened her mouth, she might scream out, "No! With my past, I'm not fit to wed any man and certainly not someone who expects an angel!"

"Speak up, please," the judge looked at her.

"Yes, I—I do," Sassy managed.

"Hunter, do you take Sassy to be your lawfully wedded wife, to love and to cherish for all eternity?"

"I will." His voice was strong, determined, with no hesitation. Even inebreated, he exuded a possessive triumph.

"The ring, please," the judge said.

Hunter took her mother's ring in his big hand and slipped it on her finger. Sassy looked down as the judge droned on about circles of love, circles of gold. Her mother's wedding ring. The little gold heart was worn from years on Maureen's finger. Her mother had made a great sacrifice because she loved Mike Malone so much; but that's what love was all about: sacrifice. Sassy stared down at the heart, certain in her soul she could never love this man that way. It was wrong to use her mother's ring in this sacrilege.

"Get on with it, Judge," Hunter hiccoughed.

"If there is anyone present who knows a reason why these two should not be wed, speak now or forever hold your peace."

The room was so silent that Sassy heard Grandpa wheeze and the wind blow against the house. Sassy

115

found she was holding her breath. Hunter shifted his feet impatiently. "I said get on with it."

"It's just part of the ceremony." The judge shrugged and pulled at his mustache. "Very well, with the authority vested in me by God and the Territory of Washington, I now pronounce you man and wife. You may kiss your bride, Hunter."

He turned toward her, put his big hands under her chin, lifted her face up to his very slowly. Then he kissed her, his lips barely brushing hers, so different from the passionate, bruising kiss of only minutes ago.

It was over. She was now Hunter's wife. The enormity of it swept over her. Then the judge, his wife, and the old man were crowding about her, offering warm wishes and congratulations.

"Lands sake, too bad there wasn't time for a party," the plump lady said. "We should at least have a shivaree."

Sassy didn't even know what that was. "Maybe some other time," she said and handed back the lace tablecloth. "Isn't there something we're supposed to sign?"

Hunter looked alarmed.

What was it, Sassy thought? Maybe the wedding had been a sham, a hoax to get her into bed. No, the Stones looked too wholesome and honest.

The judge relit his pipe and dug through a cluttered desk for the legal documents. Sassy signed with a flourish; but when she handed the pen to Hunter, he dropped it on the floor, too drunk to write.

The judge picked up the pen. "I'm not sure he's sober enough to sign anything, Ma'am. Maybe later—"

"Can I sign for him?" Sassy asked. Hunter was indeed swaying dangerously as if he were about to pass out and fall across the desk.

The judge shrugged. "I suppose under the circumstances . . ." He looked at the drunken man dubiously, sighed, and shook his head. He handed Sassy the pen and she signed Hunter's name. Grandpa yawned and made his mark on the paper, turned, and shuffled back to bed.

"Hazel." The judge smiled and took a deep puff. "Let's not delay these young people; they'll be eager to retire."

Sassy felt a flush rise to her face, but Hunter grinned. "Right. This time next year, you'll be filling out birth records for our first son. Come, Sassy."

She said her goodbyes once more and saw Hunter slip the judge some money. He threaded her father's ring on his watchchain although she had to help him to keep him from dropping it. Then she was going out the door into the cool, wet night, the ragged wild flowers still clutched in her hand. Holy Mary, what in God's name had she done?

Hunter took off his jacket and draped it around her shoulders. It felt still warm from his body heat and smelled faintly of leather, tobacco, and the masculine scent of his skin. "I'm sorry," he said, "I forgot there was supposed to be a ring."

"It doesn't matter," Sassy said, a bit grim. She'd made this deal and now she'd try to make the best of it. Maybe when he sobered up, he'd regret it, too.

"It matters to me," Hunter said as they walked to the horse. It snorted a greeting, and Hunter fumbled with the reins, but managed to untie them. "I intend that you will have the best of everything. When you ride down the street in your carriage, everyone will say, 'There goes Hunter's lady, isn't she beautiful? Look at her clothes and her jewels.' "

"It doesn't matter," Sassy said again, realizing she was yet another possession to this cold, proud man. He would display her along with the fine furnishings, his piano, and his wealth.

He swung up on the horse, reached down his hand to her. "I've ordered a fine carriage from San Francisco, but it hasn't arrived yet. We can ride double."

She let him lift her up before him. "We can manage as far as the hotel."

"We're not going to the hotel; we're going home." He clucked to the horse and they started down the steep street, headed out of town.

Home. It wasn't home to her and never would be. It was Hunter's house. "You might have asked what I thought."

"Would you really want to stay at the hotel tonight with fifty curious women straining their ears against walls and our door to hear the slightest sound?"

"I—I suppose not." She was already dreading what she must endure in his bed, remembering the unleashed passion of the man earlier tonight. Worse than that was the thought that she might not be able to fool him.

Hunter felt the girl tremble in his embrace as the Appaloosa clopped along the muddy road out of town. "Are you cold? You're shaking."

"No."

Then she must be afraid. He could understand that. No telling what kind of horror stories she'd heard about virgins on their wedding nights. He would have to control himself, be very gentle that first time. It would be difficult, since he had literally ached for this innocent's ripe body from the first moment he had seen her. Now she belonged to him and he could slake his lust in her arms tonight. His very first virgin. All his women had been sluts and whores.

He held her close as they rode, trying to warm her with his big body. When the lightning cracked again across the sky and she flinched, he held her against him protectively. "It's all right, Sassy Girl. I'll take care of you; you're mine now."

She buried her face against his chest and he kissed her soft hair. She seemed so very young, so vulnerable, not like the fiesty, fiery female who had enticed him with her stubborn independence and pride. Of course her nubile body had enticed him, too. She was made to bear children, to satisfy a man. He felt his maleness harden against her as they rode through the woods and into the hills. He was literally aching with his need. He'd have to go slow with her since she was so young and innocent, but it was going to be worth the wait. He imagined getting her home to his own big bed.

The thought of having her naked among the covers made him draw his breath in sharply and, without thinking, he laid his hand on her thigh. Even through the fabric of her skirt, he could feel the heat of her skin and imagined its white silkiness against the darkness of his own. She stiffened under his hand.

"You're my wife, Missy," he reminded her. She sighed, then relaxed as if realizing he could do anything he wanted with her ripe body and it was her wifely duty to accommodate him. The fact that she did not protest emboldened him to move his hand to her slender waist and then up under the big coat to her breast.

119

She took a deep breath, but did not object. Mine. He cupped her breast, feeling her nipple against his palm as the horse clopped along in the cool rainy night. In his mind, he already had her in his bed, his mouth pulling at those nipples. A year from now they would be swollen with milk for his son. When the child was satisfied and asleep, Hunter would make love to her and drink of her breasts.

A son. Knowing what he did of his own father, did Hunter dare sire a child? Suppose it inherited . . . ? No, he would not worry about that tonight. He would imagine the pleasure of taking his bride to bed. That made him think of the house. "The house is pretty crude right now for an Eastern lady; but as soon as I can find some skilled workmen, I'm going to build you a castle on that hill. It will have the best of everything; nothing that Hunter owns is ever secondhand or second-rate."

"Why is that so important to you?" She sounded almost fiery again.

He'd never thought about it. Yes, he had; many times. Over and over as a young child, he had remembered that nightmare that was not a dream. "My mother . . ."

No, he couldn't tell her; she wouldn't understand the pain and ridicule a half-breed boy had suffered. They rode on in silence. The mist had turned into a fine, cool rain and Sassy burrowed her face against his chest and he bent his tall frame protectively to keep the wet and cold away from her. He was still drunk and he knew it. He'd been a fool not to stay in the hotel. However, he wanted to enjoy his new bride without anyone eaves-dropping at every creak of the bed or his moans as he exhausted himself plunging into her body. Besides, suppose she should change her mind and go running into

120

the hall in her nightgown? Out at Hunter's Hill, even if she protested, there would be no one to keep him from taking his husbandly privilege.

It seemed like forever they rode through the light rain with the thunder rolling faintly. It was the kind of growing storm that might last several days. He smiled to himself. There were worse things than being trapped inside by bad weather on your honeymoon.

He glanced down at Sassy who had drifted off to sleep against his wide chest, her foolish little bouquet still clutched in her hand. She didn't look fiesty right now; she looked tired and vulnerable. What had driven her to marry him? His money? Sheer desperation that no other man seemed interested and she hadn't been able to find a job? No doubt she would be furious if she knew to what extent Hunter had gone to to make sure she had no other choices.

The Appaloosa stepped in an uneven place in the road, joggling her, though she was cradled in his arms. Sassy sighed in her sleep and he brushed his lips tenderly across her forehead without even thinking about it. Almost he could learn to love this flame-haired imp. He frowned and shook his head, steeling his resolve. No, to do so would put him in her power as his beautiful, worthless mother had done his father. The wild mixed-blood Indian beauty had almost destroyed Clayton James before that fateful night when . . .

He must not think about that long-ago night, but he would never forget the screams and the curses and the blood . . . so much blood . . .

No, Hunter would not become a slave to this beauty's love. A man needed a wife to preside at his table, show off his wealth with jewels around her pretty neck, give him sons. Respectable ladies weren't meant to be play-things anyway, not like the girls at Lulu's. No man would ever laugh at Hunter as they had his father. His woman was a lady who would never think of wanting a man, any man, between her silken thighs. No, a respect-able lady only endured a husband's embraces, knowing it was her duty to produce sons for him. Once he had put a baby in Sassy's belly, Hunter would be thoughtful enough to take his lust down to the low whores at Lulu's Lovelies and not subject his wife to his animal appetites.

He was almost sober now that they were nearing home. He thought about tonight with both anticipation and dread. Hunter had never taken a virgin before. Sassy, despite her fiery nature, would surely lie there rigid and terrified the first time. That didn't appeal to him even though he hungered for her body. Maybe if he got her drunk before he took her, she'd relax and it wouldn't hurt her so much when he rammed his big maleness through the delicate silk of her virginity. Yes, that's what he'd do; he'd get her drunk.

That decided, he concentrated on the road, seeing the faint lights of his house up ahead, gleaming through the misty rain.

It seemed forever before he rode up the drive and around to the barn. A sleepy stablehand came running out to take the horse. Hunter instructed him to give the stallion a good rubdown and feed, then dismounted, Sassy still in his arms. The man looked at her wide-eyed.

"I married tonight," Hunter said softly. "This is my bride." Turning on his heel, he strode toward the house, carrying the sleeping girl. A lady. *My* lady, yes, mine alone.

Was she really asleep or only pretending? Sassy stirred

in his arms as he entered the back way, closing the door behind him. He decided not to awaken Cookie, and Swede was probably out at the logging camp . . . or drunk down at Lulu's. Hunter felt wet and weary. What he needed was a roaring fire and the whiskey he kept in the master bedroom. Hunter hoped Kitty wasn't asleep in his bed. He knew the house well enough to find his way down the hall in the dark. He carried the girl into his room and laid her on the big bed. She stirred as he fumbled for the ornate oil lamp on the bedside table and lit it.

The girl yawned and stretched lazily as she gradually came awake, throwing off his coat. All Hunter could concentrate on was the way her taut breasts strained against the delicate pink fabric of her dress as she arched her back. His manhood began to throb hard as stone. God, how he wanted her! He had to fight a terrible urge to throw himself across her, rip her dainty lace underthings away, and ram into her.

No, he reminded himself and went over to the ornate walnut chest to get the bottle; whiskey first, and when you've got her drunk enough, at least you won't hurt her when you take her virginity. As tired and cold as they both were, he ought to wait to claim his husbandly rights. Then he took another look at her ripe body spread out on his big bed in a tumble of petticoats and full skirts, the long fiery tresses across the pillows, and poured a tumblerful. He couldn't wait; he wanted her too badly. He would take her tonight.

Chapter Seven

Sassy came awake gradually, wondering where she was. Her muscles had felt so cramped and now she was finally spread out on something soft. She stretched again, looking about the dimly lit room. She recognized the intense face staring down at her with desire and sat up with a start. "Where are we?"

"My bedroom. Or maybe now I should say *our* bedroom." Hunter set the crystal tumbler next to the potted fern on the bedside table. "You seemed wet and cold. I thought I'd fix you a whiskey."

"Aye, that sounds good. I'm awfully tired." From the expression on his face, she could tell he would not take that as an excuse tonight. The next hour would be a time of reckoning. Holy Mother of God, just what had Sassy let herself in for? She listened to the rain on the roof for a long moment. When he found out he'd been cheated, that she wasn't a chaste virgin, he would probably throw her out into the storm. Sassy shivered. That was the least he would do. He had a terrible anger and passion.

"Are you cold? I saw you shiver."

"No." She stood up slowly.

He put his hands on her shoulders. "Your clothes are damp. Here, let me help you undress."

"No, I can manage, thank you." She pulled away from him, wanting to delay the inevitable as long as possible. She looked toward the massive fireplace. "A—a fire would be nice," Sassy gulped, wondering how long she could stall this virile bridegroom.

"All right, I'll build one." He went to the hearth, knelt there. "The adjoining room is your dressing room. You'll find everything you need. I ordered your trousseau in advance from San Franscisco. Let me light you a lamp."

She took the small oil lamp and paused, watching him. His shirt strained over his lithe muscles as he worked. Wide-shouldered and narrow-hipped, she thought, a powerful man—a stallion of a male. When Hunter came into a woman, she would know he was there.

Outside lightning crackled and thunder rolled. The rain now drummed the roof in torrents. Hunter cocked his head and listened. "We got here just in time. The way that sounds, we may not go out for several days."

Several days. Even if she could fool him into thinking her innocent, he'd expect to mount her continuously. This man wanted sons for his empire. She took another look at his lean, hard body hunched on one knee before the fire he was coaxing into flame. He had a strange jagged scar, and she wondered how he had come by it. He looked potent enough to put a child in her the first time he took her.

Hunter turned and looked up. His gaze burned into hers, passionate and intense. "Aren't you going to change?"

His impatient expression said he was holding himself in check, but not for long. If she didn't hurry, she was going to find herself pulled down and taken right there on the hearth.

"Of course." Holy Saint Patrick, deliver her from the lustful appetites of men. She recalled the taste of his mouth as he had lifted her up on his horse and kissed her savagely, arousing instincts in her she hadn't known existed. She forced herself to smile at him coquettishly. "Fix yourself a drink, too. After all, we've got all night."

"You're right, Missy; I've waited a long time for a bride, no use rushing it. I want to savor it awhile."

A glimmer of an idea occurred to her. If she could fill him with enough whiskey, he might never know whether he'd gotten a virgin or not. It was the only hope she had.

She looked around at the big bedroom in the glowing light, at the dark, ornate furnishings and the massive bed that would suit the lord of a manor. On the heavily carved bedside table sat an elegant oil lamp, a potted fern, and a tumbler of whiskey big enough to knock a sailor unconscious. As he poured himself a drink, she crossed the thick Persian carpet to the dressing room.

Sassy held up her lamp with a shaking hand and inspected the place. Hunter had spared no expense. Three wardrobes and two big chests, a table covered with silver-handled hairbrushes and fancy perfume bottles, a delicate porcelain washbowl and pitcher. She set the lamp down, reached for a luxurious towel and scented soap. The longer she stalled, the more he would drink. *Sassy, my girl, you might just pull this off.* She brightened at the thought.

She took off her damp clothes, hung them tidily over a towel rack, and kicked off her shoes. While she washed with the water from the pitcher, she listened to him moving around in the other room. How much whiskey could he hold and how long would it take him

126

to drink it? Would he think she was trying to escape her wifely obligations completely tonight by rendering him impotent? She shook her head at that thought. James Hunter was probably more of a stallion of a man with his belly full of liquor than most men were cold sober.

She dried herself with the thick, Turkish towels, wrapped herself in one, and sat before the mirror and sampled the perfumes. Then she unpinned her hair, letting it cascade down over her shoulders to her waist, and began to brush it.

"What's taking you so long?" he called impatiently.

"Have another drink. I'll be there in a minute. You want me to be pretty, don't you?"

"Missy, you'd be pretty to me with your hair a tangle and your freckled nose smudged."

She was touched by the declaration. He almost sounded like a real bridegroom, a man in love. No, she shook her head and looked at the worn gold ring on her left hand. No, he wasn't in love with her; he was in love with a marble statue on a pedestal. The rain drummed down as she arose with a sigh and opened a wardrobe, examining the nightdresses.

If she had hoped for a modest flannel one, she was disappointed. They were all the finest of fabric and lace, but sheer enough that when she held one up to the lamplight, Sassy had no doubt she could read a book through it. She chose a pale green one, put it on, looked down. She might as well be stark naked. "Didn't you buy any nightdress warm enough for a cold night?" she called.

He laughed, sounding relaxed and good-natured. "That's what I'm here for."

The whiskey must be working. How long could she stall him? She returned to brushing her hair.

More time passed. "What are you doing in there?" Now he sounded annoyed. "Am I going to have to come in after you?"

"I—I'm coming." Bless the saints, he sounded ready to kick the door down. She studied it, toying with the idea of slipping the lock. The door appeared solid and strong, but she was certain it couldn't withstand an assault by that determined half-breed. There was nothing to do now but go to him and hope for the best. She said a prayer to her patron saint as she dabbed on perfume, picked up her lamp, and returned to the bedroom.

Hunter leaned against the mantel, smoking a cheroot and sipping his whiskey. He had stripped off his shirt and was bare-chested. When she entered, he stared at her, and she feared she had disappointed him. "Lord God," he whispered in a tone of awe, "you are the most beautiful, desirable . . ."

She had never seen such intense longing on a man's face before, and it scared her. She couldn't possibly live up to his expectations. She extinguished her lamp and set it on the chest of drawers. They faced each other in the dim glow of the table lamp and the fire.

He looked her up and down. "Turn around."

She started to protest, then decided it was useless. Sassy turned slowly in a circle, feeling like a harem slave on an auction block awaiting a decision as to whether she pleased the master enough to buy her for his pleasure. "We've done this before. Do I meet with your approval?"

He sipped his drink, the smoke from his cheroot drifting upward in a crooked trail. She saw the sudden hardness bulge in his pants and flushed, looked away.

"Why do you ask, you minx? You want compliments?

128

All right, I've never wanted a woman like I want you right now."

"I didn't mean—"

"Yes, you did." He regretted instantly his admission that he desired her. Angrily, Hunter threw his cigar into the blazing fire and looked her up and down, feasting hungry eyes on her curves through the sheer nightdress. "You women are all alike, even the ladies among you, I suppose. You aren't satisfied until you have a man in your power, groveling, offering anything if you'll only . . ." His voice trailed off as he remembered his wild, beautiful mother. Only at this moment could he understand the way she had enslaved his father—and the other men. He recalled that final tragedy . . .

With a shaking hand, he set his whiskey on the mantel, preferring to drink in the beauty of his bride. Sassy stood barefooted in the lamplight, her long hair hanging down her back, catching the glow and reflecting it like a forest fire. Through the sheer nightdress, he could see creamy pale skin, generous breasts with rosebud tips that begged for a man's mouth, a waist so small he was certain he could span it with his two big hands, and hips and silken thighs that could take a man to ecstasy . . . or insanity. He stared at the apex of her thighs and the dark red curls there. He fought an almost uncontrollable urge to kneel before her; clasp her to his lips; kiss those thighs, that font of pleasure; caress her with his mouth until she, too, lost control and they went down in a tangle of pale gossamer nightdress and long red hair to the thick carpet and a frenzied embrace.

He hadn't realized he was so drunk until he started to move toward her and swayed on his feet.

She looked nervous. "Is there something wrong? Do I not please you?"

"Believe me, you please me." Hell, he was probably scaring her, innocent as she was. He'd have to go slow or he'd terrify her. Even though his blood pounded in his temples and his manhood throbbed with wanting, he knew he'd have to take his time. Hunter had waited long years for this beautiful virgin and he couldn't spoil everything by throwing her down on the carpet and riding her in hurried lust like he would a cheap whore at Lulu's place.

She shifted her weight from one small foot to another, uneasy. He needed to get her to relax if he were to glean any enjoyment from this wedding night. "Have a drink." He motioned toward her tumbler of whiskey.

"All right." She picked up her drink from the bedside table. "Why don't you have another? You look like you could use it."

"You're right." He felt as if he could use it, too, although his brain warned him he'd had plenty already while waiting for her to change clothes. The sheer frustration of having to wait when he was throbbing with need sent him stumbling to the chest of drawers to refill his drink. The slight scent of her perfume lingered on the air and he imagined putting his face in the cleft of her breasts and inhaling that fragrance. "So here we are."

"Yes, here we are," she said in a timid voice and sipped her drink.

If he could just get her drunk enough to relax, maybe it wouldn't hurt her so much that first time. It was important to him that he not hurt her. She seemed so fragile and defenseless standing here barefooted, looking up at him like a small, innocent schoolgirl. She was too young, way too young for a man who had lived as hard as he had. But she was his wife and he had a right to pleasure himself with her body. Her experience was a blank tablet, just waiting for him to write on it, to teach her. She might even learn to like it, to want it.

No, he shook his head, that would be expecting too much. Real ladies didn't want it; he'd overheard his father say that. A real lady endured it, lying cold and unresponsive while a man sweated and humped between her thighs until he finally emptied himself into her and hoped she'd give him a son for his efforts. Hunter returned to the fire, stared into it, remembering that was why his father had temporarily left his elegant wife for the wild Indian slut who had enthralled him. Hunter stared at the red-haired beauty. Could a lady never learn to act like a hoyden so a man could have the best of both worlds? It might be worth the time to try and teach her. If he could get her through that first time without hurting and scaring her. . . . He'd go slow and get her drunk.

Sassy barely sipped her drink and glanced at the potted fern next to the bed. First chance she got, she'd pour her drink into the planter and he'd never know the difference. What was the half-breed thinking right now? He looked uncertain, but he couldn't be as worried as she was. In the awkward silence, the fire crackled. She took a deep breath, aware of the scent of tobacco, the wood fire, whiskey, and her own perfume. She studied the rippling muscles of his bare chest. She imagined him lying naked on her spread-eagled body, his dark skin

131

contrasting with her pale body as he moved rhythmically, his powerful hips ramming his seed deep within her while his mouth demanded what her breasts had to offer. "So I am now Mrs. James Hunter. Shall I call you Jim?"

He winced, then recovered. "I—I really haven't any legal right to my father's name. I just took it."

"What do you mean?"

She couldn't tell if that were bitterness or embarrassment on his handsome face. "He never divorced his wife to marry my mother."

A bastard. He was telling her he was a bastard. So he had secrets, too. Even though she didn't want to feel for him, she couldn't help herself because of the vulnerability in his eyes.

"Does it make any difference to you?" He paused with his glass halfway to his lips.

"No." She shook her head, torn between wanting to laugh and cry. How ironic: two people married under names that weren't legally theirs. She was tempted to tell him the truth about herself but held back. Her secret would make a difference to him. Another man had taken her virginity. That was something most men could not forgive. "What shall I call you then?"

He took a big swig of whiskey. "Call me Hunter. That's what everyone calls me."

"Very well." He turned to stoke up the fire, and she poured her drink into the potted fern.

When he turned around, he noted her empty glass. "Are you feeling all right?"

"I—I suppose." What was it he expected her to say? Was he trying to get her drunk? For what purpose since her body was his to use now that they were wed? "I drank the whiskey too fast, and I'm beginning to feel unsteady."

He looked pleased but more than a little drunk himself. "Come here." He motioned and, reaching behind him, set his glass on the mantel. "I want to kiss my bride."

Heart hammering hard, she placed the empty tumbler on the bedside table and crossed the thick velvet of the rug. She went into his embrace. Her nipples, two points of fire through the filmy nightdress, pressed against his bare, dark flesh. His manhood throbbed against her, hot as if he had a fever.

"Don't be nervous, Sassy Miss." He opened her nightdress and pulled her close so that her bare breasts were against his naked chest. His lips caressed the side of her face. "What I'm going to do may hurt a little, but I've got to make a woman of you before you can really be my wife."

"I—I know that. I know I'm supposed to submit to your needs." She couldn't stop herself from shaking at the heat of his lips and the tip of his tongue grazing her ear. With all the men who had used her, she had never known desire until she'd met this one. Sassy had thought she was in love with Brett, but she had never experienced a physical craving for him like the heat that Hunter ignited when he touched her. Passion crept up her belly like a flame from the throbbing of his maleness against her to the burning in her nipples scorched by the nearness of his chest.

He was drunk, swaying as he held her, and his breath was whiskey warm. "I intend to take my time, give you all night if need be."

"Perhaps," she looked up at him as his hands stroked

133

her bottom, her back, dreading the discovery that would disappoint him, "perhaps we should wait until tomorrow night. We're both so tired and—"

"Tomorrow night, too," he whispered urgently against her lips. "I want you too bad to wait. I want to teach you, Sassy, teach you how to pleasure a man."

She almost laughed aloud at that, laughed to keep from weeping. She knew how to pleasure a man, all right! Greedy Brett had forced her to learn because he wanted the profits her ripe body could earn. She was the best and most popular whore upstairs; even Marylou, who managed the girls, said so. In a way, she almost felt sorry for the madam, because Marylou was in love with Brett; but he used any and all of her girls. Since Sassy had never felt desire herself, she could coldly concentrate on creating pleasure for her paying customers. It was ironic. Now she fought the tears that came to her eyes.

Hunter look concerned. "Sassy, don't cry. I'll try not to hurt you. I've got to possess your body; that's the only thing that will put out this fire you've built in me."

How many men had said something like that to her? Many; too many since Brett had seduced her. She blinked and the tears overflowed.

Hunter kissed her tears away drunkenly, swaying on his feet. "Sassy Girl," he whispered. "Oh, my innocent Sassy Girl."

Innocent. Oh, how she wished she were! What a bitter, bitter thing it was to have to fool her bridegroom. Guilt washed over her and she began to sob.

"What is it? Tell me." He kissed her face, her eyelids, her lips.

Despite his entreaties, she knew she could never,

never tell. This was a secret a woman took to her grave. If a wife weakened and told, tomorrow and forever she would regret it. No man could love a woman so much that he could forgive her kind of past.

He swore softly as he hugged her to him. "If you're that afraid of me, damned if I'll do it. I'm not that bad a villain." He took a deep, shaky breath and stepped away from her. Perspiration gleamed on his dark face as he struggled for control. "I need another drink."

He stumbled to the mantel, got his glass, and filled it to the brim. "Let me pour you another."

She nodded, handed him her glass. As much as he had already consumed, she didn't know what kept him on his feet. He handed back her drink and flopped down in the big wing chair, staring into the fire. "Hell of a wedding night!" he muttered.

She listened to the rain on the roof and watched the brooding man at the fire. He was kinder and more considerate than she had expected. She had thought James Hunter would throw her across the bed the moment he got her into the house, rip her dress away, and take what was now legally his. Sassy poured most of her drink into the fern and went to him hesitantly.

He seemed to be having trouble focusing his eyes. "Those lovely, long legs must be hollow," he mumbled, looking at the glass in her hand. "You ought to be almost unconscious by now."

And he soon would be, Sassy thought, as he sipped his drink. Some of it ran down the corners of his mouth and dripped onto his bare chest. "Hunter, are you going to sit here all night?"

"I might as well." He sounded grumpy.

She felt almost sorry for him now that the little bit of

liquor she had drunk was spreading through her system. "Maybe if you'd start all over and move a little slower—"

"Slower, hell! I'm usually on and off a woman in less than the time I just spent kissing you!" He reached up, caught her hand, pulled her down into his lap. "I hope it'll finally be worth the wait."

"Only you can be the judge of that," she whispered. She was leaning against his male hardness and it throbbed strongly, making her think thoughts she had never imagined before. Impulsively, she kissed him, tasting the liquor on his mouth and then she bent her head and licked the drops of whiskey off his bare chest with a slow kiss.

His eyes widened and, for a long moment, he only gasped and closed his eyes. "Oh, Missy," he murmured, "don't do that or I may forget I said I'd wait."

He was so drunk, he would never remember any of this tomorrow, Sassy thought. She didn't object as his hand slipped inside her sheer nightdress, cupped her breast. She started to pull away.

"No. Kiss me again," he whispered.

She obeyed, tasting the heat of his mouth, the whiskey on his lips. His hand stroked the areola of her breast, making the nipple swell with desire. He set his glass on the small table next to the chair, tangled that hand in her hair and held her tightly against his lips. His tongue explored the deepest part of her, sucking her tongue into his mouth in a rhythmic probing that reminded her of a man's thrusting. When his thumb stroked her nipple, she couldn't stop herself from arching her back, pressing against his hand, and moaning softly.

"So a lady can want it," he whispered a bit drunkenly against her lips. "Please want it, Sassy. Learn to like it, because I intend to touch every nerve ending in your pretty body and make you shiver for my touch."

"No!" She shook her head to clear it and tried to pull away, scared of the effect he was having on her, but the hand tangled in her hair didn't release her. He bent her head back and kissed her throat. She was certain he could feel the pulse pounding there as his lips brushed up and down her neck. He made her feel submissive, powerless. No man had ever affected her like this before.

"No," she whispered again, but she found herself pressing against the fingers that teased her nipples.

"Yes, Sassy," he said urgently, "yes. Don't let it scare you. It won't hurt if you want it."

His hand slipped between her breasts, stroked down her belly and touched between her thighs. He still had his other hand tangled in her hair, gripping the back of her head so he could pillage her mouth with his tongue. He tasted of liquor and she smelled the masculine scent of his aroused maleness, the perfume on her own heated body.

His fingers stroked the bud of her womanhood and she quivered at his touch, afraid of the newfound feelings this man was creating in her. It had to be the whiskey, Sassy thought desperately.

He pulled away from her mouth, sighing. "God, you're wet; you feel like silk." He gasped deeply as he stroked her—touching, caressing, demanding.

She had a terrible urge to spread her thighs, mount him right there in the chair, and ride him, pleasuring them both.

137

But his hand on the back of her head pressed her face against his nipple. "Bite me," he gasped. "Bite me." His fingers stroked her thighs until she trembled. With her sharp little teeth, she nipped at his chest while he pressed against her mouth and groaned. "If you weren't a lady, a real lady, there're a thousand things I'd like to do to you."

His words brought her back to reality. Bless the saints, was she losing her mind as well as control of her body? This couldn't go any further or he'd have her spread-eagled on the rug before the fire, ramming into her. When he stood naked before the fire like some primitive savage and her blood did not shine scarlet on his dagger, he would know the truth.

She managed to struggle up out of the chair and stood up. "Let me get you another drink."

"Damn it, a drink isn't what I need right now." He grabbed for her, but she eluded him, picked up his glass.

"Yes, it is." She moved, hips swinging, to the chest of drawers, knowing the dim lamplight silhouetted her nubile body and the sheer green gossamer hid nothing of her charms. Once more she was in control, knowing how to prolong a man's anticipation. He'd drunk a lot but he was still virile—ready, willing, and able to perform. He must be some kind of man.

He stood up, swaying on his feet. "Forget whiskey."

"All right." She turned toward him.

He crossed the floor, swung her up in his arms. "Pretty lady, you've got what I need."

He staggered. She'd be lucky if he didn't black out with her in his arms. All she could do was hope he wouldn't remember anything tomorrow.

He had a difficult time maneuvering across the room

to the bed, but they made it. Then he leaned over and blew out the lamp. It was a wonder his breath didn't catch fire, Sassy thought.

He stood up, defined by firelight as he pulled off his pants and tossed them aside. His maleness, freed from the restrictions of the fabric, jutted out before him. He was a lot of man, Sassy thought, even for a woman who wasn't a virgin.

He came to bed, crawling in next to her. The firelight cast a glow over the room.

Very slowly, she opened the front of her nightdress and arched her back. "Is this what you want?" she asked innocently.

With a soft moan, he fell across her, his hands squeezing her breasts up into two points for his greedy mouth. Now it was her turn to gasp as she pushed against his hot, wet mouth, asking—no, demanding—that he suck her breasts until they hurt. She wanted him between her thighs, no matter the consequences. Now he had one hand under her hips. "Spread out for me, Sassy Girl. Open and let me take you, make a woman of you!"

She obeyed his command and felt him fumbling, awkward in his hurry. And just before he took her, Hunter passed out.

Disbelieving, she lay still, gasping for air, feeling his mouth on her breast, his maleness against her inner thigh. Both frustrated and relieved, she waited a long moment, covered and dominated by his virile body. Finally, she managed to crawl out from under him and pulled a sheet up over them both. Would he remember in the morning that he hadn't consummated this union? Perhaps she had just put off the reckoning awhile; but, at least for tonight, he didn't know she was a whore.

What made her nervous and kept her awake for a long time listening to the rain was that a man had made her want him physically. It couldn't bring her anything but trouble.

At last, she slept. Once in the night, she was awakened by Hunter moaning and thrashing about, his skin wet with sweat as he muttered. A nightmare, she thought. He's having a nightmare. Sassy took him in her arms and held him close, patting and whispering to him as she might a frightened child until he put his face against her breasts and dropped off to sleep with a weary sigh. She held him until she, too, slept.

When she awakened, it was still raining and a gray dawn hung outside the window. Hunter, burrowed in the covers, slept heavily. As big as he was, with his ebony hair tousled and his face at peace, he looked almost like a little boy.

Sassy crept out of bed, slipped on the sheer nightdress, and looked around the sumptuous room. There had to be a heavier robe than this. For the first time, she noticed a pale blue velvet wrap across the bench at the foot of the bed and put it on. The first day of her new life as the wife of a prominent, powerful, and very rich man. Mrs. James Hunter. *I have no right to my father's name.* She wondered what the older Hunter had been like?

How had she gotten herself into a mail-order marriage like this clear across the country from where her trouble had all begun? She paused, looking out the window at the early morning rain, and thought about her family in Boston, wondering what time it was in New York City, whether Brett was still looking for her, and if he had ever gotten her letter.

Brett stood by the open porthole, looking at the water. At least he was out of New York City. It had never been his kind of town, too dirty and full of immigrants, although his favorite cities—New Orleans and San Francisco—were getting almost as bad. He pulled out his pocket watch, snapped open the ornate gold cover, and noted it was almost time to dock. He stared at the small daguerreotype in the watch, although he had looked at it a million times since his parents' death. Mother wasn't a great beauty, but her elegance and fine family made up for that. How much Father looks like me, he thought with a sigh. So handsome; so tall.

Brett snapped the watch shut and stroked his pencil mustache absently, remembering Papa's father. The last time he had ever seen him, the old man had been in an asylum, a frightening place for a small boy to visit. Sadly, his father had inherited Grandfather's madness. The thought scared Brett and he shook his head, turning away from the porthole. Brett preferred to think about the happy days with his beloved mother before Father took them to San Francisco. Brett was half-grown before the big mansion was built. Times there were stormy, his parents always arguing when his father wasn't out of town on business. Papa might have been losing his mind even then.

Brett crossed to the washbowl and got out his razor and shaving mug. As he lathered his face, he studied himself. Was there any possibility he'd go insane, too? It worried him. Same straight, dark hair, eyes, cleft chin, and mustache. No, he shook his head, his good looks and height were about the only thing he'd inherited from Father. He smiled grimly at himself. He certainly didn't have any of the money left. Of course he'd only gotten half anyway. How was a spoiled college boy supposed to know about investments? He hadn't realized it wouldn't last forever. His elegant mother must be spinning in her grave to see her son reduced to gambling. The Brett family had always been welcome in the most elegant of social circles.

Well, there had been a few other black sheep. Brett grinned, thinking about his two cousins. There had been gossip about Cousin Bart Brett being found dead in his place of business in Chicago a few years back. Auntie, Bart's mother, said he'd been murdered by a trusted employee who robbed the hotel's safe. Brett had done some investigating. The Velvet Kitten wasn't a hotel; it was the classiest whorehouse in Chicago, but of course Auntie would never know that. Poor thing, only two years ago, another son, Lon, had been killed by a mob in Denver. So Brett wasn't the only skeleton in his mother's family closet.

He finished shaving and got the crumpled letter out again, rereading it with both relief and sadness. So Sassy Malone was dead. That meant she couldn't put a rope around his and Marylou's necks with her knowledge. Still, he'd had a passion for her ripe body. Of course he was too good a businessman to let that passion prevent him from making a profit by putting her upstairs at the Black Garter after he'd seduced her. All these poor Irish girls seemed to have big, starving families to support; and, in these hard times, some of them were doing it with their bodies. Still, Sassy had built a fire in him that no woman had done before or since; certainly not his business partner, Marylou, or any of her other whores.

Of course Marylou was in love with him and she did a good job of running the business upstairs, so he'd kept his interest private. Sassy. Good name for that fiesty tart. He'd often wondered if that were her real name? So many whores changed names as often as they did addresses to cover their tracks.

He put the letter away. When he'd gotten it weeks ago, he'd gone to the parish priest at the small church to see if it were true. The old man vaguely remembered the incident, but no details. When Brett looked down at that grave, he felt both sad and relieved that he was safe at last.

Where was Marylou now? He ought to let her know that, with Sassy dead, they were both free from prosecution. He smiled. Hell, let the slut sweat and worry. Marylou was from North Carolina, but she'd left there years ago. After fleeing New York, she was probably back in New Orleans or maybe San Francisco where they both had connections. Like a bad penny, she'd turn up again, or Brett would hunt her down when he needed a new stake for a big deal.

In the meantime, in New York, a new, crusading police commissioner had closed down the Black Garter. He was almost out of money, Brett thought as he returned to the porthole to look and smell sights and scents of the teeming port. Marylou was always good for a stake. Yes, New Orleans and San Francisco were his favorite towns; and he had a friend here in San Francisco: John Pennell, if he were still in the business. Maybe he could work for John or borrow a little money from him to tide him over. With a little luck, Brett'd soon open a high-class place with the best of dealers, fine liquor, and beautiful women. He sighed again. Too bad Sassy was dead; she'd been a gold mine.

Chapter Eight

Hunter stirred behind her and Sassy whirled around, but he settled down and continued to sleep. Would he remember that their marriage had not been consummated last night? If not, he'd expect to awaken with the scarlet stain of her virginity on his body. What to do?

Sassy went into her dressing room and was pleasantly surprised to find a pitcher of warm water with fresh towels and soap. At least he had some servants. Quickly she refreshed herself, then took the warm, soapy washcloth and went into the bedroom.

Hunter lay sprawled on his back, sleeping peacefully. Very slowly, Sassy pulled the cover back. His dark, muscular body contrasted sharply with the white sheets. Her gaze swept over him. Even in the relaxed state, here was more man than she had ever seen. No wonder he had been hesitant, fearful of hurting a virgin. Maybe he wasn't the unfeeling brute she had thought. She began to wash him, almost holding her breath that he might awaken. Instead, he smiled in his sleep and mumbled some girl's name, then another. Sassy frowned and resisted the urge to give him a whack with the wet cloth.

No doubt he was dreaming of past and pleasurable encounters. Of course there was no logical reason it should annoy her and she knew it. Still . . .

His maleness began to respond to her touch, and she marveled again at the size of him. Troubled, she recalled last night and her unexpected response to him. Aye, in the past she had pretended passion because it brought her good tips, but even her atttraction for Brett had not made her body burn with desire. But last night. . . . She remembered her reactions to the touch and the scent and the heat of this man in those moments before he had passed out. It was unbelievable that she had actually ached for him, had wanted him thrusting deep into the very core of her. When she thought of it, she remembered the taste of his mouth, her own pulse pounding harder, her disappointment when he dropped off to sleep. Was she losing her mind? He was just a big male animal after all, no different from the rest of them.

Sassy pulled the covers back up over him; hung the towels and washcloths up to dry in her bathroom; and, after a moment's consideration, poured the bowl of washwater out the window and closed it against the rain.

Now what? She took a deep breath as she returned to the bedroom. Did she smell coffee? Aye, it was definitely coffee. She looked at Hunter, but he slept peacefully. With enough liquor in his belly to pickle him, when he woke up, he was going to feel as if someone had taken a logging axe to his head. She doubted he'd want any breakfast, but she'd best go meet the servants and bring him back a pot of strong coffee.

She tiptoed into the dim hall, following the inviting

scent. From what she could see in the pale light of dawn, the house was as grand as it had seemed last night, almost as fine as the Van Schuyler mansion in Boston where her mother had worked part-time as a servant. Sassy paused in the dining room. A large space, it contained an ornate dining-room suite, china cabinet, and chandelier; but paper work, ledger books and pencils were strewn across the big walnut table. She spied a cobweb on the chandelier, and the house smelled dusty as if the servants weren't doing their job with lemon oil, rug beaters, and feather dusters. Probably Hunter, like most bachelors, wasn't too concerned with sparkling-clean windows and highly waxed floors.

She followed the sounds of banging pans and the aroma of coffee that drifted through the house. She imagined a sweet, plump old-lady cook, warm and friendly like Bridget O'Malley, Mama's friend back in Boston. Bridget, bless her heart, was Mrs. Van Schuyler's personal maid and had been the one to help get Maureen a job at the Van Schuyler estate. Sassy had tried to get a job there after Mama died, but Mr. Van Schuyler wouldn't hire any more Irish. Lately, Papa had been keeping company with the plump and pleasant Bridget.

A smile on her lips, Sassy swept into the kitchen to meet this queen of the kitchen. "Hello, I'm the new mistress, I'm so glad . . ."

Bent over the big black stove was a gray-haired man in his late sixties who smelled of vanilla. White flour dusted his brawny, hairy arms, and his white apron was at variance to his rough, logger clothes.

Sassy looked around the kitchen. Its tidiness contrasted sharply with the rest of the big house. She herself

146

felt out of place. "Oh, I'm sorry, I was looking for the cook."

"I'm Cookie. What are you doin' here? Hunter don't usually bring his doxies to the house."

"I—I'm Mrs. Hunter. We were married last night." She drew herself up to her full height, but she wasn't very tall.

"Oh, Jesus! Now I've gone and done it! I beg your humble pardon, Ma'am." The man wiped his hands on his apron in confusion and she noticed he limped when he crossed the floor. "I just expected to get more notice so I could do a wedding cake."

"A wedding cake?" This brawny old timberman didn't look like the kind who could open a can of beans.

"I'm partial to angel food myself, but I make a Lady Baltimore that would melt in your mouth, so—"

"Are you really the cook?" She managed to close her gaping mouth.

"Yes, I am, Ma'am, ever since I got injured a couple of years ago. Hunter looks out for his men and I was with his father before him. I do hope I didn't hurt your feelings none; Hunter would be mad as a bee-stung bull if I insulted his bride."

"N—No Cookie, that's quite all right," she stammered, looking around the tidy kitchen. It smelled of cinnamon and spices just as he smelled of vanilla. "How much help is there?"

He shrugged and returned to rolling out biscuit dough. "Sometimes we get a cleaning girl, but then some fella marries her and we're back on our own. I do the best I can to keep help. Besides the boss, it's just me, Swede, and Kitty."

"Kitty?" She imagined a blonde maid who spent as

much time between the sheets with the master as she did changing them. "Kitty?"

"Yeow." An oversized yellow tomcat came out from under the wood stove and looked up at her balefully. Its ears were ragged and it carried its broken tail at an odd angle.

Cookie smiled and tossed the cat a bit of ham. "The boss picked him up as a starving stray down on the dock—probably jumped off a ship. Hunter's a soft touch."

"I—I didn't get that impression. Hello, Kitty."

"Yeow?" The cat glared at them both with lemon-colored eyes as if annoyed at being disturbed. Unlike other cats, Kitty did not come over and rub up against her ankles. He only looked at her and wiggled his ragged ears.

"I like cats," Cookie said and tossed the tom another bit of bacon. "My Polly always kept a couple. Brings back memories of the days before she got sick . . ." His voice trailed off and he sighed, then shrugged. "Hard to realize she's been gone twenty-four years next winter. Now, Missus, will you be wanting breakfast served here or in your room?"

Sassy picked up a cup from the cabinet, liking this big, brawny man and his kitchen scent. "I thought I'd take coffee back to the bedroom, thank you. I'm not sure your boss will feel like eating."

"Hung one on, did he?" Cookie smiled.

She was taken aback at the cook's frank question. "I suppose you might say so."

"He's like the son I never had, Hunter is. I worked for his daddy. Here, Missus, let me get you the good china." He took the mug from her hand. "Hunter

148

bought it for his lady and I was beginning to think we'd never get to use it."

"Why, thank you, Cookie. Is something wrong?"

The man was staring at her with frank curiosity. "No, Ma'am, it's just that judging from what Hunter said he wanted, you aren't quite it."

"Is that good or bad?"

He hesitated. "Frankly, I was dreading the kind of wife I expected him to bring home."

She warmed to him and smiled. "Cookie, I think you and I are going to be very good friends."

He reddened. "Hope so, Ma'am. Hear not many ladies came in on the boat."

"Didn't you come down to the dock?"

He shook his head, embarrassed, and returned to his pans.

"I don't remember seeing you at the dance, either."

He kept working, not looking at her. "Hunter tried to get me to, but I figured that since there's so many fellows to choose from and not that many ladies, none of them would be interested in a crippled old codger like me."

Immediately, she thought of Ellie. "There're some lovely, mature ladies among the women."

His kind face lit up with interest, then he shook his head. "I been married and don't think anyone could replace my Polly. Me and Kitty do okay here at Hunter's."

She watched him dust the flour from his hands, limp into the dining room, and return with a delicate, china coffeepot, cups, and tray.

"Cookie, what's your real name?"

149

"John, Ma'am; from the Bible. My mother and Polly both read a lot of scripture."

"Well, John, I think several of those ladies are looking for housecleaning jobs if they don't marry."

John poured strong, savory coffee into the pot, put it on a tray. "Good. I'd like at least a full-time lady, but she must like cats. The last one was mean to Kitty; he clawed the daylights out of her, and she quit in a huff."

"Yeow?" The big tomcat looked up at her, but it rubbed adoringly against the cook's legs.

"I'll look into it then." Sassy took the tray and started down the hall.

"Ma'am, if I may be so bold, what's your name?"

"Sassy."

The big man appraised her and nodded. "Fits you, all right."

"Funny," Sassy grinned, "that's just what the boss said. By the way, John, from now on, instead of eating in the kitchen, I'd like to start using the dining room." She picked up the tray.

"And move Swede's things?"

Who or what was Swede? "If anyone questions my orders, tell them to talk to me about it. I intend to be fair, but things need a little shaping up around here."

"Swede won't like his papers and things moved."

Sassy reached for a spoon. "And just who is 'Swede'?"

"The boss-man's bull. He's Hunter's idol, been with him and his daddy before him longer than I have."

"Bull?" She had a sudden vision of a beefy male cow charging about the dining room.

"Bull o' the woods," he said and returned to his biscuit rolling. "He half-raised Hunter after . . ."

150

She waited, but he paused as if he had already said too much. "Will this 'Swede' be in today?"

"He's at the logging camp—maybe come in tomorrow or next day."

Straightening out this bachelor household would be a real challenge, Sassy thought with a sigh, reaching for the sugar bowl. She picked up a spoon and stirred sugar into the coffee. The brew looked strong enough to corrode the spoon. Idly, she wondered if she were up to running this household or if it were even a job she wanted. Was her impetuous decision to marry Hunter something she would regret? She was in the marriage now; too late for regrets. "What does the boss like in his coffee?"

"Black and strong, that's all."

"John, I know you weren't expecting me—"

"Yes, I was, Ma'am. I just didn't know when. He's been on a real tear the last couple of days; I figure you're the reason. Hunter's stubborn, always gets what he wants."

The thought rankled her. If she'd been able to find a job or another man even the least bit interested in marrying her, Sassy would have had a choice. "The boss has met his match," she said. "You'll find I'm stubborn, too. I don't intend to let Hunter walk all over me."

She thought she saw a glimmer of admiration in the old man's rugged expression. "I see your spirit matches your hair; maybe you're the right choice after all."

"John, you and I are going to be great friends. We'll talk later." She picked up the tray, turned on her heel, and walked out of the kitchen.

John's gaze followed her. Sassy. It suited her, and it was good to have her in the house. John ached for the

151

sight of a wholesome woman, someone like his Polly. He'd learned to cook during the long drawn-out months when she lay dying and someone had to take care of her because they had no children. Had anyone told Miss Sassy about what had happened that long-ago fatal night? John had been there; he would not forget that horror if he lived to be a hundred.

Secrets. He wondered what the new missus would think if she knew John's secret? When Polly's pain got so bad she was begging him to end it, John had finally overdosed his beloved wife with laudanum, held her in his arms and wept as she died. Some would call it murder; it was against the law. But Polly had died a long time ago in another place and time, and he'd never told anyone what had happened.

Polly. How he missed her plump, comforting presence in his life. He was just so damned lonely. John reached for the big bottle of vanilla in the cabinet and took a long swallow. He'd sworn to Polly he would never touch a drop of whiskey, and he never had. John Fitsroy was a man of his word.

He put the biscuits in the oven and leaned against the stove, the cat rubbing against his legs. The boss's lady was all right, though a little thin for John's taste; he liked women with no sharp bones who appreciated food. Yet Miss Sassy seemed like a good sport, not snooty and cold like he'd been dreading. John wondered if in that batch of belles, there might be one plump, mature lady who liked cats and might be interested in a crippled old geezer who wasn't rich or handsome?

* * *

Tray in hand, Sassy returned to the bedroom. Hunter still slept, and the steady rain dripped in a slow rhythm on the roof. Sassy set the tray down on the bedside table and poked up the fire, adding another log to make a cheery blaze on this cool, wet day. The room, she noticed now that it was morning, was a beautiful blend of forest greens and burgundies, with the finest of furnishings. She imagined herself and Hunter sitting together before the fire in the matched wing-back chairs. He would be reading a book, and she would be sewing, a friendly, purring kitten curled up on her lap. Kitty. She smiled ruefully, thinking of the big, hostile tomcat with torn ears. Well, a man who picked up stray cats couldn't be half so hard as he tried to appear.

Hunter mumbled in his sleep and she sat down gently on the edge of the bed, sipped the strong, sweet coffee, and watched him. He stirred and his eyes blinked open. Then he put his hand to his head and groaned.

"Head hurt? I brought you some coffee."

He started as if he hadn't known she was there, struggled to sit up, groaned again. "What happened?" He stared at her as if trying to place her.

He had been drunker than she thought last night. That explained his behavior. "Hunter, don't you remember? You demanded I marry you."

He sat up in bed, cradled his head in both hands, and moaned. "And did you? What a question! Of course you did. A lady like you doesn't end up in a man's bedroom without marriage."

She set her cup on the bedside table, held out her hand with the gold ring. "You didn't give me much choice. I think if I hadn't married you, you were going to abduct me. Now that you're sober, if you're having regrets—"

"Regrets?" He caught her hand as she started to get up. "Missy, you're the one who must have regrets. I'm sorry if I didn't treat you with respect. I suppose I behaved like a beast." He looked troubled.

"You don't remember anything?" She sat back down on the bed, relieved. "You were so drunk, I signed your name to the paper. I suppose it's legal, though." She held up her left hand. She'd turned the heart on the ring around to signify she was taken.

Hunter blinked. "I remember that much; I didn't even have a ring for you. I'll make it up to you, Sassy. I'll get you some fine jewelry."

She shrugged, thinking about his refusal to wear her father's wedding band. He didn't want commitment or obligation. "It doesn't matter."

He looked at her, hesitant to ask what he really wanted to know. "We—we've had our wedding night?"

"You don't remember that either?"

He cursed under his breath. "I've been obsessed with getting you in my bed since the first moment I saw you. Now it's happened and I don't even remember it. I—I hope I didn't hurt you."

He looked stricken, and her heart softened. "No, you didn't hurt me."

He glanced down at the covers and she hastened to add, "I washed us both up."

"Damn me for a drunken, rough brute," he muttered. "I probably took you like some slut—no way to treat a real lady."

A real lady. She was too conscience-stricken to look

154

him in the face. "You'd had too much to drink," she soothed him, patting his hand. "Don't worry about it."

"I am worried about it," he insisted. "I wanted you bad enough that nothing else mattered; I was crazy with lust. Whatever I might have done last night, I swear I'll treat you with respect from now on. I wouldn't want you to think you'd gotten a bad bargain."

He was the one who had gotten the bad bargain, Sassy thought, thankful for his memory lapse and feeling more than a little guilty. "I made the bargain; I'll not welsh on it."

He tucked a pillow behind his back, struggled into a sitting position. His bare chest looked massive and she looked again at the white scar on the brown body. His face furrowed as he struggled to think. "I—I recall lifting you upon the horse and the feel of you in my arms." He looked at her in a way that sent a shiver up her back. "I remember thinking one night in your arms would be worth everything I owned."

Sassy smiled self-consciously. "It makes me nervous for you to talk like that, Hunter. I'm just a woman, after all, not a goddess."

He caught her hand, kissed her fingertips. "You're more than a woman, Sassy; you're Hunter's lady. Now that you belong to me, whatever you want, you'll get; whatever you ask, I'll try to do."

"My own knight," she said, "ready to slay dragons for me." She motioned toward the scar. "What's that?"

"Nothing much. Let's talk about something else. "What's a dragon?"

She had a feeling that he was distracting her to keep from answering questions about the jagged scar. "It's—

it's, well, just a dragon; something knights fight to protect damsels from."

He gave her a rare smile and, when he did, he looked
almost like a little boy with that one stray curl hanging
down. He brushed it out of his eyes. "Sassy Girl, you
have never had a protector like me before. Men will doff
their hats with respect as your carriage rolls past and
say, 'There goes James Hunter's wife.' "

She swallowed hard and glanced away, unable to look
him in the face. If he ever found out her past, he would
divorce—or perhaps even kill—her for making him the
laughing stock of Seattle. However, New York City was
a long, long way from here. Maybe God would allow
her to make a fresh start and the stormy man need
never know her past. "I promise I'll be a good wife to
you, Hunter. You won't ever regret this."

He looked at her, baffled. "I don't expect to. I'm the
luckiest man in the world." He reached for his coffee,
took a sip. "God, what a headache!"

She smiled as she drank her coffee. "I presume you
don't want any breakfast?"

He made a wry face. "You presume right. Maybe
later we'll have big steaks and a bottle of wine right here
before our fire. After that . . ."

She realized he was staring. She glanced down. Her
robe had slipped open, showing the swell of her breasts.
Instinctively, she reached to pull her robe closed, but he
caught her hand. "Don't be too modest," he whispered.
"You're mine now and I don't think I'll ever get enough
of the touch and the taste and the sight of you."

She felt herself blush at the hint of passion in his
voice. This virile stud intended to keep her flat on her
back with her thighs spread, Sassy thought. She wasn't

156

sure what her own emotions were. "I'm your legal wife, Hunter, and as such, whenever you want me—"

"That's what I dreamed of hearing you say since the first moment you stepped off the boat and I saw the sunlight sparkle on that reddish hair." His voice was soft, gentle.

She laughed. "Suppose I hadn't been the one that Mercer gave the letter to?"

"I would have reneged on the deal," he declared. "I knew which one I wanted the moment I saw that pert little freckled nose."

"You were so forbidding, so dour. I was afraid to admit I had the letter."

He set their coffee down, pulled her to lay her face against his brawny, naked chest, and stroked her hair. "Don't ever be afraid of me, Missy," he whispered. "Love and friendship, that's what I'm offering you. The only one who needs to be afraid is any man who even looks at you."

She closed her eyes, listening to his heart beat against her face as he stroked her hair. She had never felt as safe and protected as she did at this moment. "Maybe it's lucky I couldn't find a job and none of the other men showed any interest in me."

He cleared his throat awkwardly. "Isn't it though? See? You were meant to be my bride."

Something about his voice bothered her, but she couldn't put her finger on it. "When you feel better, I'd like to see the whole house and hear about the place."

"All right, Mrs. Hunter, but let me finish my coffee first."

Sassy looked down at the worn gold ring on her finger. Would Maureen have approved of the big half-

157

breed? Probably. Maybe he was a lot like Papa: rough around the edges, but all-male, protective, and passionate. She stood up. "I'll get dressed."

"You'll find the clothes I had sent up from San Francisco in the dressing room."

"How did you know what size to buy?"

He sipped his coffee. "I didn't, so I bought clothes in several sizes. You can give away any you don't want."

Sassy thought of her friends and their frayed dresses. It was a dream come true. "Thank you, Hunter."

"Don't mention it. I've got plenty of money."

In the dressing room, she opened the wardrobe doors. "Praise the saints," she exclaimed, "I've never seen so many clothes!"

"Like 'em? There're shoes and jewelry and lace underthings, too. I wanted to give my wife the best."

Something about his tone sent her back to look around the doorway. "You didn't have to buy a wife, Hunter."

"Didn't I?" His face looked dark, tragic. "Sassy, I know what I am. Not many back-East ladies would marry a half-breed bastard, and there're some other things you don't know—"

"I took you for better or worse," she said. "As far as I'm concerned, nothing matters before you met me."

"If you say so." But she could tell he didn't believe her.

Sassy bit her lip. *I wish my past wouldn't matter to you,* she thought. But somehow it was different for a woman. It didn't seem fair. She went back into the dressing room and turned her attention to the clothes. So many to choose from. She thought about the poverty of her family. Could she figure out a way to send them money without Hunter asking too many questions? Surely she would have a household allowance to spend as she wished.

She chose a pale willow-green dimity with a low-cut lacy bodice accented by tiny pearl buttons down to the waist and dainty pearl jewelry. The handmade leather slippers fit perfectly and a petticoat with yards of ruffles made her feel even more feminine. She tied her hair up with a green ribbon and dabbed lilac water between her breasts and behind her ears.

She could hear him stirring in the other room as she did her hair; and when she returned to the bedroom, he was almost dressed, although his shirt was still unbuttoned. He paused in pulling on his boots, stared at her.

"Do you like it?" she picked up the edges of her skirt, whirled around.

"Come here to me."

She approached him hesitantly. He put both hands on her shoulders and studied her. "So very young and innocent," he whispered, "and more than I ever dared to hope." He smelled of shaving cream and his hair was damp. "Mrs. Hunter, you could almost make me forget my headache. Funny the way you affect me; I had you last night, but I already want you so much this morning I can hardly think of anything else." His manhood throbbed against her.

She was abruptly shy at the thought of making love to him, having to pretend to be as innocent as he thought she was. "You promised to show me the house."

He smiled, kissed the tip of her nose. "I did, didn't I? Looks like it's going to keep raining for several days; and, after all, we have the rest of our lives to make love."

The rest of their lives. It sounded so secure, so permanent. She didn't love this strangely volatile-but-gentle man yet, but she now thought she might learn to.

He took her hand and led her through the various rooms. "It's the finest house in the area, but I've dreamed of building something even grander and better for my lady. There's going to be a world of work for construction men, if we can get them to come out here."

"This place is still big enough for a large family," Sassy said, thinking of her family in their cramped slum and some of the other poor Irish construction families she knew.

He looked momentarily troubled. "I shouldn't even think of producing children."

"What?"

"Nothing." He shrugged. "We'll begin on that this very evening," Hunter said and brushed a wisp of hair away from her forehead.

She blushed like a schoolgirl. "Aye, I'd like many children."

"I'll do my best." Hunter smiled. "And now to show you that piano you schemed to get but I was determined you'd play only in my own house."

"You're a stubborn man when you want something, aren't you?" He was a lot like the Malone men and more like her than she wanted to admit.

"Sassy Lady, if you only knew how much!"

She thought about his remark and wondered as he led her into the big library. The piano was near the fireplace and the walls were lined with shelf after shelf of fine books. Rich leather furniture and oriental rugs completed the decor. "Bless the saints!" she breathed in awe. "It's the most wonderful room I ever saw!"

"It meets with your approval?" He leaned against the mantel and seemed pleased to watch her touch the piano and examine titles in the bookcases.

"Oh, Hunter, to have so many books is something I've always dreamed of! They must give you a great deal of pleasure." She pulled several volumes from the shelves. "These look like they've never been opened."

He shrugged. "Sassy, I've got an empire to run; I seldom have time just to read for pleasure."

"But you miss so much!" She whirled about the room in pure delight. "Here's what we'll do: Every night after dinner, we'll sit in here and read or I shall play the piano for you."

He looked uneasy. "I don't know whether I can spare the time for such nonsense—"

"Of course you can!" She touched his cheek. "You said you'd do anything to make me happy."

"You drive a hard bargain, you red-haired vixen." He kissed her forehead and gathered her into his embrace. "I wanted a lady so my children would be learned and cultured, but I didn't expect you to force it on *me*."

"It will be fun, you'll see." She whirled out of his arms, sat down at the piano. It was as dusty as everything else in the house. She wouldn't hurt his feelings by mentioning the lack of housekeeping, but Sassy decided that in the next few days she would make it sparkle. "What song would you like to hear?"

"I don't know." He shrugged and lit a thin cheroot, broke the match in half, tossed it into the fireplace. "We've been isolated here; play some of the songs that have been popular back in civilization."

"All right. Here's a song that's loved by soldiers on both sides of the war, 'Aura Lea.' "

161

He stood behind her as she played and sang: *"Aura Lea, Aura Lea, maid of golden hair, sunshine came along with thee, and swallows in the air."*

"I like red hair better," Hunter murmured and put his hands on her shoulders as she played.

"Aura Lea, Aura Lea, take my golden ring; love and light return with thee, and swallows with the spring."

She couldn't remember when she had felt so satisfied, so content. If she could only do something to help her family and didn't have that terrible secret hanging over her! Sassy played several more songs, and Hunter listened quietly. Outside, as time passed, the rain dripped rhythmically.

John stuck his head in the door. "Boss, I fixed a light meal. Want it served in the library?"

Hunter nodded, looked at the clock on the mantel. "Yes, Cookie, and then you can have the day off." The cook nodded, grinned, and disappeared.

Sassy stopped playing. "My! Is it that late already? How the time has flown!"

Hunter bent to poke up the fire. "Yes, it did, didn't it? I don't know when I've had a more enjoyable morning."

"See? I told you so. I really like your cook. But why does he smell so strongly of vanilla? He can't be putting vanilla in everything."

Hunter shook his head. "There's a lot of alcohol in vanilla, Sassy, but he doesn't touch whiskey. He's a shy, lonely man who adored his sick wife and took care of her 'til she died. He worked for my father until. . . . Well, anyway, I think Cookie's got some things he's never told me, never told anyone—things that eat at him."

Don't we all? She thought, but she didn't say it. Maybe

162

her husband was a kinder, more sensitive person than she realized. She thought about plump, shy Ellie. Lonely people. People with secrets. Maybe I'm not the only one. "Hunter, this place really needs some cleaning; what about hiring a housekeeper?"

"Good idea if you can find one who can get along with Cookie and Kitty. We haven't had much luck keeping help."

Sassy brightened, her mind already busy. "Fine. After we eat, we'll sit and read." She stood up.

He paused in poking the fire and looked at her. "Since we were just wed, I think we have more compelling things to do with our time than read."

His meaning was only too clear, and Sassy contemplated the hours ahead nervously. The house would be empty except for the two of them. The virile half-breed intended to get what he hadn't had last night; enjoying her ripe body as many times and in as many ways as he wished. As her legal husband, it was his right. And this time, he wasn't drunk.

Chapter Nine

Sassy sat down on the leather sofa before the fireplace, folding her hands in her lap to keep from fidgeting.

The cook limped in with a butler's tray, set it up before the sofa, bowed slightly. "Miss Sassy, I got out all the good china and even the linen napkins."

"Thank you, John. I'm sure the food is wonderful."

He beamed at her, took the lids off the dishes with a flourish, nodded to Hunter, and left the room.

Hunter, standing before the fire, smiled wryly. "Well, you've been a busy little bee already this morning. I see you've made a conquest. Cookie usually serves me at the kitchen table out of a tin plate."

"And no doubt sharing with Kitty, too," she said and began to serve their plates.

"As a matter of fact, Kitty usually ends up *on* the table. He's some cat!"

Sassy motioned to him to join her. "You wanted civilization and class brought to Washington Territory; that's what you'll get, linen napkins and all."

"That's right," he conceded as he sat down beside

her. "With you as their mother, I expect my children to fit in anywhere and not be ashamed. They'll know which fork to use—unlike their father."

"Oh, Hunter, it isn't hard to learn proper manners; you've probably got a book on that subject in your library. Spread your napkin on your lap and start on the outside with the silver, working in as each course is served."

She was thankful her mother had been a real lady who knew those things and that she had had those months with Miss Merriweather to brush up on proper etiquette.

"Would you like some wine?" Before she could answer, he filled her glass.

"Not so much!" she protested with a gesture to desist. "You know what happened last night after too much to drink."

He only smiled. "Have some roast beef; you'll find in spite of his oddities, Cookie is a very good cook."

Sassy marveled at the food as she began to eat. Obviously, even in a primitive place like Washington Territory, if you had money and the means, you could live like royalty. The roast beef was juicy and succulent; the hot rolls dripped with melted butter. Clams and fish and a rich chocolate dessert rounded out the menu. It had been a long time since she had eaten so well. The wine was imported, she thought, and she couldn't resist draining her goblet after she tasted it. Hunter promptly refilled her glass, although he appeared to drink little himself.

"Watch out," she warned as she sipped her wine. "You'll have me as drunk as a mourner at an Irish wake."

"I'm counting on it," he answered and he didn't smile as he filled her glass again.

"You aren't drinking much," Sassy noted.

Hunter shrugged. "I'm just losing the headache from last night, so I'm going easy on it today."

She'd had too much already, she knew, and she suspected he was deliberately getting her drunk as she had him the night before. However, it was an excellent vintage and she was tense about what was to come later. Sassy drank and ate as slowly as possible.

He frowned. "At the rate you're going, you'll still be eating dinner when Cookie serves breakfast in the morning."

"It isn't as if we don't have all afternoon," she said. The wine was beginning to affect her, she thought, sipping it and staring out at the steady rain.

"I can wait," he said. "I've been waiting all these years to share luncheon with a lady. Have the house and furnishings met with your approval?"

"Oh, it's wonderful, Hunter." She looked around the room, thought of everything she had seen in the house. "It only lacks one thing that I can think of."

"What did I forget?"

"A silver tea service."

He looked blank as he pushed the dishes aside. "A what?"

She remembered her mother's wistful memories of her early life. "In wealthy families, there's always a silver tea service with the family's monogram engraved on it. The lady of the house serves tea or coffee at socials when other ladies come to call. A silver tea service is something you pass on to your children and grandchildren. But, of course, it isn't something I really need."

"Do all *real* ladies have one?"

He looked so perturbed, she shrugged it off. "Washington Territory probably isn't too concerned with frivolities like that. Besides, I doubt the local general store would carry them. It isn't important."

"It is if all ladies have one." Frowning, he refilled her glass.

Sassy started to protest that she already had had so much her thinking was muddled, but his look brooked no argument. She drained the goblet, wiped her lips daintily, set the glass with the dirty dishes.

Hunter stood up, took the butler's tray into the hall, and closed the door. Then he sat next to her on the sofa. His hand fingered a curl that had fallen from its ribbon near her throat. "Once the weather breaks," he said, "I won't have nearly so much time to spend with you."

"Sometime I'd like to ride out with you and see how your men cut the timber and get it to market." She was attempting to make conversation, but her mind was on his fingers stroking her hair.

"If you wish." He touched the tiny pearl buttons at her throat. His hand felt warm, slowly as he unbuttoned them.

She raised her head, lips half-opened, and looked at him.

"You were worth waiting for," he murmured and he bent his head, put his other arm around her, and kissed her.

Sassy gasped at the hot domination of his mouth on hers as his tongue slipped between her lips and his free hand continued to undo her buttons. She stiffened just

167

a moment; and his mouth, still on hers, whispered, "Don't fight me, Sassy, you're mine now."

Hunter was her husband. He might endure a little hesitancy, but she was expected to let him do what he wanted with her body. It was her wifely duty. Knowing that, she threw back her head in surrender and let his blade of tongue explore her mouth.

She felt his hand opening her bodice, pulling at her lacy chemise. And then it cupped her breast, the thumb trailing lightly across the nipple. His mouth went to the pulse-point in her throat and she gasped for air, her chest heaving. It unnerved her to think he could take control of her emotions like this. A fire started between her thighs and worked its way slowly up her belly to her breasts where his hand stroked and teased and touched.

He had pushed her back against the cushions in the corner of the sofa, half-reclining with him partly on top of her. She felt the hard heat of him throbbing against her thigh, and an aching void in her wanted the big, hot maleness of him as deep as he could go. She whimpered and his mouth against hers said, "Don't protest, Sassy Girl. I want you and I want you to learn to want me. Relax and let it happen. Relax."

For this he had gotten her tipsy, she thought in a daze. She could give herself to him as wantonly as her emotions drove her, and he'd think it was the wine.

Then she couldn't reason anymore, only feel as his lips caressed her throat and moved down to fasten on her nipple. For a moment, she was stunned by the sensation his greedy mouth created and then she gasped and pulled his face against her breast, tangling her fingers in his black hair.

He lay half on her, his hand fumbling with her skirt,

gradually brushing up her leg until she felt his fingers under her delicate pantalets.

A gently bred girl would probably protest. "No, you shouldn't," she managed to gasp, and yet she couldn't keep from opening her thighs to his stroking touch.

"Even a lady might learn to like this rather than just submit to it," he whispered against her breast, and his breath felt warm on her nipple. "You're wet, so wet, Sassy Girl. That makes it easier for me."

His long fingers were probing her, playing her nerves like a violin. She began to shake violently.

Immediately, he was apologetic. "I—I know that isn't proper to do to a lady. I don't mean to shock you."

Shock her? He had had her on the brink of succumbing to her own passion. She regained control of herself. "It's all right. After all, we're married."

"I'll take it slower. Last night, I'm sure I didn't treat you like a lady. I'm sorry for that."

"You were drunk," she answered, still giddy from the wine and the touch of his fingers that had left her wanting more. The intensity of her feelings surprised and scared her.

"Such a waste," he murmured, "as badly as I wanted you, not to remember every moment of our wedding night." He reached to peel off one of her silk stockings. As he inched it down, he kissed her bare thigh.

The warmth of his lips on her skin and the tingle of his tongue brushing along her thigh raised feelings in her she didn't know she was capable of. He had her stocking and shoe off now and was kissing the instep of her foot.

"Such tiny feet," he murmured. "I didn't know a woman's foot could be so sensual."

In truth, Sassy hadn't known either. The tease of his lips on her instep, planting kisses on each toe, made her want more. "Take the other one off," she whispered and closed her eyes.

Again his lips followed the silk stocking down her slim leg. "You have long legs for such a small girl, Missy." His mouth was now working its way back up her leg, kissing her dimpled knee. "May I?"

She was a bit baffled. "May you?"

"You're a lady," he whispered. "Even though you're my wife, I can't take you like some common—"

She held up her hand to stop him from saying that word. She had a feeling that if he pronounced it, he would look into her guilty face and know what she was. "You're asking permission?"

He looked uncertain, a bit embarrassed. "I thought that a husband was expected to ask his wife if she would accommodate him."

She felt heady with the wine and her power over his big body. "Hunter, I thought you took what you wanted."

That was all the permission he seemed to need. He breathed heavily as he looked down at her, opening his pants, pushing up her dress. "If you had refused me, I don't know whether I could have stopped." His body was between her thighs now, his two big hands under her small hips, positioning her for his thrusting, his mouth sucking hard on her breasts. If she had wanted to stop him she couldn't have. This wasn't going to be a prim, civilized coupling; this was going to be primitive and passionate. Her hair came loose from its pins and fell down over him as he penetrated her.

"Oh, God, you're hot! Hot as liquid fire! Sassy, Sassy!"

She locked her legs around the back of his powerful thighs and felt him thrust deep and sure. For a moment, she wasn't certain she could hold all of him. Each thrust went even deeper, pushing up into the very core of her. Aroused and eager, she reminded herself that she must not like it too much. He expected his innocent bride not to share his passion, only the act itself. Still, she wasn't sure she could not react to his virile loving. She gasped aloud.

Immediately, his mouth was on hers again, his eyes anxious. "Am I hurting you? I—I don't mean to, Sassy, but I never wanted a woman this way before."

"I—you're not hurting me," she whispered and closed her eyes, meeting his body thrust for thrust, willing him to go deep . . . deeper, to thrust against the most sensitive part of her, fill her with his hot rush of seed.

He put his tongue far in her throat even as he penetrated the intimate most velvet cavern of her body, demanding and dominating. Just when she thought she couldn't ride this crest of emotion one moment longer, he groaned and gasped, stiffened. She felt his male juice spurt hard into her womb as his greedy mouth sucked her nipples into two points of inner fire.

She had never come this far before emotionally, as if she were walking on the edge of a knife-blade. What was it her mind and body wanted? Always before, she had lain waiting for the customer to spend himself so she could get up and collect her money. Now she wanted something for herself. What would he think of a supposedly refined girl who gave way to passion— gasping, biting, and digging her nails into his back?

Then the moment passed as his body relaxed and he lay on her, breathing hard. "If this is what love with an innocent virgin is like, no wonder every man wants to marry one! Did I hurt you?"

She took a shuddering breath and that emotion that had almost swept her away subsided, replaced by frustration. "No, you didn't hurt me. Did I—did I please you?"

"Please me?" He kissed her lips, her face, her eyes. "Oh, my naive lady! You could enslave me with that body of yours. It scares me how you affect me."

He kissed her again, sighed and got up slowly, buttoned his pants. She pulled her skirt down, upset but unsure exactly why. She had wanted something more. She watched him at the fireplace, leaning against the mantel. When he lit a smoke, his hands shook noticeably.

"No other woman has made you feel this way?" she asked innocently, yearning to hear him say it again.

He frowned and smoked. "I shouldn't have admitted that; you'll take advantage of my weakness as Springtime . . ."

There was something tragic in his dark face, some deep hurt behind those eyes of blue ice. She went to him. He slipped one arm around her, staring into the fire as he smoked.

"Hunter, tell me about your parents."

He shook his head. "Too painful. I've got bad blood, Sassy; I only hope my children don't inherit it. I probably shouldn't even father any."

She leaned against him, thinking if she could unravel this mystery, she might understand the man. "What was your mother like?"

172

In the silence, the rain beat a steady rhythm on the roof and a log on the fire crackled. When she took a deep breath, she inhaled the fragrance of his tobacco, the log fire, and his male scent. For a long moment, she was not sure he had heard her or that he would answer.

"I was very small, yet even I realized she was beautiful. *Toma Alwawinmi.* It's Nez Perce, means 'Springtime.' She was like spring, sometimes soft and warm, I suppose, sometimes stormy as spring weather and wild as the wind." He spoke so softly that she barely heard him and maybe he had even forgotten Sassy was there, maybe he talked to himself. "Beautiful, dark, and passionate; mixed-blood, white and Indian—Salish, Paloose, Nez Perce. She attracted men like a bitch in heat attracts the pack."

Had Hunter been the product of a chance encounter? "Did your father love her?"

"Love her?" Hunter laughed without mirth in his haunted eyes. "He worshiped her, thought she was an angel; then he found out the truth and . . ." He shook his head. "I told you I had inherited bad blood. My mother's people don't like to disturb ghosts by talking about them."

There was so much more she wanted to ask, but the look on his face told her she had pushed as far as she dared for the present.

He yawned. "Missy, you've worn me out. What about a nap on a cool, rainy afternoon?"

They returned to the big bedroom, listening to the rain as they settled down to rest.

"Maybe it was a lucky twist of fate after all that I couldn't find a job," she sighed.

"Uh huh." He grunted and pulled her against his chest.

"Strange," she thought aloud, "the first day I arrived, I had a lot of suitors; the next, they all stayed away from me as if I were poison."

"It wasn't you, it——" He blurted, paused. "Never mind."

"Never mind what?" A suspicion began to build in her mind. Surely he wouldn't have stooped to that. She leaned on one elbow and looked down at him. "Hunter, you knew I wouldn't marry you as long as I had other options."

"Forget about it, I said." He reached up and rumpled her hair. "You were meant to belong to me; I knew it from the first moment I saw you." His eyes flickered, closed.

"Hunter, did you have anything to do with that?"

"Do with what?" He yawned again.

Her suspicion grew. "Was I tricked into this marriage? Did you order people not to give me a job or other men not to consider me as a bride?"

"Now why would I do that?" His voice was faint, sleepy.

"Because if I had no alternatives, I'd marry you."

"And it's worked out well, hasn't it?" He smiled with his eyes closed, obviously pleased with himself.

She was not to be put off. She was every bit as stubborn as he was. "Hunter, don't be evasive. Did you use your power and wealth to keep anyone from offering me a job?"

"The wife of a rich man doesn't need a job. Now hush and let me nap."

"What did you say to the other men?"

"Nothing much."

"But you did say something?"

"Missy, why must you pursue this like a bulldog hanging onto a bone? From the first moment I saw you, I was determined to possess you."

She was getting madder by the moment. "And I had nothing to say about it! No decision to make!"

"You said 'yes,' didn't you?"

"And if I hadn't?"

"Are you determined to have this out?"

"I am!"

"All right, damn it!" His eyes opened and flashed with stubborn blue fire. "I would have done anything to get you."

She managed to keep her voice calm. "What did you do?"

"I merely passed the word there were to be no jobs offered and that I'd kill the man who married you before he ever spent a single night in your arms. Now, are you satisfied?" He rolled over on his side, his back to her.

She'd been tricked! That she had been bested and out-maneuvered hurt her pride. If he'd do something as ruthless and arrogant as scheming for her hand, what else was he capable of? Damned if she'd stay in this marriage! She knew better than to go head to head with this stubborn half-breed. Sassy forced herself to keep her voice steady. "All right; I just wanted the truth, that's all."

"Sometimes people are better off not finding out the truth," he said softly as if lost in an old memory.

"I'll grant you that," she agreed, thinking of her own sordid past.

175

"Are you upset?"

"No." Sassy wasn't upset; she was so angry, she was shaking. She lay down quietly, so furious she wanted to pound his brawny back with both fists but she decided against it. This savage barbarian would probably put her across his lap and spank her bottom for it, adding insult to injury.

She would not live with the glib, self-satisfied rascal. She would move into town and determine what to do later. Perhaps she would annul the marriage—no, she couldn't do that; this marriage had been consummated. Her fury built as she realized he had made sure of that before she found out how she had been tricked. She was so angry she couldn't think straight. Perhaps she would take some money from his wallet and go to San Francisco. Perhaps. . . . One thing was certain, she couldn't do anything until he dropped off to sleep. Hunter would never simply allow her to pack up and leave him.

Sassy forced herself to contain her rage and lie quietly for a few minutes, listening to his steady breathing as he dropped off to sleep. Then she sneaked out of bed, trying to decide on a course of action. Could she borrow a horse and make it back to town before Hunter woke up? What would happen then, where she would go, what she would do wasn't her main worry now. Her anger dominated her thinking. James Hunter might influence the residents of Seattle with his power and money, but Sassy wasn't going to be bullied.

She slipped on her shoes, not bothering with stockings or pantalets. She had to get out of here fast. He was sleeping so peacefully he snored, but he smiled in his sleep like Kitty dreaming of catching birds. Sassy had to

176

fight an overpowering urge to get a pitcher of cold water and splash him. No, then she'd have to confront him. As it was, he might sleep till Judgment Day. She went through the coat he had worn last night, took some of the money. That would cover the cost of ship's passage; and when she could afford to, she'd return it to him. Sassy Malone might once have been forced to be a whore, but she was no thief.

Quietly, she tiptoed to the back door. The rain had dwindled to a fine drizzle. Sassy slipped out the door to the barn. She wasn't even sure she could saddle a horse since the Malones had never been prosperous enough to own one. Which was the fastest horse here? The master's, no doubt. She paused before the big Appaloosa's stall, hesitating. The stallion might be dangerous. If she took another horse and Hunter came after her, the Appaloosa would catch her before she could get to town. That's the one she must take then. What was its name? It was one of those things Hunter had mentioned in casual conversation.

She looked at the black spots on its snowy rump, just the size of black silver dollars. "Poker Chips," she remembered aloud, and the horse whinnied. "Okay, Poker Chips, let's go to town."

Somehow she managed to get the bridle on and pushed her full skirt up her thighs as she mounted like a man. She nudged the horse out of the barn and into the rainy afternoon. It was a spirited horse that danced and snorted, wanting to run, but she managed to keep it reined in as she headed down the road toward Seattle. She began to have second thoughts as she headed toward town. She had taken his money and his horse. Sassy had a feeling that no one dared take what belonged to the moody half-breed without severe repercussions. Well, Holy Saint Patrick, she'd turn the stallion loose to return to its own barn when she was about to board a ship. She'd tie a note on the bridle saying not to look for her. She'd return his money when she could.

Now she gave the stallion its head and it took off at a gallop, throwing mud everywhere. What she lacked as a rider, Sassy made up in sheer bravado. She hung on for dear life as she headed toward town. The Appaloosa evidently didn't like having any rider but Hunter on its back; it laid its ears back and snorted. Everything that belonged to Hunter knew it and accepted the fact, she thought with annoyance, everything except Sassy. She was not some docile cat or horse that must obey its master.

After several miles, the stallion was lathered and blowing. She did know enough to realize she had to cool the horse out. Reluctantly, she slowed to a walk, looking back over her shoulder. The muddy road behind her was silent and empty. How long would Hunter sleep? Maybe he was a reasonable man after all and, realizing how she felt, would let her go in peace. Despite his avowal otherwise, he might even be regretting his bargain, since he'd been drunk when he married her and had satisfied his lust for her body. Aye, maybe he wouldn't come in hot pursuit. He didn't seem that reasonable, but the possibility that he might be gave her reassurance as she walked the horse.

Now just how was she going to explain her reappearance in town the next day after her wedding? Surely the Stones had told everyone about the marriage. Maybe Judge Stone would help her—no, probably not. Sassy

178

shook her head. Everyone seemed to be either a friend of or financially controlled by James Hunter.

She nudged the stallion into a lope. Even though the rain had turned into a light mist, her clothes were wet and the fabric clung soddenly to her curves.

Was that thunder? Too rhythmic. Sassy realized the sound was hoofbeats, drumming on the trail behind her. She glanced back, saw the outline of a big man on a sorrel galloping toward her. Reasonable? He looked furious! Lashing the stallion with her reins, she galloped toward town. Behind her, she heard a sharp whistle.

Immediately, her stallion slammed to a halt, dumping Sassy over his head into the mud. Even as she scrambled to her feet, grabbing for the reins, Hunter whistled again and the horse whinnied, jerked its head wildly, and took off back up the trail to the man.

She stood, soaking wet and muddy, feet wide apart, hands on her hips, facing him with righteous anger, but a bit afraid as he galloped up. "Hunter, just what do you think you're doing?"

"Damn it, Sassy, you scared me half to death when you fell. Why didn't you tell me you couldn't ride?" He swung down off the horse, frantic. "Are you hurt?"

"No! No thanks to you! I've changed my mind and we'll have the marriage annulled!" Sassy tried to grab the reins out of his grip. He caught her hand and they struggled.

"If you aren't the hottest-tempered little——! You can't have this marriage annulled, not after I've bedded——"

"Oh, you're no gentleman, James Hunter, or you'd not rub my face in that!" She fought to get away from him.

"I never claimed to be a gentleman; I didn't lie to

179

you, Missy! You knew what you were getting!" If she hadn't been so muddy and wet, he would have had an easier time of it hanging onto her. As it was, he half-tore her bodice as they struggled.

"Let go of me, you rotten trickster! I've heard some low, conniving tricks in my life, but this takes the cake!"

They struggled in the mud of the road and went down, rolling as they fought.

"Sassy, I'm trying to keep from hurting you! Stop fighting me or at least tell me what I've done!"

She turned her head and tried to bite his hand. "You rascal, acting as innocent as a church bishop! Do you deny you tricked me into marriage by making sure no other man would marry me or offer me a job?"

"No, I don't deny it; it was the only way I could get you." He had her arms pinned now and used his body to hold her down. "When I want something bad, I go after it."

"You dirty—I've changed my mind! I don't want to be your wife!"

"It's a little late for that now, isn't it?" He lay on top of her in the mud, stormy and stubborn.

She fought to get out from under him, but he was too big for her. The hard maleness of him pressed down on the vee of her thighs even as his chest pressed against her breasts. "You can't own me or make me obey you as your horse does!"

His face was dark as thunder. "You're mine, Sassy! I want you bad enough to do whatever it takes to keep you!"

Chapter Ten

Hunter bent his head and kissed her. "This is no way for a lady to act—even a hot-tempered hellion like you. Sassy, I'm offering you my kingdom. All you have to do is reign over it and let me make love to you."

His mouth caressed hers as they lay in the mud and his hand went to her breast, massaged her nipple through the wet cloth that clung to her curves.

She must not lose control and arch her body to press against his hand. She must not allow him to think she liked his touch. She must not. . . . "Let me up."

"Are you going to behave like a lady?"

The mud was cold. Her temper began to cool. Aye, he had been ruthless in what he'd done to claim her. On the other hand, he was a rich and powerful man. Her family needed whatever money she could send them. She'd be a fool to let her pride prevail when she had no place to run or anyone to help her. She had no alternative. She'd bide her time until later. "Perhaps I was a bit hasty."

He stood up then and offered her his hand; when she took it, he pulled her gently to her feet. "Are you hurt?"

She shook her head.

"I'm sorry I was so rough; I was trying hard not to hurt you." He whistled and the two horses came at a gallop.

"Hunter, does everything you own obey you?"

He smiled ever so slightly. "Except you, my lady. Maybe that's why I find you such a challenge."

Now she got a good look at the small mare that Hunter had ridden. She was almost a duplicate of Hunter's stallion, except the beautiful mare was a sorrel with red-flecked hips while Poker Chips was black with a spotted rump. "Such a fine mount," she said.

"I bought her for you, Sassy, the first day I saw you," Hunter said gently. "She's almost the same color as your hair. I was going to present her to you the first sunny day we could go riding."

"For me?" Sassy was almost overcome with emotion as she patted the mare's soft muzzle. Hunter was trying to bribe her to stay; she knew that, yet never in her life had she owned anything so fine. "What's her name?"

He shrugged. "You name her. She's yours."

Sassy stood in the mist, patting the mare's nose. "Suppose I still want to go?"

"There is the possibility that after last night and this afternoon you are even now carrying my son."

She felt her face flush crimson. "That was crude."

He shrugged. "I'm a crude, primitive man; I need a lady to civilize me."

"You didn't answer my question." She looked up at him.

"Do I need to?" His expression was possessive and stormy. "Here, let me help you." He offered her his cupped hands and she let him boost her up on the mare.

"I've bought you beautiful riding outfits, a fancy side-saddle, and silver bridle. I don't like you riding astride."

"Why not?" She tossed her head haughtily as if she weren't smeared with mud and glared at him.

His eyes burned into hers. "I don't want anything between those silken thighs but me."

His possessive tone enraged but embarrassed her all over again. Sassy whirled her mare, dug her heels in, and galloped toward the house; but Hunter fell in beside her easily. Gradually, Sassy slowed to a walk. "Just how did you know I was gone so soon?"

"When you left our bedroom door ajar, Kitty came in and hopped on the bed. I thought it was you rubbing against me until he meowed in my ear."

That ornery cat! Sassy thought in disgust. *If I'd just remembered to close the door, Hunter might still be asleep.* All right, so Hunter had wanted her badly enough to do whatever it took to get her. There were worse things than being worshiped and idolized.

He rode along, saying nothing.

"Is it all right if I name the mare 'Freckles'? "

"Name her what you please. I'll breed her to Poker Chips, and we'll have a good colt next year for our son."

Did he really care about Sassy or was she only like a fine-blooded mare to be bred to provide him heirs? *By Hunter out of Sassy.* She shivered and Hunter said, "I didn't stop to grab a jacket when I realized you were gone, but Cookie will have a pot of hot coffee and a warm bath ready."

She wasn't shivering because she was cold, but she said nothing. They rode in silence. Now that her anger had cooled a little, she studied her mother's ring on her finger. What would Maureen have advised her to do? She cast a covert glance at him. He still wore her father's ring on his watchchain. *Despite his words,* she thought, *he's still not ready to make a final commitment to me or this marriage.*

He swung down off the horse, came around, and held up his hands to her. She slid into his arms, and a lanky stablehand appeared to take the reins of the two horses. He looked at Hunter and grinned. "Good ride, boss?"

Hunter nodded. "We both had a good ride, although mine was better than hers."

She remembered him lying on her, his maleness evident even through their clothes. She felt the blood rush to her face.

"Missus enjoy her ride?"

Everyone here owed his loyalty to Hunter. No one would help her if she decided to leave again. "As the master said, he had the best of it."

Hunter swung her up in his arms and carried her toward the house.

"Hunter, I can walk."

"As tired and bruised and cold as you are?" He didn't put her down.

"I wouldn't be tired and bruised and cold if it weren't for you."

"Nor if you'd stayed where you belong. I didn't appreciate being awakened from a sound sleep to go out in the rain to chase down my wife."

"Hunter, you should have let me go. I'm not sure we can make this marriage work."

His face above hers was grim as he carried her in the back door and down the hall to the bedroom. "Because you're a highborn Eastern lady and I'm a half-breed Injun bastard?"

"That's not what I meant—"

"Don't try to explain yourself, Missy. You're mine now, whatever regrets you're having, and I intend to give you more wealth and luxury than you ever dreamed of. All you've got to do is be my lady and give me sons."

She wanted to scream at him that she realized now that was all he wanted from her, but her nerve failed her. He stood her on the floor by the fireplace next to a big copper tub of steaming water.

Sassy gathered her courage. "You don't say anything about love; you just keep telling me you want me."

"I do want you, damn it; too much! That's what bothers me; I didn't expect this complication." He held her close and glared down at her, anger on his dark features. "I like being in control."

She looked up at him a long moment and, without thinking, asked, "What are you afraid of, Hunter?"

"Nothing. I fear nothing—except maybe being made to look the fool, being humiliated before other men as my father was."

She could only guess at the torture behind those haunted blue eyes. Holy Mary, talk about looking the fool and being humiliated by other men, if Hunter knew Sassy's past, his fury would be something to fear.

"Are you cold? You're trembling. Quick, now, let's get out of these wet things."

"I can take my own clothes off," she protested as his fingers fumbled with the buttons of her dress, but he stopped her with a gesture. "It's my right and privilege," he said softly. His fingers were warm on her breasts as

185

he unbuttoned her bodice. Slowly, he removed his own shirt. "The tub is big enough for two." Was he asking or telling her he meant to share her bath?

She felt from the way he was staring at her that he might take her right there on the thick carpet before the fire. How many women had Hunter used for his passion while he looked for a proper virgin to be his bride? It was ironic and maybe all he deserved that he'd gotten a whore. His thumbs traced slow circles around her nipples and she was once again surprised by his ability to arouse her. Of all the men who had used her body, including Brett, none had ever made her want them . . . until now. She willed herself to pull away from his teasing hands and finished stripping off her muddy clothes.

"I've not seen you completely naked in broad daylight."

Nor I you, she thought with defiance, but instead she stood still, letting him appraise her like a slave.

He shook his head, swore softly.

"What's the matter?" She looked at him with sudden alarm. "Do I not please you?"

"I must have really hurt you last night, or you injured yourself when you fell from the horse; you've got bruises on that fair skin. I never noticed those two small moles, almost like beauty marks, on your left hip."

"Are you through inventorying your possession?"

"If only I could possess you," he whispered. "You're holding me at a distance."

Sassy climbed into the water, sighed loudly. It did feel good. "Oh," she breathed and leaned back in the long tub. "I didn't realize I was so cold."

He continued to study her. She knew her body was

186

half-hidden by the foamy suds, but that didn't keep him from staring. "Looking for more bruises, Hunter?"

"You know what I'm staring at; don't be so self-satisfied." He undressed and stood before the fire naked. Modestly, she tried to avert her eyes, but she couldn't stop herself from peeking at him. "And are you looking for bruises, too, Sassy?"

She felt her face flame. "You rascal! I wish I were seeing lumps on your hard head."

"Move forward and I'll get in behind you."

"I'll not share my bath with you!"

"You'd have poor Cookie and the stablehand carry another tub of water in here? I suppose elegant ladies aren't concerned with the plight of tired servants."

She gritted her teeth and inched forward, very aware of his body as he climbed into the tub behind her, his long legs straddling her so that she fitted into the vee of his thighs. He felt huge, throbbing against her hips as he pulled her against his chest. "Give me the soap and I'll wash your back."

She handed him the expensive cake of perfumed soap and the sponge and closed her eyes, reluctant to admit even to herself that she liked the protection of his big arms embracing her . . . Or was it imprisonment?

He washed her back so gently he surprised her. Then he reached around and soaped her breasts and belly. She felt her nipples swell beneath his soapy fingers. Now he pushed up the curls from the back of her neck, kissing the nape. "You have the most desirable neck," he whispered, "the kind that kindles passion in a man."

"You are kindling your own passion," she retorted. "I'm just taking a bath."

"Have it your way." His hands soaped her belly,

moved down to her thighs, stroking again and again. She was thankful he couldn't see her face as she closed her eyes and sighed.

His hands didn't cease their caressing as he kissed her shoulders and her neck. His breath felt warm on her wet skin. In spite of her misgivings, she relaxed and enjoyed his touch. "Ah, my Sassy Lady. To think that no man but me has ever touched this silky skin, seen your body."

He half-turned her in the water, resting her against his bare chest as he kissed her. She had not realized such a big man could be so gentle. She found to her surprise that she returned his kiss, slipping her arms around his neck. Her face pressed against his chest, and, without thinking, she kissed his nipple.

He gasped audibly. "Careful, Sassy, you don't want to carry this too far in a bathtub."

She looked up at him and smiled. "We could get out of the tub."

"We could, couldn't we?" He cupped her small face in his hand. "The water's getting cold anyway."

He stepped from the tub, reached for a towel, wrapped her in it, and lifted her out. "Hmm, you smell good." He took a deep breath. "Like scented soap and soft, wet skin." He carried her to the big bed.

She protested. "We'll get the sheets wet."

"How like a woman to think of that at a time like this." He lay down next to her. "Believe me, that's the last thing on my mind." He trailed his fingers across the swell of her breasts just above the towel. "Are you still angry about what I did to get you?"

"Does it matter?"

"It matters."

She was having a hard time sorting out her feelings

about Hunter, distracted by the trail of kisses he blazed across her throat. "I—I never dreamed a man might want me that much."

He kissed her wet, bare shoulder. "You were perfect—beautiful, chaste, a prize any man would fight to claim."

She was glad her eyes were closed so he couldn't see the truth in them. His mouth sent shivers down her frame. "Oh, Hunter, suppose I weren't perfect? Suppose—?"

His mouth covered hers, cutting off the confession she was almost ready to blurt out. His tongue flicked lightly between her lips; then he sucked her tongue rhythmically between his lips. He pulled the towel away from her breasts. "These will suckle my sons," he whispered and bent his hot mouth to them, causing her to arch her back, willing him to nurse. His hand sought the bud of her femininity. "Other men will envy me and want you as they see you pass by, but I am the only man who will ever lie on your belly and put his seed in you. You'll never know another man's touch, that makes you rare and special."

She knew then she could not confess; he would never love her enough to understand, forgive the ridicule it would bring upon him if others knew her past. Brett James and New York were a long way from here, and who knew what had happened to Marylou Evans? The madam might even be dead or have gone back to the South. Sassy had a rare opportunity, she thought as Hunter kissed the cleft between her breasts. She had a chance to close the door on her own past and bury her secret forever. Could she learn to love Hunter? Did it matter how she felt when he worshiped her? If Sassy could become the lady Hunter thought she was, he need never know the truth.

His lips brushed her skin in feather-like motions as he kissed between her breasts and moved lower. When he made light, flicking touches with his tongue in the hollow of her belly, she couldn't stop herself from tangling her fingers in his black curly hair, making a soft, helpless noise in her throat.

"Yes, Sassy," he whispered as his tongue touched her navel, "you didn't know you could like that, did you?" His mouth moved lower still.

"What—what are you doing?" Surely he wasn't about to put his mouth there.

"Put your hands above your head," he murmured. "I have a terrible urge to do something to you, my innocent, that I have never done to another woman."

"But—but not there!"

"Don't try to stop me, Sassy," he commanded, and his breath felt like liquid flame on the bud of her womanhood. "I want to possess you, all of you, no matter how shocking it may seem to a lady."

Sassy forced herself to keep her hands above her head as his mouth kissed both her thighs. She belonged to him now and the half-breed was powerful enough to do anything he wanted to her. She was nothing but a pretty toy, a pleasurable amusement. She dared not stop him, no matter what it was he wanted to do.

"Spread your thighs," he said.

"Hunter, I don't think—"

"Spread them."

She complied, not really sure what he was about to do. No man had ever touched her with his mouth before, no matter how drunk or lustful he was.

190

"My innocent lady, I'm going to teach you passion so that you can pleasure me more." And then his mouth touched her there.

For a moment, she could only react with shock as the wet flame of his tongue caressed her; and then she writhed under him, but his big hands held her down. She breathed loudly through open lips, gasping for air as his hot, hard blade of tongue began to explore her. Then she couldn't stop herself. She grabbed at his hair, holding his mouth against her, wanting him to kiss her deeper still. She locked her long, slim legs around his muscular shoulders, afraid he might stop before he gave her what she hungered for. Never had any man made her want him as she now wanted Hunter. "More . . . oh, Hunter!" she gasped, writhing under him. His hands tightened on her small waist, pulling her to his mouth as he explored every nerve, every sensation her body was capable of. The stabbing motions of his tongue caressed her, made her burn with unknown passion.

"Surrender to me, Sassy." His breath was hotly insistent against her velvet place. "Let me lead you, teach you."

She felt as if she were being swept away by a rushing tide that she did not understand and had never experienced before. In some ways, perhaps she was a virgin— Hunter's virgin. And just as his tongue reached deep, setting her whole being aquiver, she stopped fighting for control and surrendered to his domination. "Teach me," she whispered from the black whirlpool of emotion. "Oh, Hunter, teach me."

He taught her all right. She who had had many men had never been swept away with passion as she was now that she surrendered totally to his will.

He smiled at her bewilderment after it was over, kissed her with the taste of herself still on his lips. "I knew I could bring you to passion," he murmured as he kissed her. "I knew you were like a flower waiting to open up to love for the right man. Touch me, Sassy Miss. Touch me."

She lay spent and satisfied in his arms; but when she touched him, she knew he was engorged and throbbing with seed and she spread herself. "You want a child," she said. "Let me give you one."

"I won't last long, not the way I want you," he warned through clenched teeth.

"I'm your wife, Hunter. Use me for your pleasure and to produce that dynasty you crave."

He needed no further urging. He bent her legs, put his hands under her small hips and drove into her hard and deep. She felt him throb all the way to her womb. He came up on his knees and rammed hard into her again; and, on the second stroke, he froze in mid-motion, pouring himself into her while she tried with her body to squeeze every precious drop from his.

Chapter Eleven

The first gray light of dawn awakened Sassy. For a confused moment, she was not quite sure where she was, then sighed with relief as she realized she slept curled in Hunter's strong arms. She had not felt so safe and secure in a long, long time. Smiling to herself, she remembered last night. Her new husband was a more-than-adequate lover. Up until now, she had always thought the pleasure of sex was reserved for men.

He had had restless nightmares again last night, but she had taken him in her arms without awakening him, soothing him until he had relaxed and drifted into deep sleep. She wondered what unfinished business or haunting memory from his past brought those on and what it would take to stop them? Somctime when she felt more secure, when there was friendship and trust with the love he felt for her, she'd ask him about his secret agony and hope he didn't inquire about her own.

Sassy slipped out of bed without waking Hunter and went to the window. The day looked a bit gray but appeared to be clearing.

Coffee. She took a deep breath and smelled coffee.

Good old John. He wasn't the round, jovial domestic of her dreams, but he could cook and she liked him.

Quickly, she washed her face, brushed her hair, and put on a frilly pink morning dress and slippers. Closing the door softly behind her to keep the cat out, she tiptoed down the hall.

Suddenly, she heard an angry commotion that made her jump: Someone was pounding a table with a fist. "By jingo, Cookie!" a male voice shouted, "who moved my ledger books?"

"Miss Sassy says to start serving meals in the dining room."

"So Hunter finally got his 'lady,' did he? I hope she don't put doilies and ribbons on everything in house!"

That accent; slightly foreign. This must be the formidable "Swede" she'd already heard about. Sassy took a deep breath and sailed into the dining room to confront a big, blond man who might have been forty-five or fifty. "Maybe not ribbons, but a little cleaning wouldn't hurt a thing."

Immediately, the big man jerked off his cap and turned her way. Sassy almost gasped aloud. Once he might have been handsome, but the left side of his scarred face looked as if someone had taken an ice pick to it. "By jingo, Ma'am, I didn't know you heard—"

"How could I not when you were shouting loud enough to wake the dead?" She had the advantage, and she was not going to be bullied by the bachelors in this household. The cook grinned and limped toward the kitchen, leaving a scent of vanilla in his wake as he abandoned the field of battle to Sassy. She squared her small shoulders. "You must be Swede. I've heard Hunter speak of you."

194

"Yes, Ma'am." He fumbled with his hat. "I'm pleased to meet you, Mrs. Hunter." He ran his hand through the curly blond hair which was streaked with gray. *A rough-hewn logger,* she thought and wondered about his scarred face. "Ma'am, the crew was expectin' to be invited to wedding."

And Swede had expected to be best man. Sassy thought about Hunter's drunken abduction. "We—we decided to go ahead on an impulse."

"The town not too happy folks didn't get party. If weather clears, they might come out anyway."

That hardly registered with Sassy, as intent as she was on the problems at hand. She looked squarely into his bright blue eyes. "Swede, why don't we sit down and have some coffee while we're waiting for the boss to join us?"

"Yes, Mrs. Hunter." Although his words agreed, his expression was definitely hostile. One more obstacle in her path. How was she going to deal with this potential enemy?

"You may call me Sassy." She smiled at the big man and indicated a dining chair. John hurried to put crisp linen on the table and limped in with coffee as the pair sat down.

Swede looked ill at ease with the dainty cup in his hand. "By jingo." His voice carried a definite accent. "Hope I didn't upset you, Miss Sassy. Boss wouldn't like."

"I'm not your average, prissy, swooning lady," Sassy said, studying him while she sipped the strong, hot brew. Why did he look familiar? No doubt, like everyone else in town, he'd come down to the dock and out to the picnic for the ladies. *Wouldn't she have remembered a man with such a scarred face?* "I won't tell him if you won't."

He looked relieved, less antagonistic. "Hunter's talked nothing but marriage since Mercer took his letter."

She decided she could deal with this burly, rough man. He reminded her of her papa and all the tough construction men she'd met. "You've known my husband a long time?"

He nodded, proud. "I been his bull o' the woods and done his books for years. I almost raise the boy. Before that, I came west with Clay."

Clay? She didn't have any idea who the Swede was speaking of, decided not do delve into it. "Tell me about a 'bull of the woods.' "

"Foreman, I guess you'd say, Miss Sassy." He shrugged shoulders almost as wide as Hunter's or her father's. Construction and timber men must be a lot alike. 'I boss the timber beasts."

"The what?"

"Crews that fell the trees, get them out of the woods and down the skid road for market."

"Swede," she gave him her warmest smile and then glanced around the cluttered, dusty room, "don't worry that I'm going to invade your territory and meddle in my husband's business. However, I do think that a man who is an important part of Hunter's empire like you are should get more respect and not have to work on the dining table."

"Beg pardon, Ma'am?" His bright blue eyes widened. Of all the things this tough old lumberman had expected, Sassy thought, it probably wasn't that Sassy would insist he deserved more respect. "I miss meaning; English never good after all these years."

Sassy sipped the strong, bracing coffee. "Back East, a manager or an accountant always has an office so no one disturbs his paperwork. Do you write his business letters, too?"

Swede shook his head. "Not much letters to write. Anyway, I know numbers. I not so good with the writing and reading."

"But you are probably the most important person who works for Hunter," Sassy insisted. "As such, you deserve an office and your own desk."

He blinked. "Desk?"

"A *big* desk," Sassy said.

He considered for a long moment. "By jingo, yes, I am important!"

She turned on her charm. "I have a great deal to learn about Washington and timber, Swede. For my husband's sake, I don't want to appear stupid. Can I count on you when I need help?"

The hostility faded and his brawny chest puffed out. "Why, sure, Miss Sassy. Now I met you, I see why boss married you. You not what I expect."

"I'll be having some dinners for Hunter's business associates and leading citizens, so you see why I need the dining room. Of course, you're always welcome at our table."

Swede beamed at her. "Why, yes, Ma'am."

"What I was thinking was that one of the rooms here should be turned into your office so your paperwork won't be disturbed. Besides a desk, I think you should have a big leather chair like other important businessmen have."

Swede leaned back in his chair, picturing her suggestions. "You know, Miss Sassy, you right. Nice to have office; we just never bother before."

Point won, Sassy thought. "It's worth bothering about. I'll look into it right away."

Kitty wandered into the dining room and paused by Swede's chair, his crooked tail in the air, his ragged ears wiggling. "Yeow?" He rubbed against the man's leg.

Sassy held her breath, somehow expecting the rough man to kick the cat.

Instead Swede leaned over, picked up the yellow tom, and stroked it. "Boss not up yet, Kitty, but Cookie maybe have nice bite for you."

The smell of bacon frying wafted through the air and the cat licked its chops, jumped down, and scurried for the kitchen.

Despite his bluster, Swede was a placid, gentle giant, Sassy decided, one of those men who could always be depended on. "How did you and Hunter get acquainted?"

Swede wrapped both big hands around the coffee cup and smiled. "I was his father's friend since I come over from Oslo as a boy; worked the Maine forests first. That's where I met Clay, came west with him."

She had jumped to the conclusion that the senior Hunter's first name had been James, too, but Hunter hadn't said anything about being a junior. Clay Hunter. She wanted to know the secrets about Hunter's birth so she could unlock the puzzle of this strange, haunted man.

She watched the weathered man. Once he had been handsome, she thought.

The big Swede appeared lost in memory as he sipped his coffee. "Try to turn both sons into timbermen like Clay wanted. Older one too spoiled and used to easy life; finally took his half of inheritance and wasted it; don't know where he is now."

Sassy leaned closer, intrigued. Of course the older son

would be Clay Hunter, Junior. "I didn't know Hunter had a brother."

"Half-brother," Swede corrected. "Hunter's mother was wild, pretty Indian girl Clay love. His fancy wife was back East—"

"Swede," Hunter stood in the doorway, his shirt collar open, his face as brooding as an approaching summer storm. "I doubt Sassy is interested in all that past history." His blue eyes held a cold warning.

The older man colored. "You're right," he said in embarrassed confusion. "You know I always look out for you, boy."

"I know you do; you always have. I wish you'd just think before you speak."

The tension was so high Sassy felt obligated to step in. "Well, good morning. I thought you were still asleep."

"So you thought it a good time to snoop and pry into things that don't concern you?" His eyes looked like azure ice.

"Don't blame Swede. I was asking questions and he was just being polite."

Hunter's scowl didn't change as he sat down in the host's chair. "Don't pry, Sassy. I really resent your using your womanly charms on my men. If you want to know something, ask me."

He wouldn't trust her enough to share his heart and thoughts with her, she knew, but she didn't say anything. She regretted having created trouble between these two. There followed a long, awkward moment of silence. Swede stared at the flowered design on his cup and Sassy fiddled with her spoon.

John limped through the door with a huge, steaming platter of bacon and ham.

"Well," Sassy said a bit too brightly, "it appears Kitty did leave a little bacon for us after all!"

The three men laughed and the tension was defused.

While John heaped the food on each plate, Hunter looked around as if seeing the linen cloth and the fine china for the first time. "We going to live like this all the time now, Cookie?"

The old man paused in his serving. "Miss Sassy says we should live like civilized folk."

Hunter looked at Sassy. "I didn't realize getting married was going to turn things upsidedown this fast."

Sassy gave him a winsome smile. "You did say you wanted a lady who could bring the niceties and etiquette to Washington."

"I did say that, didn't I?" Hunter conceded. "Swede, you let her move all your ledger books?"

Swede sipped his coffee. "Miss Sassy says I important; need office."

"With a desk," Sassy said.

"*Big* desk," Swede corrected.

The cook, fighting a laugh, grabbed up the coffeepot and hurried back through the door. Sassy had a distinct feeling that he was chortling over his stove.

Hunter leaned back in his chair and eyed her. "It appears you've been a busy little thing again. I wonder where I ever got the idea that ladies were meek creatures who never meddled in their husbands' business."

She heard a faint chuckle and knew John must be listening on the other side of the door. She gave Hunter her most winsome look. "I'm not meddling, Dear; I'm just attempting to get my dining room back. You are expecting to be entertaining important citizens now that you're married, aren't you?"

He favored her with a begrudging smile. "I suppose that does fall into your sphere then."

Sassy waited like a dutiful, obedient wife. He certainly had some stodgy, old-fashioned ideas that needed to be changed, but she mustn't move too fast. Slow pressure could gradually wear down granite.

Hunter reached for his coffee cup. "Swede, is it all right with you?"

The logger rubbed his scarred cheek a long moment. "If Miss Sassy want put account books in barn, I do it."

Hunter sighed and made a gesture of defeat. "I'll see about the desk and chair. Now, my Sassy Miss, what other changes are you planning?"

"Do you really mind?" She must not appear too triumphant.

"Would it matter if I did?" He raised one eyebrow at her. "I have a feeling that you're stubborn and determined and that once you set your mind on something, you go right ahead on."

"Are you talking about me or yourself?" Sassy paused in spreading her napkin on her lap and gave him a challenging look.

"She know you well, Hunter!" Swede grinned and a lock of curly blond hair fell across his forehead. He brushed it back and sipped his coffee.

John reappeared with a light, fluffy omelet, big biscuits, more coffee, and a bowl of wild strawberries and thick cream. When he passed her, she caught the decided scent of vanilla and wondered again about introducing the lonely man to her friend, Ellie?

With the men's attention diverted by the food,

Hunter relinquished his concern for household matters and his disapproval of Sassy's prying and involvement. Relieved, Sassy allowed herself to eat.

While the two men talked business, Sassy smeared wild honey and fresh butter on a biscuit and contemplated her next moves. The house needed a good cleaning, and she would hire household help to take the load off old John. Besides, Ellie needed work, and there was always the possibility . . .

She sipped her coffee and scrutinized Hunter's profile as the two men talked. First his stubbornness in claiming her had fascinated her. However, after last night and his virile and gentle lovemaking, she was beginning to think she could learn to love this man and be happy as his wife. The past was behind her and the future looked promising. She imagined the two of them sitting at this same table on their fiftieth wedding anniversary surrounded by their children and grandchildren.

The only tragedy was that her own family, the Malones, could never be a part of this happiness. How she would like to have them here on holidays, all sitting around the table. Papa, Hunter, and Swede were somewhat alike and would enjoy each other's company. Too bad they must never meet.

The men finished eating and John brought the coffeepot in to refill the cups.

"John," Sassy said as she laid her napkin aside, "you are indeed a wonderful cook. I think the boss should hire more help so you wouldn't have to work so hard."

Hunter paused with his cup halfway to his lips. "More help?"

"See, Boss? Miss Sassy agrees with me. We need a full-time housekeeper."

"By jingo, and don't forget big leather chair," Swede said.

Hunter looked at Sassy with amused admiration. "You've been here a few hours, you red-haired minx, and you've got my whole empire in revolt."

She gave him a fetching smile as she stood up. "Do you really mind if I make a few tiny changes?"

"Tiny?" He grinned as he picked up his coffee cup and rose from the table. "Sounds as if you're turning the place upsidedown whether I like it or not. I didn't realize any changes needed to be made."

Very slowly, Sassy raised her head and stared up at the cobwebs festooning the chandelier.

Hunter's gaze followed hers. "Funny, I never noticed that before. All right, Missy, do whatever you like. Just don't put too many doodads and ribbons on everything."

"Shall we take our coffee into the library, gentlemen?" Sassy made sure she didn't appear too triumphant, but already her mind was busy with tasks and changes.

The three of them went into the library where the cook had a fire going to warm the morning chill.

"Oh, Hunter," she said with enthusiasm, looking around at the hundreds of books, I do love this room! I'll bet you spend a lot of time here."

"Not really," Hunter shrugged as he settled himself in a leather chair and lit a cigar, broke the match in half. "As I told you, I'm too busy with my business to waste much time reading."

"But it's such an enjoyable way to spend an evening," Sassy insisted, "don't you think so, Swede?"

The big man glanced at Hunter, uneasy. "Like Hunter, I spend free evenings playing cards with the crew at lumber camp or with girls at either the *Illahee* or—"

"Swede," Hunter cut in, "that isn't a subject that would interest a lady."

"I forget. We never had real lady around before, Miss Sassy." Swede turned a flustered red as he sat down on the sofa.

There must be a couple of whorehouses in Seattle, Sassy thought. She intended to keep Hunter so interested, he wouldn't be going there anymore. She looked around at the hundreds of books. "Swede, isn't this a wonderful library?"

He shook his head. "Don't read much."

"Oh? You miss so much if you don't read."

"He manages just fine," Hunter said. "Lots of people can't read very well and they do okay."

It hadn't occurred to her that a man doing her husband's bookwork might have problems with reading. "I'm sorry, Swede," she said gently. "I didn't mean to embarrass you."

The logger looked at her. "You read good?"

She nodded.

"You teach me more?"

It annoyed her that Hunter hadn't taken the time to help this man. "Aye, but I've no supplies, no primers."

Swede brushed a graying blond curl out of his eyes. "Maybe you help me, Miss Sassy, and I teach others."

"I'd love to, Swede." She gave him a warm smile.

"Good idea," Hunter nodded. "You buy all the pencils you need. I'll tell the general store to let you have whatever you want and put it on my bill."

"Some things I might not be able to get in Seattle."

"I'll authorize my bank to let you have a weekly draw."

"Oh, Hunter, you won't be sorry. There's probably a

204

lot of men in your crew who can't read. Swede and I will open up new worlds for them."

He made a face. "Most of these tough old lumberjacks have gotten along just fine all these years without reading. I can see them sitting in my library with a book of Shakespeare."

Sassy merely smiled. She had decided that under that tough exterior, this man—who helped stray cats and disabled people—was not as insensitive as he wanted to appear.

Kitty wandered into the room, jumped up in Hunter's lap. He scratched the cat's ragged ears. "I suppose you'll be putting a ribbon around Kitty's neck, too?"

Swede finished his coffee. "By jingo, I bet if anyone could do it, Miss Sassy could and make the old devil purr while she tied the bow."

"No doubt," Hunter said dryly.

"I may stop at that," Sassy said.

The big Swede looked toward the piano. "Well, now, Miss Sassy, do you play? Hate to think Boss ship that thing this far for nothing."

Hunter said, "Of course she plays. She tried to buy my piano from me. Play us something, Sassy."

She felt as if she were being exhibited in a museum as *Hunter's Lady*, but she went to the piano and sat down. "Any song you'd like to hear, Swede?"

"Just play something pretty." He sounded wistful.

"Here's one that's been popular during the war." She began to play and sing: "Aura Lea, Aura Lea, maid of golden hair; sunshine came along with thee, and swallows in the air."

When she finished, there was a long silence broken only by the logs crackling on the fire and the mantel clock ticking. Swede, blinking as if he had something in his eye, went to stand by the window. "Real pretty, Ma'am," he whispered, his mind far, far away. "Real pretty. Knew a yellow-haired girl named Leigh once; guess she wait a long time before she give up on me; married another man."

Sassy wondered at the regret on the man's scarred face. What memories had her music dredged up?

Swede stared out the window, but he saw nothing except a picture from a time long ago. To him, the pretty blond preacher's daughter who had loved him would be forever young. He should have stayed in Maine and married her; instead, he went off to the West with Clay. The other woman had been dark and wild. In her arms, he'd forgotten the innocent Leigh, betrayed a trust, thrown away his principles. Nothing mattered but making love to that tempting Jezebel. He was as weak as all those other men. His confession had led to murder. He should have carried the burden of guilt silently instead.

Secrets and regrets. Swede's conscience often drove him to drink and to Lulu's embrace. He could never acknowledge his own son because the boy would hate him if he knew. *Leigh. I was such a fool, but I can't undo the past. I threw it all away for a few nights in that other woman's arms. There is hell after all, just like your father said.*

The cat meowed in the silence and brought Swede back to the present with a start. "Thank you, Miss Sassy. For just a moment . . ." He didn't finish.

"Yes, that was nice, Sassy." Hunter got up from his chair, letting the cat slide to the floor. He crossed the room and tossed his cigar into the fireplace. "Swede, we've lost a lot of time the last couple of days. What do you think we should do next?"

Sassy watched Swede turn around from the window and wondered again about him.

"Well," the logger said, "got to see about snaking that timber off south slope."

They returned to business. It was evident that Hunter respected and admired Swede. She was glad she had won the logger over. Sassy's mind wandered. "If you two will excuse me, I've got a thousand things to take care of as lady of the house."

They nodded absently, involved in their conversation about timber. Sassy left to inventory supplies and make lists of things she needed from the general store. She put on an apron, tied up her hair in a kerchief, and searched out a feather duster that looked as if it had never been used. There was just so much to do! Sassy had not felt this happy or hopeful in a long time. Yes, this marriage was going to work after all. Already she was beginning to love Hunter in spite of her caution. Deep in her heart, she now felt she could become the woman he thought she was. The past was dead and buried. She had a bright, new future ahead of her.

She paused in the dining room and studied the ornate walnut sideboard. She imagined a fancy silver tea service gleaming there such as the one her mother had once owned before she had to sell it to help pay the family's passage over. Sassy saw herself at a garden club or social gathering of the respectable ladies of Seattle.

One lump or two? She mouthed the words as she pretended to pour for the mayor's wife. The doctor and the minister's wife had come, also. As Sassy poured, the banker's wife said, *Mrs. Hunter, we would be so pleased if you would accept the chairmanship of the library committee and we'd also like you to help raise money for the symphony.*

"Aye, if you ladies insist," she smiled modestly and held out a cup. "I'd be honored to chair such a group for the most respected ladies of Seattle and for such a worthwhile cause." She picked up the imaginary monogrammed silver teapot. "One lump or two?"

Sassy heard a noise and whirled around. Old John watched from the kitchen door, eyes wide. "Who you talking to, Miss Sassy?"

She felt foolish, having been caught in her daydreams. "I—I was making swipes at the cobwebs on this chandelier, of course. Bless the saints, it's so dusty. I simply must clean it!"

Remembering what Swede had said concerning a party, Sassy warned the cook about having some cakes and other food ready just in case a few people actually turned up later, then forgot about it as she began to clean with a vengeance. Tomorrow, she'd see if Ellie would like to come work as a housekeeper.

Hunter and Swede, in the meantime, had moved the ledger books into the new office and were intent on their business discussions. She heard them as she passed with her brooms, polishes, and feather dusters. Hunter frowned. "A lady shouldn't ruin her hands that way," he said. "She should have Cookie bring in some of the men to do that." She nodded, knowing she would begin again when he wasn't looking. They stopped midday for a bite of lunch and then, since the day was clearing, Hunter announced that he needed to go out to the timber lease with Swede.

"How long will you be gone?" Sassy asked, thinking

208

of how much cleaning she could get done with the men out from underfoot.

"Till supper," he smiled. "I expect by the time I get back, you'll have moved all the furniture and turned things upsidedown."

She didn't smile. "You know me better than you think." She turned to the timber boss. "Swede, will you be joining us for supper?"

He shook his head. "Thank you, Miss Sassy, but no. Besides, you two are honeymooners."

"And we appreciate that," Hunter put in quickly before Sassy could say anything, slapping the other man on the back.

The minute they were out of the house, Sassy got down to serious cleaning. On Hunter's orders, John brought in two men to assist with the heavy lifting. It would take her several weeks, Sassy thought happily, but with some help, she intended for the whole place to sparkle. Already most of the furniture gleamed with polish, the cobwebs were gone from the chandelier, and the lanky stablehand had cleaned the dirty windows.

From the kitchen drifted the aroma of beef roasting and cakes baking. Sassy smiled as she sniffed the delicious scents. She was beginning to feel like a real wife. Hunter was going to build her a mansion on a hill. They would have many children and would be just like any prosperous, married couple. There would never be a breath of gossip about the Hunters. A generation from now, her children would be prominent citizens. No one would ever know the scandal in Mrs. James Hunter's past.

In her zeal, Sassy scoured, dusted, waxed, and polished, and ignored the sun's gradual move toward the far horizon. She would work a while longer, then stop and clean herself up before her new husband returned for dinner.

Abruptly, Hunter walked in the door.

"Oh, bless the saints, I lost track of time!" She jumped up, wiping her hands on her apron. "You've caught me looking a sight!"

"And what a sight." He pulled her to him, kissed the tip of her freckled nose. "I see smudges on that pretty face, Sassy Girl." He took the corner of her apron, wiped her cheek. "What have you been up to? The whole place smells like soap and wax."

"Of course, I've been cleaning. And I've got a list of supplies I need. Is it all right if I go into town tomorrow and get some things?"

"Anything you want." He kissed her.

"Thank you, Hunter." She hugged him. "Give me a minute to clean up while you fix yourself a drink."

The sky was turning pale pink and purple with the sunset. Sassy pulled off her apron, quickly tidied herself up, and joined Hunter in the dining room. He took her in his arms and kissed her again. "I've been waiting all day to get back to you."

Sassy took a deep breath. The look in his smoldering eyes told her he intended to take her right to bed, make love to her till dawn. If any man was virile enough to make love all night, it was the big half-breed.

Before she could answer, he pulled her to him, ran his hands down her back, cupped her small hips. Teasing her lips with the tip of his tongue, his hand went to stroke her breast. "Sassy," he whispered, "let's forget about supper and get right to the dessert."

Chapter Twelve

Sassy pulled away from him. "After John has worked so hard on dinner, I don't think we should hurt his feelings."

"What about my feelings?"

She favored him with her most seductive smile. "There's time enough for what you have in mind later. At least let me wash my face."

He sighed in resignation. "Okay, I hope it's worth waiting for."

"That's up to you." She looked at him innocently, then turned and went down the hall to brush her hair and dab on some cologne before she reappeared for supper.

Even Hunter appeared impressed by the crisp, table linens and the sparkling chandelier. "You've been a busy little bee all day, haven't you?"

"You said you wanted a lady." Sassy took her seat and spread her napkin over her lap. "This is the way ladies live and run a house. Having regrets?"

He looked at her a long moment, shook his head.

"No, you've fulfilled every dream I had, Sassy Girl. I only hope I don't disappoint you."

She shrugged his comment off. "I came into this with my eyes wide open, Hunter, not expecting a prince on a white horse; I suspect I'm more realistic than you are."

His dark face furrowed with puzzlement as he sipped his burgundy. "I wanted a princess; I got a princess. What more is there to know?"

"Nothing," she said, wanting desperately to change the subject. "Nothing at all. Tell me about your day."

John interrupted to serve the roast—crisp on the outside, juicy inside—with potatoes and fluffy hot rolls. The food was excellent and plentiful. Sassy couldn't help thinking as she took a second helping that this was more meat than her family would see in a week. Tomorrow, maybe she could go into town for supplies and attempt to send a small amount of money to her father.

Finally Hunter leaned back in his chair and sighed. "I don't know when I've enjoyed a meal so much. You're being here, Sassy, made all the difference between just filling my belly and really dining. Shall we take our wine with us?"

"Let's." She had enjoyed both the meal and talking with him. If he wouldn't delve too deeply into her past, maybe this would work after all.

They went into the library and Hunter said, "I suppose it's proper to ask if you mind if I smoke."

"Hunter, it's your home. You can smoke if you wish."

He lit a slender cigarillo, broke the match in half, threw it in the fireplace.

"Why do you always do that?" Sassy asked.

"What?" He stared at her, baffled.

"Break the match in half."

"Oh, that." He shrugged, took a puff. "Have you ever seen a forest fire?"

Sassy shook her head.

"It's something that scares the hell out of timber men. Imagine a big blaze out of control, driven by the wind for hundreds of miles, with people and animals unable to outrun it. When I touch that match tip, I know it's too cool to start a fire."

The images he brought to mind made Sassy shudder. Were forest fires what he had nightmares about? Sassy wandered over to the piano. This afternoon she had cleaned the keys and polished the wood until it shone. Idly, she picked out a melody with one hand.

"Play me something." He leaned against the mantel and sipped his wine.

Sassy set her wine on the piano, sat down on the bench. She played some of the Civil War songs: Stephen Foster tunes, "The Last Rose of Summer," "Lorena," and finally, "Aura Lea."

Now she paused and sipped her wine, and Hunter sighed and threw his cigarillo into the fireplace. "I really like that last song."

"Why?" she smiled. "Were you wanting a girl with golden hair?"

He shook his head. "You know better than that. I'm in love with a red-haired minx. I meant it has such a haunting melody. It certainly had an effect on Swede."

He had never said he loved her. She wanted to hear him say it, but she couldn't ask. He might not mean it. Pride of possession and love were two different things. "It does have a haunting melody, doesn't it? Sometime maybe Swede will be able to join us for dinner." Sassy

213

walked over to the bookshelves, searching through the titles.

"I wonder if a hundred years from now, it will still be popular?" he mused.

"Who can know?" She paused before a bookcase. "Oh, Hunter, there're so many novels to choose from I can't make a choice! What's your favorite?"

"I told you I seldom read." He looked annoyed. "I'm too busy to be bothered with make-believe stories; that's for ladies and children."

"All right, I'll choose one for each of us and every night, we'll read a little."

Hunter groaned. "I can think of better things to do with a pretty girl than sit and read."

"We can do that, too, but later." She studied the titles, overwhelmed.

"Besides," Hunter drained his wine glass, "my eyes are bothering me; I think I got dust in one of them."

She didn't believe him. He was trying to get her in bed early and she wasn't ready to end this evening. "I tell you what; I'll choose a book and read to you."

He looked resigned as she chose a book and sat on the sofa. Hunter promptly lay down with his head in her lap. "I may enjoy this after all."

"Oh, you're terrible!" she said as he reached up and nuzzled the underside of her breasts. "Be serious now and let me read."

"What's it about?" He didn't sound enthused at all.

"It's about King Arthur and his knights of the round table. Have you read this one?"

"If the table's made of wood cut from my trees, I might have read the lumber profit sheet, otherwise—"

"I know, I know. But you're missing something. Don't

the Indians tell tales around the campfires and the loggers tell stories?"

"That's different. It isn't the same."

"Yes, it is, too. Before King Arthur was ever written down, there were old legends about him."

Hunter wiggled his head deeper into her lap. "If you're going to read me something, it should be something useful, like how to cut costs in the timber business. What's this King Arthur about?"

"It's about fighting and honor and a beautiful lady who becomes his queen."

"The sooner you start, I guess the sooner you'll quit—if I don't go to sleep in your lap first."

She ignored his cynical comment and began to read aloud. Sassy was a good reader and in moments, it seemed as if she were in the midst of ancient England. Hunter was a bold knight and she the fair Guinevere.

Once in awhile as she read, she glanced down. Hunter had begun by looking bored. Gradually he seemed to hang on every word. Finally Sassy was too tired to read any further. She paused and closed the book.

Hunter said, "Why did you stop? That's not all the story, is it?"

Sassy shook her head and laid the book aside as she cleared her throat. "I'm tired and my voice has given out."

"But I want to know what happens," he protested.

"Tomorrow you can finish the story yourself."

"Tomorrow I'll be out on a timber lease," Hunter said. "I won't have time to read."

"Well," Sassy yawned, "I suppose I could continue tomorrow night."

"I hope you're not tired," Hunter whispered. "I've got an idea about what to do with the rest of the evening." He pulled her face down to his and kissed her.

She started to protest that, yes, she was tired, but his tongue slipped between her lips and his hand reached up to massage her breasts. His mouth tasted hot. Even as her nipple swelled against his hand, she couldn't stop herself from pressing against his fingers.

He looked up at her, his eyes intense and bright blue in his dark face. "I want you, Sassy, want you bad."

A slow fire spread from her breasts, down her belly to the vee between her thighs. She closed her eyes, overcome by the feelings aroused when his hand stroked her breasts.

He stood up suddenly, swung her into his arms, and carried her down the hall to their bedroom. The full moon shone through the window, illuminating the scene. He laid her on the bed, then began to undress in the moonlight while she watched. His manhood was large, engorged and hard, erect and ready.

She started to sit up, to undress herself, but he caught her hands. "No, give me the pleasure."

Very slowly he undressed her, making an erotic ceremony of it. He caressed and kissed her skin as he unbuttoned or pulled off each item. Her pulse pounded in her ears by the time she finally lay naked on the velvet spread. He knelt between her thighs. "Tonight, Sassy, I'm going to teach you to want me, not just lie there like a proper lady, waiting to be used."

"I thought that's what ladies were supposed to do," she said in a small voice.

"It is," Hunter answered, as he leaned over her

breasts. "But I think I want my lady to learn to want me as much as I want her."

"What—whatever you say; I'll try."

He kissed her, his lips brushing ever so gently across hers. She returned his kiss, her tongue touching his lips shyly at first, then bolder until his mouth opened and she explored farther, tasting the hot sweetness as he sucked her tongue deep in his throat.

She lay gasping with excitement as now his lips moved across her ear, her throat. "Sassy . . . my Sassy . . ."

His breath felt like silk on her skin and his hands stroked her hair and then her body. She trembled with anticipation as his fingers ran down her belly to her thighs. He touched her femininity and she gasped aloud and couldn't stop herself from moaning.

"Do you want me, Sassy Lady? Say it. . . . say it."

"I—I can't." She felt sudden shyness at his demand.

"Maybe you're too much of a lady," he whispered.

"I—I thought that's what you wanted." Nothing mattered but the way his fingers stroked her.

"I want you to surrender to me body and soul. I want more than your body, Sassy Sweet; I want all of you, want to dominate you, own your very being. Surrender to me."

These were new feelings for her. In an ironic way, she was a virgin. Always before, men had used her, and she had feigned passion because it pleased her customers. The emotions Hunter evoked in her were real, so very real.

Hunter rolled over on his back, pulled her on top of him. "I can go deeper, Sassy Girl, if you'll let me; let me go to your very core."

She hesitated, feeling his maleness big as a stallion's between them. She was surprised to realize she wanted to mesh with him, take him as deep as he could go. Very slowly she raised up and slid down on his manhood.

"Easy, baby," he whispered. "I don't want to hurt you."

"Hurt me," she demanded. "Hurt me good!" She felt him thrusting deep within her.

Hunter groaned aloud, reached up and caught her breasts with his hands, pulled them down to his greedy lips. "Ride me, Sassy," he begged against her nipple. "Ride your stallion; ride him hard!"

His powerful hands spanned her small waist now, slamming her up and down with his sheer physical strength. She whimpered at the feel of him penetrating her.

"That's it, Sassy Girl," he urged. "Come with me; come with me."

She needed no further urging. She rode him hard while his hands held her waist, grinding her down on him until her inner being was filled by his maleness. She wanted his seed deep within her; she ached to be bred, to have her belly swell with his child. She yearned to nourish him with rich milk from her breasts.

Her hair had come loose from its pins and fallen down over both their naked, writhing bodies in a curtain of silky flame. She felt him throbbing within her.

"Come, Sassy Baby," he whispered, "just a little more. I want to take you with me. Come."

She didn't even know what he was talking about. Still a sheen of perspiration began to break out over her naked body as she rode him wildly. Her heart pounded madly. Why hadn't he already finished? She had never had a man take so long. Most barely took one stroke and were through, but Hunter seemed to hold on, hard as a steel rail while she worked herself into a frenzy with his touch and his penetration.

He arched his back, thrusting still deeper within her. "Not until you come with me, Sassy. Not until you come."

She was intent only on stopping this deep inner ache that his rod and his touch and his mouth were building in her. He ground her down on him one more time. Then he gasped as he began to give up his seed deep inside her. She felt the hot rush into her womb, and then she remembered nothing else because her own body convulsed, squeezing him, wanting every drop he could give her. It was the most wondrous, fearsome emotion, like being sucked down a dark, unknown whirlpool. She didn't care where they went as long as they went together. She clung to him as they were swept away. "Hunter, darling, oh, Hunter!"

When she finally came to, she lay in his arms and wept while he kissed her face and eyes. "Sassy, Sweet Sassy. Did I hurt you?"

"No, I—I don't know what's the matter. I've never experienced anything like that before."

"Of course you haven't, my innocent little bride." He cuddled her in the hollow of his shoulder. "It's all right, Sassy Girl," he crooned as he kissed her. "I—I didn't know it could be like that, either." He sounded thunderstruck. "I didn't know what I'd been missing with what I was paying to get from—never mind, you wouldn't know anything about that anyway."

Whores. He was talking about whores. Sassy was certain she had never given any customer an experience like this; not for any amount of money. Nor had she ever experienced something like this emotion that had swept over her, not even with Brett when she had thought herself madly in love with him. Could this emotion be love? She didn't even want to think about it. Holy Saint Patrick, she couldn't imagine anything better.

Sleepy, she yawned. She could put all her worries behind her now like a nightmare from which she had finally awakened. She had everything: wealth, social position, and a man who adored her and had made her his legal wife. No one knew her past and no one ever would. Brett James and his madam, Marylou Evans, were thousands of miles away, and they thought Sassy was dead. She was safe, safe in Hunter's strong arms, where she drifted off to sleep.

The next to the last thing she remembered was her husband reaching to pull the sheets over them both without moving her out of the hollow of his shoulder. The last thing she remembered was his gentle kiss brushing across her forehead. "Missy, you're more than I ever dared hope for."

And he was more than she had ever dared hope for, Sassy thought as she burrowed deeper into his arms, resting her face against his brawny chest. She knew now that she was in love with Hunter, hopelessly in love with her new husband. In spite of all the pitfalls and mistakes she had made, God intended to give her a second chance. For the first time in years, Sassy slept a peaceful, dreamless sleep.

* * *

A sound awakened her. She blinked and listened.

Hunter sat bolt upright in bed. "What the hell—?"

She came up on one elbow, listening. It sounded like many people laughing and singing. "You don't suppose—"

Sassy hopped out of bed, ran to look out the window into the moonlit night. Wagon-loads of people came down the twisting road toward the house; others rode horseback. Many of them looked drunk. The noise of their laughter and singing cut through the still night.

"Oh, I plain forgot!" She put her hand to her mouth and whirled to face Hunter. "The shivaree! I forgot!"

"The what?" He was out of bed, grabbing for his pants.

Sassy reached for her clothes. "Remember the judge mentioned a shivaree and Swede said the whole town might turn out tonight if it stopped raining?"

"Oh, great!" Hunter grumbled, running one hand through his rumpled, curly hair. "So now we've got to get up and serve drinks and food all night to a bunch of drunks!"

"Don't be a spoilsport!" Sassy hurried to her dressing room, grabbed a hair brush and a ribbon. She called back over her shoulder. "You must be well-thought-of or they wouldn't bother."

She felt giddy and lighthearted. Hunter loved her; her secret was safe, and the future looked promising. A few drop-in well-wishers didn't seem like a problem.

From out front, she heard the wagons creak to a halt and the off-key strains of "For He's a Jolly Good Fellow" reverberated.

221

Hunter had lit a lamp when she returned to the bedroom, her hair at least pulled out of her face. "It could be worse," Sassy laughed. "They could have caught us earlier as we were making love—"

"For that, I would have killed someone." Hunter slipped his arm around her. "I hope Cookie has something to feed them."

"Aye, he was baking cakes and roasting extra meat, just in case; then I promptly forgot about it."

Hunter peered out the window. "Well, I see Swede is leading them. I ought to wring his neck! Looks like he's even brought all the girls from the . . . never mind."

She pretended she didn't know what he was referring to as she kissed his cheek. "I can hear John banging around in the kitchen, so he's awake and got things moving. We'd better go see what else we can do to help."

Hunter picked up the lamp and they started down the hallway arm in arm. "Maybe they'll only stay a few minutes, have a drink, and leave."

From outside, came the strains of ". . . de camptown ladies sing dis song, doodah . . . doodah."

Sassy smiled in spite of herself. "I wouldn't count on it. Sounds like they're in the kind of mood to sing all night and stay for breakfast."

He paused in the hall, faced her. "Happy, Sassy?"

"I'm happy, Hunter, Darling, happier than I ever dreamed I could be."

"I like to hear you call me that." His free hand cupped her small chin.

"What?"

"Darling."

What she wanted to hear him say was "I love you,"

but she didn't ask. It wasn't the same if you had to ask. She wasn't a wife; she was a trophy, a possession.

He bent his head and kissed her. "I'm glad I've got you, Sassy Girl. I'm proud to show you off as my wife."

It wasn't "I love you," but it would do for now. "I love you, Hunter, Darling. From this day forward, there'll be nothing but happiness in our future."

Heavy banging on the front door interrupted them. "Let us in!" A dozen drunken voices shouted, "We've come for the party! Let us in!"

Bang! Bang! Bang!

Hunter swore under his breath, but he smiled. "I suppose we have to open it or they'll tear it down."

"You open the door and try to delay them while I help John get some food on the table."

"I don't think they want food; they want drinks!" Hunter flung over his shoulder as he set the lamp on a table, headed for the door.

The old cook already had most of the lamps lit, including the big dining room chandelier, and was supervising two stablehands. "Miss Sassy, I got half-a-dozen cakes out and I'm slicing roast beef now. It'll be okay, as long as the liquor holds out."

"Fine, John." She looked around, assessing what was needed as she heard the crowd coming through the front door, still singing. She meant to take her role as the wife of a prominent resident seriously. Hunter's future position in this area might depend on how his lady conducted herself. "Do make a big pot of coffee, John; strong coffee. I think some of them need it."

John paused, shook his head. "Like Swede, they don't want coffee; they want whiskey, but I'll make it anyhow." He disappeared into the kitchen.

The table looked good, Sassy thought critically. It was covered with every type of food. At least Swede must have reminded the cook that the crowd was definitely coming. She wished again that she owned a silver tea service. The belles would be so impressed. However, something like that couldn't be bought in Seattle.

Abruptly, a crowd surrounded her—a slightly drunk, good-humored crowd of loggers, girls from the ship, shopkeepers, a couple of girls in gaudy dresses and painted faces. So even the local whores have turned out, Sassy thought as she greeted one and all warmly and accepted congratulations and good wishes.

Gertrude came to her, smiling. "Sassy, guess what? Will's asked me to marry him and he loves kids."

"Oh, Gertrude, I'm so glad for you both." She hugged her. "I hope you two will be as happy as Hunter and I are."

Gertrude pushed up her spectacles and peered into her face. "Are you really happy, Sassy? Mildred said he had almost kidnapped you from the street."

Sassy winked. "Hunter is a very impulsive fellow. I'm happy, Gertrude, happier than I ever thought possible." It was true, she realized with wonder; misery was behind her.

"What can I do to help?" Gertrude asked. "The table looks lovely."

"Did Ellie come?"

She nodded. "I had to beg her, but she's here somewhere. Little Timmy's asleep back at the hotel; the maids said they'd check on him."

"Please go find Ellie; she's great help and the cook could probably use her."

Gertrude left, moving through the crowd, glad that

MORE PASSION AND ADVENTURE AWAIT... YOUR TRIP TO A BIG ADVENTUROUS WORLD BEGINS WHEN YOU ACCEPT YOUR FIRST 4 NOVELS ABSOLUTELY *FREE* (AN $18.00 VALUE)

GET
FOUR
FREE
BOOKS
(AN $18.00 VALUE)

ZEBRA HOME SUBSCRIPTION
SERVICE, INC.
120 BRIGHTON ROAD
P.O. BOX 5214
CLIFTON, NEW JERSEY 07015-5214

Sassy was happy. She hoped she got a happy ending, too. None of her friends knew Gertrude's secret. She had never been married, although she and Tim had planned to wed. They had given way to passion once when he got sudden orders for the front. Her beloved Tim was dead within days, never knowing about his son. Tim had no family and hers had thrown her out for disgracing them. After struggling to support little Timmy as best she could, Gertrude had signed up for the mail-order brides, hoping to make a fresh start. Would she tell the man she married? Maybe, if she felt she could trust him to love her anyway.

Gertrude located Ellie in the front hall, brought her back to the dining room and Sassy.

Ellie looked around, her eyes wide. "This is the most beautiful house I've ever seen; I'd love to work here."

Sassy hugged her. "I could certainly use some help. Gertrude, if you don't mind, you stand here at the end of the table and serve. Ellie, our cook needs some help."

John limped in from the kitchen just then, carrying a big tray of sandwiches.

"John," Sassy said, "these are my friends from the boat, Gertrude and Ellie."

He smiled as he set the tray on the table. "All the beauties of the East must have come here at the same time."

Ellie smiled and ducked her head. "And all the hand-some, smooth-talking gentlemen seem to be in Washington. I don't remember seeing you at the dock or the social."

The man blushed. "Wouldn't have been any point; I figure the most attractive ladies like you were already spoken for."

225

Ellie paused, tongue-tied.

Sassy said, "John, Ellie's real choosey, just like you. Maybe if you'd find her an apron—"

"Oh, I'd love to help." Ellie forgot her self-consciousness and began bustling about. "I could get the trays ready."

"I'd be delighted for some advice," the cook said. "Come on in the kitchen, Miss Ellie, and tell me what you think we should do about serving the cakes."

The pair disappeared into the kitchen and Sassy grinned and winked at Gertrude. "Have you ever seen such a quick, mutual attraction?"

"Not since I met Will," Gertrude said and smiled.

From the library floated the off-key strains of someone banging out "Oh! Susanna, oh, don't you cry for me! I come from Alabama with my banjo on my knee."

Sassy gestured. "I'd better go greet the rest of the guests and protect my poor piano! Hunter must be in the library with Swede, Judge Stone, and his wife."

"Mildred's in there, too," Gertrude said. "She's found herself a middle-aged storekeeper."

"Why, then we've all found someone. Aren't we lucky?" Sassy left the dining room and elbowed her way through the crowd toward the library. Everyone along the way wanted to shake her hand or wish her the best. She couldn't remember when she had been so happy. Now her friends seemed to be finding love and happiness, too. She paused and spoke to Will. "I hear you've asked Gertrude to marry."

The logger blushed. "I know I ain't near good enough for someone as sweet and pretty as her, but I'll do the best I can. And little Timmy is the son I always wanted."

"You'll make a wonderful pair." Sassy patted his shoulder, realizing he was sincere. Maybe everyone on that ship was going to have a happy ending, just like in the fairy tales. Sassy was glad. Since she was so in love herself, she wanted everyone else in the world to be. She maneuvered through the people.

The library was crowded, too. A plump woman dressed in purple stood with her back to Sassy near the piano, talking to several men. When she gestured, the blonde's fat hands moved and the light reflected off the many rings on her fingers. Something stirred in Sassy's memory. What was it?

She looked around for Hunter. He stood talking to Swede a few feet away, and the burly logger looked more than a little drunk. "Hell, Swede," she heard him say, "did you have to bring the girls? What will my wife think when she gets a look at Lulu?"

"Someone talkin' to me?" The fat woman drawled as she whirled around.

Sassy grabbed onto a chair to keep from collapsing as she stared at the woman, blinked, looked again.

It had to be a nightmare, Sassy thought, struggling to keep her expression as frozen as her heart. Any moment now, she would wake up in Hunter's arms, beloved and secure, her past behind her, her secret safe. The plump woman looked into Sassy's eyes and started in surprise, then smiled.

There was no mistake. It was Marylou Evans.

227

Chapter Thirteen

Oh, my God. . . . Sassy stared into Marylou's eyes. Only a moment ticked past; but, to Sassy, it was eternity. No one around them seemed to notice. The singing and merrymaking continued loud and unabated. Past Marylou's shoulder, she saw Hunter visiting with Mrs. Stone and the judge. The piano rang out loud and off-key as a quartet of drunks sang, "Oh, don't you cry for me, I come from Alabama with my banjo on my knee."

Marylou moved first. To Sassy, she drawled, "Mrs. Hunter, I hope you don't mind the town shivareeing you. It's an old custom in some parts." Her pale eyes bore into Sassy's brown ones.

"How—how nice of the town to turn out." Sassy managed to regain her composure, at least on the surface.

"Not at all. Your husband is influential hereabouts." Her tone dripped like slow southern molasses but her expression mocked Sassy.

What to do? Any moment now, surely Marylou would announce to the world that the girl known as Mrs. James Hunter was in reality one of Marylou's former whores. She waited, hardly daring to breathe, dreading to see the look on Hunter's face, the shocked sneers of the crowd. Instead, Marylou brushed a crumb off her full purple bodice. Her lips barely moved. "Be in town tomorrow."

Sassy whispered. "Yes."

"I'll watch for you."

"Your place?"

"No, I'll find you." Marylou blended into the rowdy crowd as some of the loggers pushed forward to greet Sassy and wish her well.

Glancing around, Sassy realized that no one had seen the brief exchange.

Would the evening never end? She needed time to think, to decide what to do. Sassy pasted a smile on her face as she greeted people, seeing that everyone got a drink or another slice of cake. Inside, she was crying at the cruelty of Fate. Holy Mary, how ironic that just when she thought she was safe, one of the only two people in the world who knew her secret should turn up in her own house! Occasionally she glanced toward the fat madam, her rings catching the light as the woman gestured. Sassy's future lay in those plump hands.

Hunter strode over, slipped his arm around her. "Having a good time?"

"Of course." She forced herself to laugh to keep from sobbing. She would not break down just because her world was in pieces. In only a few hours, she had married, fallen madly in love with her new husband, and made plans for a lifetime of happiness. Now all that was about to be destroyed. Sassy loved Hunter too much to lose him and lose him she would if he should find out about her past. She would do anything to prevent that; but could she?

He hugged her to him as another grizzled old logger came up to shake hands, comment on the beauty of the bride, and wish them well.

Sassy felt like a puppet, automatically smiling, nodding as crowds thronged around the couple. Tomorrow she would get some answers, but that was hours away. *No matter how far and how fast you run, you never escape from your past,* Sassy thought. *It is part of you forever, so you need to do life right the first time.* She had lied; she had schemed; she had done all the wrong things, maybe, trying to straighten out her life, make a fresh start. *God is not mocked.* She was going to have to pay for her sins and in the very worst way—not with her life, but with the love of the man who in a few short hours had become the center of her universe. She would not, could not give Hunter up. Yet that seemed to be the price she was going to be forced to pay.

Finally, the noise died down as people tired and sobered. Even Swede yawned and pulled out his watch. The judge and his wife suggested loudly that it was time to load up and leave the newlyweds in peace which led to some sly winks and smiles. Sassy felt herself blush at the innuendoes. Of course then she and Hunter felt obliged to urge everyone to stay for one more drink and most of them did. Gertrude and Will had eyes only for each other, and Ellie kept stealing pleased, embarrassed glances at the cook, who smiled back. At least some people were happy, Sassy thought, but then they surely didn't have personal secrets to hide as she did.

At last Sassy stood with Hunter at the front door as the crowd straggled out. She drew a sigh of relief when the wagons creaked away and Hunter closed the door, leaned against it. He took a deep breath. "Whew! I didn't think they would every leave!"

Sassy laughed as she looked up at him, her mind busy with her problem. "Oh, they were just having a good time."

"Some of that crowd aren't the kind a lady would normally have in for a social." He slipped his arm around her shoulders.

"Oh?" She kept her eyes big and innocent.

He kissed the tip of her nose. "I forget you're too naive to know what I'm talking about."

She felt too guilty to even look at him. She was weary of lying. Her conscience ached to tell him the truth and be done with it, but she was in a trap of her own making. *So this is what hell is like,* she thought. *Not fire and brimstone like they tell you, but something a thousand times worse; living in fear that someone you love will finally discover your secret.*

"Missy, you're awfully quiet; what are you thinking?"

"About what a wreck this place is and how much cleaning it will take." She looked around at the empty glasses and the clutter.

He smiled. "And I thought it might be something *really* important. Worry about it tomorrow; let's go to bed."

"I'll need some cleaning supplies," Sassy said as they walked away from the door arm in arm. "I need more polish."

He shrugged as they paused in the dining room and looked at the table littered with crumbs. "You want to give a list to Cookie?"

"Why don't I go into town myself? I'm not sure what

all I'll need, and I want to talk to Ellie about working part-time out here."

"Fine. However, I have to go out to the timber tomorrow; I figure Swede will have such a headache that he won't feel like talking, much less working."

Sassy drew a breath of relief. Hunter wouldn't insist on going with her. She wanted to be able to confront Marylou alone. John limped into the dining room just then and picked up a stack of plates. The old man looked tired. Even Kitty had curled up under the sideboard sound asleep.

"Just leave it all, John," she said. "It's been a long night and you can clean up tomorrow. Thank you for doing such a good job."

He nodded. "Thank you, Missus. I sure did like your friend; she's a fine figure of a woman."

Hunter looked from one to the other. "Gertrude?"

The cook reddened. "No, the mature one; sweet-natured and got a little meat on her bones. I like a woman with a healthy appetite; she'll appreciate my cooking."

As he started to leave the room, Hunter said, "Oh, Cookie, by the way, the Missus wants to go into town tomorrow. Take the buggy and drive her."

Sassy shook her head, struggling to keep the alarm out of her voice. "There's no need of that. I'm perfectly capable of driving a buggy."

"Don't be silly. You've never driven a buggy, have you?" Hunter frowned.

She had to admit she hadn't.

"Besides, no lady would travel that road unescorted and you'll need him to help you with the packages."

"But he's so busy, and I think I can drive—"

232

"Sassy, there's no telling what kind of trouble you might run into along the way or what kind of trail trash might turn up who don't know a real lady from a tart." Hunter's voice was firm, "Now if you want to wait a day or two, I'll drive you myself—"

"I—I really need those supplies," Sassy interrupted. "I guess John can drive me." She dared not argue too much. Hunter would wonder why she wanted to go alone. Maybe she could send the cook on an errand in Seattle.

Hunter yawned. "All right, Cookie, after breakfast, you're to drive the missus."

The old man nodded and grinned, extinguishing the oil lamps. Hunter put his arm around Sassy's shoulders and they went down the hall to the bedroom. "We can still get a couple of hours of sleep," Hunter said as he undressed and got in bed.

However, Sassy didn't sleep. She lay in the hollow of his shoulder listening to him breathe and staring at the ceiling. She had never known such torment as she knew now. Hunter was a proud man who couldn't bear to have other men belittle him, laugh at him, humiliate him. She could only imagine his fury and his hurt when he discovered he'd been made a fool of.

Why was that? What secrets did this moody man hide behind his cold blue eyes? Would she ever know? Perhaps he had been a loner too long to ever trust another person with his innermost hurts and dreams. This passionate, savage man might also be capable of violence.

That didn't frighten her; what frightened her was hurting him, losing him. She lay her face against his warm chest, listening to his heart beat as the moments ticked

233

past. *Let love and friendship reign.* She touched her wedding ring in the darkness. She loved this man more than life itself and if she lost him, she didn't want to live. Yet, she couldn't count on his devotion outweighing his pride. Maybe it was only just. She had worked as a whore, stolen another woman's identity, pretended to be something she was not. Sassy tried to pray, attempted to make bargains with God, but the words wouldn't come. Whatever happened, she must protect Hunter. What to do?

The new day dawned slowly, spreading pale gray light through the window. She got up, put on a blue velvet robe, and went into her dressing room to splash cold water on her eyes. The woman who stared back at her from the mirror appeared to be carrying the weight of the world on her shoulders.

At breakfast, Hunter seemed unusually cheerful as he ate his steak and eggs. "Sassy, you've hardly said a word. You aren't coming down sick, are you?"

She forced herself to smile. "Bless the saints, no. I'm just tired from last night; that's all."

He grinned at her with evident approval. "You made a wonderful impression. I'm proud of you, Sassy. You were a great hostess."

"I tried hard, Hunter." She played with her napkin. "I want you to be proud of me."

"I am proud of you. You remind me of that queen in that story; what was her name?"

"Guinevere?" She raised her eyebrows.

"Yes, you remind me of her. Maybe we can continue that story tonight."

"If you wish." Her mouth felt so dry she could hardly swallow. "Hunter, I—I'm not perfect. Even Guinevere had her faults."

"Not my Sassy." He stood up. "All I hoped to get was a lady; I didn't expect to find such a jewel of a wife." His eyes mirrored his caring.

She became flustered, whether because his admission was so heartfelt and sincere or because she felt so guilty, she wasn't sure herself. "I—It isn't like you to talk like that, so tender and vulnerable."

"I trust you, Sassy, and somehow, I know you won't let me down or take advantage of the way I feel about you."

"Oh, Hunter, I love you so!" Her vision seemed suddenly blinded as she stood up, went into his arms.

He hugged her to him. "Hey, what's this? Tears?" He kissed them away. "Maybe you're too tired to go into town today; maybe you should wait or send Cookie."

She managed to gain control of herself, shook her head, and kissed him. "Aye, I'm tired, but I need to get supplies and I'd like to pick them out myself." She was terrified that if she didn't go into Seattle and meet Marylou, the woman would come out to the house or, worse yet, track down Hunter and tell him what she knew.

He turned toward the door. "I'll see you for supper. Have a good day, sweet."

"Have a good day . . . darling."

"On second thought," he paused in the doorway and favored her with a devilish grin, "I suppose I could delay my departure for a few minutes if you'd like to go back to bed."

She made a shooing motion. "Oh, go along with you! We've both got things to do and that can wait till tonight."

"Spoken like a wife of fifty years." He laughed and reached for his hat.

Fifty years. Right now she would give thanks to know that he might want her fifty weeks or even fifty days from now. She watched him leave, then went to get dressed for her trip to town. Once she would have reveled in the wardrobes of expensive clothes she had to choose from along with all the matching shoes, hats, parasols, and jewelry. Now none of that mattered. Absently, she chose a blue silk dress and fine kid-leather pumps. Her underthings were of the softest silk and trimmed with imported lace. She put her hair up in a chignon with pearl combs.

It was late morning before John helped her up into the back seat of the buggy. For once, she was glad that the old man seemed preoccupied, because she didn't feel like making small talk. They drove into town at a leisurely pace. The countryside was beautiful and wooded; the scent of sun-warmed flowers and the tangy scent of Puget Sound touched her senses. Any other time, she would have enjoyed it, but now she was too immersed in her problems.

John drove down the steep street and stopped to assist Sassy from the buggy in front of the general store. "I got a list of my own for the house and some of the help, Ma'am. I need to drive down to the mill and the stable."

Sassy nodded, watched him drive off. She squinted, gazing up and down the street, wondering if Marylou were looking for her. Where was she expected to wait? Was she being watched even as she stood here? Not knowing what else to do, she took her list from her reticule. The bell tinkled over the door of the general store as Sassy entered and closed it behind her. A dozen scents assailed her: coffee and spices, leather, and new dry goods.

A bent, thin man came out of the back room, wiping his hands on his apron. "Mornin', Mrs. Hunter. Sure enjoyed the shivaree last night."

"Yes, it was fun, wasn't it?" She held out her list. "My husband said to put anything I need on his bill. I hope you have most of these supplies."

"Yes, Ma'am." He rubbed his hands together as if in anticipation of money. "I do hope you don't hold it agin me about not givin' you a job, Ma'am. Hunter made it clear I wasn't to hire you, said he didn't want his lady workin' as a clerk——"

"That's quite all right, Mr. Johnson." She cut him short. "I understand."

He looked a bit shamefaced. "Your husband is a very important man, Mrs. Hunter, even if he is a half-breed. Not many in these parts would cross him."

Would they delight in seeing him humiliated and shamed because of her? She would do anything in her power to prevent that.

Old Mr. Johnson peered at the list. "Some of this I'll have to dig out of stock in the back room, ma'am, if you'd care to maybe go over to the hotel and have a cup of coffee while you wait."

Where would Marylou try to contact her? She didn't want to be seen with the madam in the hotel dining room where all the still-unclaimed brides would soon be having lunch. "I'll just look around while I wait, Mr. Johnson; perhaps I'll see something else on your shelves that I need."

"Yes, Ma'am." The prospect of a bigger sale delighted him.

The bell tinkled behind her, but Sassy didn't turn around. The shopkeeper peered past her shoulder and his tone changed from one of respect to a sneer. "Be with you in a minute, Lulu. Got to take care of Mrs. Hunter first."

That molasses-slow drawl. "That's quite all right, Bill. *Ladies* always get first attention; I know that."

Sassy glanced out of the corner of her eye as Marylou paused by the door, closed it, sauntered down the aisle, stopped to look at something in a glass showcase.

The storekeeper shuffled off to the back room. The only sound was the creak of the floorboards under Marylou's hefty frame and the clop-clop of horses passing outside. Somewhere, a man whistled for a dog.

Sassy drifted casually down the aisle, paused to finger a strand of blue ribbon on a shelf near the glass case. "Is there some place we can go?" she whispered.

Marylou peered into the case and shook her head ever so slightly. "What safer place than this?"

Sassy thought a minute. Of course she couldn't be seen anywhere with Marylou; people might talk, but she hadn't planned on negotiating with her in the middle of a general store with the owner liable to walk back in any time. "What is it you want?"

"Me?" Her jewels flashed as she touched her chest with mock surprise. "Why, Sassy, you hurt my feelings! And we were such good friends, too. Hunter know about you?"

Sassy moved to look in the same showcase. There was a dainty gold bracelet there that any other time she would have hungered for. "Of course he knows, so there's nothing you can tell him."

Marylou smirked and her heavy white face powder

238

accentuated the lines around her eyes. "Liar! You wouldn't have come if you weren't afraid. Many are jealous of his power and money. Some would like to see him taken down a notch."

Sassy glared at her. "I'll do anything to protect him!"

The woman studied her. "You really do care about that half-breed bastard, don't you?"

"Don't call him that!"

"How ironic. I'll bet you don't know that Brett—"

"Spare me your chatter. What is it you want?"

"I want to make a deal," Marylou whispered and held up a dress as if trying to make a decision. "You keep quiet about my being wanted for murder and I'll keep your secret."

Could she trust her? Sassy fingered a spool of yellow ribbon.

"We both keep our secrets," the madam urged. "Texans would call it a Mexican standoff."

"Aye, it's agreed then." Sassy heard the creak of a buggy as John pulled up in front of the dirty shop window.

Marylou looked in that direction. "Here comes old Cookie, but I reckon we've reached an agreement."

Sassy nodded. "Where's Brett?"

"I ain't heard from him." Her heavily powdered face wrinkled as she frowned.

"Of all the places in the world to end up, I wouldn't have come to Seattle if I'd known you were here," Sassy said through gritted teeth.

The woman shrugged. "Kid, it's a small world; few places to hide nowadays. It's more ironic than you know."

"What do you mean by that?" Sassy glanced around to make sure the clerk hadn't come back yet.

"Nothing. I just know more secrets than you do. Funny, I would have thought you'd recognize the handwriting."

Sassy was thrown off-guard. "What?"

"Never mind." Marylou laughed and looked Sassy over. "Your life might not be worth a Confederate dollar if he knew about you."

"Or yours, if you told him." Sassy countered.

She smiled and studied her rings. "They do say kings used to kill messengers who brought bad news. So we both keep our mouths shut, and—"

Sassy heard Mister Johnson reentering.

"Just wanted to thank you again, Mrs. Hunter, for being so kind and democratic to all of us last night," Marylou drawled in a loud voice.

"My husband would expect nothing less from me," Sassy answered as she went back up the aisle toward the clerk.

Behind her, Marylou said, "Bill, I can't seem to make a decision on a dress. I'll come back later."

He nodded and Sassy heard the bell tinkle behind her. She managed to keep her relief under control. "Did you find everything on the list, Mr. Johnson?"

"Most everything." He hesitated, thumbs hooked in his apron straps. "Mrs. Hunter, I ain't one to meddle in other folks' business."

I'll bet you aren't, Sassy thought, but she kept her face immobile. "Yes?"

"You bein' new in town and being a sheltered Eastern lady, Ma'am, you might not know . . ."

"Might not know what?" Sassy gave him her most innocent, big-eyed stare.

He fumbled with his apron. ."That woman; well, you'd be shocked to know what she is." Condescending scorn etched his voice and thin face.

"Why, Mr. Johnson, I have no idea that you're talking about; perhaps you'll tell me?" Sassy looked up at him, feeling a bit ornery at his self-righteous airs. No doubt Bill Johnson was one of those who patronized Marylou's place on Saturday nights and prayed for her soul on Sunday.

His wrinkled face turned a mottled red and he ran his finger around his collar as if it were choking him. "Well, Lulu and her girls . . . that is, she runs a place . . ." He paused. "She just ain't a proper person for a lady like you to be talkin' to; everyone thinks you was real kind not to ask her and her girls to leave last night."

"I really don't know what you're hinting at, Mr. Johnson, but I'm sure a fine, Christian gentleman like you doesn't engage in gossip."

"Your husband wouldn't want you to be seen talking to Lulu," Johnson blurted out, "and he'd give her hell for even saying good morning to his wife."

The bell tinkled again and they both turned. The old cook limped in. "Miss Sassy, you ready?"

"Almost, John." She spoke to the shopkeeper. "You did remember the fancy salmon for Kitty?"

"Yes," Johnson grumbled and glared toward the man at the door. "Seems to me like Hunter spoils that old cat and the cook, too."

"Why, Mr. Johnson, I don't remember that he asked you, but I'll pass on your opinion to my husband," she said it a little too sweetly.

"Oh, Mrs. Hunter, please don't," he groveled. "He'd have my hide. I—I'll finish your order." He disappeared into the back room.

Sassy motioned to the man to enter. "Cookie, is there anything you'd like besides more vanilla?"

The old man hesitated a long moment. "I—on second thought, Miss Sassy, I don't think we need vanilla."

"Oh? Is there anything you want personally, John? You worked so hard last night."

He stared longingly into a showcase that featured a red silk cravat. "I was just doin' my job, Ma'am."

She made her decision from the look on his face. The clerk came out of the back room with more packages. "Mr. Johnson, see that this red tie goes on Hunter's bill."

"Yes, ma'am, but maybe you should ask your husband first—"

"Wrap it," she snapped.

"Yes, Mrs. Hunter." He hurried to do her bidding.

She turned to the cook. "John, after Mr. Johnson loads the things in the buggy, go call on my friend Ellie and see if she'd come out and help clean up after the party."

John grinned from ear to ear. "Yes, ma'am."

Her mind was already back on her problems. "I've got to go to the bank; I'll join you two at the buggy soon."

She turned and swept out of the store, listening to the bell tinkle faintly behind her.

She was surprised to discover her hands were shaking from the encounter with Marylou Evans. At least maybe for the time being, she didn't have to worry about Marylou telling Hunter. Would the woman contact Brett? Brett thought Sassy was dead and buried. *Hand-*

writing. How could Marylou know about that letter Sassy had written if she hadn't heard from Brett?

The bank. Sassy went down the wooden sidewalk, lifting her skirt to keep it out of the mud. The men she passed doffed their hats respectfully. "Morning, Mrs. Hunter. Nice party to your house last night."

She nodded to each and continued on her way. It felt good to be treated with respect. However, if Marylou told the secret, men would soon be leering and propositioning Sassy. Hunter would hear rumors. . . . She didn't even want to think about that.

No matter what, she needed to get some money to her family. She had given Papa a small sum when she last saw him, but by now, with the hard times and the way the Irish were being discriminated against, Mike and the children could use more help.

The banker rushed to her side as she entered. "Morning, Mrs. Hunter. Everyone's talking about the shivaree." His hair had been slicked down with Macassar oil until it gleamed like wet black paint.

"I'm glad you enjoyed yourself," Sassy said. "I need to send a small amount of money every month."

"Being as how your husband is one of our biggest depositors, I'll be pleased to oversee that, Dear Lady."

Sassy named a sum and an address. "I'd like this sent every month to a Mr. Mike Malone."

His eyes mirrored curiosity.

"A carpenter who's been injured and is unable to work," Sassy explained. "And he has children."

"Ah, of course; an old family employee." When he nodded, his slick black hair gleamed in the light. "I think that's most commendable of you, Mrs. Hunter, to take on that responsibility."

"I could hardly do less," Sassy said. "My husband said I could draw on his account."

"Of course!" He wrote busily in his ledger books. "Why, anything your husband wants, I'll be happy to oblige. We're delighted to have you in our bank, Ma'am."

In minutes, Sassy had the details worked out and left the bank. It would be almost impossible to hide the withdrawals, no matter how small they were. What would she tell Hunter? She was so very, very weary of lying. How she longed to face Hunter, tell him the whole truth, have him embrace her and say, "I love you, Sassy, nothing else matters." But of course she couldn't tell him. Not many husbands were friends as well as lovers. But no man could be expected to be understanding and supportive about finding out his wife used to be a whore.

The day had turned muggy. She walked back to the buggy where John was loading up the last box. He climbed down to assist her into the buggy next to her friend Ellie. The plump widow seemed so delighted to be there she was actually talking without being prodded.

Sassy said, "I—I'm developing a headache, Ellie. Why don't you sit up next to John and visit?"

Having made the two of them happy, Sassy sighed with relief. She didn't have to make small talk any longer and could think about Marylou Evans. She opened her parasol to keep the sun off her freckled face and relaxed in the back seat. Lost in thought, she only half-heard the old man cluck to the horse as the buggy pulled away.

* * *

244

Lulu watched Sassy from behind the lace curtains of her parlor as the girl got into the buggy and drove off. Of course she couldn't blackmail that snippy little bitch because Sassy might just contact the authorities back in New York and the murdered man had been rich and important. Everyone thought it had been self-defense, but Sassy had overheard and seen the whole thing, so the girl knew better.

"Wonder where Brett is?" Lulu asked herself aloud as the buggy disappeared down the road. He was slick and clever. Had he fled New York by now, one jump ahead of the law? He had connections in many cities, including New Orleans and San Francisco.

Lulu went over to her desk. The chair protested her weight as she sat down. She picked up her pen. How much did Sassy really know about the letter? Not that it made any difference. Should Lulu write or wire Brett and let him know where Sassy was? She'd have to find him first. Lulu missed him terribly. This might be a way to lure him back to her arms. Or maybe not.

There was a plate of cookies on her desk. She ate two while she fiddled with the pen. Killing that customer had been Brett's idea, but Lulu could go to jail or hang, too, since she'd helped. That thought dismayed her. She touched her throat under her double chin.

She listened to the girls stirring awake and drifting in to eat breakfast. It occurred to her she hadn't been up before 10:00 A.M. in years because whores worked so late at night. Not like on the dirt-poor southern farm where, a pretty red-neck girl with no shoes and not enough to eat, she'd been up before daylight to milk cows. Lulu had run away from the crowded shack and found out men would pay to do something her step-brothers had been doing to her since she was twelve. With her body, she could finally buy enough to eat. It was amazing how important food could become when you've known hunger, she thought now as she bit into another cookie.

From her customers, young Lulu had heard about a gold strike in Georgia and went there. The government was busy pushing the Cherokees off the land in Georgia so white men could find the gold. Lulu took up with a handsome ne'er-do-well Welshman who had a Cherokee wife and son. Evans hadn't found any gold, but he talked wistfully of strikes to be made in Nevada and California. They left the wife and child behind and drifted on. She took his name, but soon learned he had nothing else. Evans was a dreamer who would always be looking over the next hill for a pot of gold and finding nothing. Half the time, Lulu supported them both with the earnings of her body.

The Comstock Strike came, but Evans didn't find any treasure; he got sick instead. By then, Lulu was weary of him and his empty dreams. She abandoned him and went her own way. Years passed so very quickly; her age and weight caught up with her. She changed her first name and became a madam, procuring girls. For the first time, she'd been foolish enough to fall in love—with a charming, worthless gambler, Brett James. He didn't care about her; she was smart enough to know that. Brett didn't care about anyone except Brett, partly because he'd been spoiled by a doting society Mother while his father built business empires and neglected them both. Still Lulu and Brett had had a good partnership going at the Black Garter until that killing.

She leaned back in her chair, eating cookies and scattering crumbs. She stared at her rings. Her jewels were her security. Someday, their value might support her . . . or at least pay for a fancy funeral. Fine funerals were important in the South.

When Lulu had fled New York, she'd gone first to San Francisco. Lulu had run into an old acquaintance of Brett's, John Pennell, who was looking to add some white women to his place, the *Illahee* in Seattle. Seattle. She'd heard Brett speak of it once. It sounded like a place where she could hide out until the New York police lost interest in the murder. In her heart, there was always the hope that she and Brett could be together again if she got a business going—if not in New York, maybe New Orleans or San Francisco. Lulu simply cut Pennell out of the deal, came up to Seattle with some new whores, and went into competition with him. Everything had been fine. Until Sassy turned up.

Lulu twisted her rings again. What to do? From a woman's point of view, Lulu almost sympathized with Sassy, knowing she loved Hunter. Of course, he probably wouldn't believe Lulu if she told him. She smiled to herself. On the other hand, she knew someone Hunter would believe. Should she do it? Lulu smiled and made her decision.

Chapter Fourteen

Sassy breathed a sigh of relief as she stepped out of the buggy in front of the house. Now that she had met with Marylou, she dared to think that her secret might be safe. While it wasn't the ideal situation, at least she had bought some time for herself.

John refused to let either her or Ellie help unload the buggy, insisting it was not work for ladies. The stablehands were unloading it as she and Ellie went inside. Both women changed clothes, tied up their hair, put on aprons, and began cleaning with renewed vigor. Sassy was preoccupied with her problem, but Ellie ended up in the kitchen area every chance she got.

By the time Hunter showed up for supper, the house smelled of wax and furniture polish and the windows sparkled. Hunter looked startled when he walked in. "Am I in the right house?"

Sassy ran into his arms, hugged him. "If you're looking for the home of Mr. and Mrs. James Hunter, yes."

He kissed the tip of her nose, then frowned as he took one of her small hands in his big ones. "You've got to stop working so hard, Sassy; you're ruining your hands. Ladies are supposed to have soft, fine hands."

"So I'll use a little glycerin and rose water on them; they'll be all right. I had to get the place to rights before I hired more servants or no one would stay. She took off the scarf that bound her hair. "I had the time and nothing else to do."

"Let's have a drink while Cookie finishes dinner."

Something about his tone bothered her. "He's taken Ellie back to town, so he's not cooking tonight."

Hunter raised one eyebrow. "Are we about to lose a cook?"

She laughed as they went into the library. "No, I think we're about to gain a live-in, permanent housekeeper if everything works out the way I plan. I've fixed supper myself tonight."

He didn't laugh, but gestured her toward a chair. "Sit down, Sassy. There's something we need to talk about."

Oh, Dear God, Marylou had told him. Very slowly, Sassy untied her apron and sank onto the sofa.

Hunter went to the sideboard, poured himself a whiskey, and brought her a glass of sherry. "I had to go into town this afternoon to pick up some new saws."

"Yes?" She sipped her drink, not even tasting it.

From his expression, he was choosing his words cautiously. "Bill Johnson told me you exchanged a few words with Lulu Evans."

She gave him her most innocent look and held onto her glass with both hands so he wouldn't see how they trembled. "You mean that plump lady in purple who wears all that white face powder and jewelry? She came up to me while I was waiting for him to finish filling my order; she wanted to thank me for the lovely party."

He chewed his lip thoughtfully. "Sassy, I'd rather you weren't seen even speaking to her; she's not someone a lady should know."

"I suppose you and Mr. Johnson are better judges of that than I am."

Touché. Hunter's face reddened. "I—I'll not deny that. Lulu is . . . well, just not your kind, Sassy."

She looked him in the eye and sipped her sherry. Because she felt cornered, she was rebellious. "What kind is she?"

He ran his finger around his collar as if cornered himself. "You're going to be shocked, but since you asked, her girls sell . . . their favors to any man who has the price." The distaste and scorn in his voice and face were unmistakable.

"I see; but you've been a customer?" What she wanted to scream at him was that the girls who sold themselves because they needed the money were no worse than the men who bought them, but she dared not. There would always be a different set of standards for women, no matter how hard women tried. She couldn't change that, and she could lose her man over it.

"That's just something men do; if that makes us hypocrites, I'm sorry, but that's the way the world works. I hate to be blunt, but I knew you wouldn't have any idea what she was. If Swede hadn't been so drunk, I'm sure he wouldn't have invited the whole town, including Lulu's girls, out here last night. He gets on binges sometimes and loses his judgment."

"Please don't be hard on him," she pleaded, relaxing. Her secret was still safe. "Swede didn't mean any harm by it; and, after all, it's done and over."

"Did Lulu say anything else to you?"

Sassy looked up at him blankly. Had she? There'd been something about a letter. . . . or had she only imagined that? "Nothing important, I think; she just thanked me. Why?"

"Nothing." He took a deep breath. "I smell roast chicken and hot rolls. Do you really know how to cook?"

She was as relieved to have this conversation end as he seemed to be. "Aye, I can cook. Let's have dinner."

"Sassy, I don't want you to think I'm being hard on you; I've had to fight for any shred of respect I got. Some still jeer at me as a half-breed Injun bastard."

She hadn't realized he was so wounded inside. If she didn't watch her step, he'd be hurt even more. She wasn't sure what to say. They went into the dining room.

Hunter said, "After my mother died, I was raised by her people until my father sent Swede searching for me. Swede taught me the timber business. It was hard to learn to act and think like a white man."

"So why did you?"

"Money," he said softly, lost in the past. "I only saw my father a couple of times. I reminded him of something he wanted to forget after he returned to his wife." He brushed a lock of black curly hair from his eyes. When those two died, I inherited half my father's estate and discovered that money translated into power. Maybe someday I'll be able to help my people when they can no longer help themselves."

"Perhaps the whites have taken all the land they intend to take and they'll leave the Indians alone."

Hunter shook his head. "In the end, the whites will

251

have it all and any warrior who protests will be in prison or hanged like Leshi."

"A friend of yours," she guessed.

"He fought the whites when they invaded the area; people were killed. They gave him a trial, of course; and Crosby, the lawyer, really tried to get him a fair deal, but he could do nothing. Leshi was hanged. No man wants to die with a rope around his neck; it's better to die fighting."

"Hunter, have you ridden as a warrior?"

He looked at her a long moment. "When we knew they had come to stay at the place they now call Seattle, we fought them, but it did no good. I learned you can't defeat white civilization with guns and lances. Money and power are what wins."

She knew now where his scar had come from and she was troubled by the brooding look on his face. Hunter had bigger ambitions—politics? More power? He wanted a wife white men would respect. She would be a hindrance and a liability to him if the people of Seattle knew her secret. "Let's eat," she said, not wanting to think anymore. "I'll serve."

The food was delicious and Kitty, sitting by Hunter's chair, begged until they fed the cat to keep it quiet.

Hunter sipped his coffee. "Great meal! I never guessed you were so talented, Sassy; what other things are there about you that I don't know?"

"What do you mean?" She looked up quickly.

He shook his head. "Nothing, Sweet, just making conversation."

"Oh." She felt flustered. "I—I'm just preoccupied with everything I'm thinking about doing to the house, and I've worked hard today cleaning." There was so much she wanted to ask; but she was afraid if she probed into his background too much, he'd retaliate with questions she didn't want to answer herself. They drank their coffee in silence. Then Sassy leaned back in her dining chair and put down her napkin. "Shall we read?"

Hunter frowned. "I have a headache, Sassy. I'm not sure I feel like reading." He stood up.

"Oh, I'm sorry. Can I do anything?"

He followed her into the other room. "I suppose it might help if you'd rub the back of my neck." Immediately, she set her coffee cup down, came around behind him as he sat on the sofa, and massaged his neck and shoulders.

"Ahh! That's good!" He closed his eyes.

She rubbed the sinewy muscles of his wide shoulders. "Maybe, if you don't feel like reading, I could play or read to you."

"If you like."

She played the piano while he smoked his cigarillo and watched her, contentment etched on his chiseled features. When she finished, he smiled. "If you only knew how many times I've pictured a scene just like this: my wife playing the piano I bought for her. Everything is perfect, Sassy."

Perfect. How she wished she had met him before she had become involved with Brett James. She would give anything to be able to go back and wipe out her past; but the past is set in stone and can't be changed, no matter how much one regrets it. "I'll read some more of King Arthur and his knights if you'd like."

He shrugged. "If you wish."

"If you'd rather I didn't—"

"No, that's fine." He patted the sofa. "I don't want this evening to end. Bring your fairy tale and come read to me."

Sassy got the book and sat down on the sofa. Hunter promptly put out his smoke and settled his head in her lap. "This could become a habit."

She smiled as she looked down at him nuzzling against the underside of her breast. "I presume you don't mean the reading aloud?"

"That, too," he admitted. "I didn't think fiction could be so entertaining, but maybe I've been missing something by sticking strictly to business books."

Sassy began to read aloud. In moments, the walls faded away and time was lost. The world was as big as her imagination and nothing was impossible. She transported them to a long-ago land of adventure and knights in armor. The words on the printed page came alive as she read; and Guinevere, Lancelot, Galahad, and King Arthur lived again.

Finally she tired and stopped reading.

Hunter said, "Why did you quit? That's not the end of the story, is it? I want to know what happens next."

She laughed and laid the book aside, rumpled his hair. "As interesting as you find this, it's hard to believe you've seldom opened all these wonderful novels."

He reached to pull her face down for a kiss. "I told you I was too occupied with business to waste time reading," he said. "Besides, you're reading them aloud makes them come alive for me. How does the story end?"

She sighed. "Do you really want to know? It's not a happy ending."

"I thought love stories always have happy endings."

She thought about her own life. It probably wasn't going to have a happy ending either. "Queen Guinevere betrays the king with his most trusted knight, one who has been almost a brother to him. She and Lancelot end up unhappy and paying for their sins."

"If they betrayed Arthur's trust and made a fool of him, that's all they deserve."

"You expect too much of people, Hunter. Humans make major mistakes; that's what makes them human."

"*Weak* people do. There's no excuse for it."

Kitty hopped up on the sofa and Hunter stroked the yellow cat. "I don't think I want to hear any more of that story. Maybe tomorrow night you can read something else."

"I'm beginning to feel like Scheherazade."

"Who?" He looked up at her blankly.

"You know, the girl who married the stern ruler in the *Arabian Nights*. He expected perfection, too, and always killed the girls the next day after he'd slept with them. However, Scheherezade began a story and didn't finish it, so he kept her alive so she could tell the end the next night. But then she began another story and he kept her alive to hear that one. After awhile, he fell in love with her, and she didn't have to keep making up stories. They were more than lovers, they were friends; and he was willing to accept her just as she was."

"I can see that—especially if she looked like you, Lady." He kissed her again and he smelled like pine needles, sun, and tobacco.

She held him close, wishing this would never, never end and that there were no secrets to hide. "I'm ordering some primers so we can help Swede. And probably some of your crew would like to learn to read."

255

"We?" He looked annoyed. "Sassy, I really don't have time. Some of the Indians don't even speak English. Why don't you do it?"

"Your attitude surprises me." Sassy scratched the cat's ears. "They all need to learn a little reading and writing if they're going to deal with whites."

"Maybe Swede'll help with numbers, but he won't be much help with teaching anyone to read; his English isn't good enough."

"That's why I thought you'd help." Sassy was peeved by Hunter's lack of interest. "There're children here, aren't there? Maybe I could organize a school."

He yawned. "Why not? I'll even pop in now and then to see how things are going. Now let's go to bed." He stood, swung Sassy up in his arms. The cat lay curled up on the sofa and never stirred as he carried Sassy out of the room.

She slipped her arms around his neck and kissed his face as he whisked her down the hall. "I wonder what history will say about a group of women who came clear across a continent to marry men they'd never met."

"If it's remembered at all, everyone will talk about how romantic it was," he murmured as he lay her on the bed. He bent and kissed her throat.

"Tonight," she whispered, "tonight I want you to give me your baby." If she carried his child, could he possible hate her or turn his back on her, no matter what he discovered?

"I'd like that," he said as he reached to unbutton her bodice. "I'd like that very much; except . . ." A troubled expression crossed his dark face.

"Except what?"

"Nothing. Do you—do you believe traits can be inherited?"

"Like freckles from me and blue eyes from you?" She smiled, but he didn't.

"That wasn't what I meant. Never mind." He kissed her as if trying to drive a troubling thought from his mind.

They made love leisurely, gently, without the lust that had driven them before. They savored every slow moment, the touch and the taste and the scent of each other's body. When they finally meshed together in a rhythm of mutual fulfillment, she begged him for it. "Please, Hunter, oh, please."

He answered her by emptying his seed deep in her womb while she clung to him, unwilling to release him until he had given her every drop her body craved. Afterward they lay in each other's arms, sated. She had never felt so loved and protected as she did at that moment, lying in the circle of his powerful embrace as they dropped off to sleep.

The next morning looked warm and pleasant as they finished their breakfast and made plans to go riding.

Sassy wore only a filmy chemise as she dug through her wardrobe. "What shall I wear?"

"What difference does it make?" He came up behind her, kissed the nape of her neck. "You'll be beautiful in anything you choose."

"Don't start that or we'll never get there." Sassy pulled away from him with a smile. "You promised to take me out to the timber lease. I want to see what goes on."

He kissed her bare shoulder, his lips nibbling along her skin until she felt goose bumps break out. "All right, if you insist."

She turned in his arms and returned his kiss. "We'll finish this later."

"How about now?"

She could spend the rest of her life in his embrace and never get enough. In her mind, the clock was already ticking away their time together and there was nothing she could do but pretend that everything was normal. "How about twice as much later on tonight?"

"Sold! And I won't forget about it."

She gave him a teasing, winsome look. "I don't intend you should. Now let me get dressed without your putting your mouth all over me."

He cupped both hands over her breasts. "Is that a complaint?"

"You know it isn't, but you did promise me a ride in the country."

"All right!" He threw up his hands in defeat, backed away.

She chose a butternut-colored riding dress with a big hat to keep the sun off her delicate complexion. "I swear, there's probably nothing so fine in all San Francisco."

He paused in pulling on his boots. "You ever been in San Francisco?"

She shook her head. "Just saw it from the *Continental*. Have you?"

A troubled look of memory crossed his dark features. "Once when I was a boy. I found my way to my father's estate . . ."

She waited for him to continue, but instead, he

shrugged. "It's a long story and not very interesting. Someday maybe I'll take you there."

"To your father's estate?" His look made her wish she hadn't asked.

"He's dead, Sassy, and his legitimate son inherited the mansion. I meant San Francisco."

She waited for him to say more, but he turned moody, troubled. She almost asked about his father, about the past, then decided against it. Like everyone else, Hunter had secrets, too. Did anyone ever *really* know another person, know him deep down, know his feelings and innermost thoughts, his most intimate secrets? Were Hunter's secrets any worse than hers?

"Let me look at you," he said as she finished dressing. She whirled around. "Like it?"

"You are what I always dreamed of," he said softly. "You even look like a lady. When you pass by, men will show respect and doff their hats, not like . . ."

She waited, but he said no more, although she could tell he was preoccupied. They went out to the barn where the lanky stablehand grinned at her as he led the two horses out. Freckles, her dainty mare, wore an expensive silver-trimmed bridle and a sidesaddle.

Hunter helped her to mount. "You look beautiful, Sassy, with that big hat and your dress sweeping almost to the ground."

"Now if I just knew how to ride," she laughed sheepishly.

"It won't take you long to learn," Hunter said. "You have a real talent for it." He swung up on Poker Chips and they rode out of the yard at a walk. "Are you happy, sweet?"

"I don't know when I was ever so happy," she admitted.

"Good. I intend to make your happiness my first priority so you'll stay with me always."

"You couldn't run me off with a stick." She smiled at him, but he didn't smile and she wondered again what it was that made him so serious, so possessive, so remote.

He was right, she thought as they rode along. She was beginning to get the hang of riding and actually enjoying herself. The air felt warm and the breeze smelled of pine needles and wild flowers. If Washington Territory weren't the most beautiful place in the world, she thought with contentment, it would do until that perfect spot came along. Up ahead in the distance, the sound of axes rang out and echoed through the hills. She heard a distant shout of 'Timber!' and the reverberation of a giant tree crashing down.

"Is this dangerous work?" she asked.

He nodded. "Logging is not for weaklings, Sassy. It takes hard, tough men, but the world needs our lumber."

She realized now that Hunter had earned those wide shoulders and hard muscles. "How do you get the fallen trees out of the woods?"

"Right now, ox teams drag the logs out and we roll them down the skid road to the docks where they're loaded on ships. I wish there was an easier way."

"What about railroads?"

"Not here yet. We hear they're building a railroad completely across the country, but that will take several years. Then maybe we can hook a spur line from the timber country to it. Right now, we have to send timber around the Horn by ship. In some areas, they're floating logs down rivers or man-made flumes."

They rode into the logging camp and Swede came out to meet them. "By jingo, Hunter, Miss Sassy is even prettier than I remember."

Sassy blushed and Hunter laughed as he dismounted and came around to help her down. "Yes, she is, although as much as you had to drink, I'm surprised you can remember anything."

Swede's scarred face reddened and he grinned. "Seems I seen a certain blue-eyed Injun boy in that shape a time or two."

"But never again." Hunter glanced at Sassy fondly.

Swede apologized to Sassy for bringing the drunken crowd out to the house while she assured him she wasn't offended. The crew had gathered for coffee and they stood about, gaping at Sassy. She noticed many of them looked like they had Indian blood and she wondered if they would work for anyone but Hunter.

"Boys," Hunter said, "for those of you who weren't around for the party the other night, I'll be sending over a keg of beer; but I did want you to meet my wife."

A cheer went up as they pulled off their caps, twisting them in big, rough hands while murmuring shyly. Sassy did her best to put them at ease. Most of the crew trooped back toward the woods. In the distance, the sound of axes rang out once more.

Swede said, "Miss Sassy, would you like to look around?"

"I'd love to," she said. "Can we go out and watch the boys cut the trees?"

"They call them fallers," Hunter explained. "They're

261

so skilled they can make a tree land inches from where they tell you it will."

"I'm impressed."

They tied up the two horses by the crew's shack and Swede handed Hunter a pair of heavy boots with sharp, steel spikes on the soles. "Don't forget your corks, Boy; you might need them."

Swede also wore the calked boots with the spikes as did some of the others. She wondered about these tough, hard men who lived by cutting and selling the giant trees to feed the lumber needs of the world. The three of them walked through the woods toward the sound of ringing axes and saws.

Sassy said, "What are the spiked boots for?"

"We call them corks," Hunter told her. "When a logger's walking a fallen tree, it keeps him from slipping. Pretty useful in a fight, too."

"By jingo, I'll vouch for that." Swede shrugged and reached to touch his scarred face. "I not even remember what this one was about. Hope if it was over a woman, she pretty enough to be worth it!"

She was shocked when both men laughed, but she realized these were rough, savage men used to co-existing with death and danger.

Deeper in the woods they saw loggers felling trees and stopped to watch them work. Sassy knew then how Hunter had come by those powerful arms and shoulders. Those axes looked big enough that she wasn't even sure she could lift one, much less swing it. Only big, brawny men like Hunter and Swede could survive in this work.

Hunter looked around. "Where's Clegg?"

Swede shook his head. "Had to fire him this morning.

262

Show up to work so drunk he barely standing. Clegg a troublemaker anyhow. Soaking up booze at Lulu's by now."

Hunter frowned. "We need every man we've got to make that contract deadline. There's a lot of money riding on it, but you did right, Swede. This isn't the first time we've had problems; Clegg's been nothing but trouble off and on all the years he's worked the timber country."

Up ahead in the forest, a giant fir appeared almost sawed through. It trembled on its base.

"Timber!" Someone yelled and the men scattered.

Swede gestured toward a small yellow flower. "It fall about six inches to the left of that."

Sassy looked at Hunter. "Can he call it that close?"

Hunter grinned. "If Swede says it will, it will. Nobody knows timber like he does."

"Clay did," Swede said.

"Don't mention him." Hunter frowned.

The big tree trembled again and creaked and groaned. Sassy held her breath, fascinated. Around her, sweating men watched in rapt silence or made bets on where it would land. With a roar, it crashed down. Limbs on nearby trees were torn away as it fell. For what seemed like an eternity, Sassy watched the big tree falling. Dust churning up, it landed, seemed to bounce, and settled on the forest floor. Birds flew away, squawking, and a startled doe bounded through the forest.

Sassy took a deep breath of the scent of fresh sawdust and bruised needles. The men shouted and threw their hats in the air.

Hunter gestured toward the tree. "What'd I tell you?"

Sassy looked closely. Through the dust, she saw the

trunk of the fallen giant lay almost exactly where Swede had said it would, scant inches from the little yellow flower.

Hunter bent to put on the calked boots. "Let's get cracking, men. You buckers ready?"

"What're 'uckers?" Sassy asked as Hunter climbed up on the giant log.

"They trim the branches off and cut it up into shorter lengths so we can move it." The sharp spikes of Hunter's boots bit into the bark. "Someone get that ox team and throw me a chain."

Sassy felt a need to relieve herself and looked around at the men. "If no one minds," she said to Hunter, "I'll walk back to the crew shack and ... ah ... get myself a drink of water."

For a moment, she thought he would protest; then he seemed to understand. "Want me to go with you?"

"No, I can find my way. I'll be back in a minute."

"Stick to the trail, Sassy," he yelled. "You get out in these woods, you could get lost and we'd never find you."

"Don't worry," she called over her shoulder as she retreated down the path. "I'm not about to do that."

She started walking toward the shack. The forest was beautiful and she felt at peace as if she had finally found where she truly belonged. A rabbit peeked out at her from behind a bush, a butterfly flitted through the lacy shadows. Behind her, the axes rang again and Hunter shouted orders to the men. This was Hunter's world and she felt at home here, too. If it weren't for Marylou, Sassy would feel she was in heaven.

She found a private copse, relieved herself, and then

started on to the crew shack. She'd have a cup of icy cold water from the stream.

It seemed a lot farther going back than it had coming. A person could get lost in these endless miles of forest and never find his way out. The thought made her shudder.

Abruptly, a man stepped out of the woods onto the trail ahead of her—a big, powerful man taller and heavier than Hunter but older, maybe in his mid-forties.

She started and took a step back.

He swayed, grinning with yellow teeth, his ugly face covered with a stubble of beard. "Didn't mean to startle you, Little Lady."

Sassy paused and frowned. "I told Hunter I didn't need an escort," she snapped. "I'm perfectly capable of finding my way back."

His blue eyes glared at her as he swayed and only then did she realize he might be drunk. "So you're Hunter's woman."

She didn't know what he expected her to say. She drew herself up primly. "Yes, I'm Mrs. James Hunter. If you'll let me pass, please, I can find the camp by myself."

He held his hand out. "Don't you want some company?"

Alarm bells went off in her mind. She glanced behind her. Once again in the distance, the sound of axes rang out. If she screamed, she wasn't certain they could hear her and it hurt her pride to think she might have to ask for help. "You're drunk. If you don't get out of my way, I'll tell Hunter you annoyed me."

He swore a string of curses. "So that rich half-breed bastard got hisself a wife." He advanced on her slowly.

"Why don't you give a white man a little of what you've been giving that red-skinned sonovabitch?"

She slapped him hard even as she turned to run. He moved fast for such a big man, fast as a striking snake. He grabbed her, clapped his hand over her mouth, and pulled her to him. She struggled to break away while he held her against him. He smelled of sweat, dirt, and cheap whiskey.

"Now, Honey," he said against her ear, "old Clegg only wants five minutes of your time. Nobody but the two of us will ever know what happened." He dragged her off the path into the woods.

Sassy fought him. This brute was both drunk and powerful. Worse than rape, the logger might kill her, leave her body in the woods never to be found. He had one arm wrapped around her waist, the other dirty hand over her mouth. He was big and she was helpless. Her heart pounded in terror.

"Honey, I like it when women fight me, makes it more excitin'!" He breathed against her ear and she gagged on the scent of rotted teeth and cheap whiskey as he half-dragged, half-carried her. "I'm gonna get my mouth all over you!"

He whispered dirty words about what he intended to do to her body, what he would force her to do to him. The drunken logger pulled her even deeper into the woods and she knew she wasn't big enough to stop him from carrying out his threats. Sassy was going to be raped!

Chapter Fifteen

She'd rather die, Sassy thought as she fought him with her last desperate ounce of strength. She managed to turn her head so she could get her mouth open. She bit down on his hand, tasted blood.

"You little slut!" He struck her, cursing, jerked his hand away.

This might be her only chance. Sassy screamed even as he clapped his hand over her mouth again. "You bitch! I know these woods like a map; they'll never find me—or you either!" She clawed, trying to delay him, hoping Hunter had heard her scream.

Somewhere behind them, she heard a shout. "Sassy? Sassy, where are you?"

She bit and struggled, slowing her captor. Behind her in the distance, she heard men crashing through the woods. "Sassy? Mrs. Hunter? Where are you?"

She scratched her abductor's face and when he slapped her, she screamed, "Hunter! Help! Help me!"

Clegg dragged her to a small clearing. With all her strength, she brought her knee up and caught him in the groin. He turned her loose with an oath, bent double in his pain. Sassy stumbled to her feet, tried to run, tripped over a root, and fell. Her abductor grabbed her, tearing her dress as his hands held her fast. "No, you don't, you little bitch! I may need you to get out of here!"

"Sassy? Sassy, where are you? I'm coming!"

She had to delay this brute of a man. She scratched at his dirty, bearded face as she fought to escape. Behind them, she heard the sound of men crashing through the underbrush.

"Clegg! Let her go!" Hunter's voice cracked like a whip through the trees. She looked up, sobbing with relief as the loggers came out of the woods. "Let her go or I'll kill you, so help me God!"

"Get back, Hunter," the drunk snarled, "or I'll break her in half!" He had her bent over his knee. "She won't do you no good if I hurt her!"

"You hurt her and you'll know what Indian torture is, you slimy bastard!" The fury on her love's face distorted his handsome features. "Clegg, this is between us!"

The man hesitated. "I don't stand a chance against your whole crew, Hunter; I'm using her for a hostage."

"Let her go!" He moved, silent as any warrior.

Clegg had his arm around her waist. "If I fight you and win, can I walk away from here? Do I have your word?"

Hunter hesitated, and when he did, her captor twisted her arm and Sassy cried out in spite of herself. "Yes, you've got my word. Don't hurt her; for God's sake, don't hurt her!"

Sassy protested, "Don't give your word. He doesn't intend to keep his!"

"Boss, she's right! By jingo, that drunken—"

"Swede, I don't have any choice. All right, Clegg,

Swede will keep the boys back. You whip me, you walk free."

"How do I know you'll keep your word?"

"Because I don't intend you'll be able to walk," he said softly. "I intend to kill you."

The brawny logger laughed. "I've waited a long time, you half-breed uppity bastard!" He let go of Sassy and she ran to Hunter, fell sobbing into his arms.

He hugged her to him briefly. "Sassy," he brushed her tumbled hair from her eyes, "are you hurt?"

"Don't fight him, Hunter," she implored. "He's drunk. He's crazy."

He glared at the bruise on her face. "He do that?"

"Hunter, it isn't bad; I—I'm not worth it!"

Hunter swore. "Clegg, you've hurt my woman. Now I'll kill you for it!" He handed her over to Swede.

"No, Hunter," she sobbed and tried to pull free. "Oh, Swede, stop him!"

"Miss Sassy, Clegg has it coming. The boy, he take care of hisself!" Swede hung onto her and she struggled, watching the two big men advance on each other with their spiked boots. She glanced up at Swede's scarred face and knew what was coming but she was helpless to stop it. All a female could do was watch when stallions fought over her.

The two moved to the small clearing, peeling off their shirts, circling each other warily as the crew waited.

Clegg whined, "Hunter, it don't do me no good to fight if Swede finishes me off."

"I told you, you sonovabitch," Hunter said in a cold voice, "if you whip me, Swede will let you walk. But I aim to stomp you bloody!"

This was going to be a fight to the death, Sassy

thought with disbelief, between two powerful, half-naked men in spiked boots. She had a vision of gladiators in a Roman arena. "Hunter, no! Don't fight him!"

"Keep her out of this, Swede," Hunter ordered as he faced Clegg without even looking over his shoulder.

"Yes, boss." The man grabbed Sassy's arm even as she tried to run between them.

The two faced off warily, circling each other, looking for a weakness, an opening. Clegg was the bigger man, but Hunter had the advantage of youth. All Sassy could do was watch as the two men charged and meshed, powerful, naked chests and arms rippling with strength, glistening with sweat.

"Hunter! Look out!" She shrieked as spikes flashed in the sunlight and corded leg muscles struck like hammers, leaving smears of scarlet blood on naked flesh. The set, stern looks on the other men's faces told her that here, deep in the Washington woods, no one would move to stop this primitive fight, no matter how bad, brutal, or bloody. This was to the death!

Once again the two faced each other, circling warily. Blood gleamed on their sweating, half-naked bodies. The crowd watched the pair, awaiting the outcome. Sassy could do nothing because Swede clenched her arm.

Clegg looked as if he had more experience in battling with the spiked boots. However, Hunter was faster on his feet and his anger made him dangerous. Hunter dove in under the other man's guard, one boot coming up to cut the logger across the belly. The man swore and screamed. Hunter dodged away, but Clegg grabbed him in a strong bear hug, lifting him off the ground. "Now, you Injun bastard, I'll break you in half!"

He snarled. Hunter caught him in the eye with his elbow, and the other man's grip loosened for an instant. Still Hunter did not quite escape his powerful arms as they meshed and rolled across the forest clearing, dirt and leaves sticking to the red smears on their bodies.

Hunter broke free by sheer strength, but Clegg's heavy boot flashed and cut him across the chest. Sassy screamed as Hunter fell and Clegg brought his weight down on Hunter's left hand. "Now, you brown sonovabitch, let's see you fight one-handed!"

Hunter groaned and staggered to his feet.

Sassy tried to pull out of Swede's arms. "Someone, do something! Can't you tell he's hurt?"

"Keep her back, Swede!" Hunter ordered, not looking her way. Again he circled the other.

Clegg was tiring, even Sassy could see that. The man might have been old enough to be Hunter's father. Though he was bigger and taller, he was not the superior physical specimen Hunter was with one hand out of action. Hunter moved quick as a striking snake, one of his calked boots catching Clegg in the shoulder, sending him stumbling backward.

Both looked weary and in pain, Sassy thought as the two faced each other, smeared with blood and sweat. The scent of it drifted on the air along with their labored breathing and their boots crunching on the layer of leaves and twigs.

Horrified, she watched the drama play out. Hunter's arm hung limp and Sassy knew that hand might be broken, leaving him at a terrible disadvantage now as he backed slowly away from his opponent. Hunter, she knew, was left-handed. Only his wits and cunning could save him. Clegg rushed forward, squeezing him like a vise, a triumphant gleam in his dark eyes. This time, he'd break Hunter's ribs. He muttered against Hunter's ear, forcing the life from him.

An insult, Sassy thought, noting the way he grinned as he said it. But it incited Hunter to fury. Swearing, and using his great strength, Hunter once again managed to bring his elbows up and catch Clegg in the face. He dropped Hunter with a cry, then charged in like a maddened bull, attempting to stomp him as Hunter hit the ground. The half-breed was too fast for him. He rolled out from under Clegg's slashing boots and struggled to his feet. His breath came in such agonized gasps that everyone in the silent, watching circle heard. He looked weak from loss of blood.

"All right," Hunter gasped, "now I intend to make sure you never hurt another woman!"

Before the logger realized his intent, Hunter drove forward, boots slashing. Clegg retreated, sweat and blood dripping down his knotted muscles. Too late, he understood that while Hunter was hurt, he was also driven by an all-consuming hatred and revenge. What Clegg had done to Sassy, whatever he had whispered to Hunter, drove the half-breed past human endurance and reason. However, with his injured hand, Hunter was at a disadvantage. Clegg got in one lucky blow that caught him off balance. Hunter stumbled backward over a log and fell, grabbing for Clegg's boot just as the logger put all his strength into a brutal kick. Spikes flashed as Clegg's boot came down towards Hunter's groin. Hunter caught the boot and twisted. Clegg screamed in pain as he landed heavily on the ground, striking his face against the rough bark of the log.

Hunter swayed to his feet, breathing hard. Clegg rolled away from his foe, moaning.

"Kill him, Hunter!" A chorus went up. "He deserves it! Stomp him!" Like a circle of savage wolves with no mercy for the cowardly defeated, they watched.

Hunter hesitated, breathing hard. "Sassy? His life is yours. Do you want him dead?"

"Oh, Hunter, no!" Sassy wept and ran into his arms. "Don't kill him over me; let him go!"

He held her against him. "I've got a right; any frontiersman would say so."

She shook her head, feeling nothing but revulsion for the groveling, whimpering man. "Clegg isn't worth it. Let him live. Are you hurt? I was so scared for you!"

"It's okay, baby; everything's okay now." He held her with his good right arm and turned toward his men. "Swede, escort Clegg to town, see he gets a month's pay and is on the next ship out." To Clegg, he snarled, "If I see you in these parts again, I'll kill you."

The logger never looked up. He continued to roll and moan, "Oh, God! I'm hurt! I'm hurt."

Swede hauled him to his feet. "You lucky to be alive!"

Sassy examined Hunter's bloody hand. "Oh, Dearest, I've got to get you home. Does it hurt?"

"Not bad," he said, but his face told her he lied.

They recovered the horses and mounted up, although Swede and Sassy wanted to wait for a wagon. It seemed a million miles back to the house where Sassy sent John riding into town for Doc Maynard. She put Hunter to bed and washed the dirt and blood off him. "Holy Mother of God! Your body looks like he took an ice pick to it!"

He grimaced with pain as he reached out, cupped her

small face with his right hand. "I'm okay, Sassy. Did that bastard hurt you?"

She wondered again what Clegg had muttered to him as she shook her head. "Just tore my dress, that's all."

He lit a cigarillo with an awkward hand. "Get me a drink, Sweet, while we wait for the doctor. Clegg should have known that no one touches anything that belongs to me!"

She ran to get him a whiskey, wiped the sweat from his agonized face. "Is there anything else I can do?"

"Just be here, for me, Baby; that's what counts." He touched the tip of her nose. "I've waited a long time for a lady like you. I'll not have every tramp on the West Coast think he can rough up Hunter's woman and get away with it."

She thought of all the men she had had, how they would laugh if they knew that this man idolized her, thought she was special and pure. "I'm afraid your hand may be broken."

He grimaced and sipped his whiskey. "Maybe not. But it looks like if there's any writing for me to do, you'll have to take care of it for awhile."

"Aye. Good thing we've got Swede to do the book-work." She reached for a washcloth and wiped Hunter's face, inspected the puncture wounds on his arm and body. "You loggers fight rough."

"When there's something worth fighting over," he murmured and pulled her to him to kiss her. "That sonovabitch will pass the word no one can treat a lady like that in Seattle and get away with it!"

* * *

Lulu watched through the lace curtains of her parlor as Hunter's cook rode into town at breakneck speed. A few minutes later, Doc's buggy headed back up the road.

What was going on out at Hunter's Hill? Was there any chance the big half-breed had found out Sassy's secret and beaten her half to death? Hunter was passionate and dangerous enough, maybe, if he ever found out he'd been made a fool of. On the other hand, she'd seen the way he looked at that little red-head as if she were his whole world. There was always the slim chance that he loved Sassy enough not to care about her past. No, no man could love a woman that much.

Well, Lulu would have to wait for the details until Doc returned to town. She twisted her rings and sat at her desk, considering the checkmate situation she was in. She'd sent wires to Brett's acquaintances in every big city she could think of. Where was he? Still in New York? His parents had been killed together in a buggy accident in San Francisco near their estate. Lulu knew Brett still had connections there—and in other places such as New Orleans. She'd only really come here thinking he might finally even get desperate enough to ask a relative for help. Hadn't the handsome, charming rake always known how to take advantage of everyone when he needed them? He certainly had played Lulu for a fool, using his good looks and personality, and *she* should have known better. Now that Sassy Malone was too innocent to know a rascal when she saw one.

I'll swan, wasn't it ironic how things turned out? Lulu smiled to herself, reached for a cookie. Who would have ever believed that with all the people in the world such a triangle could come about?

Lulu chewed and watched the late afternoon sun slant through the lace curtains. She had one advantage: She knew something Sassy and Hunter didn't, and that knowledge gave Lulu an edge. Secrets. Everybody has one; some big, some small. The most important secret Lulu and one other person might be the only two in the world who knew, although Brett might suspect. So far, Lulu hadn't figured out how to use that secret to her advantage; and besides, she felt kindly toward that other person. Now the small secret. . . . She measured the power of that knowledge against the pleasure she would get from telling Sassy. No, she shook her head, she'd better keep her secrets as a hole card.

With the sun setting, Sassy lit the bedroom lamp, looked from Hunter's freshly bandaged hand to Doc Maynard's wrinkled face. "So you can't be sure whether it's broken?"

"Not till the swelling goes down." Doc snapped his bag closed. "But he's tough as a pine knot. One thing for certain, he won't be using it for awhile."

"But, Doc," Hunter protested, "we've got a contract to meet and we've lost time already."

"Swede can get the timber out," Doc said.

Sassy said, "He's in town right now loading Clegg on an outbound ship."

"Good riddance!" Doc snorted and scratched his head. "I treated him just a'fore I came out here; he'll live."

Hunter sighed. "Sassy, I suppose for a couple of days you and Swede will have to run things. I won't be able to handle a pen or an axe."

276

"We'll manage," she assured him. "I don't know much about bookwork; but, between us, it'll get done."

Doc turned toward the door. "I'll be back out in a day or two. There isn't much to do now except keep a clean bandage on it and let him mend. If it were anyone but this healthy young stud, he'd probably get blood poisoning or lockjaw."

Hunter grumbled. "I've got a business to run, Doc. I have to be back in action in a couple of days."

"You heard Doc," Sassy said firmly.

The old man paused in the doorway. "Take it easy, Hunter," he said. "Swede handled the timber business for your father for years; he can do it for you."

Hunter frowned blackly. "Let's not talk about my father."

Sassy, sensing the abrupt change of mood in her husband, took the older man's arm. "Never you mind, Doc. We'll manage just fine." She walked him out to his buggy. "Doc, did you know this family?"

"That was a long time ago before I came here." He set his bag on the seat. "They do say his father went back to his wife after the tragedy."

"The tragedy?"

Doc nodded and climbed into the buggy. "Then his mother's Injun relatives raised him."

"Doc," she admitted, "I'm not sure I know what you're talking about."

"I just assumed you knew . . ." Doc hesitated. "A man's background, good or tragic, makes him what he is, I reckon. Not many men would have come out of it as well as Hunter has, although he's moody and maybe a little hostile for it."

"Aye, he struck me that way, too, at first," Sassy

277

agreed. "However, beneath all that hard crust, I sense something gentle and tender; but he's not one to trust women."

"Because of his mother," Doc blurted out, then seemed distressed that he had spoken before he thought. "Forget I said anything. There was an older child by the wife, I hear, but Hunter seems alone except for you and Swede. Don't fail him, Ma'am." He clucked to his horse and drove away.

More mystified than ever, Sassy stared after the buggy as it disappeared into the darkness. Perhaps sometime when she knew him better, Hunter would open up to her, or maybe Swede would fill in the missing puzzle-pieces. If she understood his past, perhaps she could help him. Help him? She couldn't even help herself at the moment. She could only hope that Marylou Evans kept her part of the bargain.

She went back inside. Hunter had dozed off, the furrows of pain in his dark face smoothing out as he slept. The ragged yellow tomcat lay next to him. What kind of person would pick up stray cats and yet respond with such savagery to another man? She looked down at Hunter, wondering about the lonely, tragic child he might have been and what was it in his past that made him that way? If the time were ever right, she would ask Swede.

By the time John had dinner ready, Hunter had awakened. She fed him because he handled a knife in his right hand so awkwardly. Then she curled up on his bed and read to him until he finally dropped back to sleep.

Quietly, she readied herself for bed and extinguished the lamp. He slept restlessly, muttering as if in a nightmare. No doubt his injured hand throbbed. Sassy gathered him into her arms and stroked his hair until he drifted into a deeper sleep. However, she herself could not sleep. She kept reliving the bloody, brutal fight she had witnessed and—in a sense—caused. Before she had only guessed how much fury and violence Hunter might be capable of, now she knew for certain.

Suppose someday some man from her past should turn up in Seattle, recognize her, and make a smart remark? There was no doubt in her mind Hunter was capable of killing a man. Suppose he found out the man spoke the truth? She shuddered, realizing she might be in danger herself. However, people change and memories fade. Perhaps in half-a-dozen years, even those who had once known her would no longer connect the highly respectable Mrs. James Hunter to the old Sassy Malone.

She dozed off, remembering her childhood. Her mother had been an elegant lady who had fallen in love with one of her titled father's hired hands. She was disowned and all she had left was her silver tea service, which she sold to pay the Malones' passage to America.

In Boston, they discovered the grim prejudice against the Irish and what poor really meant as the family multiplied. Mike Malone tried hard, but Maureen, who had once lived in a fine house, now worked part-time cleaning the wealthy Van Schuyler's home. It hurt Mike's pride, but they needed the money badly. Sometimes Mama had taken Sassy with her.

Sassy smiled now, remembering. The Van Schuylers had a piano in their music room. When no one was about, Maureen taught Sassy to play it.

Three years ago, things had gotten worse when Mama died of hard work, poverty, and pneumonia. The next year, Mike had fallen from a scaffold at a construction site, and it appeared the Malones might actually starve. At the age of seventeen, in sheer desperation, Sassy had gone to New York, looking for work. If she hadn't been so young and naive, she might have realized what she was getting into.

Brett James was everything to turn an innocent girl's head—handsome, charming. He was an older man of the world who hired her to wait tables in his saloon. Within a month, he got her drunk, told her he loved her, and seduced her. Too late, she discovered that what was upstairs over his establishment was not really a hotel at all. Brett's plump hostess, Marylou Evans, was not a hotel manager but a madam. Sassy was trapped in a big-city bordello.

The only bright spot in this living hell was the money that her family needed so desperately. She sent it all back to her injured father who was naive enough to believe she made that much in tips as a waitress. If it hadn't been for the murder Sassy witnessed, she might still have been working as a pretty whore in Brett James' place.

Murder. She remembered putting her ear against the door and listening to Brett and Marylou talk.

"Damn!" he grumbled, "Albert Huntington is in town and won big at poker last night. I stalled him, but we don't have it. He's demanding payment, says he's almost bankrupt."

Sassy peeked through a crack in the door, watched Marylou admire her rings. "I hear he's from an influential family and married to some Philadelphia society dame. What can we do?"

He ran his finger along his pencil mustache, a frown on his handsome face. "My games are crooked. He knows it and might go to the police. I think we'll kill him and be done with it."

"And get hanged?" She reached for a sugar cake.

"Not if it's self-defense," Brett said.

"That little pip-squeak ain't gonna—"

"Stop stuffing your fat face and think," he snapped. "I have two derringers. We'll lure him into the alley. You say he's insulted you. I'll draw on him, shoot, and, as he falls, you slip the other derringer into his pocket. You'll swear he was armed and drew on me but I got him first. With no evidence to the contrary, his elegant wife won't ask for an investigation; she'll fear the publicity."

Sassy leaned against the door, wondering whom she should tell. What to do? Even a whore couldn't stand by and let cold-blooded murder happen without trying to stop it. If only she'd known they'd planned it for that very night!

Then it was too late to do anything. Even as she tried to signal him from the window, the scrawny little businessman confronted Brett and, in seconds, lay dead in the alley with a gun in his pocket. Brett and his fat madam looked up and saw her. Their expressions left no doubt they would kill her to cover the crime. After all, the police wouldn't be interested in a poor Irish whore found dead in a gutter.

Murder. Sassy came awake with a start, thinking she heard the man moan, remembering the sound of the derringer as Brett pulled the trigger. She lay still, her heart pounding, as she relived the killing. After a long moment, she realized the moan came from Hunter.

She was safely in bed with her husband in Washington Territory. At least she was safe for the moment. Sassy got up, took a wet cloth and sponged his face. He settled down and slept while she stroked his face.

What would Hunter think if he knew she'd overheard the plans for, then witnessed, a murder? That night Sassy had fled Brett's place and secured a position as personal maid to Sophia Merriweather. Yet she feared the pair would search her out to silence her.

The mail-order-bride trip had seemed like the perfect escape. Now Marylou had turned up here in Seattle. Why had she chosen such an out-of-the-way place? Maybe, like Sassy, she didn't think anyone would know her here.

She snuggled closer to Hunter's muscular chest. In his arms, she felt safe. Merciful saints, if Hunter ever uncovered her history, he might be an even bigger danger—a proud man who'd been made to look the fool.

At least Clegg was on a ship out tonight, so that ended one threat. Now if she and Swede could handle the business for the next few days, they would take the burden off Hunter until he had partially recuperated.

The big man patted her in his sleep and Sassy smiled and drifted off to sleep herself. Holy Saint Patrick, how could she worry about the future when she had a man who idolized her as this one did?

Clegg thrashed around in the ship's bunk and listened to the chain rattle as the anchor was slowly raised. His head still ached from the liquor and, now that he was sober, he felt each throb of pain as his pulse beat. He should have resisted the urge to taunt Hunter about his mother as they fought. That Springtime was one sweet piece; even Clegg had had her when he was just a half-grown boy. But then, who hadn't? Clegg might have sired her bastard himself. She had always behaved like a bitch in heat, but that night the wealthy timber man caught her . . .

Damn that Hunter—and Swede, too. In a few more minutes, the ship would get underway and he'd be happy as hell to see the end of Seattle and her people.

A sound. Was it a rat? Clegg raised up on one elbow, the hair standing up on his dirty neck as he imagined a sly rodent scurrying across the hold. Two things Clegg feared: rats and fire. No sound. Maybe he had imagined it.

At least Swede had paid his fare when he put him aboard. Clegg had survived crimpers before, being shanghaied onto some tramp ship where he'd be worked like a slave and thrown overboard if he complained.

The old ship creaked and groaned as it made ready to sail. Another sound; closer. Could he use one of his spiked boots on a rat?

"You Clegg?" A form appeared in silhouette.

Did he recognize that voice? He didn't think so; but how to be sure? "Who is it?"

"A friend."

He felt around for something, anything he could use as a weapon. "I got no friends."

"Someone was willing to bribe the guard to get you off this ship; I'd call that *real* friendly."

Hunter, he thought, as he saw the outline of the tall form in the dim light. Hunter had changed his mind and was luring him out to throw him over the side. No, he remembered Hunter's hand. He wouldn't be using it for awhile. So maybe he'd sent someone. "You try to throw me overboard, I'll shout like hell!"

The other laughed. "Now why would you want to do that when I've come to help you?"

"Don't give me that." Clegg sat up slowly. "How do I know I can trust you?"

"I'm here, aren't I? This ship is leaving. You going with it or do you want to take your chances with me?"

Rats and fire. If he stayed aboard, there were always rats. "Who are you or who sent you?"

The silhouette gestured. "Come on. You'll like what I have to say."

It took all his energy for Clegg to sway to his feet. Whatever the stranger was offering was better than staying aboard this old tub. The night was as dark as hell's bowels. He followed the shadow up the ladder and out across the deck. Rats and fire. Fire might someday get him; but, at least this time, the rats wouldn't.

Chapter Sixteen

Sassy savored a second cup of coffee as she sat in the wing chair across from Hunter in the bedroom. "How's the hand?"

He glanced from the cup of coffee he held awkwardly in his right hand to his bandaged left hand. "Swelling's gone down, and it's stopped throbbing. I don't think it's broken."

"Twenty-four hours can make a big difference," Sassy said. "At least with Clegg sailing out last night, there's one problem gone."

Hunter stretched his sore muscles and grimaced. "So where is everyone?"

"Swede's out with the crew trying to get that timber cut for the contract. John's gone to town for the mail and supplies and, if you want my opinion, to call on Ellie."

"I don't know what he sees in your friend, but at least, he hasn't reeked of vanilla the last couple of days."

She sat on the arm of his chair. "He's happy and not lonely now. I'm going to hire Ellie as a full-time house-keeper to hurry this love match along."

"Sure. My wife isn't supposed to work so hard. By the way, let me know if Cookie brings back a package."

"Oh? What'd you order?"

He winked. "Surprise for you, you minx. Something from San Francisco."

Immediately she leaned forward. "For me? What?"

He laughed, enjoying her curiosity. "I said it was a surprise."

She knelt by his chair. "Tell me."

"If I tell, you won't be surprised. I want to see your face when you open it." He put his coffee cup on the chairside table, stroked her hair.

She couldn't remember mentioning anything she wanted. "Why do you torment me? You shouldn't have mentioned it if you didn't want me to wonder."

He made a face. "You can wonder all you want, but you'll have to wait. I won't tell you, my freckle-faced pixie, even if you get me in bed and work your wiles on me."

She raised her eyebrows. "Would it help?"

"Why don't you try it and see?"

"You're a conniving rascal." She laughed.

"I do have one little something I picked up in town, something from the general store. Look for a little box in the chest of drawers."

"A present for me?" She went to the chest, found the box, came back.

His blue eyes smiled. "Bill Johnson said you were eyeing it."

"I don't remember anything in particular." Sassy opened it slowly, savoring the moment. Her family had been too poor for many gifts. "Oh, Hunter," she gasped as she saw the gleam in the light. It was the small gold bracelet. "This is expensive."

286

He shrugged. "I can afford it. It's the least I can do when you had to provide your own wedding ring."

Tears came to her eyes as she glanced first at her finger and then at his watchchain. Hunter couldn't quite bring himself to make that final commitment.

"What's the matter? You don't like it after all? I'll take it back."

"Oh no, I love it!"

He watched her. "If my hand weren't banged up, I'd put it on for you."

"I can do it." She hooked the clasp and held her arm up so Hunter could see. "I feel like a kid at Christmas."

"Good. I want to do nice things for you, Sassy, spoil you with my money."

She looked at him a long moment, then raised her face and kissed him ever so gently. "I love you, Hunter. I'm so glad we found each other." She waited, hoping he would say he loved her, too.

Instead, he cupped her face in his good hand. "My wife," he whispered. "It seems almost too good to be true—such a beauty and mine alone."

A possession, that's what she was to him, a trophy to be kept on a pedestal.

Kitty jumped up in Hunter's lap, breaking the spell. He patted the cat absently, looked toward the window, and frowned. "I ought to be out in the timber with the boys."

"Humph!" she snorted. "A lot of good you'd be with one hand. In a couple more days, you'll have that bandage off, although you'd better take it easy awhile."

"Isn't it amazing that I've managed all these years without you to mother and nag me?"

"I'm just taking over John and Swede's job. Don't you like my taking care of you?"

He studied her critically, and when he spoke, his voice was soft, tender. "I like it and you know it. I've been without a woman to look after me most of my life. I didn't know what I was missing." He stuck a thin cheroot between his lips, lit it awkwardly with his right hand.

"What about your mother?"

"Springtime?" He seemed lost in his own thoughts for a long moment while the smoke curled up around his head. "She was never much of a mother, really. Besides, she died when I was a very small boy."

"What happened to her?"

He frowned. "I don't want to talk about her, not now, not ever."

Once again, he turned cold and remote. The sweet intimacy had been lost and she wished fervently that she had never asked about the wild beauty. Hunter fidgeted. It was going to be hard to keep him occupied for the next several days until his hand healed.

"I'll tell you what," she suggested. "This afternoon, I'll have John pack a basket and we'll take the buggy and go on a picnic."

"You're spoiling me." He smiled slightly.

Sassy stood up. "That's a wife's privilege." She heard the creak of a wagon approaching and went to the window. "It's John coming back. He'll bring the mail in here, won't he?" How she wished she dared let her father write her, but she was afraid Hunter would get the mail and wonder who Mike Malone was. He might even open her letter and read it, find out her background.

Hunter shrugged, bored. "No, he'll probably pile it up for Swede like always."

She drew a breath of relief but she couldn't help but be surprised. "You don't read your own mail?"

288

He made a gesture of dismissal. "Sometimes. It's mostly dull paperwork and Swede deals with all that. I'm usually too busy to be bothered."

"Well, Swede is gone and you've got nothing to do, so I'll get it for you."

"I don't feel like messing with it," he complained, but Sassy was already out the door and down the hall.

She found the mail on the temporary desk that had been set up for Swede until the new one was shipped from San Francisco. She sorted through it quickly. Nothing for her. She was both relieved and disappointed. She missed her family. Sassy carried the mail back to the bedroom.

"You're right," she admitted. "It looks like dull business mail. Want me to open it for you?"

He held up his bandaged hand. "Have you forgotten? I'll look at it later."

"I could open it and read it aloud."

"That would make it a little easier, wouldn't it? I suppose you could even answer it if I dictated to you."

"I'd be glad to. That'll take some of the load off Swede, too." She opened the first letter. "Henshaw and Sons Lumber Company thanks you for filling their order and payment is being sent to the bank."

"Good. Read the next one." He leaned back in his chair and smoked his cigar.

"Willoby, Clinton and Dawson Law Firm says they have been unable to collect from the client in California. Do they have your permission to sue?"

"Hell, yes!" Hunter said. "When Swede gets here, I'll dictate a letter—"

"Swede's got too much to do now." Sassy reached for

289

a paper and pen. "Dictate what you want and I'll write it."

"You know," he said, stretching his legs out before him as he smoked his cigar, "I could get used to having you as a secretary. I didn't know ladies could be anything but ornamental."

She paused, her pen poised over the paper. "I'm not good with figures, but I read and write as well as anyone. Tell me what you want to say."

The morning passed pleasantly with Sassy reading the mail aloud, then answering as he dictated.

"Hunter, it really is awful to burden Swede with all this. You ought to at least read your own mail."

"I told you I was busy. I suppose I need to hire someone to take over the office and get the bookwork off Swede's back, but it's hard to find someone out on the frontier who can even read, much less handle business mail."

In the early afternoon, they took a picnic basket and went for a buggy ride out to the woods to check with Swede.

"Swede," Hunter asked, "you think you'll meet that shipment date?"

"By jingo, hope so. I be leaving this afternoon to check things at the far lease. I camp in woods tonight, check things tomorrow, and report back."

"Good," Hunter grunted. "Sassy's dealt with the mail this morning; she may end up running the whole office."

Swede winked at her. "I wouldn't mind that one bit." His bright blue eyes twinkled. "I hate paperwork."

"I told Hunter he should deal with it himself, but he says he's too busy. I think he hates it worse than you do and is making excuses."

The two men exchanged glances.

"Boss right; don't like to be bothered," Swede explained. "I usually do the best I can, but I not speak or read English too good." He brushed a graying blond curl out of his eyes.

"I don't mind, Swede," Sassy said. "I'll give it a try for a few days." She and Hunter got back in the buggy.

The big logger slapped him on the shoulder fondly. "Boss, tomorrow, I let you know about timber on far slope."

"Fine." Hunter nodded. They said their goodbyes and drove back to the house in the late afternoon sun.

Sassy played the piano for several hours to amuse Hunter and then they had an early supper of fresh salmon broiled in butter, an excellent wine, and pears baked in a honeyed brandy sauce.

Hunter got up from the table stiffly. "My muscles hurt from all that stomping I got."

"I think a good soak in a tub of hot water would do you good," she suggested.

He gestured with his bandaged hand. "Just how am I supposed to take a bath with this?"

"Easy." She got up from the table. "I'll have John heat some water. I can bathe you."

He grinned. "Sounds good to me."

In less than an hour, he was sitting in a steaming tub in their bedroom with his bandaged hand held carefully out of the water.

Sassy knelt by the tub and began to wash him.

He closed his eyes in evident pleasure. "If I'd known I could enjoy this so much, I would have had my hand stomped a long time ago."

She smacked him with the washcloth. "You're just like some oriental potentate, luxuriating in your bath, enjoying a woman waiting on you."

"Why don't you get in here with me?"

"Because what you've got in mind isn't bathing."

"How do you know what I've got in mind?"

She sudsed his brawny chest, ran the washcloth across his nipples. "I see that look in those blue eyes. You'd forget yourself and get that bandage wet."

"What about when I get out of the tub?" He reached for her with his good hand, pulled her against his wet, soapy body, and kissed her.

"We'll see." It took all her willpower to pull away from him and finish sudsing his muscular body. He stood up and she wrapped a towel around his lean hips. His manhood was erect and hard.

He stepped out of the tub. His body still wet and smelling of soap, he pulled her to him, kissed her. The towel came loose and gradually slid to the floor. She felt his maleness insistent and big between them. "You can't put any weight on that hand," she reminded him.

"I don't intend to. You make love to me, Sassy."

He stood in the dim lamplight, naked and glistening, all male, like a dark Greek god.

She slipped out of her clothes and kissed his wet nipples while he pulled the pins from her hair and let it tumble down her shoulders to her hips. Her kisses inched down his belly very slowly. He moaned. "I can't take that!"

"Try," she said and kissed his navel, gradually going to her knees before him, bringing her kisses ever lower. He gasped, tangled his good hand in her red hair, pressed her face against him, wanting more.

"Sassy," he gasped. "If you don't stop . . ."

She didn't stop.

With a groan, he bent over and lifted her from the floor, slipping one arm around her tiny waist, lifted her to the bed.

"You're a greedy little pixie," he whispered, "the kind of passionate woman men dream of and you're mine."

"Just yours, Hunter," she whispered, straddling him. "Only yours for the rest of our lives." He had unleashed something wild and untamed in her that couldn't get enough of his hard, virile body. She slid down on him and again he was big, throbbing. She felt him all the way up to her navel. "I want you to put a child in me," she whispered. She lowered her breasts to his mouth.

"I—I'm almost afraid of the kind of child I would father," he whispered reluctantly. "There's something you don't know about my family."

Secrets. Hunter had some, too. She waited, then realized he wasn't going to tell her what he meant. But she was Woman. She would not be fully fulfilled until her belly was big with his son, her breasts swollen with the promise of milk.

She brushed her nipple against his mouth. He wrapped his one good arm around her, pulled her down against his lips, and sucked her breasts into two sensitive points while she rode him for her own fulfillment. It was violent and passionate, rutting and meshing like two wild things. He thrashed under her but she was merciless, riding him hard. Sassy did not stop until he had exploded inside her, putting his seed deep in her womb. She didn't uncouple from him, but lay on top of his body while he gasped for breath and stroked her hair.

"Sweet, I feel like I've been used for stud service."

"You mind? I want your child."

"You give me too much pleasure to worry about anything else," he admitted. He wrapped his arms around her and they slept, her velvet vessel still holding him inside her.

In the woods, Swede came awake suddenly in his blankets and listened. By jingo, he was getting as jumpy as Kitty. He must be getting old, although he wasn't yet fifty. He lay quietly in his temporary camp and listened. An owl hooted in a tree and he heard a deer run through the nearby woods. What had startled it? A fox? Bobcat? Swede wasn't afraid although he was halfway between the two timber camps without another human around for miles. This was his domain. He'd spent most of his life as a logger and he knew the forests and its inhabitants.

At dawn, he'd be on his way to the east camp to check the timber cutting there, then he'd report back. He thought about Hunter. Secrets. Hunter must never know. He would think less of Swede for it. How many times had Swede yearned to tell him? Swede knew what hell was, he thought now as he stared up at the blinking stars. It wasn't a faraway place of flames; no, it was worse. A man makes his own hell with his conscience . . . if he has one.

Swede must keep his secret forever. Once he had tried to ease his conscience by confessing and it had led to violence and murder. He lay still, remembering the past and the sweet, gentle girl he had loved before he became dazzled by the Jezebel. Sometimes when the need for a woman was overpowering, he succumbed, got drunk, put his ruined face on Lulu's big breasts. When he made love to her, Swede pretended she was the little blond daughter of a Lutheran minister. Once lately when Swede was very, very drunk and especially vulnerable, he thought he might have told Lulu his secret. He prayed he hadn't.

Did everyone in this world have a secret? He nodded, thinking about all the people he had known. Had that pert new wife of Hunter's guessed at his? She was a smart girl, that Sassy. The longer Hunter waited to tell her, the more humiliated he would be. Not that Swede hadn't tried to help with his own limited abilities, he just didn't know much about it. Sassy. She would make Hunter a good wife and give him fine sons. Swede wanted to be around to see that passcl of kids, even though he could never acknowledge . . .

Again a sound. This time Swede sat up in his blankets. It might be something bigger than a bobcat or a fox. It might be a bear. He wished that he had a rifle with him or at least an axe.

Then he laughed aloud at his own fears. "By jingo, Swede, you gettin' daft!" He had no enemies that he knew of and Clegg was safely on a ship. Most forest animals would run from a man and Swede was big enough to handle almost any emergency. He feared nothing but God's vengeance; but then, hadn't he paid enough for his sins already?

He lay back down and relaxed, starting to doze off again. A step. His keen ears heard the crackle of leaves.

Swede came up out of his blankets in a fighting crouch. "Who's there? By God, who is it?"

A man stepped out of the shadows into the moonlight, and Swede stared for a long moment at the form, the glint of the moonlight on the rifle barrel. "Clegg?"

"Yeah, you dumb Swede, it's me."

"How'd you get off ship? I gave crew strict orders—"

"I had a friend." Clegg laughed and moved closer.

If he kept the man talking, he might get close enough to take that rifle away from him. "We talk, Clegg."

"Talk?" The man waved the gun wildly, his unshaven face grimy with sweat. "I didn't come to talk, I came for revenge; first you, then that damned Hunter."

Swede didn't care what happened to him much, but Hunter was different, so very special to him. Swede must protect him at all costs. "I got bottle in pack, Clegg. We sit down, have drink, talk—"

"He's stomped me all over," Clegg snarled. "I look almost as bad as you do now!"

Swede winced at his cruel words. "Hunter mean no harm, Clegg; you had his woman. Hunter kill any man who touch her; everyone in woods know that."

"And I'll still have her, just like I had his Injun ma. He might even be my son; wouldn't that be a laugh?" Clegg grinned with crooked, yellow teeth. "After I tie him up and stomp that handsome face to bloody pulp, I'm gonna have her right in front of him, let him watch me do it to her before I kill him."

"And that's the reason I got you off that ship," said a voice in the shadows.

Swede whirled toward the voice. It was both familiar and unfamiliar. "Who the hell—"

"You know who. You've made me sweat enough on a

logging crew and I swore someday I'd get you for it."
The handsome man stepped out of the shadows.

"You!" Swede blinked in disbelief. "Never expect to
see you—"

"I never expected to see you again, either, you old
bastard." He moved closer. "I always wondered what it
was you said that night—"

Swede shook his head. "I never tell you. Sorry I tell
Clay; nothing but trouble from telling secrets."

Clegg looked from one to the other. "Did I miss
something? I don't understand what the hell you two
are talking about."

The newcomer frowned. "Never mind, Clegg. It
doesn't concern you."

Time. He must stall for time until he found out why
they were here. Swede tried to think what to do, turning
his head slightly, watching Clegg with the rifle. "So why
you come to Seattle?"

"What a question! I came to see my dear brother."

Swede shook his head. "That not reason; you always
spoiled, never care about anyone but yourself."

The other scowled and the cleft in his chin deepened.
"I want to know what caused my father to go beserk?"

Swede backed slowly away. "I not tell. You not use it
against Hunter." If he could make it to the forest, he
knew it like the back of his hand. He might lose them
both among the towering timber.

The other grinned, moved closer. "You stubborn old
bastard. I guess that's one secret I'll never unravel. Well
then, I suppose there's no reason to prolong this."

For the first time Swede saw the big axe. Swede
turned and tried to run, but he tripped over a root and
fell. Even as he struggled to get to his feet, he glanced

back over his shoulder and saw the moonlight glinting on the axe blade as it came up.

Instinctively, he threw his hands up to protect himself. The younger man swung with both hands, putting all his strength into it. Swede saw the moonlight glint on the steel as it came down. *Now my son will never, never know,* he thought with both relief and regret in that fraction of a second before the axe took off one of his protecting hands and split his skull in half.

Chapter Seventeen

Sassy and Hunter were finishing breakfast in the dining room when they heard a horse galloping up to the front of the house.

Hunter said, "Now what?"

Sassy had already jumped to her feet. She waved John away as she hurried to the front door and opened it to the logger who had just dismounted. She recognized the lanky, buck-toothed boy as one of Hunter's crew. "Oh, hello. It's Bob, isn't it? Nice to see you."

"Biff," he corrected, pulling off his cap. He twisted it in his hands, looked around. "Ma'am, sorry to disturb you, but I need to see the boss."

"Here I am." Hunter came out of the dining room. "Why are you in such an all-fired hurry?"

Something about the man's expression caused her to go to Hunter's side. "Is something wrong?" she asked.

The young lumberjack acted as if he were attempting to think of a way to put it, finally gave up, and blurted it out. "It's Swede, Boss; he's dead!"

"What?"

"Somebody split his head wide open with an axe!"

Hunter's swarthy face went white and Sassy cringed at the mental picture that came to her mind of the blond hair soaked with blood, the bright blue eyes staring sightless into Eternity. "Hunter, are you all right?"

He took a deep breath and a little color returned to his hard face. "I—I'm fine. Come into the library, Biff; tell me what you know."

Sassy followed and poured them each a glass of brandy. The window was open on this warm summer morning. A bird called. A bee drifted through the open window and out again into a sky the color of Hunter's eyes.

Hunter gulped the brandy, and his hand shook. "Now," he said, "calm down. Maybe it's a mistake. Maybe it's someone else."

"No." The lanky boy shook his head and leaned back in his chair. "No mistake. Even if the hair was almost black with dried blood, you could tell."

"Spare the lady the gruesome details," Hunter snapped.

"Beg your pardon, ma'am." Biff colored and reached for his drink. "I ain't much used to being around real ladies—"

"Quite all right," Sassy put in quickly "But, as my husband asked, is there the slightest chance of mistaken—"

"No, ma'am, it's him all right."

She looked at Hunter. He closed his eyes and swallowed hard. She had known he was not nearly as cold as he appeared to be. His father's logging boss was the oldest, closest friend Hunter had.

Biff cleared his throat. "Well, you know, Boss, he was supposed to turn up at the camp at the far slope at dawn and never got there, so someone went back along the trail."

Hunter looked devastated. "Where'd they find him?"

300

"Still in his blankets where he'd bedded down last night. Looks like someone came up behind him and maybe he half-turned to look at his killer."

For a long moment, the only sound was the ticking of the mantel clock. She tried not to imagine the scene of Swede awaking to an attacker. In her mind, she saw the flash of the axe blade in the moonlight and heard him scream, scrambling too late to escape.

Hunter swore softly but thoroughly under his breath. "Swede didn't have any enemies. I don't know who'd want him dead."

"What about Clegg?" Sassy asked.

"His quarrel was with me," Hunter said and drank his brandy. "Besides, Clegg was put on that ship last night."

"That's right, Boss." Biff nodded. "I helped Swede get him to the ship after Doc saw him."

Another long silence. She watched Hunter. His face was a frozen mask of fury and grief. He looked at his bandaged hand. "And me too damned stove up to do anything about it!"

Sassy went to his side. "Maybe it was a robbery."

Hunter shook his head. "Swede never had any money on him and he didn't have any enemies that I'm aware of."

Biff asked, "Boss, now what?"

"I—I don't know," Hunter said, "but I intend to get the bastard who did it."

Sassy's heart went out to this shattered man who was her husband. Maybe he hadn't realized himself how much he depended on his bull o' the woods. She put her hand on his arm. "Why don't I take Biff to the kitchen while you try to make some decisions?" she offered.

"Good idea." The big half-breed sighed.

"Come with me." She led the way out of the library, the logger trailing in her wake. "John will fix you something to eat and then you can report back to camp. The boss will have to make some plans; he'll let you know before you leave what to tell the others. Do you know our cook?"

The boy nodded. "Cookie befriended me back when he was still a faller."

"Then maybe you ought to be the one to tell him," Sassy said. "I think he's known Swede for almost as long as Hunter has." She didn't want Hunter to have to break the news to John.

Sassy returned to the library. Hunter sat with his face in his hands, the yellow tomcat rubbing against his leg as if it sensed something was very wrong. Sitting on the arm of his chair, she put her arm around his shoulders. "I'm sorry," she said. "I'm so sorry."

He cleared his throat. "Swede was more than just a logging boss," Hunter murmured. "He was my father's best friend, so he felt obligated to look out for me after my father died."

"I'm sure there was more to it than obligation. You were probably like the son he never had."

"I suppose that's right." He stared at the blank wall. "When I find the bastard who did this . . ." His voice trailed off, but his expression left no doubt as to what the killer could expect.

The cold, hard look on his vengeful face frightened her and she wondered what the older Hunter had been like and what traits her husband had inherited from him. "Let's not think about vengeance now, dearest. We've got to decide what to do. Is there a family cemetery?"

Hunter shook his head. "My father is buried in San

302

Francisco with his wife. I don't know where my mother . . ."

"Maybe we should start our own graveyard," she put in quickly. "Most families of property have one. Maybe Swede wasn't exactly family, but he'd surely be pleased to be the first one buried in yours."

Hunter brightened. "There's a little rise I know in a clearing that has a view of Puget Sound; Swede was fond of the place."

It was warm outside, Sassy thought; it needed to be done soon. "Late this afternoon?"

He stroked the cat absently. "Yes."

"I'll see to the details." She left him, seeking out cook and logger in the kitchen. They would need a lot of food for a funeral crowd. She found John shaken, but stubbornly making bread.

"I'll get some food sent out from town," she began, "so you won't have to——"

"Begging your pardon, Miss Sassy, but I want to do the food myself for Swede's friends." His reddened eyes blinked back tears. "Besides, it gives me something to keep me occupied. Is Hunter okay?"

She nodded. "He's still in shock but he'll rally."

With the old cook supervising the funeral meal, she sent the logger to spread the word and find a carpenter to craft a coffin. Then she returned to Hunter, who stood at the library window, smoking a cheroot. "I'm not sure I can run the business without Swede."

"You feel that way now," Sassy said gently as she slipped her arm around his waist, "but in a few days, when your hand heals, you'll pull it all together, get a new bull o' the woods, take over the ledgers and reports yourself."

"Sassy, you don't understand. I can't . . ."

She waited for him to continue, but he let the words hang on the air like the pale blue smoke from his cheroot.

"Hunter, what was Swede's real name?"

He shook his head. "Funny, now that you ask, I don't know his real name. It never seemed important."

Her husband was so alone, Sassy thought. Wasn't there anyone who could take part of the burden of the business from him? She voiced her thoughts aloud. "Do you have any relatives?"

"Of my father's family?" He shook his head. "Just my older half-brother; I haven't seen him in years."

"Is he still alive?" She tried to think of someone who might bolster this solitary man.

He shrugged. "I don't even know. Like any young boy, I looked up to my older brother, but he wasn't pleased when Father left half his estate to his bastard. He didn't feel I was entitled to anything, and maybe I wasn't. My mother was just a mixed-breed whore while his was a lady with a legal marriage."

Sassy winced at the word, but abruptly, she understood much more about him. He needed to talk, to face his ghosts. "What was she like, your mother?"

"Toma Alwawinmi," he whispered, staring out the window. "I was only two or three when she died. Beautiful, but as wild as the wind. Her name meant 'Springtime' in the Nez Perce language."

Springtime. Sassy envisioned the passionate, mixed-blood girl. She must have had a mane of hair as black as Hunter's. Did she have blue eyes like his? "Your father must have loved her very much."

Hunter surprised her by making a sound of disgust. "Lusted for her, maybe. Every man who saw her

304

wanted her, wanted her enough to throw away everything—wealth, family, reputation, friendship. Nothing meant as much as having her, and Springtime would sell or give her favors to any man who had the price or took her fancy."

"Did your father know?"

Hunter shrugged. "I think he didn't want to know and wouldn't face it until . . ." He paused but then continued. "Other Indian children would snicker when I passed and I knew their elders gossiped about her."

Pieces of the puzzle slipped into place as she imagined the lonely, outcast child who belonged in neither world and whose mother was a tramp. He craved respectability; Hunter's pride meant more to him than love. What a bitter, bitter joke Sassy had played on him without meaning to. How people would laugh and whisper behind his back with glee if they knew his wife was as common a whore as his wild mother!

"What about your father's widow?"

Hunter hesitated. "You ask too many questions. I thought I told you she was dead, too."

"Maybe you did; I forgot."

"Swede tried for several years to turn my brother into a lumberman, but he didn't think it was suitable work for an educated gentleman."

"But you cared about him anyway." It was more a statement than a question. She had caught the affection in his voice.

"Yes. I suppose that's stupid." He looked sheepish. "He was so impressive to a lonely young kid."

She laid her head against his shoulder. "Maybe he didn't hate you; maybe it was just a natural reaction to his having to share the inheritance. What happened to him?"

Hunter shrugged. "Heard he lost most everything and went back East. He had a wild streak, and there was something else." He bit his lip, shrugged. "Hell, maybe we both inherited Father's worst trait."

Outside, a hammer tapped and a saw rasped as the crew began to construct the coffin. Hunter started. "I wish I knew why this had to happen and who did it." He clenched and unclenched his one good hand, and his rage frightened her. Had he inherited that tendency toward violence? Would her life be safe if he ever found out her past? "I liked Swede," she whispered. "I liked him a lot. He wouldn't want you to take justice into your own hands."

"My father did," Hunter replied softly, but she knew better than to ask what Clay Hunter had done. She had to wait and bide her time, and maybe someday he would tell her what troubled him so.

The day seemed endless. A wagon covered with a tarp delivered the body. Sassy caught Hunter's arm. "Don't look at him."

"Someone who cared about him should—"

"I'll see to everything. Did Swede own a suit?"

Hunter laughed without mirth. "A suit? No, I don't think I ever saw him dressed up."

"Well, he was about your height and weight, I'm sure one of yours would fit him."

"Get Judge Stone to say a few words at the services; Swede would like that."

"Does he have any relatives that we should notify?"

Hunter's brow furrowed. He lit a cigarillo awkwardly, broke the match, tossed it away. "I don't know; I don't really know very much about him at all except that he was my father's best friend and was always there for me. I never thought much about it till now." He shook his head. "I always just accepted him at face value and never cared about his past."

If only you were willing to do the same for me, Sassy thought. "Why don't you try to get some rest?"

"Rest, hell, I've got a killer to hunt down."

His tone and expression scared her. Instinctively she knew he could be as merciless as any savage warrior who ever roamed these forests. "Hunter, you can't do that today; it isn't fitting, and, besides, you want to be here to pay your respects." She had to keep him busy on this the longest of days. "Maybe you could occupy yourself a couple of hours with paperwork."

"With this?" He held up his bandaged hand.

"I didn't think. I'm sorry."

Hunter looked around. "I'll read awhile." But he paid little attention to which book he grabbed off a shelf as he settled into a chair.

Sassy selected one of Hunter's suits and a pair of his good boots from the wardrobe. She handed them over to Biff and studied the rough-hewn coffin. "Oh," she said. "We'll need a lining."

Biff hesitated, drawing her attention. "If it won't offend you, ma'am," he stammered.

"What do you suggest?" Sassy asked.

"Swede spent a lot of time at Lulu's Lovelies. It's a—uh—place in town. For entertainment."

"Yes?"

"One of the boys from the lumber camp rode into

307

town with the news. Lulu and the girls was wonderin' if you'd be offended if they came to the services? Lulu sent a purple-satin comforter to line the coffin."

Could she bear to face that woman again? She must not think of herself. "Anyone who was a friend of Swede's is welcome to come. And, Biff, use the comforter; Swede would like that."

John limped out with a big pot of coffee for the men. "Miss Sassy, I got a lot of food ready."

"Thank you, John. I know Swede was a friend of yours, too. You both looked out for my husband."

For just a moment, his wrinkled face trembled and tears came to his blue eyes. "I had been waitin' to tell everyone Miss Ellie says she's going to marry me."

"Congratulations," Sassy said and tried to smile.

Biff sipped his coffee. "We're all afeared Hunter will be like a crazed grizzly run amok when his wounds heal. Does he own a gun?"

"I—I don't know," Sassy said.

John shook his head. "Hunter hates guns; far as I know, he don't even own one, because . . . never mind."

"Oh?" She waited, but he said no more. Of course she had seen Hunter in action with those spiked boots; he didn't need a gun. She walked back to the house with the old cook.

He paused in the doorway. "I'm glad you're here, Miss Sassy. If you weren't, Hunter might do something crazy, like his father."

She waited expectantly, but he had obviously said more than he had meant to already. She wasn't hungry herself, but it occurred to her Hunter might feel better if he ate. In the kitchen, she got a big plate of roast beef, fresh bread, and a hunk of warm cake, and tiptoed to the library. Hunter had the book propped up before him, but his gaze was vacant.

"Hungry?" She tried to sound cheerier than she felt. "I brought you something to eat."

He closed the book. "I've been reading."

"Uh huh." She set the plate on the table next to the sofa, reached for the book. "Your mind must be a million miles away or you'd have noticed you've got the book upsidedown."

He looked startled, then chagrined. "I do? Oh, of course I do." He shrugged. "I haven't really been reading; I was thinking. Can't remember such horror since . . ."

She waited. The silence sounded loud to her. "Want to talk about it?"

He sighed, shook his head. "Some secrets are too dark to share or too horrible to be forgiven."

She almost asked if there were any connection to his nightmares, then remembered that he didn't know she was aware of his restless sleep. "Eat. You'll feel better."

"Now you sound like Cookie," he grumbled, but he reached for the plate.

"Has he been with you long?"

"He worked for my father, too, just like Swede. He was there; I heard them arguing."

She waited, watching the pain cross his dark face. She rested her hand on top of his, not saying anything. Sometimes a touch, a reaching out, meant more than words.

"I—I was so little and I couldn't do anything; I didn't do anything to stop him."

The silence hung heavy between them and, in the background, she heard the sound of hammers banging, banging. "I love you, Hunter," she whispered. "I'll always love you, no matter what."

Love and friendship. She had reached past the barricade, she saw it in his troubled blue eyes as the words tumbled from his mouth. "Oh, Sassy, something terrible happened that night!"

"Did you see it?"

He stood up, began to pace. "I—I don't know."

"Then how do you know it was terrible?"

He didn't answer, he paced—agitated, disturbed. Was it possible that he was attempting to deal with a horrible truth he couldn't bear to know?

"Never mind." She slipped her arms around him and he pulled her to him, kissed her hair. "You were only a little boy; whatever happened wasn't your fault."

"I should have tried to stop him, but I was afraid," Hunter whispered and hugged her to him so hard she feared he would break her ribs. "I should have tried."

She didn't know if he were talking about his father, John, or Swede. And with his mental agony, she couldn't do anything but let him cling to her. She was surprised to feel him shaking. "It's been a long day, dearest, and a bad one, with Swede's death." She looked out at the late-afternoon sun. "People will be arriving soon, and you've been under a lot of stress."

"So was my father. I may be just like him! If I've inherited—" He left the thought unfinished, stalking from the room.

Lulu stood in front of her wardrobe, nibbling a sweet and deciding what to wear to the funeral. It was a sad time; she had been genuinely fond of Swede. She pulled out a deep lavender-gray dress and held it up for inspection. Yes, this would do nicely.

She heard a step behind her, turned, startled. "I'll swan! Where did you come from?"

He smiled, put his hands in the pockets of his stylish coat. "Now is that any way to greet me?"

He was as handsome, as charming, as ever. Her gaze swept over him from his expensive boots to his fine hat. She resisted an urge to fling herself into his arms. "You're the last person I expected to see. Anyone know you're in town?"

"No, and don't you tell."

"You here to stay?"

"Depends on the kind of reception I get." He favored her with that charming smile.

He didn't care about her, she knew that in her heart, but someday, maybe he might learn to. "From me or him?" Lulu turned away.

"Both. Honey, I've missed you!" His arms went around her ample girth from behind and his tongue caressed the rim of her ear. "I know that telegram was just an excuse to get me here."

Now Lulu almost wished she hadn't sent it. Hunter's brother; so handsome; so sophisticated. "I—I don't have time for that; I'm getting dressed for a funeral."

"I heard the news when I arrived. Too bad."

"Too bad? Is that all you've got to say?" She pulled away from him. "You ain't changed much."

"You wouldn't like me if I did, Honey." He kissed the back of her neck and sent shivers up and down her body. "We were good together. It could be that way again."

She knew better than to hope; but once, long ago when she had been younger and slim, he had wanted her, at least for a little while. Gradually it had become merely a business partnership with her providing most of the money. "I been meaning to take off some weight," she drawled, brushing crumbs off her ample bosom.

"You're just right, like always." His hand went to her big breast, stroked her. "You're all-woman, sexier than these little boney things you hire."

He turned her around and his mouth covered hers in a way she had not been kissed since they had parted company. For the moment, she forgot he had lied to her and used her in a million ways. With his mouth on hers, his hands pulling her against his hardness, she could pretend he really cared. She found herself clinging to him. "I—I ain't got time for this. I got to get dressed for the funeral."

"Then keep me in mind for when you get back," he murmured. "This place making any money?"

So that was it. "Flat broke as usual?"

"I've got some deals working."

"Uh huh. How much do you need?"

"Honey, you hurt my feelings!" He poured himself a drink. "Go ahead to the funeral."

She eyed him, jealous of his charm to other women. "Just in case you were thinking about it, don't sample my girls while I'm gone."

He paused with the tumbler at his lips, winked. "Now Honey, you know you're the only woman I ever really loved."

She wanted to believe him; but deep in her heart, she knew better. With a sigh, she dressed for the funeral.

The sun was low on the horizon as the procession wound its way behind the wagon carrying the body to that little rise Swede had liked.

Strange, Sassy thought as Hunter helped her from the buggy, *the first body buried in our family cemetery is not even kin.*

Most of the loggers and many of the townsfolk had driven out to pay their respects; even Marylou—no, she now called herself Lulu—and some of her girls had come. Lulu's eyes were red in stark contrast to her heavily powdered face. Maybe the old madam had a soft place in her heart for Swede after all.

Sassy and Hunter followed the six sturdy loggers who carried the pine box. Judge Stone and his wife joined the procession along with Asa Mercer, Doc Maynard, Sassy's friends, and Seattle's most respected citizens.

The mourners gathered at the grave as a bird trilled and a breeze ruffled the big firs. Sassy took a deep breath and smelled the scent of pine and wild flowers.

Judge Stone spoke, but Sassy only half-listened in her sorrow. ". . . maybe men who commit heinous crimes like this spring from bad seed or are throwbacks to Cain, who slew his brother. Let us hope that the killer doesn't pass on this violent nature to his descendants."

Sassy had her arm linked through Hunter's. She felt his sudden tension and glanced at his pale face, too numb to listen closely as the judge rambled on. A man cleared his throat, and a young whore sobbed. John, next to Ellie, wiped his eyes on his sleeve; and Sassy swallowed with difficulty. She hadn't known Swede long or well; and yet, she had felt an unusual relationship to him. Or maybe it was only that they both cared so much about Hunter.

Concluding his remarks, Judge Stone addressed Hunter. "Would you like to say something?"

There was a long silence and Sassy thought he would refuse, but then Hunter spoke in a voice so low, even she had to strain to catch his words. "Swede was my friend since I was a very little boy. Before that, he was my father's best friend and trusted bull of the woods. Yet, I really don't know much about him, not even his real name. He was a private man, and maybe there was something in his past that he wanted to forget."

There was a murmur of agreement through the crowd. Hunter cleared his throat. "If I could say one thing to sum up Swede's life, it would be this: He could be counted on and was a man worthy of trust. Swede was like a father to me, and I'll miss him every day of my life." A murmur of 'amens' ran through the crowd as Hunter finished.

Now other men spoke, recollecting stories of Swede in the timber industry—small personal anecdotes that didn't tell much about the man at all. He had taken most of his secrets to his grave.

Finally, the plain pine box was lowered into the hole and the judge was inviting those gathered to step forward and sprinkle a handful of fresh dirt on the coffin. It made such a loud sound, Sassy thought dully as she tossed a loose clod against the wood and remembered her mother's funeral. Then the loggers picked up their shovels and filled in the grave. Sassy breathed deeply. The smell of turned earth mixed with the scent of Puget Sound. In the distance, thunder rumbled.

Mrs. Stone and Marylou—Lulu—had brought flowers and spread them across the mound when the loggers stepped back. Then she and Hunter were surrounded by neighbors pushing forward to shake Hunter's good hand and offer condolences. She glanced over her shoulder as they left the clearing. The fresh grave looked lonely and bleak.

However, there was no time to be pensive and sad.

All important ceremonies ultimately end with food, Sassy reflected as the crowd gathered at the house. Ellie was at John's side, helping him serve, aided by the faithful Gertrude and her Will. Even Mildred seemed sweet and sympathetic as she dished out quail, succulent fish, roast beef, and wild-berry pies. Dusk came, and the mourners continued to talk and to eat. Hunter ate little as he wandered through the group, greeting friends and associates awkwardly with his one good hand. Would the day never end? Finally, the last of the mourners loaded up and left in the darkness.

She linked her arm in Hunter's, listening to John, Ellie, and the hired girls moving through the house, picking up dirty dishes and glasses. "It's been a long day. Why don't we go to bed?"

"I can't sleep; I've got to kill a man."

Sassy winced. "Oh, darling, let the law handle it."

"There isn't any law; that's why some people come here."

"At least wait until tomorrow." By morning, maybe he would feel differently.

He nodded. "Too dark to start tracking now anyway." They started down the hall. He paused at the open office door, taking in the letters and contracts scattered on the desktop just as Swede had left them. "Damned paperwork; Swede took care of so much I never even thought about."

"Let's not look at any of it tonight," she soothed. "Maybe you'll feel like sorting it and reading it later."

"Funny. So funny," he muttered.

She wondered what memory had reclaimed him but didn't ask.

They entered the bedroom, undressed in the dark.

315

Hunter went to the window. "I never thought of a time Swede wouldn't be around. My father depended on him, trusted him; I did the same."

He idolized Swede; even Hunter's lady couldn't live up to that image of perfection. Hunter still saw the older man as his hero. Swede surely had human failings, just like everyone else, but her husband preferred his people on pedestals.

She slipped her arms around him. "Let's see if we can get some sleep."

"Sleep?" he pulled away from her. "Somewhere out there is the snake who killed my friend and he's alive! I can't sleep thinking about that."

"God evens things out in the end, Hunter."

Hunter snorted. "I may not be patient enough to wait for heavenly justice. I may take it out of God's hands."

She tried not to let her shock register on her face. "Hunter, you don't know what you're saying; you're tired."

"I keep thinking about what Judge Stone said about bad seed. I'm not sure I have a right to have sons."

He wasn't making any sense as far as she was concerned. "Hunter, you're tired," she repeated wearily. "Everything will look different to you tomorrow."

"Sassy, there're things you don't know about me, things that might make a difference—"

"I know all I need to know." She took his dark face in her two small hands and stood on tiptoe to kiss him. "If two people love each other, can't they just close the door on the past and pretend their lives began the moment they met?"

He jerked from her grasp, retreating to that remote

world inside his head. "I can't sleep. I—I think I'll sit up and read awhile."

"Do you want me to stay with you?"

He shook his head. "Go on to sleep. You'd be bored watching me read."

"You aren't going out, are you?" She was worried.

"No, I'd be a fool to be out looking around in the dark. I just want to think."

She was too exhausted to stay awake herself. "Why don't you get yourself a brandy or some hot milk and bring your book to bed?"

"That sounds like a good idea. Maybe I will. Go to sleep, Missy."

It was pointless to argue with him; he had withdrawn into himself. "All right. If you need me, call."

She went to bed, but she could hear him pacing in the library. In a minute, she would get up and go check on him, she thought drowsily.

Sassy awoke with a start, wondering what had pulled her from her dreamless sleep. Horse hooves pounded in the drive, and she tensed until she realized it was someone arriving, not leaving. Relaxing, she listened to Hunter's footsteps, the opening of a door, and muted voices.

Curious, she donned robe and slippers and tiptoed down the hall. The voices were low, the words mostly indistinct. " . . . was just thinking about you . . ." she heard Hunter say. "It's been a long time."

" . . . passing through town . . . heard what happened . . . sorry . . ." The other man's voice had a different accent than Hunter's but sounded vaguely familiar. "I'm willing to let bygones be bygones if you are."

"I was never angry with you . . . ought to stick together . . . start over . . . blood is thicker than water."

Sassy's curiosity got the better of her and she tiptoed to the library, peeked around the door. The vaguely familiar voice was apologizing for the past again. The tall, dark-haired stranger stood with his back to her.

Hunter said. "I got married several days ago."

The other said, "Congratulations. I heard about it in town. Everyone says she's a real lady."

"She's better than I deserve," Hunter said. "If she knew everything, she'd probably go back East."

Without thinking, Sassy stepped into the doorway, planning to protest his statement and tell him that she loved him and that nothing else mattered to her.

Hunter smiled when he saw her, motioned her in. "Sweet, my half-brother was in town and heard the news, so he came by."

Alarm bells sounded in her head, yet there was nothing she could do but come into the room, hand outstretched. "I'm so happy to meet . . ."

The man turned around, a smile on his handsome face. He had a cleft in his chin and a pencil mustache. "Why, Hunter, she's as pretty as everyone said she was." He walked over, caught her numb hand in his.

It was a nightmare come true. Sassy stared up at him in horror. Maybe she was still asleep and, any moment now, she would awaken and find she was safely in bed next to her husband.

The handsome man grinned as he squeezed her shaking hands. "I'm so glad to meet my new sister-in-law. I'm Brett; Brett James."

Chapter Eighteen

Sassy stared open-mouthed at him as Brett held firmly to her hands. This couldn't be happening; she must be asleep and in the middle of a nightmare. It was too big a coincidence that she had come completely across the continent to escape Brett and Marylou only to meet them again in Seattle.

Brett smiled without releasing her and looked at Hunter. "Isn't that sweet? She's speechless. No doubt she's a trifle shy, just like all real ladies."

Hunter frowned. "Sassy, are you all right?"

"I—I'm fine." Sassy found her voice, pulled her hands free, took an involuntary step backward. "It's been a very exhausting day." To Brett, she said, "I—I didn't expect—"

"To ever meet your brother-in-law?" Brett asked smoothly. "I doubt that my younger brother ever expected to see me again, either; but I was here and learned of the terrible, terrible thing that had happened to Father's dear friend and felt it was time to let bygones be bygones."

Sassy ran her tongue over her dry lips. She wanted to

weep and protest; no! No! Just when she had found love and thought she was safe, God was going to get even with her after all. "I—I believe I could use some sherry."

While Hunter poured her a glass, Brett grinned at her. "She really doesn't look well, Hunter. Perhaps your sweet wife is already in the family way."

Sassy felt the blood rush to her face.

"I didn't mean to embarrass you, Ma'am." Brett made a sweeping bow. "I'm afraid I've spent too much time these past years in rough, low company. I forget how to deal with genteel ladies."

Sassy sat down, afraid her shaky legs might give out under her. She forced herself to appear calm and sip the sherry Hunter handed her, but inside, she was screaming.

Hunter poured whiskey for himself and Brett. "I know we were never close, Brett, but sudden death makes people see things in a different light."

"I had just been thinking the same. Blood really is thicker than water after all, isn't it?" Brett was his old charming self, Sassy thought as he held his glass up. "Cheers!" He took a deep drink, sighed. "Ah, my brand. I think I was the one who gave you your first taste of liquor—got you drunk and sick, as I recall."

Hunter didn't smile. "I suppose I was a nuisance, following you around that summer. It was lonely for an Indian kid in the lumber camp with Swede trying to turn us both into timber men."

Brett wiped the whiskey from his pencil mustache. When he frowned, the cleft in his chin deepened. "Father's idea; Mother was shocked. The Bretts moved in a different social circle."

"You went to college while I was sweating out in the

woods; Clay never thought about educating the Indian kid."

Brett looked around the room. "Well, you've done all right for yourself, little brother: big house, wealth, pretty wife. What else could a man want?"

"Respect," Hunter said and reached for the humidor of expensive cheroots on the mantel. "Deep inside, I still feel like the Injun slut's kid with people snickering behind my back. I want to be socially acceptable, send *my* son to college."

"It's no big thing, little brother."

"Not if you grew up in a mansion with servants as you did, hobnobbing with the elite of both coasts."

He offered the cigars to Brett, who took one, sniffed it appreciatively. "Hmm. Finest imported. Good taste in everything." He looked at Sassy.

"I try."

Sassy stared from one to the other in a daze, not knowing what to do. If only she would wake up and find that Brett's arrival was part of that dream. She wanted to scream, cry, and attack Brett James with both fists. Most of all, she wanted to run away, but if she did, Brett would tell her husband her horrible past. She had a crazy idea that as long as she stayed in the library, he wouldn't tell.

So she clenched her hands around her sherry and stalled for time. "I—I don't understand how you two can have the same father, yet have different last names."

Hunter flushed and paused in the act of lighting both cigars. "I told you, Sassy, I have no right to my Father's name. 'Hunter' is my Indian name." He checked the match, broke it in half before tossing it in the fireplace.

321

"No right," Brett muttered, "but the legal son only got half the estate."

"You can't hold that against me." Hunter leaned against the mantel. "I was a half-grown boy, didn't even know what a will was until that lawyer contacted me."

Brett forced a laugh. "Doesn't matter. Hey, if I'd gotten it all, I'd have lost it *all* on wine, women, and gambling—instead of just half. The old man's probably spinning in his grave, as hard as he worked, schemed, and struggled. He always said I took after the Bretts."

She looked from one to the other as they smoked, felt the tension between them in spite of their vows of brotherly friendship.

Brett moved quickly to make amends. "Ah, I hold no grudges." He flashed his most ingratiating smile and sipped his whiskey. "Life's too short for that. Besides, you took your half and built an empire. Me, I lost mine, don't even have a job. I'll level with you, little brother. I'm down and out like the prodigal son. I didn't just 'happen' to be in the area, I came hoping you'd be willing to give your big brother some help."

It would have made a touching, heart-wrenching scene, Sassy thought, if she hadn't known Brett well enough to know he hadn't a sincere bone in his body.

Hunter's expression softened. "You're not as proud and haughty as you once were. I admire your sincerity, Brett."

"That's about all I've got left—sincerity," Brett said, his brown eyes downcast and humble. "I sure don't have any pride left or I wouldn't drop in on you, hoping you might give me a stake or make a place for me."

"We'll talk tomorrow." Hunter gave him an encouraging pat on the back.

Brett wanted to stay, Sassy realized with a sinking heart. She'd hoped he wanted a loan or could be bribed to go away. Why should he, Sassy thought bitterly, when he could blackmail her forever to keep his mouth shut? How could she get the amount of money Brett would demand without Hunter's noticing? It was hard enough to send small sums to her father.

"Clay James' legacy: two sons," Hunter sighed, downing his drink.

"Yes, chilling thought, isn't it?" Brett sipped his whiskey. "To think either one of us might inherit that trait. Did you tell your wife—"

"Shut up, Brett."

Now they had her full attention and she looked from Hunter's tortured face to Brett's arrogant one.

"Oh, I'm sorry." Brett reacted in embarrassed confusion, "I just assumed Sassy knew about the skeletons in our family closet." He looked deep into her eyes. "Every family has some."

"Except Sassy's family." Hunter looked at her proudly and tossed his cigar in the fireplace. "I'm damned lucky that an elegant lady from Boston would have an old backwoods half-breed like me."

Sassy felt her face burn.

"Oh," Brett said, "she's blushing! A true lady if I ever saw one, little brother—modest and virtuous as well as pretty. I've met a lot of women, Hunter, but looks like you've really gotten a prize. What is it the Bible says about 'a virtuous woman, her price is above rubies'?"

She had to get him off this subject he kept nibbling around before Hunter became suspicious. "Mr. James, did you know Swede very well?"

"Oh, please, dear sister-in-law," Brett implored, "do

call me Brett. After all, we're family. No, I didn't see much of him; he was usually on a timber lease. Last time I saw him, he came to the house the night my parents died."

"I didn't know that." Hunter stared at him.

"Swede and Father went into the library, closed the door, and talked."

Hunter looked fascinated. "About what?"

Brett shrugged. "Business, I guess. Then Swede left. It was later that night that Father. . . . Well, we won't bore your wife with our family skeletons." Brett took out his watch, flipped it open, stared at the daguerreotype. He looked at the younger man. "Do you have any idea who would want to kill Swede?"

Hunter shook his head. "I suspected a logger I'd had trouble with, but Clegg left last night on the ship."

Brett's handsome brow furrowed. "Oh, yes, I remember the captain saying something about that. I think I arrived on the same ship that rascal left on." He looked at Hunter's bandaged hand. "This Clegg do that to you?"

"Yes. We had a set-to with calked boots. He tried to touch Sassy."

"I don't blame you." Brett smiled, and the cleft in his chin deepened. "She's such a lady!"

The blood froze in her veins, but Sassy managed to get her glass to her lips and sipped the sherry. She felt the warm, bracing taste all the way down and only half-listened to their conversation. There didn't seem to be very many happy memories these half-brothers could share, so Brett filled the silence with news from New York and the East Coast, boasting of the important business deals he had made before falling on hard times.

The yellow tomcat, wandering into the library, paused before Brett, and Sassy observed the slightest withdrawal on Brett's part. She knew he hated animals, but he leaned over to pat Kitty. Kitty raised his back and spat at the man as if abruptly faced with a bad dog. Inwardly, Sassy cheered the cat's reaction. Kitty was evidently a good judge of character.

Hunter was chagrined. "I don't know what got into that cat," he apologized.

Brett grinned. "Oh, after he gets to know me, I'm sure we'll get on famously."

So he intended to stay. Holy Mary, what was she going to do? Sassy knew she couldn't object without raising questions in her husband's mind. All she could think of now was how long would it be before Brett told Hunter that his respected lady had once been a whore in Brett's establishment and that Brett himself had taken her virginity? Since he hadn't already blurted it out, he must be playing some angle. "I think we should all get some rest," she said.

Brett grinned. "I think you and I are going to be very good friends, Sassy. Why, I feel like I've known you a long time already. Why don't you show me to the guest room?"

She wasn't about to be left alone with Brett. "I'm very tired—"

"Let me get you settled," Hunter offered. "Sassy Girl, you look weary. Go on to bed. We boys can manage on our own."

Suppose Brett told Hunter when she left the room? There wasn't anything she could do about that now. She said her good nights and went back to bed, where she could pound her pillow and muffle her cries. It wasn't fair.

Hunter had mixed feelings about his brother's turning up after all these years, but he wanted to do the right thing. It didn't take long to show Brett to the guest room, but when he came to bed, Sassy appeared to be asleep. "Sassy?"

No answer. He climbed in beside her, but couldn't sleep. Sassy stirred restlessly, and he had a sudden intuition that she wasn't asleep, either. Then why was she pretending?

He stared at the ceiling, lost in reverie, as the hours passed. Most of the memories were sad and lonely, except those involving Swede. Hunter hadn't seen Brett since the reading of the will, which had been a stormy scene.

Sassy. Her attitude baffled him. She had been very cool toward Brett. In fact, she had been almost hostile. Why? He listened to Sassy turn over and yearned to reach for her, but something held him back. Did she resent Brett as the prodigal son coming late to get into his brother's share of the James wealth after frittering away his own?

Damn! His hand hurt when he moved it. Well, at least with his hand bandaged, it would be awhile longer before Sassy found out. He supposed he should go ahead and tell her, but he feared she might laugh.

Laughter. Hunter winced, remembering. Once again he was a ragged little half-breed waif who belonged nowhere. Even the full-blooded Indian children chased him, throwing rocks and screaming, "White man's bastard! Killer's bastard!"

Springtime had called her son Small Hunter and he kept that name because he had none of his own. He knew that when a white man claimed a son, he gave it his own name, but Clayton James had never offered. It was only years after the man's death that Hunter had appropriated the James so he would have two names like the white men.

He would never let himself think about the tragedy or discuss it with anyone. How old had Hunter been? Two? Three? No one even knew he had been a witness to it all. Not that he remembered much of anything except his terror, although he still had nightmares. Sometimes his mind tried to find its way through the haze, but he always woke up sweating and shaking before he could remember the details.

After Springtime's death, Hunter was sent to his Indian relatives. Swede checked on him now and then, but mostly the foreman was away in the forests, fulfilling the role of James' second in command. He never knew Hunter had ridden with the war parties in that ill-fated fight against the whites invading Seattle. Hunter saw little of Swede except for the summer that, under Clayton James' orders, he tried to turn the two boys into timber men. Swede had never been one to drink, but he had begun to.

Clay James avoided his youngest son—memories of the mother, no doubt. He moved to San Francisco with his elegant, wealthy wife and older son. He was rich and powerful enough to be above the law. Springtime was dead and no one did anything about it.

Hunter remembered his mother with mixed feelings.

Her white blood had mixed with Salish, Paloose, and Nez Perce, creating a girl as beautiful as the mountain flowers and as wild as the wind with her long black hair, dark eyes, and sensual body. When Clay was gone, he trusted Swede to look out for the West Coast timber cutting—and to keep an eye on his woman. His caution was in vain. Springtime had no morals and men were drawn to her like a pack of dogs following a bitch in heat. Her sloe-eyed beauty could have corrupted the most moral of men. And did many times. Hunter often hid behind furniture, as silent as a shadow, and watched. He was too young to comprehend what they were doing, but still he felt shame.

Eventually, Clay James heard the snickers. He was wild with rage and jealousy. Springtime denied everything, and Clay grabbed the child up and shook him, demanding to know what the child had seen, what men had been there.

Hunter felt only terror at the fury and the madness he saw in Clay James' brown eyes as the man interrogated him. Swede, protecting him, insisted that Hunter was a child and could not understand.

The little boy learned to hide, shrinking into himself to avoid notice. His father, drinking heavily, would pace and rage at Swede.

"She's beautiful, Clay," Swede would agree. "Men draw to her like steel to magnet. She make any man betray everything for a night in her arms."

"She's just an Injun whore," Clay muttered. "She's not a lady; every man lusts for a whore, but he expects to marry a lady."

"By jingo, Clay, you got lady; why don't you go back to her?"

"Springtime's like a fever in my blood. Wanting her will destroy me. I've got two women, a son by each, and I'm miserable." He paced and drank and swore. "You're my friend; I trust you. Look after my interests here." Clay paused, uncertain madness gleaming in his eyes. When he frowned, the cleft in his chin deepened. "There're rumors of gold in California, that means growth and a market for all this timber. I could move my wife and son out to San Francisco, make it a little easier for me."

Swede leaned back in his chair. "You move Springtime to San Francisco?"

"You think my wife would stand for that? Right now, she thinks I stay out here on business. She'd find out." Clasping his hands behind his back, he resumed his pacing. "I married a homely woman so I'd have the Brett family money to finance my business deals. I'm a pitiful sonovabitch. Married to a rich, elegant lady and can't stay away from an Injun whore!"

"Don't blame yourself, Clay." A blond curl fell down over one eye when Swede shook his head. "Always there's women like Springtime around ever since Eve and Jezebel. Women like her, they make a man forget everything."

Clay slapped him on the back. "I don't know what I'd do without you, old friend."

The big man fumbled with his cap. "By jingo, let me go back with you, Clay. Put someone else in charge here."

Clay shook his head. "There isn't anyone I trust like I do you, Swede." He slammed one fist into his palm in a fury, his dark eyes gleaming with an insane jealousy.

"Keep her away from other men for me. I'd kill her if I caught her with anyone else; I'd kill him, too!"

Hunter shivered in his hiding place, frightened by the rage in his father's voice. He didn't come out for a long time after his father had left.

Swede sat with his head in his hands. Hunter barely remembered wondering if the man were sick, angry, or very tired. He crept over to him and the big man hugged him a moment. "By jingo, I can't even tell you," Swede whispered. "Not ever."

Sometimes when Clay James went out of town, other men came to see Springtime and the boy would hide and watch his beautiful mother, her long black hair cascading down her naked shoulders. The men, usually drunk, would bring Springtime gifts or money.

They would rut and paw at each other on her bed and, in the pale moonlight, the perspiration would gleam on their naked bodies, the man between her thighs, kissing her full breasts. Springtime would claw bloody scratches down his back as she bucked under him. "You bitch!" the men would always gasp. "You whore! Slut, how many other men do you sell yourself to?"

And Springtime would laugh like the gentle sound of rain and assure each man he was the only one.

But Swede knew the truth, and he and Springtime would argue when the men were gone. Hunter, making himself small, hid inside himself and watched and listened.

"You pretty slut," Swede would rage, "you keep this up, Clay will hear. He crazy; his papa die in asylum. He find out, he might kill you!"

"Then don't tell him."

330

"He's my friend; he trust me."

"Some friend!" She laughed softly, her voice a soothing purr. Sometimes at night, Hunter thought he heard his mother's voice. He knew she was no good, but he loved her for the times she held him close, rocked, and sang to him. That almost made up for the neglect when she drank, for the way the countless men treated him and the way the other children of the Indian camp sneered at the little half-breed bastard.

Sassy stirred and Hunter came back to the present. He was no longer a little boy, hiding in terror the night the unspeakable happened, the night his father showed up and surprised the beautiful Springtime with a man. Hunter shuddered and turned over. He would not let himself think about that, not that he could recall much anyway. His mind had blocked most of it out of his memory.

First his father's voice outside. "Springtime, you here?"

A familiar voice talking to Clay. Hunter couldn't remember his words.

"Oh my God!" His mother's voice. "I didn't expect—"

"Springtime? Where are you, you bitch?"

The man in his mother's bed was grabbing for his clothes, heading for the open window by the bed.

The naked beauty held onto the man, beseeching him as Clay James cursed and broke the door down. "Oh, God! Don't leave! He's crazy! Crazy jealous! Please . . ."

The man broke free, clearing the window as Clay James crashed into the room, his eyes wild with madness. "All right, you slut! I can't take any more of your cheating!"

331

"No, Clay, I—I wasn't—"

The little boy didn't move. Like a wild thing, he had learned young that safety lay in stillness when faced with danger.

His mother was screaming, begging. He should help her. He should . . .

Shotgun. His father had a double-barreled shotgun. Hunter remembered the roar, the way Springtime's scream broke off in the middle, and the man's wild, crazy eyes. For a long second, the acrid smoke hung in the air; and the roar echoed and re-echoed, making the child's ears ring. Something warm splattered on him, something warm and wet and smelling like copper. Hunter drew himself into a ball, making himself as small as possible. He would be next.

His father was weeping, cursing. "You slut! Why couldn't you be faithful? Why . . ." He put the barrel under his chin and snapped the triggers, but he'd used both shells. With an oath, he threw down the gun and stumbled out the door and into the night. Hunter did not move. He was too afraid to cry or scream. Clay might return to kill him, too. The man who ran might have saved her, but he had panicked and saved himself instead. Who was he? The face was a blur now when Hunter tried to remember what had happened that night almost a quarter of a century before.

The child ran outside, away from the scent of sex and blood, gunpowder and whiskey. He ran blindly through that terrible darkness, listening to the echo of nightbirds the chirp of crickets. He tripped, got up, and ran on fleeing from the terror of what he had seen, running from the horror of the reality. He ran until he was so exhausted, he couldn't put one foot in front of the other

When his sides hurt so much he could not run, he flopped on the ground, gasping for air, and vomited. He must not cry. If he cried, Clay James would find him and maybe do to him what he had done to Springtime. He lay unmoving until dawn. No one came and he realized that he was a small, worthless boy that no one wanted, an outcast of a whore and a madman. A half-breed caught between two worlds.

With the dawn, Swede found him. He did not mention what had happened; perhaps he thought the child did not know. In all these years, Hunter had never told anyone, not even Swede, that he had seen his mother's murder. Swede sent the child back to Springtime's people. Nothing was done to Clay; he was white, rich. On the frontier, he was within his rights to kill his faithless squaw. He took his trusted foreman, went to San Francisco, and picked up the pieces of his life.

Swede sought Hunter out now and then on his father's behalf, but Hunter had turned his back on his white blood. He was about fourteen when he rode with the braves against the white settlement on Puget Sound, trying to discourage the whites that the Indians called Bostons from settling in the area. The tribes knew that mass settlement meant timber cut, game depleted, their young men seduced by whiskey, their women turned into whores for the pleasure of white trappers and loggers.

Hunter was wounded once in his battles against the whites. He still carried the scar, but the whites who had seen it thought it was from a logging accident.

As the years passed, he heard occasionally that Swede came sometimes to the tribe in search of Hunter, but his people would tell the white man nothing. Hunter did not want to see him, knowing he came in Clay James' stead.

Hunter listened to Sassy breathe. At least his woman would not be unfaithful to him; she was a lady. He had been uneasy that when Sassy met the charming Brett, she would be smitten by him. Instead, she had almost seemed to dislike his elegant half-brother.

Yes, Sassy was a lady. She would never stoop to behavior that would shame her man and cause other men to laugh at him behind his back. She was not like Springtime. She was a lady. Hunter thought about the only time he had ever seen Brett's mother.

He was not yet half-grown when he had decided to return to the whites. He knew that he must seek out his father. Other white men said that he was back in San Francisco, expanding his timber business and growing very rich and powerful. Of course the law had not cared what Clay had done to a squaw far to the north.

Hunter hid out on a tramp ship, and when he arrived in the city, the half-grown boy with his long hair and moccasins roamed the streets, hungry and bewildered. He had expected a small village where everyone would know Clay James. Instead, because gold had been discovered, he found a human anthill, with white people crammed together. The streets were filled with wagons and strangers in a perpetual hurry. He knew enough English to ask for Clay James, but the men he encountered merely shrugged and went on their way, not knowing or not caring.

After a fews days, Hunter was reduced to stealing food like a starving coyote and it rankled his proud heart. He did not know what to do or where to go. He belonged nowhere and had nothing. He saw a wagon-load of lumber and followed it at a distance, but it went to a construction site. He followed the empty wagon back to the lumberyard. "Clay James," he said to the teamster.

The man shook his head. "Not our outfit."

"Where?" Hunter asked.

The man yawned and pointed. "That's a big company now. What business you got with him?"

However, Hunter was already trotting down the street. It took him several more days to find the big lumberyard and there was no one there but an indifferent watchman. "Clay James?"

"This is Sunday, Boy," the watchman said. "Ain't nobody working on Sunday afternoon. Imagine Mr. James is out for a Sunday drive today."

"Where?"

The man gave him directions and Hunter began to walk. He came to a magnificent home with an ornate iron gate. Surely just one family didn't live here. Even as he hid in the shrubbery and gawked, a fancy open carriage, a phaeton drawn by a fine team of high-stepping bay horses, came down the drive. A black driver got out and opened the gate.

Hunter watched as the phaeton pulled out onto the busy street. There were three people in the carriage, including a lady—not pretty, but well dressed and haughty. The boy was older than Hunter, a younger version of the man who faced him. Clay James still had the dark eyes and the cleft in his chin, but he looked a bit grayer, a little more portly with the years that had passed. He didn't look as if he had smiled for a long time.

As the phaeton passed, men on the streets doffed their

hats respectfully to the lady and she acknowledged them with a slight nod of her head. The handsome son looked bored as if he took for granted the opulence surrounding him. The man, rich, respected, and admired, beheld his people with a regal air. He stared in surprise when his gaze fixed on Hunter, but he gave no nod or sign of recognition.

Long after the carriage had passed out of sight, Hunter remained in his shrubbery hiding place, saddened that his father had not stopped the coach and invited his younger son to ride with him.

He stood there a long time, feeling sad and alone, thinking of the well-dressed, white-skinned son, but most of all feeling envious of the respect men paid his father and his lady. He yearned for that, the respect that money and power could bring him. He, too, wanted an unattainable goddess that other men would envy and respect, not snicker at behind his back.

The boy, not knowing what to do now that he had found his father and received no sign of recognition, walked aimlessly along the waterfront. It was almost dark when he heard a shout behind him. "Hunter? Hunter, Boy?"

His father. His father had come for him. He whirled, but it was Swede. "By jingo, I been combing the city since Clay say he saw you." For a moment, he thought Swede would hug him. Instead, he held out his hand awkwardly and Hunter shook it, remembering it was a white man's gesture of friendship. Swede looked bad, as if he drank too much.

"Did my father send you to find me?"

"In a way," Swede said evasively. "Let's no talk out here on street. You hungry?"

336

Hunter had his pride. His belly had had no food but garbage from behind cafes for several days. "I will watch you eat if you are hungry."

Swede regarded him keenly. "I take it as insult if you do not share my food."

"I will eat then." Hunter gave him a grave nod.

They went to a small, out-of-the-way place and Swede ordered double helpings of steamed, buttered clams, fried potatoes, and broiled beef.

Hunter managed not to gobble. He would not have the man think he was starving.

Swede watched him eat. "I look for you over the past years. Where you been?"

"My mother's people move much," Hunter said as he put the good hot food in his belly. "Did my father look for me as well?"

Swede sighed, brushed a lock of blond hair back from his forehead. "He never forget you. Clay go back to his family; there was nothing else to do."

"Not with Springtime dead, maybe."

Swede winced and closed his blue eyes. "Don't remind me. Clay never forgot her, either, Hunter. Men sometimes destroy what they love most. The memory of that have driven him to drink. He's half-mad."

The boy paused, then continued eating. If his father were half-mad and his grandfather had been insane, that meant he might be someday, too. "You are a loyal friend to him, Swede. Did he send you to tell me to go away?"

Swede lit his pipe, carefully broke the match in two. "Small Hunter, your people's way of life is doomed. You need learn how live like white man. Clay wants I take both boys to woods for summer, teach you timber business."

"His wife know about me?" Hunter wiped his mouth.

"I don't know if she know about Clay's other life. If she does, she pretends she don't. Better for her pride."

"I saw his son."

"Brett?" Swede shrugged wide shoulders. "He spoiled college boy now, gone most time to Harvard. If he get family fortune, he waste it all."

He looked down at his brown skin, thought about his father. "Does Clay James want to see me?"

Swede hesitated, then reluctantly shook his head. "I'm sorry, but no. You remind him of her."

"I hate him then," Hunter exploded in sudden rage. "I wish you were my father instead!"

Swede grimaced. "Don't say that! To be your papa, I'd have to betray best friend, so don't even think it. Someday, Clay do well by you, boy; I got nothing. You be glad then to be his son, not mine."

His son. Yet he wouldn't give him his name. Hunter pushed back his plate, stood up. "I go now. No reason to stay if he doesn't want me."

"I want you," Swede said. "I proud if I could call you son. I teach you timber business; maybe you get rich and respected, too."

In his mind, the boy saw the elegant carriage with the regal lady riding inside, the men taking their hats off respectfully to the lumber baron. "Yes, I would like that."

It was night when they left the cafe. Hunter turned to leave, and he would always remember the tortured, troubled look on Swede's weathered face as if something gnawed at him. Hunter never saw Clay James again. Over the next several years, he learned the timber busi-

338

ness and met the sneering older son, who resented his father's half-breed bastard. And then one night, something happened that changed everyone's life forever: Clay James' final act of mad fury.

Hunter saw Brett only one more time: At the lawyer's office, where they learned Clay had divided his empire down the middle for the two boys, except for a generous bequest to his best friend, Swede. Hunter took his share and returned to the timber country, determined to build an empire that Clay James would have envied. Brett got the rest of the wealth and the fine home. Swede, however, turned down his friend's bequest and gave it to charity. He and Cookie went to work for Hunter.

Hunter glanced over at Sassy in the darkness. At least he didn't have to worry over his wife being attracted to his handsome, charming half-brother. He could tell Sassy disliked the prodigal son. What would Swede have done? Swede had character; everyone knew that, despite his occasional drinking bouts. No doubt he'd say to give the arrogant one a chance to redeem himself. It was the least Hunter could do to show respect for the murdered man.

Hunter closed his eyes and slept. Maybe tonight, he'd be too tired for troubled dreams. Someday he would remember how the nightmare ended, and then maybe he would never have it again. Whatever it was must be too horrible for his conscious mind to confront.

Chapter Nineteen

Sassy came gradually awake beside her sleeping husband. She hadn't slept well. Some bad dream.

Oh, Dear God, it hadn't been a dream at all! Sassy sat up in bed, remembering last night's events. Brett James. It was every woman's worst nightmare to have her secret past return to threaten her future just when she thought it was safely buried and she could breathe easy at last. Such horrible coincidences happened only in stories, yet her most dangerous enemy was now in her own house. Was it only an ironic quirk of fate or was God punishing her? What was she going to do and, more importantly, what were Brett's intentions?

As Hunter stirred, Sassy rose quickly. In her dressing room, she splashed cold water on her face, praying for inspiration. At the moment, she had no plan, no way of dealing with this new threat; but she had to do something. Half-brothers. Both were tall, had dark hair, and were handsome—but in totally different ways. Hunter was masculine and protective, if rough-hewn. Brett radiated an easy charm that hid a total lack of character. They didn't look much alike to her.

She brushed her hair and pinned it up. As she laced up a pale pink cotton dress, she heard Hunter stirring. She forced herself to return to the bedroom. "Good morning. You didn't sleep well last night, did you?"

Hunter, dressed, sat on the bed trying to pull on his boots with his one good hand. "You didn't either," he accused. "You tossed and mumbled."

A chill shivered down her back, but she kept her voice light. "Are you telling me I talked in my sleep? I'll bet I talked about clothes and my new gold bracelet."

Hunter shrugged. "Couldn't tell." He frowned at his bandaged hand. "Maybe we should be glad my brother showed up. I was beginning to wonder how I was going to cope with the office end of the business."

She took a deep breath. "We can manage alone. I can answer the mail, and a part-time accountant will do until your hand improves enough to write."

He pulled her to him with his good hand and kissed her. "Yes, but with Brett here that takes a lot off my back."

She wanted to scream at him, but she only said, "You're just going to accept him without any questions?"

"Now, Sassy," he murmured and kissed her forehead, "he is after all, my brother—"

"Half-brother," she corrected.

"Okay, half-brother," he conceded, "but he is blood kin. Would you turn your back on a relative who seemed so apologetic? I've never seen the proud Brett James grovel the way he did last night. It must have really hurt his pride."

Sassy murmured noncommittally. If she weren't careful, she would appear hard-hearted and selfish. Hunter

341

was vulnerable; he'd lost Swede, his best friend. Later, he might take a harder look at his rogue relative, but for the time being, Brett was going to be welcomed into the family with open arms.

Hunter kissed her again and stood up. "I smell coffee. Let's go have breakfast, shall we?"

Brett. She was going to have to face Brett at breakfast. "I—I don't feel very well. I might have John bring me a tray."

Immediately, he was anxious, peering down into her face. "You aren't sick, are you? Could you be pregnant?"

The look on his dark, handsome face bothered her. "If I were, you don't sound very happy about it. I thought you wanted a large family."

He sighed, shook his head. "I'm having second thoughts. What Judge Stone said about bad seed yesterday bothered me. I hadn't seriously considered the hazards of bloodlines. Now I'm wondering if I want to take that chance."

Had he found out already that the children's mother would be a whore? "What—what do you mean?"

"Sassy." He brushed a wisp of hair from her forehead. "My mother was a slut and she drank. Clay James was a violent and disturbed man, and . . ." He shrugged as if there were more he didn't want to tell her. "Suppose our children inherited the worst of those traits in spite of having a prim, blue-blooded lady like you for a mother?"

She almost sighed with joy. He didn't know; at least not yet. "I think you're overreacting, and anyway, I certainly don't think I'm expecting a baby."

"That's almost a relief," he said.

Sooner or later, she was going to have to face Brett; it might as well be now. "Maybe I'll go to breakfast after all." She took his arm, the condemned woman walking to her death; the mental ordeal was as bad as finally confronting Brett and getting it all out in the open. She thought about Clay James as they walked down the hall toward the dining room. Violent and disturbed. Maybe Brett had inherited his father's worst traits, but she couldn't believe that Hunter had.

Brett was already at the table, ensconced in the host's chair. He wiped his mustache with his napkin and greeted them. "Good morning, you two lovebirds. I hope you don't mind that I've already had my first cup of coffee."

"Brett," Sassy said, "you don't need to stand for me, but you're sitting in Hunter's chair."

"Oh, I'm so sorry!" He moved across from Sassy as Hunter seated her. "I always stand in the presence of a *real* lady."

"I meant since we're all family, you need not be so formal." She looked him squarely in the eye as Hunter took his seat.

Hunter said, "You didn't need to give up your chair, Brett. It was a natural mistake; and, anyway, you're the elder brother."

Brett sipped his coffee and smiled, and the cleft in his chin deepened. "Well, after all, the host's chair does belong to the man who owns and controls everything, and that's you, Little Brother."

Sassy scrutinized him. She knew now what he was after; he wanted Hunter's whole empire: Logging, land, power, and wealth. What could she do to stop him? In her vulnerable position, not much.

John entered, poured Hunter and Sassy's coffee, glared at Brett, and limped back to the kitchen. She poured thick cream in her cup and sipped the hot, bracing liquid. She felt Brett's gaze on her and met his insolent stare.

"My dear sister-in-law," he purred, "that is a beautiful dress. If I had to give that color a name, I'd call it angel pink."

Hunter smiled approvingly. "Appropriate for the lady wearing it."

Brett eyed her. "I'm sure. Why, anyone can just look at your wife and see the sweet innocence there."

He was jabbing at her, but Hunter couldn't know that. She felt like a small butterfly entrapped in a spider's web, fluttering helplessly and awaiting her fate while he toyed with her. "Mr. James, you are too kind."

"Oh, my dear," he reached across the table before she could move and covered her hand with his, "you must call me Brett; after all, we are family. Why, I feel very comfortable with you as if we had known each other before."

Hunter sipped his coffee as Sassy wrenched her hand back. "That's an interesting idea, Brother. Sassy's read me something about that—what's it called, reincarnation?"

Brett nodded. "Of course I suppose that's the only logical explanation. She looks so familiar."

Surreptitiously, Sassy rubbed her hand with her napkin to get the feel of Brett off her skin. Then she trapped both trembling hands around her coffee cup as John re-entered the room and began serving thin, fried steak, eggs, and hot, fluffy biscuits. So that was Brett's cruel game; he was going to torment her in a game of cat and mouse, almost but not quite telling Hunter about her. How long would it be before her husband guessed?

Brett said, "Married life must really suit you, Brother; you look happy."

Hunter winked at Sassy. "I am happy, Brett. You ought to think about getting married yourself."

"I would if I could find a girl as wonderful as you have." Brett picked up his fork. "The problem is all the ladies of good background seem to be taken, and who'd want anything else? Why, these days, there's no telling what you might get, even a little wh—"

"Brett." Hunter glared at him. "You know better than use a word like that in front of a lady."

"Oh, I'm so sorry, my dear." Brett looked too contrite. "The kind of women I've been around the last few years. . . . Well, I forget my manners sometimes."

"Apology accepted," Sassy said, studying her plate. She was afraid that if she looked into his eyes, she would see a sly grin. She sneaked a glance at Hunter. He was eating his breakfast awkwardly with his good hand but with evident relish.

"Brett," Hunter said, "if you really want to get married, there's a ship-load of brides, ladies every one, that you can look over."

Brett chuckled. "Who knows what came in on that boat? Why, not knowing any of their backgrounds, you just have to trust their word for what they are and where they came from."

"That's true," Hunter conceded and went on eating. "There's probably not any in the bunch on a level with Sassy."

"Oh, to be sure," Brett agreed. "Besides, what I had in mind was a rich, pretty widow."

Hunter laughed. "You won't find many of those in these parts. There's such a shortage of women here that even an elderly or a homely woman is snatched up."

"That's why I'm a bachelor," Brett sighed and pushed back his plate. "My sights are just too high, I fear."

There was a long silence in which they finished their breakfast. Sassy was so upset she could hardly eat. She prayed for a miracle: That Brett would keep his mouth shut, tire of his little game and the isolated country, and move on to some more exciting and exotic place like San Francisco.

Brett said, "By the way, Little Brother, I took the liberty of looking over your ledgers this morning before you got up. I'm not sure how good at figures Swede was." He looked grave.

"Really?" Hunter stared at him. "Well, we did get behind now and then. I thought he was doing as well as could be expected." He swallowed hard. "I relied on Swede and now he's gone."

"Well, to be honest," Brett gave Hunter his warmest, most sincere look, "my New York business has closed because of a problem involving a rich businessman from Philadelphia who had the misfortune to die on my property."

"Oh?" Hunter said, "that sounds like an interesting—"

"If Brett has plans for a rich widow and is thinking of moving on, maybe," Sassy said in a desperate attempt to change the subject, "I don't think we should—"

"But after what you said last night, Brett, I was about to offer you a job," Hunter went on. "With Swede gone, I could use a man who knows about handling the paperwork; you could stay here."

346

Her nightmare had taken a turn for the worse. Brett living here in the house. There was nothing she could do right now; if she objected too strenuously, Hunter would wonder why.

Brett leaned back in his chair. "I don't know, Hunter. I'd feel like I was taking advantage, living off my little brother's charity. Maybe I should go back to San Francisco."

"But you just got here," Hunter argued, "and with my hand injured, I really need help; it wouldn't be charity. We'd love for you to stay, wouldn't we, Sassy?"

She played with her napkin. "Well, if Brett is determined to go to California—"

"To be honest," Brett gave them both a humble, endearing smile, "I don't have any prospects there. Frankly, Brother, after the way I've treated you, I'm ashamed to take advantage of your hospitality."

"You were younger then." Hunter shrugged. "And it must have been quite a blow to you, the way they died and then finding out you had to share the estate with a bastard son."

Brett bit his lip, struggling for control. "Everything you say is true, Hunter. But now that I've had years to think about it, you've done a better job with your half of the wealth than I have."

"You've had some bad luck," Hunter said charitably as he wiped his mouth and laid his napkin on the table.

"No," Brett sighed, "I have to be very honest with you, Little Brother. It hasn't been luck; it's been riotous living, just like the prodigal son. I've lived wild and run with bad women." He looked at Sassy, then at Hunter. "It's only now that I'm older and see how happy and prosperous you are, that I realize how many mistakes I've made, where I've gone wrong."

Hunter said, "It's never too late to make amends and try to straighten your life out."

If that held true for men, why didn't it hold true for women? Sassy dared not voice her convictions. It would always be that way, she thought. No matter how 'enlightened' society became, a woman would be smart to hide her past but a man could boldly admit his transgressions and the community would admire him for it. She knew how slick Brett was, that he was worming his way into Hunter's confidence. She wanted to protect her husband, but she couldn't warn him about Brett without revealing her own scarlet past.

"In that case," Brett looked relieved, "I'd be happy to stay on awhile, Hunter; do whatever I can to mend our relationship; and try to help you in this tragic situation. Did you say you think you might know who killed Swede?"

Hunter frowned. "As I told you last night, I'd suspect a logger named Clegg, but we made sure he got on a ship."

"Well, maybe it's an old grudge from Swede's past," Brett said. "You don't really know much about him, do you?"

"Not really." Hunter shook his head. "He didn't talk about himself much. Swede was always there for me; he was a close friend and employee of Father's, but I didn't know much else."

"Funny how you find out sometimes how little you really do know about people you think you know well," Brett commented with a side-glance at Sassy. "Everyone's hiding secrets."

She managed to keep her face immobile.

"Uh huh," Hunter replied vaguely, his mind already leaping ahead to other matters. "I've got to ride out to the far camp this morning and supervise that timber cutting. Business must go on, even when someone dies."

"I'll go with you," Sassy said.

Hunter shook his head. "Sassy, this is going to be a hard ride; business, not a leisurely jaunt through the woods. You'd better skip this one."

Brett said, "I could either go with you, Hunter, or I could catch up on some of that paperwork piled on Swede's desk. Some of it looked important and I'd say there're bills that need to be paid."

"I appreciate the offer." Hunter pushed his chair back and stood up. "If you can make heads or tails of those ledgers, I'd be happy to have you take it on. The paperwork is my least favorite part of the business."

Brett had already stood up and come around to pull out Sassy's chair. "I just hope my being in the house won't put me in your way, Sassy. I *could* move into town and maybe set up an office there."

Sassy hesitated. She had just been maneuvered into an awkward position; but then, that was like Brett James, smooth, calculating. If there was one thing she didn't want, it was to be left alone in this house with Brett. "Well," she began, "I'm not sure—"

"Sassy," Hunter frowned, "where're your manners? Brett's family."

Brett's hand brushed her shoulder ever so slightly. "I hope I'm not about to cause a fuss between newlyweds."

Damn him! Damn him. What could she do? "If Brett wants to work on the ledgers," she said coolly and moved away from the table, "it doesn't concern me. I

349

was planning on working in the flowerbeds this morning or riding into town."

"Oh," Hunter said. "I think Cookie's already left. I told him when he finished serving, he could go pick up the mail, visit his lady friend, and see if there were any packages on that ship that docks today. If you needed something or wanted to go, you should have told me in time. Cookie will be back in a couple of hours."

She forced a casual show of acceptance although she felt anything but calm: She was going to be left alone in the house with Brett James. "It wasn't anything important, dear. Are we expecting a package?"

Hunter raised an eyebrow. "I told you that. It's a surprise. Now that's all I'm going to say."

"Isn't that sweet?" Brett said. "The happy husband buying gifts for his little bride."

"She deserves it." Hunter gave her a tender look and kissed her cheek. "Sassy's everything I ever dreamed of in a wife."

"And I'll bet some things you never dreamed of," Brett added innocently. "Such a treasure! You're a lucky man, Brother."

"I know it." Hunter slipped his arm around her shoulders and hugged her. "I almost have to pinch myself sometimes, wondering if I'm dreaming."

No one spoke, and in the silence that followed Sassy folded and refolded her napkin.

"Well." Brett cleared his throat. "There's work to be done, so I'll get right to those ledgers. Maybe we can have a nice supper together tonight, just one big happy family." He sauntered down the hall to the office with a proprietary air.

Sassy's mind raced as she walked Hunter to the door.

At least she'd be able to confront Brett without anyone around to listen in on the conversation.

Hunter kissed her good-bye. "If you need anything before Cookie gets back, the stablehands are in the barn."

She nodded, knowing they wouldn't come in the house unless she called them and she wouldn't dare do that.

"I can tell you're not fond of my brother." Hunter broached the subject delicately. "But he needs a job and I'm trying to help him without hurting his pride. I don't understand your attitude."

Already Hunter was questioning her motives. Her antagonism toward Brett made her look bad. How like the clever swindler to try to drive a wedge between her and Hunter. "I—I feel you're just too trusting, taking him in without asking any questions."

"That may be true," he admitted. "I used to be a dour and suspicious person; you know that, Sassy Girl. You've changed my outlook since you brought love and trust into my life."

What encouraging news, she thought ironically. She had changed him into an easy mark to be taken advantage of. Merciful saints, how could she protect him without giving her secret away?

She kissed him goodbye, then looked out the window as a stableboy saddled Poker Chips and helped Hunter mount up. He loped toward the woods and the stableboy returned to the far barn.

Sassy squared her shoulders, took a deep breath, and marched into the office. "All right, Brett, let's talk."

He turned in his chair. "My! What a hostile expression on such a pretty face. You haven't even said you were glad to see an old friend."

"I'm not and you aren't."

"Tsk! Tsk!" He clasped his hands behind his head and contemplated her discomfort. "Can't we let bygones be bygones? Can't we make a fresh start?"

"That's what I'm trying to do," Sassy snapped. "I come a thousand miles to cover my past and then you show up."

Brett leaned back in his chair with a smirk. "You should have seen your face when you walked into the library last night. It was priceless! Good thing Hunter was pouring drinks and didn't catch your expression."

"I fail to see the humor." She folded her arms across her breasts. "It isn't funny to try to escape from a sordid past and then have the man who seduced me turn up in my own house."

He grinned easily, crossing one leg over the other, cool and relaxed. "Who'd have believed it could happen? It is a real-life melodrama."

She was not going to banter with him. "What is it you want, Brett?" She kept her voice cold.

He shivered. "Such an ice princess! Want? Why, Sassy, you misjudge me! I merely want to mend fences with my little bastard brother."

"Don't call him that!"

"What? Bastard or brother?" His voice turned hard.

"You haven't changed, Brett. I won't let you hurt him."

He stroked his mustache. "I don't know how you could stop me."

"Enough, Brett. I want you to decide to move on. Tell Hunter you've changed your mind."

"You were always too innocent for a whore, Sassy," he said. "You don't know enough about playing poker."

"What in the name of all the saints are you talking about?"

"I mean you're trying to bluff me into leaving when you don't have a hole card." Brett smirked. "You can't make me leave town. All you've got on me is what I've also got on you. With Swede dead, Hunter needs me."

A horrible suspicion crossed her mind; something so ghastly, she couldn't put it into words. Surely no sane person would commit cold-blooded murder just to get a man out of his way? Sometimes Brett acted almost . . . mad. Could madness be inherited? In that case, his half-brother. . . . No wonder Hunter had doubts about siring children.

Sassy hastily dismissed the unnerving thought. "I can handle what business must be done until he can write."

"Write? Oh, my dear girl, you are priceless in your naivety." Brett fairly chortled.

"I'm afraid I don't appreciate the joke—"

"That's because you don't know what the joke is. I'm not surprised, though. Baby Brother is a proud Injun."

"I hate you for sneering at him," Sassy snapped. "Hunter is twice the man you'll ever be—"

"I presume you're talking about bed. Does that ignorant savage make you whimper? Do you claw his back?"

She felt her face flush hot and Brett snickered. "I always thought you were a cold fish, Sassy. Now I suspect you might be hot and passionate."

"Not with you, you sonovabitch!" Her temper flared out of control. "Hunter is the only man who ever made me feel that way, Brett, and I don't want him hurt; I love him too much. Why can't you get the hell out of our lives and give us a chance at a little happiness?"

"Such language from an innocent virgin! Why, Little Brother would be shocked. It's such an ironic joke that Lou was the one he asked for a favor."

"I don't know what you're talking about."

"No, I don't think you do." He spoke patiently as if talking to a dim-witted child. "Certainly if you had recognized the handwriting, you wouldn't have come."

He was talking in circles, hinting at something, but she wasn't about to admit she didn't understand. "It doesn't matter; nothing can change the way I feel about him."

"Spoken like a true heroine." Brett shook his head. "You women can be such fools for a man's lies."

The cruelty of his words stung like nettles. "Can't we, though? It cost me my virginity, and there's no telling what it's cost Marylou."

"Lou? That old tub of guts?" Brett sneered. "She had a nice little nest egg from all those years of whoring, so I convinced her to buy the Black Garter for me. All I had to do was force myself to make love to her now and then, tell her she was still pretty and young-looking."

"I can't really blame her for anything; she cares about you like I care about Hunter. She'd do anything for you."

"Sure she would." Brett brought his chair down on all fours with a bang. "You're the one I didn't figure right, Sassy. I thought you were just a scheming little gold digger trying to latch onto his money, but you really care about the big half-breed, don't you?"

"I love him," Sassy admitted, "with all my heart; and I'm not going to stand by and let you hurt him, Brett."

"Me hurt him?" He stood up. "How do you think he'd feel if he finds out the prim lady he adores used to earn her living on her back? If I describe those two little moles on your sweet fanny and he asks how I know—"

She slapped him then, hard enough that his head jerked back.

An ugly red mark spread across his handsome face and, for a moment, she saw the insane rage in his dark eyes. "You uppity shanty-Irish slut," he snarled. "I won't forget that!"

Belatedly she feared him and his madness. "Brett, what would it take to get rid of you?" she asked, inching toward the door. "If I can get you some money, will you go away and leave us in peace? I need this second chance."

"So do I," he said. "Or have you forgotten that a certain killing in New York closed me down, made me lose everything?"

"What is it you want then? You've had your half of the James estate and wasted it—"

"Damn it, it all should have been mine; you hear me, all! That bastard by an Injun whore shouldn't have gotten anything!"

"None of this matters," she interrupted. "What is it you want from us?"

"I want everything the half-breed's got," Brett snarled, "and I intend to have it, since I'll be handling the company ledgers." He indicated a contract with mock dismay. "It's a shame to discover that Swede's been swindling him all these years. That'll really hurt Hunter."

She stared at him in disbelief. "You intend to embezzle from him and make Swede look guilty?"

"Swede's dead; he won't object. Besides, 'embezzle' is such an ugly word. Tsk. Tsk." Once again, he was the charming, handsome devil who had seduced her. "Such a bad word for reclaiming what should have been mine all along."

"I won't let you get away with it. I'll tell Hunter what you're doing."

"Will you?" He sat down on the edge of the desk and looked at her. "When you do, I'll tell him about your past."

"He'd kill you for insulting me."

Brett's eyes narrowed. "Not if I handle it right. We can only guess what he'd do to you for making a fool of him."

In her mind, she saw the big, powerful man lifting her up on his stallion. Hunter could break her in half with his bare hands. "Well, I—I—"

"I can see by your face that you're afraid of his jealousy, and well you might be." He stroked his mustache. "Grandfather spent his last years in an asylum, and you surely know how my parents died, so it's in the blood. Perhaps you think that bad seed has been passed on."

"Maybe through you?"

"Don't say that! Don't you ever say that!" He was on his feet, his hands on her slender throat. Sassy gulped for air as she looked into Brett's eyes and struggled against panic.

Stay calm, she thought, *and soothe him.* Brett was mad. Could Clay James have also passed that trait to his other son? Was that what Hunter had hinted at? "L—Let's talk, Brett." Tearing herself from his grasp, she edged toward the door, speaking softly. "I keep quiet so you can take his money and you'll keep quiet about my past?"

"No, honey, I want more than that; much more. You know what a cowbird is?"

She blinked at the strange question and shook her head.

"A cowbird lays its eggs in another bird's nest; and the host bird, innocent and stupid as it is, raises that baby as its own. The baby cowbird, larger and more cunning than the host bird's own babies, gradually crowds the little ones out and dominates the nest until the others die. The host bird ends up giving its all for this one baby cowbird that isn't even its own, and it's too stupid or blind to realize it."

"I don't know what you're driving at."

"In a way, it'll be poetic justice," Brett said, "my planting my egg in Hunter's nest."

Sassy reacted with horror as his meaning became clear to her. "Surely you don't think I'll sleep with you?"

"Oh, but you will, my dear." He grinned evilly. "In exchange for my not revealing your secret. We're going to be one big, happy family; and the stupid half-breed's wealth is going to my son, not his!"

"Why, you dirty—" She turned to leave, but he caught her arm.

"Don't play the insulted lady with me, Honey." He ran his fingers along her shoulder.

"I—I'll tell Hunter about my past myself before I'd betray him!" She tried to pull away from Brett, suddenly realizing the vulnerable position she was in. He was a big, powerful man and they were alone in the house.

He clenched her arm, his eyes glinting. "Who said I was going to give you any say in the matter?" She felt the heat of his body through her dainty pink dress. "When I take what I want, you'll be ashamed to tell him, afraid of his rage, afraid he wouldn't believe you were raped. Why, with the personality he may have inherited from old Clay James, he could be a maniac!"

She struggled to break free. "I—I don't know what you're talking about."

"Oh? So Hunter didn't tell you about his mother? I figured as much. He probably didn't tell you about what happened to my parents, either. He'd be afraid; no woman would marry a crazy man's son!" He pressed up against her so hard she felt his maleness throbbing against her body.

"I—I'm not afraid of Hunter." But she was very much afraid of Brett, who had her pinned against the wall.

"Maybe you would be," Brett purred, "if you knew what Clay did." He bent his head and kissed her.

Sassy fought, but his hands caressed her shoulders. His hot lips forced hers open and he ravaged the inside of her mouth with his tongue while his hand cupped her breast.

Now his other hand clapped over her mouth. "If you were even thinking about screaming, don't. No one is here to help you, and, as you well remember, I can get rough when I'm angry."

Sassy remembered. She was so terrified, she could feel her heart pounding under his hand.

He squeezed hard again and laughed. "I forgot what nice tits you have, Sassy. I'm not going to do anything to you I haven't done in the past. Remember?"

How could she have ever thought she loved him? Brett was cruel and savage in his lust and if a woman cried out, or writhed in pain, he enjoyed it more. Fearfully, she met his dark gaze. He was crazy; why hadn't she realized it before? Could Hunter ever be as violent and dangerous as his brother?

She had to escape, to think, to decide on a course of action. Forcing herself to overcome her loathing, she made her body relax.

"You hot little bitch! So you still care about me," he murmured, stroking her nipple. "We're going to have lots of good times, Sassy, every time your trusting husband leaves the house!"

She felt like retching, but instead she pressed against his hand.

"You want it, do you?" He looked down into her eyes, breathing hard. "Once a whore, always a whore; just like that bastard's mother."

Compelled by the need to protect Hunter, she rubbed up against his body. Very slowly, he took his hand away from her mouth, but he still had her pinned against the wall. How could she escape his embrace and buy some time until Hunter returned? She leaned forward and kissed Brett, flicking her tongue across his lips.

He gasped, his dark eyes intense with passion. "You little whore," he whispered. "I intend to mount you every time I get the chance. You understand that, don't you?"

"I understand," she agreed. "I won't tell if you won't, Brett."

He squeezed her breast again. "That's a smart girl! If you knew about Clay James, you'd do anything to keep from arousing Hunter's jealousy."

Her mind was working fast, trying to figure out how to escape before he threw her across the bed and raped her. Stall. She needed time to put him off his guard. "What about Clay?"

"He never got over what he did to that wild bitch!"

"Meow?"

Sassy glanced down. Kitty had wandered into the room. She edged toward the door. "What did Clay do?"

Brett didn't seem to hear her, his dark eyes were glazed. "He was insane, you know, just like Grandfather. Everyone warned my mother, but she wouldn't leave him, even though she knew what he had done to Springtime."

A prickle of fear went up her neck and she glanced toward the door, contemplating flight. She licked her dry lips. "What—what did he do to Springtime?"

Brett laughed. "Ask her son. She was just an Injun whore, sleeping around behind Clay's back while other men sniggered."

Now she understood Hunter. What would he do to her if he ever found out he'd gotten a woman cut from the same cloth as his mother?

"Brett." Sassy eyed the door and the big tomcat rubbing against her leg. "T—tell me what happened."

"I don't know. It was years after Springtime's death that Swede came to the house one night. I was home from college." Brett whispered, his eyes unfocused. "Father and Swede talked."

"About what?"

He shook his head. "Don't know. Father went crazy when Swede left; he was wild, drinking."

She had to know. "And?" she prompted.

"He forced mother and me into the buggy at gunpoint. He wasn't like my father anymore. He was crazy."

Crazy. The word sent shivers down her back. "Why—why didn't the servants do something? Call the police?"

A shake of the head. Brett's vacant eyes relived that long-ago night. "Late. No one around."

Sassy didn't want to hear the rest, but Brett was no longer aware of her presence. "Father had a gun; he forced us to accompany him for a moonlight drive along the cliffs."

Something terrible had happened; something too terrible to tell. She saw it in his face. "Never mind."

He didn't hear her. "Crazy," he whispered. "Father kept lashing the horse, making it gallop faster and faster. Mother begged and screamed, but he laughed. I jumped and rolled just before . . ."

She waited, hardly breathing, afraid to hear what he was about to say, yet unable to break the horrified fascination that this key might unlock the puzzle.

"Over the cliff," Brett choked, his dark eyes wide and staring as he relived the horror. "In the moonlight, the sorrell's mane and tail seemed to float on air and the buggy's red wheels kept spinning. I ran to the edge. Father's laughter and Mother's screams echoed all the way down until the buggy shattered on the rocks and disappeared into the crashing surf!"

Chapter Twenty

"You—you're lying!" Sassy cried in shock. But looking into Brett's eyes, she knew this time he spoke the truth.

"You know I'm not." He spoke slowly, deliberatly, ominously. "You're afraid," he accused. "Afraid your beloved half-breed might have inherited James' insanity."

Brett certainly had. Was this a condition that progressed and grew worse? Brett hadn't been this strange when she had known him in New York City. Sassy eyed the door. Right now, she needed to concentrate on escaping from Brett.

Sassy lowered her lashes coyly, her attention on the cat brushing against her leg. "I'd forgotten how much you attracted me, Brett."

"That's more like it." He accepted adulation easily.

"Aye, maybe we're just two of a kind." She ran the tip of her tongue along her lower lip.

Breathing in short puffs, he tugged at the sleeve of her pink dress, baring her shoulder. He trailed his fingers along her skin. "That's right, Honey. You and I are just alike, and don't you ever forget it! Over the years, I may give you a whole family of sons for your half-breed to raise."

What was she going to do? She contained her disgust as his fingers traced her throat and gazed at him through veiled lashes. "How do we know Marylou won't tell everything she knows?"

"Because the fat old cow is in love with me," Brett boasted and ran his fingers down to the swell of Sassy's breasts. "That's the only reason she took part in that killing in New York. She'll keep her mouth shut if I tell her to."

She felt his body relaxing against hers as if he were satisfied that she wasn't going to fight him, that she would do anything it took to satisfy his lust. There was a lock on the inside of the master bedroom door, but the room was down the hall. Could she make it that far?

"Brett," she purred, "why don't we get us a bottle and celebrate our new understanding? We've got hours before the cook returns."

He stepped back, delighted. "Now you're making sense."

"I'm a smart girl," Sassy reminded him. "I know when I'm up against a stacked deck—like that merchant from Philadelphia."

"And you don't want to end up dead like him." Brett nodded conspiratorially. "All right, Honey, a celebration sounds good to me."

Was that the sound of the buggy creaking up the road? Of course she was only imagining it, but it would suit her purpose. "Do you hear that?" she cocked her head toward the window. "Could that be Cookie coming back so soon?"

"What?"

She'd diverted his attention, and that was all Sassy needed. She brought her knee up hard and caught him in the groin. Bent over, he cursed and grabbed for her. "You sneaky little bitch!" His fingers missed her by several inches and she ran from the room. She fled down the hall, Brett swearing and staggering after her. "I'll get you! You Irish slut! I'll get you!" Sassy ran faster.

"Yowl!"

"Damn that cat!"

She glanced over her shoulder, saw Brett trip over Kitty. The man sprawled to the floor, and the cat scampered full speed toward her. They both dashed for the bedroom.

Brett scrambled to his feet, but he was too late. With Kitty at her feet, she slammed the door. For a heart-stopping moment, she strained at the old bolt. It was rusty with disuse. Her hand shook as she struggled with it, Brett's footsteps ever closer. "Oh, please, Mother Mary, help me!"

She was going to be raped on her marriage bed. She jammed her shoulder against the door, working the balky lock, and she saw the knob begin to turn.

"Let me in, Sassy, you bitch! You'll be sorry!" The rage in his voice terrified her, and she kept her weight pressed against the door. She believed his story of his father's madness and was now firmly convinced that at least one of Clay James' sons had inherited that maniacal fury. She shot the bolt home just as Brett slammed his body against it.

Would it hold? She backed away, watching the door vibrate, horrified. Kitty, fully recovered from his encounter with the mad man, cocked his head, fascinated by the door's vibration.

"Damn it! Open up, or when I get inside, I'll make you wish a million times you hadn't tricked me! And as for that damned cat. . ."

She didn't answer, but stood gasping for breath, watching the door shake as Brett rattled the knob and threw his big body against it. The lock held, and Brett banged on.

Kitty, amusement in his yellow eyes, licked his jowls with satisfaction.

"Remind me to give you some cream." She stroked his fur in gratitude. Sassy checked the window, locked it. Brett might smash the pane and climb inside, but then he would have to explain the broken glass to Hunter; and while he might be crazy, he wasn't stupid.

Sassy shuddered at Brett's curses. Brett was capable of carrying out his threats; and, if he stayed in this house, he would seek revenge on her and the cat. Yet if she told, she would have to face the wrath of Clay James' younger son, who might be equally dangerous. She closed her eyes, calling up the image of his dark, moody face. No, she could not believe he would ever hurt her, not the gentle man who had made tender love to her. But suppose she was wrong?

Her mind raced. She needed time to deal with Brett, and the best action was to stick close to Hunter and never for a moment allow herself to be left alone with Brett. In the meantime, she would search for alternatives, or perhaps Brett would decide it wasn't worth it and move on.

Outside the door, Brett finally wearied. She pressed her ear against the wood and listened to his retreating footsteps. Suspecting a trick, she wasn't about to open the door and come out. What to do? She wanted the feel of Hunter's strong, protective arms around her, but he was at the far camp. The minutes dragged by. Kitty curled up on his pillow and went to sleep.

At last, she heard a horse's hooves in the yard and ran to the window. Brett rode out toward town. Sassy watched until he was lost from sight. Was he only riding far enough to trick her into thinking he was gone for the day? Maybe he was headed into town to talk to Marylou and have a drink with her, trying to figure his next move.

Suppose he got back before Hunter did and she was in the house alone after dark with him? By then, John would be home, but she'd be afraid to scream and Brett would know that. She didn't want the help privy to family secrets, and besides, Brett would probably tell them she had lured him into her bed and changed her mind. His charge would go unchallenged. Everyone always believed a man.

Sassy made a decision. She would ride to Hunter in the timber; and maybe, if she looked especially fetching and brought a picnic lunch, he might forget that he was very busy and, for that reason, had told her not to accompany him.

Quickly, she changed into a bright green riding outfit with a hat that contrasted strikingly with her red hair. She moved Kitty to a nest among the soft towels of her dressing room where he could snooze peacefully without being easily found. Then she ran into the kitchen; found a pan of cookies, fresh bread, homemade pickles, and fried quail that John had set aside; and selected a bottle of good wine from the pantry. A stableboy saddled Freckles for her, and in minutes, she was loping her dainty sorrel at an easy gait toward the south camp. There the crew gave her directions to the far slope, where Hunter would be by late afternoon. It was a solitary area, they warned her, suggesting someone accompany her. Agreeing for her own reasons that she couldn't be too careful, she let one of the many silent Indians who worked for Hunter guide her along the trail toward the camp. Her guide spoke little English, so she had time to think about the morning past and to try to make plans for the night ahead.

Yet in her mind, she kept reviewing the horrible image of a buggy going over the cliff at full gallop. Brett's words haunted her. Could madness be inherited? What had happened to Hunter's mother and was Swede's visit to the James' estate the cause of murder and suicide? Maybe it had been only a routine business or social call and Brett had misread the events that followed.

What was she to do about Brett? She loved Hunter and could never betray him. Yet he would feel betrayed if he found out her past, if he learned about Brett. Did both sons have their father's stormy temperament?

Rather than shame Hunter or be unfaithful to him, she would leave forever. Still, she might be abandoning Hunter to be fleeced by his cunning older brother. Whatever she decided to do would hinge on what was best for her husband. She loved him enough to sacrifice anything for him, even if it cost her her happiness—or her life.

The guide gestured that they were near the site, left her, and went back down the trail. Knowing she had disobeyed her husband's orders, Sassy took a deep breath for courage and rode into Hunter's camp.

He was sitting by a small fire and stood up as she cantered in. "Sassy? What are you doing way out here? I told you—"

"I got lonely for my husband." She reined in her mare and favored Hunter with her most appealing smile.

Accepting defeat with grace, he helped her dismount. "I was just stopping to have a bite and a cup of coffee."

"In that case, you should be glad to see me—or at least what I've brought." She held out her arms and slid into his embrace.

"You've brought yourself, that's enough." He held her close, and she put her arms around his neck and kissed him.

"Are you mad that I disobeyed you?"

"Nothing you do could ever make me really angry with you, Sweet." He kissed her again.

She wondered what kind of rage he was capable of if he knew her secret?

"Where's Brett?" he asked as he reached to take the picnic basket from the horse. "I'm surprised he didn't come with you."

Sassy thought fast. "Oh, he went off to town on an errand. John hadn't gotten back yet; even the cat was asleep, and I was bored."

"I don't like you out alone," he grumbled as he set the picnic basket down. "It could be dangerous for you."

If he only knew the danger in his own house, Sassy thought. "One of your men escorted me part-way."

He merely grunted as he tied her mare near his big Appaloosa. The two horses nuzzled each other, then fell to grazing.

Hunter grinned. "I can see some fine Appaloosa colts in our future."

Sassy laughed, too, although she didn't feel very merry. "We'll need a whole herd for all our children."

Hunter frowned. "I told you I'm not sure we ought to have children."

In her mind, she saw that buggy going over the cliff,

the horse's light mane and tail streaming out, the red wheels spinning, the woman screaming all the way down. Now she wondered what had happened to Hunter's mother? She spread out a blanket and unpacked the lunch. "What are you looking for out here, anyway?"

"I'm checking to see how dry everything is in certain areas of the woods." Hunter sat down on the blanket and reached for a piece of fried quail. "With summer, some of the east slopes get like tinder, the slightest spark or lightning could set a fire off. With a strong wind, a forest fire can be out of control in minutes; it can outrun a good horse."

Sassy examined the dry grass and leaves around her. "I guess that's why they call it wildfire."

Hunter dug into the food. "On the west slopes, there's plenty of moisture brought in by the ocean breezes, but the mountains prevent the far leases from getting as much."

She bit into a crusty piece of fresh bread smeared with butter. "Are we going to be out here all night?"

He said, "I had planned to ride hard this afternoon to get back to you; but now that you're here, maybe spending the night isn't a bad idea . . . if you don't mind sleeping on the ground with a blanket."

Sassy poured the wine. "It might be fun."

"On second thought," he gave her a smoldering glance, "I'm glad you came. We'll make love under the stars."

Brett James was still in a fury and more than a little drunk as he stared out Marylou's parlor window at the late afternoon sun. "Damn that stubborn bitch," he muttered. "She's not going to cooperate."

Marylou shrugged and reached for a sandwich. "What did you expect? Sassy loves the guy. She's not going to help you take his money." She gave him a piercing look. "That is all you want from her, isn't it?"

"Of course." He drained his glass and poured himself another. "You know I always come back to you, Honey; I like a woman with big charm."

But not big flesh, he thought as he glanced at her and struggled to hide his disgust. Fat. So much face powder she looked like a marble statue. When he had first met Lou, she had been slender; but she ate under stress. Loving Brett had given her plenty of that. That wasn't his problem. Other women smelled of perfume; Lou smelled of food.

He thought of Sassy's dainty fragrance, her waist small enough to put his two hands around. The only thing big about Sassy was her tits, and that suited him fine. He thought of the redhead safe behind that sturdy door and his anger rekindled quickly. Well, she couldn't avoid him forever, and she'd be afraid to tell Hunter when Brett raped her. He liked the idea of her belly and breasts swollen big for his child, the half-breed thinking it was his.

Just thinking about her made his manhood ache with need. "Sassy doesn't mean anything but a way to get my hands on Hunter's money."

"I just wanted to make sure," Lou sighed. "I thought maybe you were playing me for a fool again, that what you really wanted was his wife."

Brett lit a cigar. "I've had his wife, remember? I had her first. That's important to a man. He's so damned proud, he wouldn't want her if he knew."

Lou frowned. "I swan! Now I wish I hadn't let you know she was here; I feel kinda rotten about it."

370

"Careful, you're developing a conscience; bad thing for a madam."

"I've seen the way that pair look at each other, Brett; they're in love, really in love."

"What's wrong with you? Have you forgotten that little tart could have us both hanged if she opens her mouth?"

"You ain't gonna hurt her, are you, Brett? She don't deserve that."

"The hell she doesn't!" He flicked the ashes from his cigar.

Lou brushed crumbs off her ample bosom. "She loves the guy, just like I love you."

He looked at the doubt on her fat face and hastened to soothe her. "Ah, Honey, I'm thinking about you; I don't want to see you worried about hanging or going to jail. I'm figuring all the angles."

"Why don't we just pretend we never knew her?" she asked. "If we all keep our mouths shut, things can go on just as they are. Lulu's Lovelies is making money off all these loggers and you can be my partner and handle the gambling."

"Small potatoes!" Brett sneered. "I want more. He's got no right to half my father's money."

"He's got less right than even you know."

"What are you hinting at?"

"Never mind." The smug look on her white face hinted that she knew something he might like to know. Lou wasn't very smart. With a little charm and some loving, Brett might worm it out of her.

"Aw, you don't know anything that would interest me."

"Yes, I do, but I can't tell. I promised Swede."

371

"That old drunk!" Brett scoffed. "Whatever it was, he probably didn't even remember telling you."

Tears came to her eyes, and her double chin quivered. "Swede asked me to marry him, you know that?"

"Aw." He made a dismissive gesture. "All loggers ask whores that when they're drunk."

"No." She shook her head. "He meant it. I might have married him, but I'm in love with you, Brett; and now poor Swede's dead."

Tears made crooked trails down her pasty white face, smearing her makeup. He had never been so sick of a woman in his life, but he needed her for awhile longer. Brett snuffed out his cigar, giving her his most appealing look. "And I love you, too, Lou."

"Do you really?" Her eyes brightened.

"After all we've meant to each other? How can you ask?" He kissed the tip of her nose. "Things'll be good again, Honey—you'll see—once we get all Hunter's money and land."

Her fat face fell. "What're you planning, Brett? Ain't there been enough trouble? I can't sleep now for thinking about that Huntington guy. Maybe his wife loved him, too."

"Forget him, Lou. When he wasn't gambling away his company's money, wasn't he there banging your whores every chance he got?"

"And you weren't?"

"Well," he said hastily, "that was before I decided that you were the one I really cared about."

"It always hurt me, the way you looked over my girls," she said. "Hunter ain't been in here since he first laid eyes on Sassy, and you know what? I don't think he'll ever sleep with another woman; he's that crazy about her."

He'd better mend fences fast. He saw the regret and the envy in the fat whore's eyes. "He can't be any crazier about her than I am about you, Honey." He put his arms around her ample girth, dreading what she'd want next. "We'll be well off before this is over."

"Let me get this straight," Lou said. "You're just gonna embezzle money from his accounts and we'll run away together, right? I can get out of this lousy life?"

He held her close, her big breasts and belly jiggling against him. He remembered Sassy's slender waist and long legs. "Of course, Lou. That's my plan. It may take a while, though. I have to be careful not to arouse his suspicions." He smiled to himself, envisioning the many times Hunter wouldn't be around and Brett could enjoy Sassy. She wouldn't dare tell Hunter.

She kissed him. "What are you thinking about, Honey?"

"How much I want you." It was not a total lie! He needed Lou tonight for an alibi. But as he kissed her, he wondered how difficult it would be to set up an accident to rid him of the fat old whore. She might slip and fall into Puget Sound. No doubt everything she had was willed to Brett. He gave her a squeeze. "Why are you so suspicious?"

"Because although I love you, Brett, I also know you."

She knew him too damned well. Brett went to the sideboard and poured them each a drink, his mind elsewhere. Brett didn't have the slightest intention of sharing anything with the Injun bastard. If Hunter should meet with an accident, what could be more natural than that after a decent interval, the grieving half-brother should marry the rich widow? Then Brett would have it all without the tedious effort of embezzling.

"Speakin' about trust," Lou sighed, "you'd better be careful Hunter doesn't think you want Sassy."

"Why? You think he's the jealous type?"

"What's your life worth?" Lou studied the rings on her plump fingers. "I tell you I never saw a man as crazy over a woman as Hunter is over her. He almost worships her. It's something every woman dreams of."

"What do you think he'd do if he knew her past?" Brett sipped his drink.

She gave him a searching look. "I'd hate to be the one who told him. Hunter's a proud, proud man."

Brett frowned. "You sound almost sympathetic to that half-breed bastard."

"I can't help it; I like him." Lou shrugged. "Despite the fact he's tough and probably dangerous, there's something tender and vulnerable there as well . . . for the right woman."

"Women! Such sentimental fools!" Brett scoffed.

"Okay, I'll admit it." Her white-powdered face looked sheepish. "The idea of a mail-order bride was romantic and a little sad, so I helped him out a little."

"A little? That's not what you told me earlier. And how romantic is it that he ended up with a whore that I had first and who worked for you? Think how all the men would laugh if they knew!"

Lou paused and swallowed hard. "You know what's wrong with you Brett? You got no heart at all. Whores have feelings, too."

How stupid of him to offend this tub of lard. He needed her. "I'm sorry, Lou, Honey. I didn't mean to hurt your feelings."

"I've been thinking how convenient for you that Swede was killed the night you hit town."

He struggled for a properly horrified pose. "I'm surprised at you. I wouldn't stoop to that. I only killed Huntington because if I had honored his poker win, it would have broken me. You helped because you love me."

"Yes. But sometimes I stop kidding myself and know you ain't much good. Swede was good and decent at heart, even if he did fall to temptation."

"I can't imagine my old man's trusted friend and employee doing anything wrong. What would tempt him?"

"He said he never meant for it to happen. He regretted it the rest of his life. He probably should have kept his mouth shut."

So Swede had said something to Clay James that had pushed his father over the edge—his father, who had been bordering on insanity for months. "What did Swede do that was so terrible?"

"I'm not going to tell you." She drained her glass and waddled to the table to pour herself another drink.

"Okay, don't." Brett shrugged. It might take a few weeks, but he'd find out what she knew . . . if anything. Swede had been his father's most beloved and trusted friend and employee; how might the bull o' the woods have betrayed Clay?

Lou studied her rings. "With Clay's background, maybe it was only a matter of time anyway—"

"Don't say that! The James aren't crazy!" Brett paced the floor, remembering his grandfather, his father, and his mother's scream floating on the night air as the buggy fell.

"I didn't say that."

"You're thinking it." He whirled on her. "Did Swede tell his secret to Hunter, too?"

She shook her head. "After what happened to Clay, Swede said he was ashamed to tell him, not certain what Hunter might think. He didn't want to lose the boy's friendship or respect."

Brett took out his watch, opened it, stared at the daguerreotype. "My mother is dead because of Clay and that damned Swede."

Lou turned her rings over and over. "Hunter thought the world of Swede and so did I."

"Idols have feet of clay." Brett snapped his watch closed with a sneer. "Nobody's perfect."

"Hunter thought Swede was, and he feels the same about Sassy."

Brett gulped his drink. "What do you think will happen if he finds out his wife used to spread her legs to any man with the price?"

"Depends on how much he really loves her, I reckon." Lou sighed and reached for a cookie.

God, she was eating again. Brett walked unsteadily to the sideboard, refilled his glass. "Loves her?" He snorted. "Hunter's proud; he'd kill her, and you know it!"

"And he'll kill the man who tells him, I'm thinking."

Damn it, sometimes the fat old whore was very perceptive. Too bad he couldn't figure out a way for Lou to tell Hunter and let her take his fury. Hunter wouldn't have to know Brett had laid her first, unless Brett wanted him to. Brett tried to figure an angle. "There's the money."

"Forget that. Look at it this way," Lou said and bit into the cookie. "If you'd gotten it all, you would have wasted it all. Hunter's worked hard, built an empire worth a thousand times what he inherited."

Brett laughed again. "So maybe justice will be done after all. We'll call my embezzlement interest."

"And we'll get married?"

"Married?" He managed not to snort with derision.

"I thought that's what you meant. Even whores ought to have a chance to make a fresh start. Swede and I talked about it. I might have married him if some mean bastard hadn't killed him." She began to cry.

"Now, Honey." He put his arm around her. "Of course we'll get married. You just have to help me get a stake, that's all."

"Maybe we just ought to pack up and leave town." Lou snuffled and wiped her eyes with her plump hands. "Maybe if we'd just go away, that pair could be happy together. Hunter need never know her past."

"How about us being happy?" he challenged. "We need money to make a fresh start."

Clegg. Even if Brett got rid of Lou and Hunter, he still had the drunken logger to contend with. Brett couldn't risk Clegg's telling anyone who had killed Swede. What to do? Brett had no doubt that sooner or later the man would spill everything he knew. In a little while it would be dark; he couldn't do anything till then. "I'm going over to the *Illahee* to play a few hands of cards."

Immediately, Lou's plump face crumpled. "I know you, Brett; they got girls over there."

"Now, Lou, Honey, if I just wanted a girl, that's what you got here, isn't it?"

She nodded.

"So that isn't it. Besides, if I wanted a woman, I want a real one like you." He swayed on his feet. "I just heard there's a card game going on, that's all." There'd be Indian girls at Pennell's place. He wanted to revenge him-

377

self on Indian girls for the pain Springtime had caused Brett's mother.

No, as much as he'd like to lay some Indian whore, he needed to stay here so he'd have an alibi. He took Lou in his arms. He wanted a woman bad. If he closed his eyes, maybe he could pretend this fat pig was Sassy . . . at least until he could drug her.

"Stay the night, Brett," she murmured. "I'd do anything for you, you know that."

He forced himself to kiss her. "I know, Honey, and I appreciate it."

"I'm tryin' not to make you feel obligated, Brett." She sounded teary, desperate. "I'm so glad you're here; I've missed you so much."

He merely grunted. Brett's groin ached with a need that Sassy had aroused in him, but he couldn't have Sassy tonight. No matter, when he finally did, he would make her pay with pain and humiliation for refusing him this morning. He closed his eyes and began to unbutton Lou's satin robe. In a couple of hours, it would be night and he would not only have taken care of his need, he would have an alibi.

It was dark when Brett had finally satisfied himself. Lou lay unconscious and snoring from the knockout drops he'd slipped in her whiskey. He got up, dressed, climbed out the window. Making sure no one saw him, he slipped into the shadows, got his horse, and rode toward the woods where Clegg was hiding out. Brett had his alibi now and could carry out his plans. That called for three more deaths: Lou's, Clegg's . . . and Hunter's.

Chapter Twenty-One

Sassy lay in Hunter's arms under the stars while he made slow, gentle love to her. With him holding her like he was at this moment, with his lips caressing her skin, she could almost forget the problems she had with Brett. One thing was certain, she wasn't going to hurt and humiliate her proud husband even if she had to pack up and leave forever to protect him.

"My sweet Sassy Girl," he whispered, his breath warm on her ear. "I don't know what I ever did before you came into my life. I didn't realize I was such a lonely man."

"Don't say that," Sassy murmured, brushing his black curls back from his forehead as a mother would comfort a small boy. "If something ever happened to me, you could go on, maybe find another wife."

He shook his head as he raised up on one elbow to look into her eyes. "No, this is it. Some men can only care about one woman, and you're it for me, Sassy."

She didn't want to hear that. She thought about how far it was from the top of the pedestal to the mud at the bottom. It made her wince to imagine his bitterness and his fury, not to mention his broken heart if Brett made good his threat. She could not let her adoring husband find out; she could not. Nor could she ever be unfaithful to him. "You're it for me, too, my dearest. I knew it the moment I stepped off that boat and saw you sitting there so proud and foreboding on that big Appaloosa."

He laughed low in his throat. "Then why did you lead me on such a merry chase, you vixen?"

She kissed her fingertip, touched it to his lips. "Because I'm just a contrary woman, I suppose; or maybe it was the thrill of the chase."

He brushed his lips across hers. "You took a chance. Suppose I had decided you weren't worth all that trouble and had married one of the others instead?"

"Which one?" She was jealous in spite of herself.

"No one," he vowed. "I would have had you if I'd had to move heaven and earth, and now you're mine forever."

"If something should ever change your mind," she said, "remember only that I loved you above all else, Hunter."

"Nothing will ever change the way I feel about you, Sassy Girl," he said as his arms embraced her possessively. "You're mine."

"I'm yours," she agreed. She kissed him, touching and teasing his lips with the tip of her tongue until he opened for her. She ran the hot blade of her tongue deep into his mouth. He gasped, and she felt his pulse pounding harder as he sucked her tongue into his mouth, twined his with hers.

His hand stroked slowly down her body until it reached the dark red curls at the apex of her thighs. She couldn't stop herself from opening her thighs and arching her body up so that her breasts pushed against the rippling muscles of his chest. She pulled away from his kiss, gasping for air. "You know what I want," she gasped.

"Say it," he demanded, and his fingers touched the bud of her femininity. "Say it, Sassy!"

"I—I want you to touch me there, tease me there."

"And what else?"

"Nurse me," she begged, pushing herself up. "Please . . . please!"

His mouth came down on her breast, hot and wet, sucking hard on her nipple as his fingers teased their way deep into her velvet place. She gave a ragged, shuddering sigh at the emotions he brought raging from her. No man had ever stirred her, made her want him the way he did. With the others, she had only pretended, feeling dead inside.

Hunter kissed his way across her breast to the other nipple. "Now," he commanded, "touch me." He sucked hard on her breast, making her wish she had milk to give him, wishing her belly was swollen with his child. "Touch me!"

She caught his maleness in her hand; and he was big, and hard, and throbbing with seed. She squeezed him, making him moan against her breast.

His hand touched and stroked and teased her insides until she quivered.

"No," he said, "not yet. Don't waste it, Sweet; we'll go together."

And then he was on her and in her, making long sure strokes that drove her wild with slow teasing, making her want him more. She wrapped her long, pale legs around his lean, dark hips. His mouth was on hers, his muscular chest hard against her breasts as they meshed. He tangled the fingers of his good hand in her long hair as he guided her to him. He pulled almost out of her and then came down ever so slowly, impaling her against the blanket.

"Oh, Hunter," she gasped, "I can't take much more of this."

"Beg me for it. Beg me to end your sweet misery." He came down so very slowly again.

"Please," she gasped. "Oh, Hunter, take me! Take me!" It was like wildfire, she thought, being the half-breed's bride, his wildfire bride. Two untamed beings under the moon of a Washington night, naked on a blanket under the stars while they meshed and mated.

He seemed to be big and throbbing with the seed he had to give her. She could feel every inch of his dagger as he came down slowly into her. She felt the heat of him throbbing deep in her womb. "Please, Hunter, please!" Now he stopped being gentle. He rode her hard, raising almost out and then coming down with all the power behind his lean, dark hips, his flesh slapping rhythmically against hers. She tilted up to meet him, wanting every inch he had to give. His mouth covered hers, dominated hers, his tongue ramming deep into her throat even as his manhood rammed into her velvet place. She surrendered to his male domination, letting him ravage her mouth with his, but meeting him thrust for thrust, wanting him deep as he could go.

Now she began to climax, digging her nails into his lean hips, holding him captive while her femininity squeezed him, taking what it wanted from him. He made three quick thrusts and then began to shudder as he gave up his seed. She could almost feel the heat of it as it spirted into her womb. In the moonlight, they mated like two wild things.

They lay thus a long time before he sighed. "You took everything I had to give, Sweet."

"I meant to," she whispered against his ear. "I want your son."

It was perhaps the wrong thing to say, she knew it immediately. "I'm not sure you would if you knew about my father."

She did not let him out of the embrace of her arms as he lay next to her. "Tell me, Hunter. Tell me."

He shook his head. "He—Father . . ." Hunter trembled, and she knew it was something so terrible he could not bring himself to face it.

"Perhaps if you told someone, you'd feel better."

He swallowed hard. "I don't remember. Isn't that strange? I was there and I don't remember."

Or couldn't bear to face the memory, Sassy thought, looking at the expression in his bright blue eyes. Maybe his mind was protecting itself from something it couldn't bear to confront.

"I think he was insane," Hunter admitted. "Years later, he . . . Clay . . ."

"Never mind." She put a gentle hand on his. "It doesn't matter." She couldn't tell him that Brett had already told her how their father died. "About Springtime—"

"She was cheating." Even in the moonlight, she could see the pain of remembrance on his troubled face. "Other men were laughing at him behind his back."

Sassy winced. Probably the way men would laugh at Hunter if they ever found out Sassy's past. Looking at his tortured expression, she suddenly knew. "You were there. You saw it all, didn't you?"

* * *

Hunter didn't want to think about it, this terror that had reoccurred in his nightmares over and over ever since he was a little boy. Sometimes he was afraid to go to sleep, afraid that hazy horror would creep into his dreams. He nodded, swallowing. "I was hiding because I was afraid."

"Why were you afraid?"

The silence deepened as he relived it in his mind. "I was very young—maybe two or three. It was warm, the windows were open, and it was dark and late. Springtime was with a man . . ."

Sassy said nothing and he let his mind go back. Like a small shadow, he hid; and his mother and the man never knew he was there. He remembered Springtime's laughter. She had such a high, pretty laugh; but it could be so taunting, so cruel at times. "He was outside the door. I—I heard him arguing with someone, someone with a familiar voice. Maybe he was trying to delay Father. Springtime and the man on her never heard. They were making love, naked and sweaty on a bed near the window. I could have warned them, but when I saw Father burst through the door with that shotgun, I was afraid and hid behind a chair."

"Who was the man she was with, Hunter?"

He shook his head, buried his face in his hands. "I—I don't know; oh God, I don't know!"

She put her arm around his shoulders. "Didn't you see him?"

"I must have. I don't know; I—I don't remember."

She looked deeply concerned at his agony. "Don' think about it anymore; it doesn't matter."

384

"It does matter; I have nightmares about it. I could have saved her if I'd cried out that Clay was coming, but I was afraid and I hid."

"It isn't your fault; you were a little boy. You couldn't have done anything to stop it."

"I could have shouted." Again, as he always did, he felt the guilt of not helping her. If only . . . if only he had shouted a warning. He couldn't change the past that tortured him over and over. "She screamed when she looked up and saw the moonlight reflected on the shotgun barrel. His eyes were wild and crazed."

"What happened to the man?"

Hunter shook his head. "He went out the window, left her to face Clay. Father didn't get a good look at him."

"But you did?"

He tried to recall, but the man was only a blur. What he did remember was the way Springtime screamed and how it was cut off in the middle by the blast that blew warm blood and brains all over him.

"My mother lay there on a blood-soaked bed with her beautiful face shot away. Clay had the gun under his chin, trying to kill himself, but he'd used both barrels on her, and the triggers clicked. Then he threw it away and ran out into the night."

She murmured in sympathy. "Who was the man he argued with, the one who tried to delay him? Swede?"

"I—I don't remember. Maybe. He was Clay's friend; he'd try to protect him from finding out. Springtime was a Jezebel; she slept with lots of men when Father was gone."

"Don't." She soothed him as she might a child. "Don't think of it anymore, Dearest."

"So you see I have bad seed, Sassy," he muttered.

"I'm fathered by an insane killer, and Brett said Grand-father James died in a madhouse. It's in my blood."

"Maybe if you could remember everything that happened, the nightmares would go away."

"I've tried; oh, God, I've tried!"

Sassy looked into his eyes and saw that something in his brain had mercifully blacked out much of that memory. Something he didn't want to acknowledge had caused his mind to close it off to protect him. She remembered Clegg's boast. Could he have been the man who fled Springtime's bed and left her to die? "It doesn't matter, dear."

"Doesn't it? Don't you feel differently about me now?"

She thought about the fact that he might, like Brett, inherit the James' family insanity. Hunter might eventually be as wildly murderous as his father had been.

"I can see by your face what's in your mind; I would never hurt you, Sassy. I swear I wouldn't!"

Like a discordant melody in her head, she heard Springtime's scream and the blast of the shotgun blowing away her pretty face. She saw the horse and buggy going off the cliff, red wheels turning. Clay James' sons. One had taken her virginity; the other might take her life if he knew. "I love you, Hunter."

"Even after what I've told you?" he whispered, hugging her to him. "You're one in a million, Sassy Girl; I made the right choice when I picked you for my lady."

She almost said, "Not even if you knew I used to be a whore? Not even if you knew your brother was the man who took my virginity, not you?" As much as she wanted to be free of the burden of her secret, she dare not ask. He didn't love her enough to face that reality.

almost no man could love a woman that much. Sassy reached up to kiss him. "Let's get some rest."

They slipped their clothes back on and bedded down in the blankets. Hunter dropped off to sleep, but Sassy lay awake, holding him close as if he were a troubled little boy, wondering what Hunter had actually seen that long-ago night and what violence he might be capable of if he ever found out his wife was no better than his mother? She dared not let him find out, yet she would not betray him with Brett, no matter what danger she faced if Brett told. Holy Mother, what was Sassy going to do? She snuggled in Hunter's arms, wondering where Brett was and dropping off to sleep.

Brett's mind was busy with plans as he rode through the darkness to where Clegg hid in the forest outside town. Clegg came out of the shadows.

"About time! I thought you had forgot me!"

Brett handed him the bottle of whiskey he had brought. "I didn't go to the trouble of sneaking you off that ship to forget about you."

The logger gave an ugly grin as he grabbed the bottle. He took the cork out with his teeth and spat it out. "This is more like it! I was about to ride into town and get my own bottle. I want a woman, too."

"Don't be so impatient," Brett warned. "You could have caused some real trouble if you'd gone into town and been seen." Yes, he was definitely going to have to get rid of Clegg. The man was a loose cannon without much brain. If he opened his big trap about Swede. . . . but of course Brett didn't plan to let him live that long.

"Nobody bosses me around." Clegg grumbled as he

threw his head back, gulping the whiskey. "What is it you want from me?" He wiped his mouth on his grimy sleeve.

Brett winced. Such a low-class lout. What a shame an educated, upperclass gentleman like himself had been reduced to dealing with so many thugs. "I need your help in getting rid of Hunter."

Even in the dark, Brett could see the small eyes gleam. "Now you're talking! After what that Injun bastard did to me in that fight—"

"Spare me the details," Brett broke in. "Let's talk."

Clegg gestured him toward a small fire back in the shadows. "Too bad you didn't bring me a woman, too. I had me a hunger for that wench of Hunter's."

"I'll give it some thought." That would be a fitting revenge on Sassy. Brett extracted an expensive cigar from his vest. He imagined the fiesty girl on her knees begging Brett not to turn her over to this pig of a logger. While it might be interesting to watch, Brett wouldn't want to use a woman Clegg had had. Besides the logger wasn't going to be around that long.

Clegg took another slug of whiskey and stared as Brett lit his cigar. "Ain't ya gonna offer me one?"

"These are very fine Havanas," Brett said. "I don't think you would appreciate . . ." He saw the anger on the man's face, shrugged, gave him a cigar. Clegg lit up with a branch from the campfire. "You know the far slope?"

Clegg nodded. "Yep. Dry as the depths of hell this time of the year."

"Is that a fact?" Brett asked innocently. The night wind had picked up, and he examined the glowing tip of his cigar. "What would happen if long, fine cigars like these were left propped up with dry leaves and grass under them?"

Clegg studied his own fire-reddened cigar. "You'd have to be stupid not to know that. Some of them might go out, but the rest would burn down to the butt and catch that brush and leaves."

"So a dozen cigars scattered through the woods could start a big fire?"

Clegg glared at him. "I'm a logger, Mister. It goes against my grain to burn down a forest."

Brett turned his attention from his glowing cigar to Clegg. "What if I told you it was Hunter's timber lease I had in mind? What if I told you Hunter is camped out there tonight?"

"In that case . . ." Clegg stood. "When do we start?"

Brett rose quickly before Clegg could reconsider. "I brought you a horse. Between the two of us, we can do this in a couple of hours."

"With this wind, we'll have to be careful," Clegg warned. "I've heard of men getting trapped in a fire they started themselves."

"Is that a fact?" Brett held back the smile that spread inside him. "Now here's what we'll do . . ."

They rode out at a lope. Brett had sobered up, but Clegg kept sipping from the bottle. It was late and the wind blew stronger. Everything was going according to plan, Brett determined with satisfaction. Brett didn't need a drunken, loudmouthed accomplice who would spill his guts later and implicate Brett.

"Hey, Clegg, do you know where Hunter might be camped?"

He nodded. "There's a spring on the far slope makes

a good camping place. He's probably there. I want to be the one to kill him."

"Sure," Brett said, "you're entitled after what he did to you. We'll spread out when we start those fires so the woods will be aflame before Hunter knows it. With this wind, maybe he'll be caught in it." He thought with satisfaction about Sassy back at the house. As soon as he had his alibi established, he'd go home to tell the widow the sad news. Then he'd take that damned lock off her bedroom door so he could have her anytime he wanted her.

They reviewed their tactics and agreed to meet at the rock formation beside the lake. Brett gave Clegg a flint and steel in case his matches didn't work and a handful of long cigars. Brett crowed loudly once Clegg took his leave for Hunter's encampment. He hoped the logger could manage to set the fires without botching the plan. He peered at his watch in the darkness. If his strategy worked, he'd have both Clegg and Hunter out of the way before dawn and could be back at Lulu's Lovelies long before the loggers raced into town with news of the big blaze. Now, to start his own set of fires. In the distance, thunder rumbled. He considered the possibility of rain and listened carefully. The rain, he was quite certain, would hold off till tomorrow. By then, half the woods would be ablaze.

Clegg looked back at Brett as he galloped away. That damned high class snot! Brett thought he was so much better than everybody and treated others like they wasn't worth cold spit. Was there any way Clegg could double-cross that uppity bastard?

His torn and bruised body still ached from the stomp
390

ing he'd gotten from that half-breed Injun. Clegg would teach that sonovabitch, too. The other thing he wanted out of this deal was a chance at that red-haired woman of Hunter's. He wasn't sure he was able to mount a woman after what Hunter had done to him with those spiked boots, but at least he could enjoy the privilege of stripping that beauty naked and making her grovel on her knees before him.

What about Brett? He was ruthless, the kind who'd steal the butter off a sick beggar's biscuit. If Clegg didn't watch himself, Brett might even manage to place the whole blame for the fire on the logger. Clegg shuddered. He had no doubt what the timbermen would do to someone who deliberately started a forest fire: they'd lynch him. But he wasn't afraid of being strung up. There were only two things Clegg really feared, rats and fire. He grinned. His idea of the way to go was drunk and in the arms of a good whore.

The night wind increased, blowing hot against his raw face. He remembered the plan, stopped, dismounted, left a cigar smoldering, rode on. In less than thirty minutes, he had left smoldering cigars over a line nearly a mile long. With Brett matching him flame for flame and this dry wind blowing harder by the minute, they would soon have a roaring wildfire that would light up Seattle's skies.

Now to check out that campsite looking for Hunter. Too bad he wouldn't have the pleasure of staying to watch Hunter burn alive. Brett. What was he going to do about that dude? That dandified bastard would probably try to double-cross Clegg. Was there a way to do-in Brett and let him take the blame for it all? He'd have to give that more thought.

Cautiously, Clegg dismounted near the spring, tied

his horse, and crawled closer. The slight scent of a smoldering campfire drew Clegg to the site.

Two horses? Clegg watched the big Appaloosa stud nibbling grass. There was also a smaller sorrel. Who else was out here? Then he saw them asleep in their blankets in the moonlight, wrapped in each other's arms. The woman's reddish hair gleamed in the moonlight. Hunter's prissy little lady-wife. Clegg swore. If she'd lain there docilely and let Clegg get his fill, it wouldn't have taken much time; but no, she had to fight and scream. If she could give that dark Injun some, she could damned well give it to Clegg, too. He remembered the Injun whore who was Hunter's mother. Like dipping it in warm honey, he thought with a sigh. She'd been too hot and tempting for any man to turn down. Twenty-two years Clegg had been in the northwest woods and except for Sassy, he'd never seen another as desirable a Springtime. Springtime could have corrupted a saint.

Hunter's wife shouldn't have turned Clegg down. If he could sleep with Hunter's mother, he could damn well sleep with the Injun bastard's wife. Well, now the uppity bitch could die with Hunter.

He tested the wind, got upwind from the camp, and let his smoldering cigars. In a few minutes, the flames would begin to spread. The man and woman were sleeping heavily. By the time they woke up, it was gonna be too late to get out. Clegg considered running their horses off. No chance without waking the couple. Besides, the way this breeze was blowing, once those fires caught they wouldn't have a chance of outrunning the flames. They could burn up right along with their horses.

His job done, Clegg headed for the rendezvous. Already, flares of yellow and orange spread along the ground through the brush. Awakened by the smoke, the birds twittered, and squirrels chattered nervously. A panicked deer bounded through the woods in front of him.

Clegg inhaled the sooty fumes and shuddered. There was nothing he feared like fire. As a logger, he knew its power and destruction. He sure didn't want to linger none at the meeting spot. With the wind blowing just right, it could sweep over the valley near the shallow pond in less than an hour. He looked back over his shoulder. Red flames licked the base of fir and pine trees. With this dry brush and wind, the fire would quickly crown, racing through the tops of the trees, moving faster than it could on the ground.

Frightened wildlife—deer, rabbits, and squirrels—scurried past him; blindly seeking water. The pond was shallow. Even in the middle, it might not be deep enough to save the deer; and if a giant, burning tree were to fall across it . . .

He heard the rumble of distant thunder and cackled gleefully. It would rain by morning, but morning would be too late. Thousands of acres of trees would be reduced to a smoldering ruin. The one thing Clegg regretted was that he would not see Hunter and Sassy when the smoke woke them. Clegg decided not to mention the woman to Brett. That dandy might have scruples about burning a woman alive. Clegg might have had, too, if she hadn't been the one who had gotten him stomped. Sassy was more desirable than even Springtime had been, but Hunter might be as crazy as Clay James. She wasn't worth dying for.

When he glanced back, the fire was eating its way greedily through the brush. Clegg shuddered. Two things he feared: rats and fire. Rats because there had been so many of them in the shabby slum where he grew up. Even now, he could close his eyes and feel them darting across his body, nibbling his fingers and toes.

Fire. Once a street-corner preacher had screamed at him to change his ways, to turn his back on sin or burn in hell and brimstone forever. With an easy laugh, Clegg had punched the old man. He hadn't changed his ways, but sometimes he woke up sweating and smelling brimstone, remembering the preacher's vivid description.

Clegg's horse was lathered and blowing by the time he reined in at the meeting place. Brett was there before him, dark eyes gleaming with reflected firelight . . . or was he as crazy as his father?

Brett smiled as he stared at the glow on the horizon, the light reflecting in his dark eyes. "You make sure Hunter's trapped?"

Clegg nodded. "He was sleeping like a baby. By the time he wakes up, it'll be too late."

Brett laughed. "Look at that thing spread. Looks like hell with the lid off!"

Clegg shuddered. "Okay. It's done. Now let's get outta here. Fire scares me. I don't want to stay around to watch it burn."

Brett motioned him to dismount. "Sure. I've got some money hidden for you. Didn't want to have it on me. Boy, watch that fire spread!"

Brett watched the logger dismount and turn to look at the flames. Brett considered shooting Clegg in the back with one of the derringers in his pocket. He had two, the same ones he'd used in the New York killing. But why waste the bullets? Besides, if he shot the logger and the body didn't burn, Brett didn't want anyone finding a bullet-riddled body and wondering who had killed

Clegg. The best thing to do was make it look like the stupid bastard had been trapped by the fire. Like Hunter, he would burn to death.

Cautiously, Brett picked up the short, sturdy limb he'd chosen earlier. He took a step up behind Clegg, brought the club back. A twig snapped under his foot, the other man whirled around. "What the—" Clegg swore as the branch caught him across the skull, but he fell like a crashing tree.

Brett threw down the bloody club. "You shouldn't have been greedy and come back for the money," he chided. "It's cost you your life, you poor idiot!"

Was Clegg dead? If he weren't, he soon would be—cooked alive. Clegg sure wasn't going anywhere with his head caved in and no horse. Clegg had served Brett's needs, but he had no further use of the logger.

The horses reared and snorted, stamping their hooves at the scent of smoke. Brett swung up on his bay and caught the other's reins. He saw no point in leaving a valuable mount to die.

Brett took one last look at the fire sweeping the ridge. Wildfire. In a few more minutes, the forest would blaze out of control. It was a shame to waste all that valuable timber, Brett thought, but it couldn't be helped. There was a storm building; the fire might easily have been started by lightning.

He spurred his horse toward town. Tomorrow night, he would take on the role of kind-hearted brother consoling bereaved widow . . . whether she liked it or not. Right now, however, he had to get back to Seattle so he could be at Lulu's Lovelies when the loggers reported the fire. Leading Clegg's horse, Brett took off toward town at a gallop.

Chapter Twenty-Two

Hunter came awake suddenly. He lay listening, his keen senses alert to danger. What was it in the darkness that had awakened him? Very slowly, he sat up, looked around. His first thought was for Sassy's safety, but she lay next to him, sleeping peacefully, her long hair tumbled on the blanket, a slight smile on her soft lips.

The two horses gazed nearby, but Poker Chips snorted and raised his head, nostrils flaring. What disturbed his horse? More than once in the past, the stallion had warned Hunter of possible trouble. Hunter's gaze swept over the small clearing. A lifetime in the woods and years of living among his mother's people had always alerted him to any hint that something was not right long before any white man would have realized it.

Hunter took a deep breath. Was that smoke? He breathed again and looked toward the Appaloosa that stamped his hooves and eyed him uneasily. He checked the campfire—cold, just as he'd thought. And yet, that slight acrid odor was most definitely smoke.

He shook his wife. "Sassy, get up."

Her eyes opened sleepily. "Can't you wait till daylight to do it again?"

"Sassy, I'm not kidding. Get up now."

"Why? Can't it wait till morning? After last night, I want to snuggle down in the blankets and sleep."

He told himself he must not alarm her. She was his to protect. He reached for a saddle. "Don't ask any questions; just get up. We've got to go."

Sassy scowled as she watched with disbelief. He was actually saddling her horse. "In the middle of the night? Whatever it is, can't it wait until dawn?"

He glared at her. "Don't ask questions; we're going."

"But—"

"Sassy," he snapped, "stop arguing and get a move on or I'll load you on your horse bodily."

"You wouldn't dare!"

He whirled. "Don't try me, Sassy."

She was alarmed by the look on his face, but annoyed by his sharp tone. She knew Hunter was perfectly capable of grabbing her up like a doll and throwing her across her own horse. She crawled out of her blankets, began to collect the scattered picnic things.

"What're you doing?" He glanced back in exasperation.

"What does it look like? I'm packing up the camp—"

"Leave that damned stuff! Get the canteens, and wet down a couple of blankets in the spring."

Was he losing his mind? She remembered what Brett had told her of Clay James and shivered. "If you'll just give me an explanation—"

"I'll explain later, Sassy; do as I tell you." His voice brooked no argument as he reached for his own saddle.

Damn this stubborn man who expected a woman to

submit to his will without question. She had no doubt she would incur his wrath if she argued. It also occurred to her that Hunter was not usually one to be alarmed. She took the blankets and ran for the spring. "Hunter, what is it?"

"Maybe nothing," he said evasively and untied the horse.

"But maybe something," she said. "Tell me! I hate this protective, chivalrous attitude of yours."

"Don't forget the canteens."

She dipped the blanket in the water and wrung it out. As she finished her task and turned around, she took a breath and felt sudden fear. "Is that smoke?"

Now she saw the alarm on his face. "Come on, Sassy, and don't ask any questions."

A thousand questions came to mind, but she saw only Hunter's tense face in the moonlight and realized how alarmed he was. Grabbing up the damp blankets and the canteens, she ran to him. "Oh, Hunter, what is it? Is there a fire?"

"It's okay," he soothed, swinging her up in his arms and onto her horse. "There's probably nothing to worry about—"

"But you're worried. I can see it in your eyes."

"All right," he admitted as he hung a canteen on her saddle. "I think there's a small fire somewhere behind us, maybe started by lightning. The wind's coming up and blowing in our direction, so we're gonna clear out."

Her mare snorted and stamped its feet as Hunter took one of the wet blankets. "We're in danger, aren't we?"

"Sassy, I swore when I married you I'd take care of you, but you are the damndest little thing to deal with you ask too many questions. Here, wrap this blanket around you."

"I will not! If there's no danger, why would I want a cold, wet blanket—"

"Sassy, just do it for me."

She accepted the makeshift cloak although the dampness went immediately through her light dress. Poker Chips stamped and snorted as Hunter took the other blanket and canteen and swung up on his big Appaloosa.

Hunter said, "There's a small runoff pond a couple of miles to the south. With any luck, it'll have some water in it from last spring's rains. Follow me and don't lag."

Was he hinting they might not make it? Sassy needed no further urging as she took a deep breath and smelled the acrid fumes. "Lead on. I'm right behind you!"

Hunter took off at a gallop, the nervous mare following. The scent of smoke drifted through the woods. Indignant squirrels chattered in the pines and firs.

She nudged her mare up next to Hunter and shouted to him. "Can we make it home?"

"It is all around us, Sassy. We'll be lucky to make it to the pond!"

He urged Poker Chips forward. The smoke swirled through the trees, and the acrid scent made her cough. Lightning. Had lightning done this? Ahead of her, she saw a patch of sky where lightning flashed and thunder rolled. If the storm were coming in from that direction, why was the fire behind them? It didn't make any sense, but there was no time to sort it out. The dry leaves and pine needles rustled under the horses' hooves as they galloped ahead. Fire could spread across the forest floor faster than a horse could run.

She heard a crackle and dared to peek over her shoulder. Black smoke and a faint orange glow confirmed Hunter's worst fears. Now she knew real panic. Sassy struggled with her fear, almost tasting it—or was that only the caustic taste of smoke? Aware of the danger, the horses snorted as they galloped, their ears laid back, their nostrils flaring.

A bear lumbered past her along the trail, but her mare paid no attention. Two deer bolted alongside, almost brushing up against the bear, but neither paid the slightest heed to the other. Man and horse, deer and bear now shared a common enemy: an out-of-control forest fire. The wind blew in uneven bursts and, from the corner of her eye, she saw hungry flames gobbling the brush and slithering along the forest floor like angry red serpents.

She had lost all track of time, although she was certain they had only been riding a few minutes. The horses were beginning to lather as they ran. Around her, confusion reigned as rabbits with their fluffy tails afire plunged through the woods, setting dry wood and leaves smoldering in a dozen different and new directions. Birds, whirling out of the trees, sometimes flew right back into the thick, billowing smoke.

The fire climbed tree trunks like flaming fingers moving up the bark. As the fingers reached the top of a tree, it burst into flame like a Roman candle and the gusting wind caught it and blew the fire through the top of the trees. With so much more wind available near the top, the fire accelerated, catching up to the galloping horses in a deadly game of tag. She felt the heat on her face as she looked back and was belatedly grateful for the damp blanket that shielded her. Without it, a stray spark might have set fire to her abundant hair.

Hunter looked from her to the flames racing through the treetops. "Crowning!" he shouted at her. She wasn't sure what he meant, but she nodded and struggled to keep up.

Her mouth felt as dry as the hot ash blowing around her, but she dared not hesitate even long enough to remove the canteen from her saddle. The thick smoke engulfed them, and she choked and coughed.

"Are you all right?" Hunter shouted.

She nodded, hanging onto her saddle, but she wasn't certain. How much smoke would she have to inhale before she grew faint and fell from her galloping horse? She saw herself lying in the path of the racing flames, Hunter sacrificing himself to come back for her. Dear God, she hadn't come clear across the country to burn to death in the Washington woods! Sassy hung on, kept riding.

The forest, promising imminent death, was alive with frantic animals fleeing the flames. *The pond must be somewhere up ahead.* The thought kept her in the saddle and ahead of the flames. They might make it. Then, piercing the shroud of smoke, came a scream of mortal agony. She raced her mare up next to Hunter. "What in God's name—"

Another shriek.

Hunter grimaced and gestured. "Off over there! I'll look; you ride for the pond!"

It wasn't a statement; it was a command. *Stubborn man.* She hesitated only a split-second watching Hunter turn Poker Chips. Then she turned her mount, too. With the darkness and thick smoke, only the glow of the encroaching fire lit the area. In the smoldering brush to one side of the trail, a man lay on his belly, clothes aflame. Clawing frantically, he pulled himself forward by the sheer strength of his arms. Even as she reined in, Hunter was already off his horse and running to smother the fire with his damp blanket.

Sassy glanced briefly toward the oncoming flames; then, she, too, dismounted, grabbing a canteen as she went. She ran over and knelt by Hunter. "Oh, Lord, the poor man!"

Hunter glanced at her, too preoccupied to even scold her. "It's Clegg. Hand me the canteen."

"Clegg! How—" She gave him his own initialed canteen and bit back the cry that came to her lips at the sight of the logger. His shirt and much of his skin had been burned off. What flesh wasn't blackened was raw and red. He groaned loudly when Hunter splashed water on the tortured face. Sassy almost gagged. Clegg smelled like cooked meat.

The man's eyes flicked open. ". . . fires of hell," he gasped. "Preacher warned me. . ."

Sassy leaned close to Hunter's ear. "We've got to get him out of here, maybe make some kind of blanket carry—"

Hunter shook his head. Clegg was past help. Clegg, however, smiled at the sound of her voice. "Angels. I hear an angel. I'm not in hell after all."

The logger's eyes glazed over, and Hunter dribbled cold water between the man's cracked, burned lips. "Clegg, what are you doing here? You set this fire?"

". . . his idea," Clegg gasped. "He killed Swede, too.'

Sassy and Hunter both bent their heads to listen, bu

402

now the dying man only muttered about the flames of hell.

Hunter leaned closer. "Clegg, who? Whose idea? Who left you to burn alive?"

The man made a mighty effort to speak, but only sighs came from his lips as he died. Hunter stood up, meeting the challenge of the relentless fire. "Come on, Sassy. We've got to go."

She felt horror. "And leave him here?"

"He's dead. We can't do anything for him now." Hunter grabbed Sassy, swung her up in his powerful arms and carried her to the snorting horses that stamped their hooves, ready to bolt away from the terrifying flames.

As they rode out again, Clegg's dying words played over and over in her brain. What he had meant? Brett. Could it be Brett? What a wild, unreasonable idea, she chided herself. Brett didn't even know Clegg, and if he did, surely even Brett couldn't be this cruel. This was the work of a madman.

Again they were caught in the midst of panicky animals, fleeing the holocaust. A fox on the run fell and died, its furry tail on fire. A doe paused in midair looking about pitifully, and Sassy sensed it had become separated from its fawn.

Through the trees, she saw the lightning on the horizon and heard the thunder's rumble. The rain would come too late, she realized as she pulled the damp blanket around her to protect her delicate skin. By the time the rains fell, timber and animals would be burned alive. She felt the heat, smelled the scent of flames. The horses, tired and breathing hard, were flecked with foam. The roar of the crackling flames drowned out the screams of the terrified, dying animals.

A fawn came out of the woods, bleating, circling. "The fawn," Sassy shouted to Hunter. "It can't make it on its own!"

"Leave it!" he shouted back. "We can't stop!"

However, Sassy had already dismounted.

With an oath, Hunter reined in and hit the ground running. "Sassy, don't you ever do what you're told?"

She shook her head, struggling to lift the long-legged fawn. "You know I don't, so stop ordering me around!"

"Of all the stubborn—" He sighed in defeat and took the baby deer from her arms. "Go on. I'll carry it."

Sassy swung into her saddle. She marveled at his gentle strength as he mounted up, still carrying the bleating fawn. In the glow of the fire, an unlikely mix of animals waded into the pond. Bears splashed past rabbits and deer, and foxes ignored mice in the safe haven of shallow water.

That last few yards across uneven ground seemed like a million miles with the horses weary and stumbling. Only a little farther. Please, God . . .

"We made it!" She lifted her eyes to heaven in thanks as her tired mare entered the water.

Hunter dismounted in the shallows and turned the fawn loose. It bleated, searching, until a doe climbed from the pool, nuzzled the baby, and led it to safety.

Sassy swung down and led her mare deep into the pond. The cold water felt good on her hot skin. She waded over to Hunter. Cold water wasn't good for overheated horses, but they had no choice. They led both horses deeper, then turned, gravely regarding the flames. "Can anything stop it?"

He shook his head, slipped his arm around her shoulders. "Only God or nature. The wind seems to be changing direction. Maybe the fire will blow back into itself and die from lack of fuel."

She leaned against his muscular chest, drawing strength from him. "Is the house in any danger?"

"Not if it doesn't get much farther than this, although I'll lose a lot of timber. Kind of makes you think about what's really important. Looks like it'll rain toward dawn."

He kissed her forehead and she clung to him "Oh, Hunter, I was so afraid."

"You? My stubborn lady who wants to argue with me about everything was afraid? Sure couldn't prove it by me!" He sounded grudgingly proud of her spunkiness.

She watched the orange and red flames still leaping toward the sky, her mind on Clegg. "That poor man. Do you suppose he was delirious?"

Hunter shrugged. "I can see why he wanted revenge against me for hurting him in that fight, but Swede never did anything to him."

"He mentioned someone else," she said.

"Maybe just rambling," Hunter suggested, "although I've probably made my share of enemies over the years."

She felt the distant heat blow against her face in the fire-lit darkness, tasted the acrid smoke. "How's your hand?"

The bandage had come off and now Hunter looked at his fingers, clenching and unclenching them. "I suppose it's all right. I forgot about it in the excitement."

She was cold now with the wind blowing through her wet clothes. There was nothing she could do but press against him, absorbing heat from his brawny body as they watched and waited. The winds shifted, blowing back in the other direction, turning the fire into itself so that it fed on itself. It would be awhile before the fire would dwindle, but at least it was no longer advancing. She laid her face against him and he held her close. Now that the excitement was slowing, she had time to think and remembered that she still faced the terrible decisions about how to deal with Brett. The suspicion that Brett might have been involved in tonight's foul play crossed her mind, but she dared not mention that to Hunter. Besides, surely not even the blackest-hearted villain would seek such vengeance from his own brother.

Brett. In her mind, she saw the handsome, dark-eyed man with the cleft in his chin. On second thought, Brett was capable of anything. But she had no proof; and Brett could silence her with the threat of telling Hunter her past.

Oh, what a tangled web we weave, when first we practice to deceive. Sassy longed to be honest with the man she loved and admit her tawdry past, yet she feared losing him because of his unyielding pride.

In the darkness, they huddled in the pond with all the animals, Hunter's arms strong and protective around her. The flames dwindled as they stood in the water and watched. About dawn, it began to rain. Big drops spattered on the flames with a sizzle. Here and there, a great tree fell with a shower of smoldering embers. What was left of the nearby forest looked like stark blackened skeletons sticking out of the ruins.

Hunter said, "Well, in a few weeks, maybe we'll see some fireweed."

"Some what?"

"It's a flower, Sassy; it likes to grow in fire-blackened areas—a little wild beauty that brings color after a forest fire. Maybe it's God's visual promise that life does go on, that something beautiful can come of something tragic and hopeless."

She thought about her past life and wished that whatever was true of fireweed was also true of people. She hugged him to her and was equally torn between wanting to share her heavy burden of secret guilt and praying that he never would find out. She was all too certain he didn't love her enough to overlook that. Sassy stood in the circle of his embrace, watching the flames dwindle as the dawn broke faintly in the smoky east. Another day. Last night, all she had to worry about was staying alive; today she had to decide what to do about Brett.

When the rain stopped, Hunter said, "I think it's safe to go now."

The animals left the pool gradually, the fawn bleating along behind its dam. Sassy felt too weary, wet, and smudged to do anything but trudge out of the water as Hunter led the horses. She was so tired she stumbled as they came out of the pond. Hunter caught her and swung her up in his strong arms. "I'm fine," she lied. "I can walk."

"Sure you can." He didn't put her down, but cradled her tenderly against him as he walked and led the weary horses. "It's been a long time since I was that scared," he admitted. "So afraid of losing you, too."

She clung to his neck as he carried her and she thought about a small, scared boy hiding and watching while his mother's face was blown away.

He kissed her cheek as he walked. "I couldn't go through that again. Say you'll never leave me, Missy."

She hesitated. How could she promise that when if he ever found out her secret, he would order her out of his sight . . . if he didn't kill her first. "I—I'll never leave you unless I think you no longer want me," she whispered.

"I'll always want you; you're mine forever."

Forever, she thought with anguish. Oh, how she wished she could believe that.

They went home. Home to no one but a stablehand who told them everyone else was in town, fire-fighting. He promised to feed the horses and give them a good rubdown, and Hunter carried Sassy into the house.

"Seems like I'm continually carrying you into the house, both of us wet," he grinned. "Remember?"

"How could I forget?" She kissed the underside of his square jaw. "Do I look as bad now as I did then?"

"Worse. Before, you just looked like a drowned or muddy kitten; now you look like a drowned rat with smoky smudges all over her freckled face."

She began to weep, her face buried against his shoulder.

"Hey, I didn't mean to hurt your feelings. You're beautiful, Sweet, so beautiful." He kissed her.

"It—it's not that." She managed to blink away the tears. "It's just been such a terrible night, all those poor animals and Clegg. And people may need help in Seattle."

"We'll go into town after we get a bite to eat and change into dry clothes. I imagine my crew will be worried about us." He stood her on her feet in the bedroom, helped her pull off her wet garments, and wrapped her in a big, fluffy towel. "Now, you sit in the wing back while I change."

"It seems like we're reliving out wedding night, doesn't it?" she murmured.

"That's all right with me," he said, "but it'll have to wait. After all, we've got the rest of our lives."

The rest of their lives. It sounded so final, so permanent. Sassy made her decision; she loved Hunter more than anything in this world. She wasn't going to betray her husband with his brother, no matter what happened to her.

Hunter toweled his brawny chest, put on some dry clothes. "You hungry?"

"Aye, I'll fix something." She stood up, but he waved her back down.

"Sit still, Sweet. When I said 'cherish' in those vows, I meant it."

"Well, when I said 'obey,' I didn't mean it."

"I know that, you ornery little critter! Now sit still and I'll see if I can rustle up some leftover roast and fresh bread." He chuckled all the way down the hall.

Sassy leaned back in the wing chair with a weary sigh, enjoying the feel of the soft towel and the scent of food from the kitchen. With the minutes ticking away her happiness, she relished every memory she'd shared with Hunter, knowing there could be no happy end to this story. Through tears that blurred her vision, she stared at her Claddagh ring and the dainty gold bracelet around her wrist that was a concrete symbol of her husband's caring. She supposed the other ring still hung from his watch chain. Maybe it was just as well that he couldn't quite bring himself to make that most final commitment.

"Yowl?" Kitty ambled out of her dressing room, stretched, and yawned.

"Stupid cat," she smiled fondly. "I owe you for tripping Brett." Sassy went over to the bureau, poured herself a brandy and sipped it, letting its rich taste warm her all the way down her body. She returned to her chair as Hunter came into the room with cold roast beef, crusty fresh bread, and tart pickles. She hadn't realized she was so hungry until she smelled the food.

"Yowl?" Kitty sniffed the air, and she gave him a bite.

"Dig in, Sweet," Hunter said. "After we eat, I've got to go into town to see if anyone needs help. The loggers will be gathering, and we'll be able to estimate the damage. Brett's probably assessing our timber loss right now."

Brett. Oh, bless the saints, she had almost managed to forget about that villain while she sat here having a cozy meal with her husband. "Are you going to leave me here while you go into town?"

"You're bone-tired, Sassy Sweet. The fire's no threat to the house; you need some rest."

Suppose Brett showed up while she was here alone? She stuck out her chin. "I want to go with you. Maybe there's something I can do to help."

He gave in more readily than she expected. "Okay, my Sassy lady," he conceded. "When we get through eating, wipe the smudges off your face and get dressed. We'll take the buggy, go into town, and see what Brett's found out." He looked up suddenly. "What are you staring at?"

"I'm memorizing your face for all time," she said with a sad smile, "so I'll always have it, no matter what."

"No need for that, Sweet. You've got at least another fifty or sixty years to look at it."

"Sometimes we take life and love for granted," Sassy

mused, "not knowing how soon it will end. No matter what, Hunter, I want you to know I loved you with every fiber of my being."

He frowned. "You're exhausted, Sassy. We're safe now; the danger's over."

"Aye, of course." If she could only empty her heart to him, tell him everything; but of course she couldn't. "You're right, Dearest; I'm tired. Let me close my eyes just a moment, and I'll go into town with you."

"My poor baby," he whispered. She felt him take the glass from her hand and set it down. He swung her up in his arms. "My poor, tired baby," he said again. "It's been a bad night for you." He kissed her forehead.

In her mind, she saw Brett's leering face. "I'm afraid," she whispered, half-asleep.

She felt Hunter grip her even tighter. "There's no reason to be afraid, Baby; you're safe now."

She snuggled against his bare chest. Safe. She would never be safe as long as Brett was around. Sooner or later, he would catch her alone and rape her; and she wouldn't dare tell Hunter when it happened. Her own past would buy Brett's safety.

Hunter kissed her tenderly and held her close.

"Not safe," she murmured, "never . . ."

"Yes, safe," Hunter rejoined stubbornly. "You'll always be safe now, Sweet. Nothing will ever hurt you; I won't let it. You're mine and nothing will ever wreck you happiness, my Sassy lady. I promise you that."

Just how long would he keep that promise when he discovered his sweet lady was a whore? In her mind, she saw Springtime screaming, heard the shotgun blast as Hunter's father extracted vengeance. What in the name of all the saints was Sassy going to do?

411

Brett took another drink and peered out the window of Lulu's Lovelies at the smoke drifting on the horizon. The street was full of people.

Behind him, Lou said, "Brett, you ought to lay off that stuff. You haven't even had breakfast, much less dinner."

"Damn it, don't nag me," he snapped and deliberately took another sip. "You aren't my wife."

"I know that." She sounded sad, lonely. "Why don't you come away from the window? Watching that timber burn won't help anything. You probably should go out to Hunter's place and see what the losses are."

"He'd put me to work digging fire breaks," Brett grumbled. "I'm a gentleman; I don't do manual labor."

"Some would argue the gentleman part." She, too, peered out at the loggers filling the street. "A forest fire is the most terrifying thing there is. I wonder how it started?"

Brett lit a cigar. "Probably lightning."

"Too bad. Hunter and the others will lose a lot of timber. Wildlife, too. He's probably been out all night fighting it, just like most of the other able-bodied men—except you."

"Oh, but Lou, Honey, I was here with you all night, remember?"

She hesitated a moment. "Yes, of course."

He took another sip of whiskey. "Anyway, I don't know much about fighting fires. I'm waiting for Hunter to ride in and give orders."

She twisted the rings on her fat fingers. "Talk on the street is that his crew's worried about him. Cookie's in

412

town to see about Ellie. He said Hunter is out on the far slope and hasn't come in."

Brett took a big drink and affected a guise of proper concern. "You telling me my brother may be in the middle of that hell fire?" He gestured toward the horizon.

"That'd be real convenient, wouldn't it?"

"Now, Lou—"

"Don't you 'now Lou' me. I know when I'm being used." She reached for a sweet biscuit. "Why do you do this, knowing I care about you?"

He needed to soothe her. It wouldn't do to have Lou angry with him when she was the essential ingredient in his alibi. The fat old bitch needed to die and soon. "I guess I'm just a wild, bad boy," he admitted with a disarming smile. "I always come back to you, don't I?" He put his arm around her shoulders.

"Yeah, you always come back." She sounded tired and discouraged. "Because you need money or a favor."

"Tsk! Tsk! Be careful, you'll hurt my feelings, Honey."

"Brett, the only feelings you got are hangin' between your legs or in your wallet."

"And yours are between your legs and in your belly. Lou, you got a good banging last night, that should have made you happy, yet all you do is whine and bitch." He swayed drunkenly on his feet and returned to his post at the window. Anytime now, someone would find Hunter's body. Then Brett would assume the sorrowful role of the grieving brother.

"I—I'm sorry, Honey," Lou drawled. "I'm just so damned jealous. I wouldn't like to find out that you're using me, and I do know how you are about women."

He stroked his mustache, wishing she were already

413

dead and out of his way. "Lou, I'm crazy about you; but we need Hunter's power and money."

"Is that all you want from him?" She caught his arm. "I seen the way you looked at Sassy. Hunter worships her; you touch her and he'll kill you."

Brett gulped his drink. "Hell! He doesn't even carry a gun."

"He don't need to. He's powerful from years of swingin' an axe, strong enough to break a man in half with his bare hands. Brett, Honey, I'm begging you; we could forget about that pair, keep our mouths shut, and run this place. I do well here."

"My mother and her family would roll over in their graves at the thought of me running a whorehouse."

"It didn't used to bother you."

"I didn't know then just how much wealth that half-Injun bastard had accumulated."

She paced the floor, the boards creaking under her weight. "All right, then, we could go away, make a fresh start together somewhere. Sassy will keep our secret if we keep hers."

"I want more, Lou: Power and money; lots of it."

"You want Sassy, and it's gonna get you killed."

Sassy. He envisioned her small waist, big tits, and satin skin. With Hunter gone, Brett would have everything. And he'd take special pleasure in having the widow in Hunter's own bed. He'd force her to use that hot, teasing little mouth to . . .

"Brett, Honey, you ain't listening to me. Let's go away," she said, twisting her rings. "We could sell this place and start over someplace else. It ain't too late for us. We could be happy."

"I'm gonna be happy right here in Seattle," Brett

snapped. He studied the small picture in his pocket watch. "He's built his empire with my father's money."

"He's a nice guy, Brett. He'd be happy to share with you; he's so glad to have a brother."

"Share? Damn it! I don't want to share; I want it all! Just help me a little longer, Lou, and everything'll work out."

"We'll be together?"

"Sure. I got no interest in that skinny wife of Hunter's; why, her ribs stick out like a washboard." But she's got tits as big as feather pillows, he thought with a wistful sigh, and legs long enough to wrap completely around a man, pull him down into her, and hold him there while her nails claw his back to ribbons. Brett got hard just thinking about it.

A creaking wagon rumbled down the street, Hunter's loggers following it. Brett scanned the crowd of curiosity seekers that gaped at the procession, then fell in step behind the timbermen. The cortège wound slowly up the street to Judge Stone's. Brett could make out a large shapeless bundle wrapped in a tarp as the driver let down the tailgate.

His heart beat faster. Someone had found Hunter's body. As the concerned brother, he'd volunteer to ride out and tell the widow. Brett rubbed the cleft in his chin, smiling to himself. Should he tell Sassy that Hunter was dead before or after he raped her? But first, Brett was going to kill that damned cat!

Chapter Twenty-Three

Brett watched the curious crowd grow around the wagon. Judge Stone came out of his house. "There's some kind of disturbance on the street," Brett said. "Let's go see what it's all about."

"All right; if you want to, Honey." Lou didn't sound interested.

He hadn't realized he'd had so much to drink until he went outside and had to walk the distance from Lulu's Lovelies to Judge Stone's. If she hadn't held onto his arm, he might have stumbled. He had to remind himself not to hum or smile. The group of onlookers peering into the back of the wagon looked up as he approached.

"What's going on?" Brett asked.

Judge Stone hesitated. "Some of the men found something up in the burned timber. I was just about to take a look." Judge Stone reached to pull the tarp back.

Brett started and felt his stomach heave. Lou screamed and turned away. The bundle was a shapeless burned mass that might once have been human. "Oh my God! Who—"

"You haven't been out to the house all night?" Judge Stone sighed.

"No, I. . . . well, you fellas know how it is." Brett glanced at Lou.

"He spent the night at my place," Lou said.

The judge threw the tarp back over the body. "Then you wouldn't know this, but some of the men say Hunter was in the woods last night."

A sympathetic murmur ran through the crowd.

"His brother . . . just got into town."

"Terrible thing for him to see."

"He'll have to tell Hunter's wife . . . don't envy him."

Brett groaned, "I should have been with him, looking out for him instead of carousing all night at . . ."

He looked toward the sobbing madam and the men murmured understandingly. In his younger days, Brett had thought he might make a good actor. Now he staggered away, leaned against the building as if he might faint.

The old man came to his side, patted his shoulder. "I knew you'd take it hard, seein's as how you two have just been reunited."

"Maybe it's not him," Brett said as if grabbing at any straw of hope. "Maybe—"

"We found this canteen." The logger held it up. "It's got Hunter's initials on it."

Brett buried his face in his hands so they couldn't see him grin. "Oh, my God! How terrible! Where're his men? I'll need Cookie and Will!"

"They're with Gertrude and Ellie," a logger said, helping with the homeless now that the fire's out."

The judge pulled at his mustache, sighed regretfully.

417

"So sad. We just got through burying Swede and now this. Someone's got to tell Sassy."

Brett glanced at Lou. She had turned away, was talking to some of the curious who had gathered in front of the store. "Poor Sassy!" Brett said. "Oh, the poor girl! I suppose since I'm his half-brother, it's my responsibility."

Lou frowned. "Judge Stone could ride out and tell her."

Brett glared at her. "Much as I dread being the one, it is my sad duty to give her the news. She may be a bit undone, so it'll be late when I return to make the funeral arrangements."

The crowd murmured sympathetically but he saw the look on Lou's face. She knew him too well. She needed to fall into Puget Sound later this week or, better yet, choke to death on a morsel of food.

The judge said, "I'll do what I can here. Brett, you've had a lot to drink. You'd better eat something or you won't be able to face all this."

"I don't know," Brett said uncertainly. "I'm not feeling too well—"

"Lulu," the judge said, "take him to your place, feed him, and sober him up. Then he can ride out and give Hunter's wife the sad news."

The fat whore glared at Brett as she took his arm. "I'll sober him up, all right."

Brett tried to look weary and bowed with grief as he accompanied Lou. He was drunker than he thought; meal would help. His manhood throbbed with anticipation at what awaited him at Hunter's place. With Sassy alone and defenseless, he intended to enjoy her for couple of hours before he came back to town to make

418

arrangements for a big, showy funeral. After all, with all the money Brett was going to have when he married the widow, he could afford to make a nice gesture. Brett intended to give that Injun bastard the biggest funeral this town ever saw. . . . and after a decent interval, he was going to marry the widow. He was looking forward to seeing Sassy's face when he told her her husband had been burnt to a crisp.

Sassy looked up at Hunter, smiled. "I didn't think we'd be alive today; the fire reminded me how much I love you."

He wiped a smudge off her freckled face very gently. "Thanks, Sweet. Now, Mrs. Hunter, let's button that pink dress so we can go into town."

Town. Brett would be in town. Sooner or later, Sassy was going to have to deal with him. She looked at the Claddagh ring she wore and the dainty gold bracelet that bespoke her husband's love. . . . or was it only his pride of ownership?

"Hunter," she asked without thinking, "do you think couples are ever justified in keeping secrets from one another?"

She could have bitten her tongue off for her stupidity; he gave her a strange look. "I—I don't know. I suppose some secrets are better off kept; it depends on how solid the marriage is, maybe. Sassy, why would you ask a question like that?"

"No reason. Just thinking aloud." The other gold ring still dangled from Hunter's watchchain, she noted. Perhaps it was just as well that he wouldn't wear it. The marriage wasn't going to last much longer.

* * *

Because their two horses were still tired from the ordeal, Hunter had a stablehand hitch up a sorrel gelding to the red-wheeled buggy and they started into town. Neither of them said much—Hunter preoccupied with business, Sassy with Brett. In the distance, smoke still drifted from the smoldering timber.

She glanced at him. "Is it a major loss for you?"

"Yes, but we'll survive it." That boyish curl had fallen down on his forehead again. He put one big hand over hers. "As long as I've got you, Sassy Girl, everything else seems minor."

She didn't look at him, almost fearing that he might see her terrible guilt in her face. Oh, Mother of God, how she yearned to take the reins from his hands, turn the buggy around, and go back to Hunter's Hill. She couldn't stop the inevitable showdown in town. "At least the fire didn't get as far as the house."

Hunter nodded. "In a couple of years, the forest will renew itself, healing the wounds men have inflicted on it. In the meantime, the loggers can salvage some of the damaged timber, clearing away the burned areas."

She longed to be part of that rebuilding, part of the future of this new frontier. If only she could! "I'll do what I can," Sassy said. "Maybe aid some of the loggers' families; take them food."

"Good!" he nodded approval. "At first I was afraid this country was too rough for a genteel lady; but from the moment I saw you, I knew you had what it took. You're one in a million, Sassy Lady. I am so lucky that Mercer gave you my letter."

Lucky. What irony!

420

"I wonder if the ship arrived," Hunter said.

"Hmm?" He jolted her back into the routine of daily life. "Why?"

"I'm expecting a package."

The package again. She no longer cared what was in it.

"It's a surprise for you, an early anniversary gift."

"It's a long way till our first anniversary," Sassy reminded him sorrowfully. A year—a week!—from now they wouldn't be together.

"I know that, but the California Emporium found this for me; it sounded perfect, so I had them ship it."

He expected her to be curious, yet all she could think of was the upcoming confrontation. "What—what is it?"

"Something you wanted, so I was determined you should have it."

"You spoil me." She fixed her gaze on the distant horizon and the faint smoke that marred it.

"Yes, and I intend to keep doing so." He slapped the sorrel with the reins and gave Sassy a tender glance. "My life has changed because of you. I've never been so happy."

"Me, neither." At least she was honest about one thing, she thought sadly. She was too heartsick to even care what the gift was. She'd be gone before it ever arrived.

They topped a steep hill and surveyed the town. It looked like a beautiful painting, Sassy thought, this little village of Seattle with its streets full of people and the blue waters of Puget Sound, a newly arrived ship riding at anchor. Only the distant hills were ugly and burned, smoke still wafting from last night's fire. This was an area full of strong, determined people, Sassy realized.

Someday Seattle and Washington Territory would be important to the whole country. The buggy started down the hill.

"There are a lot of people in town," Hunter commented. "Loggers and ranchers. We'll find out how bad the damage is and see what we can do to help. Maybe we can donate food and supplies. I'll go to the bank."

"You're a kind person," Sassy said.

"Speaking of the bank . . ."

She stiffened at his tone, licked her dry lips.

"The banker manager tells me you've arranged to send a small check each month to a man in Boston."

She ought to tell him the truth. All she had done from the very first was tangle herself in a web of lies. Yet if she told him the truth now, she would only hurt him and she loved him too much to do that. "There's an old Irish construction man, Mike Malone, he—he used to work for my father."

"Yes?"

"He's been hurt and it's hard for the Irish to find jobs anyway. His children were near to starving, so I arranged to send them money regularly. Do you mind?" She looked at him, saw his face relax. He wanted to believe her.

"No, it sounds like something Swede would have done." Hunter sighed. "I miss him; I suppose he had faults, but he was a good man."

In her mind, she saw the big, gentle giant with his piercing blue eyes and curly hair. He looked a lot like . . . what an outrageous thought! Swede. Hunter had put his old friend on a pedestal, also. "I miss him, too."

They drove down the steep hill into town. Horses crowded the streets in front of the Occidental Hotel and the lumber mill. Hunter tied up the buggy at the hitching block in front of the general store and helped Sassy down. A young boy walked up to him, struggling with a package.

"Mr. Hunter? Here's a delivery for you—just came in on the ship."

Hunter took it with a grin and tipped the boy. "Oh, yes, something for my wife." He handed the big package directly to Sassy.

"It's heavy," she said in surprise and set it down in the buggy. "What is it?"

"Open it and find out." Hunter smiled at her fondly. "You said every lady has one."

She had to go through the motions even if her heart wasn't in it. Very slowly, Sassy unwrapped the package. Heavy silver gleamed in the morning light. "A tea service? A fancy tea set?"

It was so breathtaking that she gazed transfixed at the ornate tray and elegant teapot. Even at the wealthy Van Schuyler home, she had not seen its equal. She stared in awe, remembering her mother, who had sacrificed her heirloom silver to bring her family to America. Tears came to Sassy's eyes as she touched each piece.

"You don't like it?" He sounded concerned. "But I thought you told me every lady—"

"No, I—I love it." She wiped her eyes. "I was overcome by the gesture, that's all." *When the town finds out about me,* she thought, *no self-respecting woman will come to my parlor for tea or even speak to me on the street.*

People were gathering around the buggy now, shaking Hunter's hand, telling him how glad they were to see the couple alive. Even old Cookie threw his arms around his boss and clapped him on the back. "I been

423

so worried about you two when you didn't get back to the house, but this makes the day complete," he said and wiped his eyes with clumsy hands. "You're alive and Ellie's gonna marry me."

Sassy and Hunter congratulated the old cook, genuinely pleased that the pair had found happiness "Where're Gertrude and Will?"

Cookie gestured toward Yesler's Mill. "Helping with relief efforts, handing out food with my Ellie. I figure Hunter's Hill needs a full-time housekeeper."

"Yes," Hunter agreed. "I'm planning on remodeling or building Sassy a new house, redecorating, and hiring help."

Sassy nodded, her mind elsewhere.

Cookie said, "We're getting married in a double ceremony as soon as things settle down. We expect you two to be our attendants and little Timmy's going to carry the rings."

"Wonderful!" Hunter pumped his hand. "Sassy will arrange a celebration party and serve with her silver tea service. We'll invite the whole town. In spite of the fire life goes on and we're all going to have a happy ending."

A happy ending. There could be none for her, Sassy mourned, eyeing the building that housed Lulu's Lovelies. That's where she belonged. She watched the old cook limp back down the street to the mill.

Judge Stone and his wife emerged from their house with big smiles. "Hunter? Thank God you're safe! Your brother just identified a body as yours; he's falling apart with grief."

"Brett?" Hunter looked around. "Where is he? I better let him know we're all right."

* * *

Brett peered past the lace curtains of Lulu's window and dropped his glass. It shattered in a thousand pieces, but he was too shocked to even look down. "Good God, he's alive!"

"Who's alive?" Lou waddled to the window, peered out. "I'll swan! It's Hunter and Sassy! I thought you said—"

"I know what I said, damn it!" He strode to the sideboard, poured a stiff drink, and downed it, cursing. "Now what do I do?" He stumbled, so enraged, his hand trembled. "He's just given her a fancy silver tea service—mighty classy for a whore."

"Well, don't look so unhappy. You've got to face all those people in a few minutes." Lou played with the rings on her fat fingers. "Brett, you've had too much to drink. The judge told me to give you some coffee."

"I don't want any damned coffee!" He was in a temper. All the plans he had made, the anticipation he had had for Hunter's wealth and his woman. . . . and the damned Injun bastard had turned up alive. The body must have been Clegg's.

All his plans thwarted! He couldn't think clearly and poured himself another whiskey.

"Brett, you've had enough already—"

"Damn it, you aren't my mother! And I'll drink as much as I want! It never affects my judgment."

Prepared to argue that point, she brushed a crumb from her purple dress. "Please don't be mad at me, Brett. I love you. I—I'll do whatever you want."

"That's more like it." He was going to have to kill Hunter; that was the only solution. Maybe an ambush

425

along the road? His thoughts muddled, whiskey-blurred. Yes, it was the liquor; he couldn't be losing his mind like his father and grandfather. The possibility both terrified and incensed him. He patted his coat, momentarily re-assured by the derringers, the guns he had used to kill Huntington. But a derringer was a gambler's gun meant to be used at point-blank range. A derringer would be useless in an ambush. He gritted his teeth, hating Hunter because people crowded around him, hating him even more because he possessed Sassy.

"Right in front of everyone," he muttered. "That way, there's no whispering about what happened." Brett stared at the buggy. Red wheels. A sorrel horse. In his mind, he saw the buggy going over the cliff in the moonlight. But he wasn't insane like his father; no . . . no . . .

"Brett," Lou whined, "let's forget it and just go away. Look at how that pair is lookin' at each other; they're in love. You're actin' crazy—"

"Don't use that word to me!" He spun and slapped her. "Love! Sentimental foolishness! This is the best way, don't you understand? If it happens in front of all these people, no one will blame me."

Lou was arguing with him again, but he had no patience for her soft heart. All that mattered to him was that Injun bastard enjoying Clay James' money when he had no right to it, enjoying a woman that Brett's groin ached for. He reached in his vest, pulled out the two single-shot derringers, checked to make sure they were loaded, and handed one to her. "Put this in the folds of your dress."

"Brett, you ain't gonna—"

"Shut up," he ordered, "and do what I tell you. We'll get away with it; we did before."

"The town won't like it none."

"So what?" He replaced the second derringer in his vest. "If I've got the money, the town'll soon forget everything else. Money means power. Besides, even the judge will have to realize I had no choice."

"I thought you was gonna be more subtle about this?"

"I'm tired of waiting." His parents were dead because of Clay's obsession with Hunter's whore of a mother. Springtime was dead, but Brett could still extract revenge from her bastard.

Brett's eyes sought Sassy. The sunlight glinted on her angel-pink dress and dark red hair. He wanted her, wanted her now past all reason. He would take her brutally in Hunter's own bed.

"What about her?" Beside him at the window, Lou indicated Sassy.

He needed Lou's help on this. In a couple of days, he could get rid of the fat old bitch; but right now, her assistance was crucial. "Sassy? Aw, she'll leave town in a hurry once everyone hears about her, and no one will care. They'll know I was trying to help my brother and he lost his temper. Most everyone in the north woods remembers Clay James. They'd not be surprised if one of his sons turned violent; they know about Clay."

"I don't like it, Brett," Lou said, trying to restrain him. "Forget about Hunter. Let him keep everything; he's earned it."

"How can I forget? Everything he's got should belong to me!" He drained his whiskey and slammed the glass against the wall. It shattered into a thousand tinkling pieces.

"He likes you, Brett," Lou pleaded. "If you'd just be nice, he'd cut you in on part of it."

427

"Cut me in!" Brett threw back his head and snorted. "I should wait patiently, hat in hand like some beggar, some poor relative, hoping in his generosity, he'll throw me a crumb?"

Lou faced him. "It's Sassy, isn't it? You want her because she belongs to him."

"Now, Lou, Honey," he lied, "it's you I care about. Just think of living in that big, fine home out there on Hunter's Hill."

"We'll get married?"

"Uh huh." He patted his vest, glowering at the pair beside the buggy. "Let's go."

"Oh, Brett, I don't know." The look on her fat face mirrored her doubt and uncertainty, but she loved him. "You're drunk; this will never work."

"I love you, Honey. Help me; help me, please."

She had always been a fool for this man. He might be drunk and maybe even crazy, but she always did what he asked of her. The only thing she hadn't done was tell him Swede's secret. She owed that much to the old logger. "Let's go."

Sassy paused in the middle of the dirt street, holding fast to Hunter's arm. The street was filled with people anxious to discuss and trade stories about the forest fire. Sassy's eyes narrowed. Marylou and Brett had come out of Lulu's and approached them. The madam waddled when she walked, hesitant and miserable. Brett staggered, obviously drunk. He was more than drunk; his dark eyes shone with a strange light. She thought about Clay James and shivered. Would Hunter inherit the gradual madness?

Sassy studied her husband. Hunter, maneuvering Sassy around a mud puddle, hadn't noticed the pair coming toward them.

Sassy's heart pounded. Marylou's strained face and the grim, angry expression on Brett's forewarned her of trouble. Sassy considered the bustling crowd; surely he would not confront them on a busy street. Only a crazy man would.

Hunter, at last aware of his brother, moved toward him eagerly. "Hello, Brett. I hear you had a scare, but I'm not dead after all."

"Hunter," Brett said in a voice loud enough to attract attention, "I've just found something out, something shocking. I—I don't quite know how to say it."

"What are you talking about?" Hunter demanded.

The four squared off, the center of a curious cluster of townspeople. Sassy felt the hair rise on the back of her neck; her life passed before her.

"I said, Hunter," Brett raised his voice, "Lou here just told me something she insists you need to know. I tried to tell her to keep her mouth shut; but it's for your own good. I wouldn't want you to be the laughingstock of Seattle."

Her friends and neighbors turned, listening. Not here, Sassy prayed. Oh, God, Brett's going to humiliate Hunter in front of the entire town. "Brett," she said, "you're drunk. Go sleep it off before—"

"Before what?" He smiled innocently and the cleft in his chin deepened.

In that split second, Sassy saw the bulge in his vest and knew he carried a gun. Marylou's misery showed on her pudgy face.

"Hunter," Brett shouted and nudged Lou forward,

"you'll be shocked to hear this. It's about your prim lady's secret past."

As Sassy opened her mouth to shout a denial, she realized what the game was. This pair was about to pull the same trick they had pulled on Albert Huntington in New York. When Sassy denied the accusation, Hunter would come to her defense and they would kill him, probably slipping a gun in his pocket as he went down. Hunter would give his life to protect her honor. Within a heartbeat, Sassy made her decision.

Lou hesitated, and the inquisitive mob pushed closer.

Brett nudged her. "Tell poor Hunter what you told me."

The street fell deadly silent.

The madam cleared her throat. "I—she's one of my girls, Hunter. She used to work for me back East."

"Brett," Hunter snarled, and his voice was as low and threatening as a snake's hiss. "I don't know what this is about, but you two had better apologize to my wife or I'll—"

Even as Hunter moved, Sassy caught his arm and hung on. "No, Hunter, he—he's right! I—I was one of Lou's girls a long time ago." She couldn't hold back her tears as she looked up into Hunter's shocked face. "Don't fight for my honor, I—I'm no lady; I've been living a lie." Now she screamed at Brett. "I know what you planned, but he won't die for me; he won't fight to protect a whore's honor!" Sassy turned and fled blindly down the street toward the dock.

It was over. Hunter knew Sassy's secret. Worse, she had seen the horror and revulsion on his dark face. He would hate her forever and curse her name, but he was alive. She didn't know what would happen between Hunter and his brother now, but at least he was not going to be shot down in the street to protect her good name.

Sassy ran through the crowd and along the road, across the dock. Gasping for breath, she ran up the gangplank and onto the anchored ship.

The captain raised his head from the charts he studied and came to meet her. "Is there something I can do for you, Ma'am?"

"When—when are you leaving?"

He gestured toward the seamen on deck. "As soon as we weigh anchor. We have to catch the tide."

Then Sassy remembered she didn't have any money. Regretfully, she pulled off the gold bracelet Hunter had given her. "I—I'll trade this for my passage."

His curiosity was evident as his gaze swept over her tear-stained face, her expensive dress. "Ma'am, you don't even know where we're headed—"

"And I don't care," she choked out, "as long as it's far, far away."

She put the bracelet in his hand and the be-whiskered captain beckoned to a cabin boy. "Show the lady below, and make ready to get underway."

"Aye, aye, Sir."

Sassy managed to hold back her tears until she was in the cramped, dingy compartment. Then she lay down on the bunk and gave way to sobs. Where she was going or what she would do didn't matter. She could never forget the expression on Hunter's face as she turned and fled. He hated her, and now she had to leave Seattle forever.

Chapter Twenty-Four

Back on the street, as Sassy turned to run away, Lou saw the rage in Hunter's eyes.

"Brett," Hunter snarled, "you drunken sonovabitch!" He lunged for Brett and Lou saw a slight movement as Brett reached into his vest. He'd kill the younger man and she'd drop the other derringer into Hunter's jacket as he went down so Brett could claim self-defense. Yet she saw the agony in Hunter's blue eyes, so very, very much like his father's, and knew he loved Sassy, truly loved her. And Brett was pulling the trigger.

Never in her whole life had Lou done anything determinedly good. From the hard-scrabble days in a tobacco patch, she had looked out for herself and only herself. But something in that instant of time, maybe the agony in Hunter's eyes, caused her to throw herself between the two men.

She heard the shot from a long way off, even though she felt the barrel in her back as she lunged in front of Brett. Then the pain bit into her flesh, white hot pain like a burning poker going deep in her body. She half turned, and saw, not regret, but only annoyance i

Brett's crazed dark eyes because she had spoiled his shot. The dirt of the street came up to meet her, and she lay at their feet and watched the fight as detached as if she watched from a rooftop, a crimson stain spreading in the earth around her.

Hunter sprang at Brett and Brett backed away, the useless derringer still clutched in his hand.

"You sonovabitch!" Hunter dove for him, swinging hard. His big fist caught Brett's chin, and the small gun flew from his hand as he fell backward into the muddy street. Hunter couldn't think, he only reacted as he advanced, his rage goading him on.

Brett scrambled to his feet. "Hunter, it was for your own good! Listen to me—"

But Hunter's hard-driving fist cut his words off as Hunter hit him again. There was something satisfying in the way his knuckles connected with the other man's jaw. He put his passion and anger into his swinging blows as sweat and blood trickled down Brett's handsome face. Out of the corner of his eye, Hunter saw the judge and the newly arrived missionary pull Lou from the dirty street to the wooden sidewalk.

Brett came up swinging, spitting out broken teeth. However, he was no match for the fury that drove Hunter as he charged the older man. They meshed and went down, rolling in the dirt. Hunter felt a stinging pain as Brett landed a blow but that only angered him more. He struck Brett again and again. They were coated with dirt, sweat, and Brett's blood. Hunter smelled its coppery scent and the reek of whiskey. The throng around them grew larger as they fought, ringing the pair in anticipation of a fight to the death.

Hunter already felt dead inside, but his fury sustained

him, kept him fighting. He couldn't think about Sassy or Lulu, or anything but getting Brett.

Brett staggered to his feet, badly hurt and bleeding, his fine clothes torn and stained. He didn't look like an elegant, rich gentleman now; he looked like a desperate driven fugitive as he stumbled backward, trying to escape Hunter's punishing fists. He dropped his watch; and, in the frey, Brett stepped on it, crushing it in the dirt.

Crazy, Hunter thought. *Why, he's as crazy as our father!*

Abruptly, a light shown in Brett's dark, insane eyes and he turned and ran to where Lou lay, the judge holding up her head.

Lou looked up through a haze of pain toward the encircling crowd, the judge's kind face, the two men fighting in the street. She raised one plump hand from her torn body and saw that her diamonds were running scarlet with blood. Her insides seemed on fire.

It didn't matter. Hunter loved Sassy; really loved her and Lou had saved him for her. Brett was the one who deserved to die, even though she loved him still. She lay on the sidewalk with her blood running out on the weathered boards and watched Hunter and Brett. Brett stumbled toward her, eyes wild. "The gun, Lou! Gimme that other gun!"

The gun. Yes, the other derringer. Feebly, she reached her hand to find it hidden in her skirt. Brett needed it to save himself. She loved Brett; she had always loved Brett, but he was no good . . . no good at all.

"The gun, Lou!" Brett knelt by her, pushing the protesting judge away. "Where is it?"

434

She looked up into his insane eyes even as her failing fingers closed on the derringer. "You—you're no good, Brett. . . . true love deserves to win just once."

"He's after me, Lou; quick, the gun!"

She pulled it out of her skirt and he leaned forward, hands reaching eagerly. "I love you, Brett," she whispered. Then she shot him between the eyes.

He looked down at her with a frozen, horrified stare before he toppled over across her body.

Her vision was blurring. She was going now, she knew that, but she welcomed the escape. Her insides were inflamed, and all she wanted was to be out of this pain and a world that had always been hostile and cruel to her. But she couldn't die yet; there was something else she had to do. The judge bent over her. "Oh, Lulu, hang on. We'll get a doctor—"

She shook her head, struggled for breath. "Bury us together, then give what's left to charity. Hunter, I—I need to tell Hunter—"

"What is it, Lulu?" Hunter, deathly pale, moved Brett's body gently and knelt next to her.

She was so afraid she didn't have enough strength left to speak, but she couldn't go without telling him the secret. It was important to his happiness. "Your father . . ."

"Yes?" He leaned closer, his face bruised and bloody.

"Not Clay James . . . Swede; your father was Swede. . . . He was afraid you'd hate him, so he never told you."

Stunned by her revelation, Hunter stood up slowly, oblivious to the curious crowd in the street. *Swede*. In his mind, Hunter was a little boy again, crouching behind the chair in the darkness as his mother made love to a

435

man; that faceless man who fled in all those nightmares. Outside, a familiar voice trying vainly to delay Clayton James: Cookie. Good old Cookie. The man with his mother? Hunter remembered now that the moonlight glinted on the man's light hair. Abruptly, Clay James burst into the room with his shotgun and Springtime screamed and screamed. The man with her panicked. He left the woman to the madman's mercies and went out the window. After all these years, standing here on a Seattle street, Hunter saw the man's face clearly, that face he didn't want to recognize or acknowledge even in his dreams.

Swede. Clay James' best friend. Swede had betrayed him because of a woman and then left her to her fate in a moment of weakness, hating himself ever after. That knowledge had caused Clay James and Brett's mother's deaths, too. Secrets and regrets. Feet of clay. Everyone had them. But if Hunter wasn't Clay's son, he couldn't inherit insanity.

Sassy. A whore? Nothing mattered now but the answer. Hunter looked around. "Where'd she go?"

The silent crowd shrank back and someone gestured toward the docks. They melted away to give him room. Sassy. She was no better than his mother. He'd been lied to, made a fool of, betrayed by the only woman he'd ever given his heart to completely. How she must have laughed at him behind his back even as the people around him were smirking now. He'd been such a damned, stupid food for that freckled-faced whore. She was guilty, all right, or she wouldn't have fled. Emotion built in him and he clenched his fists and strode toward the ship. He'd warned her. . . . By God, he had warned her not to hurt him, and then she'd torn his heart out

436

with her words! His vision blurred with unshed tears as he strode toward the anchored ship.

Lou looked at Hunter's back and tried to speak. She wanted to make amends, do something right for the first time in her life, but he was gone, striding away. She could feel her life's blood running out onto the rough, wooden sidewalk. A blur of faces looked down into hers. "Judge . . . a preacher. . . . get me a preacher."

The grim, newly arrived missionary knelt by her other side. "Scarlet woman, confess your sins! Don't go to God unrepentant!"

"If—if I die with a lie on my lips, will I burn in hell?"

He nodded. "Tell the truth, woman; get right with God!"

She and Brett had destroyed Sassy and Hunter with the truth; but, in this last moment, maybe she could save their happiness with a lie. Lou managed to turn her head and look at her dead love. She didn't want to live without him. He was no good, but he was the only man she had ever truly loved.

Hell. She was going to hell because she would die with a lie on her lips, but Lou wanted to end her lonely, miserable life with a good act. "Judge," she gasped, "tell Hunter. . . . Tell everyone we lied. Never saw that girl before: she's what she said she was—a lady, a real lady."

The judge and the crowd leaned closer to catch her whispered words.

"Brett had that gun in my back, so I lied. . . . Sassy must have seen it, too, and tried to save me by lying. Tell everyone. . . . Tell Hunter." She tried to say more but she couldn't get the words out. The light was gradually fading, and even the pain was fading with the light.

"Lulu?" Judge Stone peered down at the woman. "Lulu?" He sighed and shook his head. "She's gone."

An excited murmur ran through the crowd. "You hear what she said? Sassy's no whore; she's a heroine!"

Slowly, the judge stood up. "Where's Hunter?"

A dozen people pointed toward the ship.

He felt a terrible sense of dread, knowing no one could reach that ship in time. Whatever was about to take place there, he and the crowd would arrive only in time to bear witness. He began to pray, then changed his mind. "Somebody get the sheriff!" He took off at a run toward the dock, the crowd at his heels. Hunter's pride had been shattered by betrayal and he wasn't a man to give his love lightly. Did that pride mean more to the big half-breed than Sassy's love?

Hunter strode down the dock. It was his worst night mare, people snickering and pointing. Like his mother Sassy had lied. His wife was a whore like Springtime He was filled with unnamed emotion. "Where'd she go?"

A murmur ran through the crowd and they made way for him, openly indicating the ship. Knowing his fury, she was fleeing from him. Blinded by hurt, he strode across the dock. *A lady,* he thought derisively. *My lady is nothing but a whore!*

The crowd whispered, "Wouldn't blame him for kil ing her!"

"He won't take her back—too much pride!"

"Take her back? If she were mine, I'd kill her!"

His worst possible humiliation; people whispering about his wife just as they had gossiped about his mother. He clenched his fists, focusing on the ship as he walked. He had loved her as he had never given his heart and soul to another, yet she had lied to him, made a fool of him. Love battled pride; and he was, more than anything, a singularly proud man.

He had told her that if she ever hurt him, ever betrayed him, he would kill her. He had not known love could hurt so much as he was hurting now. She had made a fool of him before the whole town. He looked down at his watchchain, at that damned gold ring. *Love and friendship*. She had given him both and she had given him neither. He paused, remembering; and, deeply pained, he marched up the gangplank and onto the ship.

The captain turned, his eyes widening at the expression on Hunter's dark face.

"A pretty red-haired girl came on this ship?"

The ship's commander shrank back in fear. "Yes. She traded a gold bracelet for passage."

Sassy sat on her bunk, hot, salty tears dripping down her face. What had happened in town? No need to worry. Hunter could take care of himself. At least by admitting her past, she had saved his life. If only the ship would get underway, so she could leave Seattle—and her heart—forever, behind. He must hate her now. She closed her mind. She wouldn't think about it.

She heard heavy steps in the hall, and then the door

was kicked wide open. Hunter stood before her, glaring. He had come to kill her. There was no doubt of the anger and the troubled passion on his dark face. "Is what Brett said true?"

"Yes." She nodded, wishing she could erase the pain from his eyes. "Please believe I never meant to hurt you. I'd give anything if I could go back and change the past, but I can't, Hunter."

"Lies. All lies," he snarled.

"Yes. I'm not a highborn Eastern lady. I'm not even Sophia Merriweather."

"Then who in the hell are you?"

She blinked back tears. "I—I'm Sassy Malone, and I'm just a shanty-Irish immigrant girl who had bad luck and hoped for a fresh start."

His voice shook with emotion. "You lied. You lied about everything."

"One thing I didn't lie about, Hunter," she said very softly. "I didn't lie about loving you. From that first moment on the dock, I loved you. I might have told you then, but James Hunter wanted a lady, so I tried to be one. I—I never meant to hurt you."

They looked at each other, and she saw his eyes go moist. From above deck, she heard the captain's shout, "All ashore that's going ashore! All ashore that's going ashore!"

His big fists clenched and unclenched. "Do you—do you love me now?"

She nodded. "Aye. I know you hate me, but know this: the day I die, my last thought will be of you."

She saw his Adam's apple move as he swallowed. His hands went limply to his sides. "I swore I'd kill you you hurt me, but I can't."

440

There was nothing left but the pain of separation, she thought dully. She heard the captain shout again. "Hunter," she said, "you'd better go; we're ready to sail."

And still he waited in the doorway, drinking her in. She saw the conflict warring behind his eyes. He tossed the gold bracelet into her lap. "I—I'll see you get money."

"I couldn't take it," she murmured.

He turned to leave, hesitated, turned around. Only then did he take the gold ring from his watchchain. Very slowly, as she watched, he slid it on his fourth finger, left hand. Commitment. A final commitment. "Sassy, don't go; don't leave me."

Puzzled, she blinked in confusion. "Hunter, don't you understand? I'm not a lady. I'm not anything at all like the wife you wanted. I'm everything you despised."

"I was a fool," he contradicted. "My pride meant everything to me. But just now, when faced with the choice, I knew that in a showdown between love and pride, only love counts. None of us is perfect; we all have feet of clay."

Sassy shook her head. "It won't work. Men will laugh and whisper behind my back."

"They will at their own peril," he promised. "Can't we close the door on the past and make a fresh start?"

She felt the agony of indecision. "Oh, Hunter, you know what I've been; you won't ever forget. No man could."

"I swear before God that we start fresh this moment. Come home with me, Sassy Girl. I'm begging you. The big house, the money, power—nothing matters without you. I love you; more than pride, more than anything in this world, I love you!"

"Oh, Hunter!" And then she was in his arms and he was holding her like he would never let her go.

"I couldn't lose you." He was weeping, too. "God, I didn't know how much I loved you until I almost let you go!"

From above, the captain's shout penetrated their elation. "Last call! All ashore that's going ashore!"

"Hunter, dearest, we've so much to talk about."

"More than you know." He looked embarrassed, hesitated. "Do you think you could teach an ignorant half-breed how to read and write?"

"What?" Then everything came crystal-clear. The handwriting on the note—no wonder it had looked familiar to her; it was Marylou's handwriting. The upsidedown book, the excuses. No doubt Swede had covered for him for years. "It isn't hard to learn," she assured him. "I'll help you. Oh, by the way, that construction man, Mike Malone, is my papa. The children are my brothers and sisters, and they live in a horrible slum in Boston."

"And you want to bring them all here?"

She bit her lip. "Aye, I know it's a lot to ask, but the house is so very big and the children and Papa would enjoy it so much. Seattle could use some good construction men."

He sighed in defeat. "Oh, Sassy, what have I let myself in for by loving you?" He swung her up in his arms and she clung to him. He opened the door and, still carrying her as if afraid he might lose her forever, he went down the narrow hall and up the steps.

Out on deck, the sunlight blinded them momentarily

A crowd had gathered on the dock. John was there with Ellie; Gertrude stood by Will and little Timmy. Mildred clutched Bill Johnson's arm. Judge Stone wiped the sweat from his brow in relief. "Thank God! Hunter, don't hurt her! I've got to tell you what Lulu said."

"Hurt her?" Hunter roared as he carried her down the gangplank. "I'd kill the man who harmed a hair on her head! You're talking about my wife and the future mother of my children, Judge."

Tears of happiness ran down Sassy's cheeks, and she buried her face against his broad chest while Hunter pushed through the crowd. "A fresh start," she whispered. "From this moment on. I love you, Dearest. I love you so much."

"Not as much as I love you," he countered. "Now let's get your silver tea service and go home, Mrs. Hunter. There're things to do if we're to be invaded by a flock of Irish relatives!"

Hunter's lady; no, much more than that, his only love. He carried his precious burden down the dock toward the buggy with the cheering crowd trooping behind.

To My Readers

Asa Mercer and his ship-load of brides is one of the most intriguing true stories of the old West. And yes, the ship actually was the *Continental,* the ship used by the Galvanized Yankees in 1864 to go off to fight the Indians. I've already told you about the Galvanized Yankees in two previous Zebra novels, *Quicksilver Passion* and *Sioux Slave.* The *Continental* was owned by Ben Holladay, the stagecoach king. After the brides' trip, the ship was used only four more years before she foundered in the Gulf of California in 1870, with a loss of eight lives.

What happened to the women who came on the ship? Two widows and eleven single women got off at San Francisco and stayed there; the rest went on to Seattle. Asa Mercer himself married one of the girls, Annie F Stephens of Baltimore, Maryland. One or two of the belles, (there's some confusion here) never married; the others found husbands and lived quiet, responsible lives as wives, mothers, and worthwhile citizens.

Asa Mercer and his wife left Seattle and eventually went to Wyoming, where he wrote a daring exposé the 1892 Johnson County Range War called: *The Ba ditti of the Plains.* Powerful Wyoming cattle barons had imported hired gunfighters as they attempted to terrorize and/or force out homesteaders and small ranchers. Novels and movies such as *Shane* have a basis of fact in the bloody Johnson County incident. Mercer and the printer were harassed unmercifully and most copies of the book were searched out and destroyed by the rich, ruthless men Mercer exposed. For that reason, an original copy is rare and valuable.

Roger Conant, the reporter who went along on the trip to cover the event for the *New York Times,* did marry, but not a Mercer belle. He ended up in California, dying in the Veteran's Home in Sawtelle, in 1915. His journal, edited by Lenna A. Deutsch, later became a book, *MERCER'S BELLES, the Journal of a Reporter,* published by the University of Washington Press.

Who else in this story are real people? Doc Maynard, Governor Pickering, and John Pennell, owner of the *Illahee.*

For those who wondered, yes, the Civil War favorite, "Aura Lea," did become popular again almost a hundred years later when a hip-swiveling Southern idol sang the old tune with new words and turned it into one of his biggest hits. The singer was Elvis Presley and you'll recognize the song today as "Love Me Tender."

Speaking of singers, the lawyer, H.R. Crosby, who ried valiantly but unsuccessful to defend the Indian, eshi, from hanging, was famous-singer Bing Crosby's randfather. A Seattle park is named for that Indian martyr.

Yesler's Mill, the Occidental Hotel, and the *Illahee* ith its Indian whores are part of old Seattle's true hisory; the other places in this story are fiction.

The term "skid road" originated in the timber country to describe the tough, rundown saloon and whorehouse areas near where the logs were skidded to market. The term has survived to describe the same type of slum, although you may know it as "skid row." Now you know its true origin.

The Claddagh ring from the Galway area with its ancient tradition of over 400 years is said to be the only ring made in Ireland ever to be worn by Queen Victoria and, later, Edward VII. Supposedly, the phrase that usually accompanies it is *Let love and friendship reign.*

While the forest fire in my story is fiction, Seattle did have a major fire in 1889 that burned 58 city blocks of the town. A good research book on Seattle is *SKID ROAD, An Informal Portrait of Seattle,* by Murray Morgan, published by the University of Washington Press.

The most destructive forest fire on the West Coast that I know of was the 1933 Great Tillamook Burn in Oregon that ravaged some 485 square miles of timber. One of the most deadly American fires that I have found in my research was the Peshtigo, Wisconsin forest fire that trapped and burned alive some 1,200 people on a Sunday night, October 8, 1871. Incredible as it may seem, the Great Chicago Fire supposedly started by Mrs. O'Leary's cow was on that very same night. Although the Chicago fire claimed only about 300 lives, it's the one everyone remembers. Here in my home state of Oklahoma, the Kiowa Indians have a crack team of smoke jumpers who fly to major forest and prairie fires across the country.

As for the Indians, there was a lot of trouble with them in Oregon and Washington in the 1840s and 1850s. The bloodshed started again as the Nez Perce fought to defend their country in the 1870s under Chief Joseph, but that's another story I may tell you another time.

The literacy campaign is one that is dear to my heart. The statistics are alarming: one in every four or five Americans cannot read well enough to hold a good job or enjoy a novel.

For those who have asked, I belong to the Western Writers of America, the Order of the Indian Wars, and the U.S. Horse Cavalry Association and spend a lot of time researching for historical accuracy because you readers have indicated that interests you.

I'm always pleased to hear from readers. Write me c/o Zebra Books and, it you include a stamped, self-addressed envelope, I'll send you a bookmark and news-letter. Foreign residents should send a postal exchange voucher (available at your post office) that I can trade or correct postage since the U.S. mail will not allow me o use your foreign stamps.

In answer to all you readers who have asked: Yes, Zebra Books has now reprinted most of my series, *The Panorama of the Old West*, and you will be happy to know I have a new contract to continue this long, long saga. *Half-Breed's Bride* is #10.) Over the past several years, my editor has forwarded hundreds of letters requesting sequel to *Nevada Nights*, my story of the Pony Express and the Paiute Indian War. I've also received lots of mail asking that the mysterious and darkly handsome ain robber, Nevada, from *Apache Caress*, be given his own book. So, by popular demand, in mid-November, 993, (December Release) Zebra brings out my tale of a Indian gunfighter who kidnaps a blond beauty from train.

447

They called him "Nevada." He was sired by a Paiute chief, but his mother was the fiery Dallas Durango, herself half-Spanish, half-Cheyenne. He was heir to the Wolf's Den ranching empire of Arizona; what set Nevada on the outlaw trail and finally drove him to return to his father's people?

Her name was Cherish, the elegant darling of her doting father's heart. Only two other things matter as much to the wealthy Amos Blassingame: his aristocratic heritage and his Trans-Western Railroad Company. He'll accept no lowly Injun bastard as his son-in-law!

Spurned by the haughty Blassingames, Nevada robs their trains with a vengeance. Then one fateful night, he captures an unexpected prize: Amos Blassingame's dearest treasure. Daughter Cherish is on her way home in her private railcar to be married. Is it revenge or love that makes the *desperado* kidnap the bride and carry her off to the rugged, wild land he is named for? His ransom demand: one night in his arms and he'll return her to her unsuspecting bridegroom. If you were Cherish would you pay his price? If she surrenders her virginity, can she forget the virile outlaw's kisses at daybreak? Remember, after that endless Nevada night of passion eventually must come the *Nevada Dawn* . . .

Come escape with me back to the romantic old West

Georgina Gentry